GOOD DIRT

# Good Dirt

A NOVEL

## CHARMAINE WILKERSON

BALLANTINE BOOKS
NEW YORK

Published in the United States by Ballantine Books, an imprint of Random House, a division of Penguin Random House LLC, New York.

BALLANTINE BOOKS and colophon are registered trademarks of Penguin Random House LLC.

LIBRARY OF CONGRESS CATALOGING-IN-PUBLICATION DATA
Names: Wilkerson, Charmaine, author.
Title: Good dirt: a novel / Charmaine Wilkerson.
Description: First edition. | New York: Ballantine Books, 2025. |
Identifiers: LCCN 2024042620 (print) | LCCN 2024042621 (ebook) |
ISBN 9780593358368 (hardcover; acid-free paper) |
ISBN 9780593358375 (ebook)
Subjects: LCGFT: Novels.
Classification: LCC PS3623.I5456 G66 2025 (print) |
LCC PS3623.I5456 (ebook) | DDC 813/.6—dc23/eng/20240912
LC record available at https://lccn.loc.gov/2024042620
LC ebook record available at https://lccn.loc.gov/2024042621

Printed in the United States of America on acid-free paper

randomhousebooks.com

2 4 6 8 9 7 5 3

FIRST EDITION

*Book design by Barbara M. Bachman*

To those whose stories
are written in our hearts.

GOOD DIRT

# Prologue

---

## ONE MONTH BEFORE

"SHHH," HER BROTHER SAYS.

She's giggling. She can't help it. She tears off pieces of sticky tape and hands them over. Just as her brother finishes with the tape, their mom calls from outside. One day, she will remember them dashing out of the room together, fingers gummy with adhesive, and, despite everything, she will smile.

"Okay, okay," says their mother. "Let's take this photo." She fiddles with her camera. "You can't show up late on the first day of school."

But her brother wants them to see what he's done.

"Mom, I want to take the picture indoors," he says. "Can we?"

"But it's so nice out here," their mom says. Behind her, the pansies and asters are in bloom. The rest is all green against the black-blue of the Sound. This, too, she will remember. The beauty of that first home. How she thought she would never want to leave.

"Let's just do this," their father says. She looks up at her dad and reaches for his hand. They follow her brother inside and into the study. When their parents see the old stoneware jar, they laugh. Great big belly laughs. That's what her brother was going for. He's put a baseball cap over the top of the jar, and on its front he has taped a handlebar mustache cut out of paper and colored in with a black marker. On the table next to it, he's stacked a couple of textbooks.

She and her brother haven't forgotten what the jar represents. Who made it. Where it comes from. How very old it is. Their father, and his father before him, have made sure of that. But in their home, they don't treat the jar like it's an antique. They treat it like a member of the family. Her big brother takes up his position next to the jar and leans in close for the snapshot.

"Say cheese!"

Now it's her turn. Then their mother sets the camera on a tripod and they take a group photo.

And thank goodness for the memory.

Because you never know, do you?

Part One

# Shattered

___

LATER, THE RETIRED COUPLE WOULD TELL THE POLICE THEY HAD run over to the Freeman place after hearing the shots. Their exact words would be *shots rang out*. But that was just a phrase that people of their generation had picked up from watching television. On the TV news, people were always saying shots rang out. In the old detective shows, shots were always ringing out. At the box office, Rambo and the Terminator and Serpico and Shaft had all made buckets of money by making shots ring out. But this was real life, in a town with one of the lowest crime rates in the nation. Few people around here had a vocabulary suited to a situation like this one.

The space between houses being what it was in these parts, it was unlikely that anyone else living along Windward Road would have heard the shots, which did not, in fact, ring out so much as make a dull *crack-crack* sound. It was unlikely they would have heard the splitting open of the antique jar when it tumbled from the table in the study. Nor could they have heard the thud of the victim's flank against the floor when he fell. What the neighbors heard for certain was the screech of the van's tires as the panicked robbers tore out of the driveway and took the first road north away from the shore, in the direction of the country club.

The neighbors had been collecting seeds from their coneflowers and black-eyed Susans. It was that time of year. They had been working side by side, knees in the dirt, murmuring to each other as they did. Taking in the clicks and chirps of their backyard. The whisper of the sea breeze through the tulip tree. The scent of fallen apples warming in the sun. But now they were hurrying past the line of trees that separated their garden from the Freemans', their shoes flattening dirt clods and snapping fallen twigs as they went. They were surprised to see the children's bicycles were still there.

Later, they would recall that this was the moment when panic set in.

*Weren't the kids supposed to be gone?* The Freeman children were almost always gone during the week, now that school had started up. They would head back out on their bikes after classes, if they came home at all. Piano lessons for her, tennis or debate club for him. The neighbors banged on the side door, now. They called out. They ran around to the front and found the entrance to the main hallway wide open. And that's when they heard it. A sound that would stay with them for years. The voice of a child, bleating like a lamb that had lost its way. A child they had watched grow from infancy. A girl who had played with their own granddaughter for most of her ten years.

It was a sound that could shatter a person's heart.

# At Least, This

———

**2018**

WELL, OF COURSE THEY HAD HOPED FOR A DAY LIKE TODAY.
If life had taught them anything, it was that a person's path still could be
lit by moments of joy, even after unspeakable loss. And here they were.
Soh and Ed Freeman smiled at each other then looked up at the window,
where they could just make out the crown of flowers on their daughter's head. Peaches and pinks. They glimpsed the dark tone of her arms
against her cream-colored dress. No bridal veil, Ebby had insisted. Just
the flowers and her granny's gown, the bodice above the flounced skirt
adjusted to fit. What a lovely young woman their child had become.

There was a glint of light from their daughter's engagement ring as
she moved away from the window. Sapphires flanking a two-carat diamond, handed down to her by her other grandma, Soh's mother. There
was no personal keepsake from the groom's mother. Not that it was
necessary, but it was the kind of gesture that those who knew the Peppers might have expected.

True, Henry's parents had hosted an impeccable dinner for the couple at their club three days before, but Soh and Ed couldn't help but
notice that Henry's mother had not embraced their daughter that
night. Hadn't kissed her on the cheek. Hadn't even taken her hand.
Henry, though, had stayed close to Ebby all evening. His arm around
her waist. His nose brushing her cheek. Love might not conquer all,
they realized, especially in a marriage between a black woman and a
white man. Even nowadays. But mostly, love still carried more weight
than pretty much anything. And they were hopeful.

Ed thought back to his own wedding day and reached out to touch his wife's fingers. Their ceremony and reception had been chock-full of guests from the black fraternities, social clubs, and summer resort circles to which they, like their parents, belonged. With all that he and Soh had inherited and were passing down to their daughter, Ed wanted to believe they had equipped their child with everything she would need to find her way in this life.

Soh tried to slow time. Savor the moment. She breathed deeply, took in the scents of the freshly mowed grass, the potted flowers along the stone path, the good dirt. The salt air coming off the Sound, a hint of chill signaling the beginning of fall. If only she could stop worrying. She looked around her garden. There were plenty of guests from the groom's side. She recognized two Fortune 500 businessmen, and that artist whose somewhat mystifying work was currently doing the rounds at the bigger museums. But there was no sign of Henry and his parents.

The Peppers were running late, today of all days.

When Ebby returned to the window, she was holding something against her torso. They saw the silvery, rectangular shape and understood. It was a framed photograph of their son, taken one morning before school. With the jar, and that impish smile of his. Typical Baz. He would have been thirty-three years old, now, had he lived. He would have been down here in the garden with them, waiting for his sister. They had lost so much as a family. But today, they were looking forward, not only back.

Within a minute, everything would change. Ebby would lean against the glass pane and they would catch the strained expression on her face. She would call her mother's cellphone, which would vibrate in the satin purse under Soh's arm. Soh would hurry upstairs to speak with her daughter. Whispers would start to circulate among the guests in the garden. And finally, Ed would walk into his home office, shut the door, and telephone the groom's father, trying to keep his cool. *Tell me this isn't happening,* he would say.

But before any of this came to pass, they were simply the mother and father of the bride, standing on the walkway leading up to the gazebo, their backs to the sea, their eyes focused on their girl, both thinking exactly the same thing: *At least, this. At least, this.*

# Small Favors

———

EVEN AFTER THE CEREMONY HAD BEEN CALLED OFF, EBBY WAS aware of small favors being bestowed upon her by the universe. Chief among them was the fact that there were no wedding gifts waiting for her at home. Ebby and Henry had asked for donations to a local charity in lieu of personal items. They had been born into families that had provided them with healthy trust funds and gifted them their first homes. They both had jobs but could pay their bills without them. There were plenty of other people who needed the extra support. The decision had been a no-brainer. On that point, at least, Ebby and Henry had been perfectly in sync as a couple.

When Ebby, too much in shock to register the full weight of what was happening on her wedding day, had insisted on walking downstairs herself to announce the cancellation of the ceremony, she immediately offered to pay back any guests who had wired funds to the nonprofit. But everyone shook their heads *no*.

"A donation is a donation," someone piped up. Funny, Ebby thought, the person who had made the comment was someone she barely knew from the groom's side. At any rate, there were murmurs of agreement all around, hugs from those who knew her well, and the blessed presence of her parents, who, having been unable to convince Ebby to stay inside the house, remained on either side of her.

She would be grateful, always, for the black hole in her memory after that. She would never remember how she ended up getting out of that garden, out of her dress, and into bed at her parents' house that afternoon. Nor would she recall eating anything the next day, or the day after that, or getting into her car. She would remember only walking into her own place a few days later, thankful for a hallway and dining table completely free of any signs of silvery wedding-gift paper. She would remember flopping on the sofa and sitting there until the sun went down, still too stunned to weep, wondering what kinds of chemicals went into paper to make it shine like silver anyway, and whether any of that stuff might be toxic.

# Ebby

---

JUST SEVEN HOURS. SEVEN HOURS OF FLIGHT, PLUS THE TRAIN and a car, and Ebby will be in a place where no one will recognize her, no one will look at her sideways, no one will cup their hands over their mouth and whisper, *It's that girl, you know?* At the racquet and swim club, at the bagel shop, at the supermarket, people back home go through the motions of being discreet, when in reality they want Ebby to hear what they're saying.

"What a shame about the wedding."

"After everything she's been through."

They want Ebby to know they know all about her.

Only they don't know. Otherwise, they would tell themselves to forget. Forget the wedding. Forget the shooting. The past nineteen years of her life have been punctuated by periodic articles, photographs, and media chatter recalling the murder of her brother, and the images of her younger self from that day. Ebby's identity has been stamped by the award-winning photo of her at age ten. Her clothing, bloodied. Her face, partially shielded from onlookers by the protective arm of her neighbor Mrs. Pitts, her friend Ashleigh's grandma.

Objectively speaking, it was an excellent photograph. Ebby can see why it won an international award. She can see why it has continued to show up in the media, especially now, with the twentieth anniversary of Baz's death fast approaching. But every time she sees that image, or a promo for that true-crime video special, or a journalist names her in connection with the shooting, Ebby feels like nothing can keep her from sliding back under the long shadow cast by the worst day of her life. Not the work she enjoys, helping clients to write better research papers. Not her family's achievements in business, science, or law. Not their long history as African Americans in New England, of which Ebby is quite proud.

And now her wedding plans have fallen apart in the most humiliating way.

There Ebby was, standing in the room that had been hers since she was ten, planning to walk down the garden path with a photo of her brother held close under her arm. She would have placed the picture of Baz, the last ever taken of him, on an easel near the steps leading up to the gazebo. She would have breathed in the cool air of the Sound mingled with the delicate scent of roses in her hair. Then she would have turned to face Henry.

Ebby and Henry had been planning a little surprise for the end of the ceremony. Instead of striding elegantly back down the path together, they would have done a little skip-dance. It had made them laugh to think of it. Surely Granny Freeman would love it, they'd said. She would chuckle as Ebby and Henry hopped past her, while her other grandmother, Grandma Bliss, and Henry's mother would try to conceal their horror at the display. Those two were more alike in their snobbishness than they would want to admit.

Ebby had been looking forward to the day after, when she and Henry would have begun a slow, lazy drive north. Seeking out the rockiest stretches of coastline, then dipping inland. Following the mustards and russets of the first leaves of autumn. Wherever they stayed, they would go walking every morning, Henry with his beloved camera and Ebby with her notebook and pencil.

"What about the Maldives?" Ashleigh had asked her on a video call. "Something island-y. Or the fjords! Or how about Victoria Falls?" Her friend was into faraway vacations. "You have to go *somewhere* for your honeymoon," she'd said. But Ebby had shaken her head.

"That's not what we want," said Ebby. Because she and Henry had talked about it at length. This was another way in which they'd been a good fit as a couple. They knew how they wanted to be in those first few days as husband and wife. New England in October was the best place in the world. And New England was their home. Only they never took that trip. Minutes before the wedding was scheduled to begin, Henry still wasn't answering his phone.

No, all those people who say, *Isn't that the girl . . . ?* don't know the first thing about being Ebony Freeman.

On the eve of her wedding day, Ebby woke up in the middle of the night, thinking that she'd heard the old jar in her father's study crashing to the floor. Later, she would wonder if it had been a premonition. She hadn't dreamed about that jar in weeks. Each time, in her dream, she would rush down the stairs toward the study, trying to stop the jar from hitting the ground, even though she'd already heard it happen. She would wake up with a drenched forehead, wishing that in her waking life, too, she could go back to the moment before she heard the jar fall.

*Just one moment before.*

In the moment before, her brother would still be unharmed. Her brother would be on his feet. Strange, though, how Ebby never sees her brother in that dream, only the jar. On her worst nights, the dream continues until she crouches down to gather up the broken pieces of pottery, cutting her hands as she tries to fit them back together. She knows her brother is lying on the floor right next to her, but she doesn't see him.

When Ebby was still seeing a therapist, the doctor used the phrase *complicated grief* and Ebby wondered why, was grief ever an *uncomplicated* thing? Despite her dream, she had dusted off that photo of Baz and the jar for the wedding ceremony. If you grieve for someone, it's because you cared for them, right? So you hold on to the memories. But Ebby needs to forget. She needs to be someone else, anywhere else. This is why she's leaving Connecticut. She is going to board a plane to France and stay away for a good long while.

# The Jar

THE JAR HAD BEEN PART OF THE FREEMAN FAMILY FOR SIX GENERA-
tions. Ebby's parents called it Old Mo because of the initials *MO* carved
just below its lip, clearly visible under the dark glaze. One of Ebby's
first words as a toddler was *oh-mow*. She and her brother used to love
their family's Old Mo stories.

The twenty-gallon stoneware pot, with its broad mouth and earlike
handles, had been a source of pride for the family, despite its origins. It
had been crafted by an enslaved man in South Carolina but would become part of a daring flight to freedom, traveling by wagon and ship
more than a thousand miles to the Massachusetts coast.

"The jar is a reminder of how you children came to be Freemans,"
Ebby's mom used to say, caressing it like a cat. She would trace her
fingers over the ridges in the glaze and along a small trail of leaves
painted in white slip down one side. Mom loved that jar, but it was
Ebby's father who had been born into the Freeman family, and it was
his dad, Gramps Freeman, who told Ebby and her brother what their
ancestors' lives had been like in the early days of the jar, after it had
made its unlikely journey to Refuge County, Massachusetts, where
their grandparents still lived.

"Tell us, Gramps," Baz would say whenever he and Ebby visited
Gramps and Granny, though they already knew the stories. They
would sit on the back porch of their grandparents' house in Massachusetts, trying to imagine what the property would have looked like in
the 1850s. Those were the days of the one-room farmhouse, before the
first Freemans added cabins for their sons. Before prosperity allowed
them to expand the main building, which grew over the years to become a gabled three-story manor restored in the Victorian style.

Their gramps's favorite details were from well before the manicured lawn and paved sidewalk and asphalt street were put in. Years before the closest town grew large enough to surround their family's land altogether.

"The only thing that hasn't really changed is that old shed out back," Gramps Freeman told them. "That became the room where the Freeman children and kids from other rural families used to learn their letters."

In the early days, Ebby's ancestors had only one door to their house and often used the jar to prop it open.

"The great strength of that jar," Gramps Freeman said, "was that its true worth was underestimated. Just like the value of the enslaved man who had crafted it and signed it at a time when people in bondage were not allowed to read or write. Just like those first Freemans in Massachusetts, who moved all the way out here to hide from the slave catchers who were crossing state lines in search of people like them." Gramps raised his brows and nodded silently in that way that he did when he wanted to be sure the kids were listening carefully.

"Most of the trouble in this world boils down to one person not recognizing the worth of another," Gramps said. "But sometimes, that can be an advantage."

The jar was typical of the kind of clay pot used to store pickled meats and such in the mid-1800s.

"At first glance, the container appeared to be pretty ordinary, but the more you looked at it, the more you could see that the jar glowed with the spirit of the earth from which it had been forged. That potter had a special touch."

By the time Ebby was born, the jar had already been moved to the Connecticut town where she and Baz were growing up, but when Gramps talked about the container, it was as if Ebby could see Old Mo sitting right in front of them. The glaze was the color of wet soil and mossy rocks at the bottom of a shallow river, a series of glistening browns and greens overlaying one another, their shapes seeming to shift along the curve of its surface. The jar had been one of her favorite things in the whole world. And she knew that had been true for her brother, too.

Ebby was barely ten years old when she heard the jar hit the floor, followed by that other sound. A dull *crack-crack* that signaled the supersonic flight of a bullet toward her brother's torso, followed by another that missed him altogether and ended up lodged in the wooden bookcase behind him. Even before she heard her brother cry out, before she reached the bottom of the stairs, before she saw the gunmen running out the front door, Ebby understood that along with that piece of pottery, something else in her life was splitting apart.

There was the moment *before* and there would be everything *after*. And in time, Ebby would come to understand her role as the surviving Freeman child. To be uncomplicated, to be successful, to stay alive. She has tried, but now she feels the only way to move forward is to find a place where she isn't reminded constantly of what was taken from her.

# Flight

———

At the airport, ebby's mother hugs her tight. here she is, twenty-nine years old, and this will be her first overseas trip alone and her first stay far from home for more than a couple of weeks. Ebby went to university a twenty-minute drive from her childhood home, worked in two offices nearby, and now reviews and edits her clients' reports from her condo in the next town over.

After high school, there was no student gap year abroad. There were no post-university rail passes for Europe. While other students packed their hiking sandals and shoved books and headphones into their knapsacks, Ebby pretended she wasn't interested in any of these experiences. She didn't want to live with the guilt of leaving her mother behind to worry.

Instead, she meets her mother once a week at the farmers market off the post road in her old neighborhood, just to spend the time shopping with her. And she still goes clamming with her dad once in a while, though not like they did when Baz was alive.

When Baz was still around, he and Ebby and Dad would make a show of grabbing a bucket, rake, and stick, walking down to the shore, and rolling up the cuffs of their jeans, only to spend most of their time watching other people hunt. Just being there used to be enough for them. There was something peaceful about seeing a person absorbed in a satisfying task.

But now, whenever Ebby goes with her dad, they fling themselves into activity. They scratch-scratch at the ground, then crouch down and pick out the quahogs and steamers by hand.

*Scratch-scratch-scratch.*

"You can search your whole life for something you'll never find," Dad once told her and Baz, his face sober, his right hand over his heart, "but if you do the work and you're patient," he intoned, letting his voice slow down and sink into his chest as he swept his arm outward, "sooner or later, you will find a clam." He chuckled then, and they snorted at Dad's clam wisdom. At low tide, after all, it didn't take much looking. But now that Ebby is grown, she sees what her dad meant back then, even as he joked with them. With all the things that can happen in life, a person needs the certainty of clams.

"Text us when you land," her mom says as Ebby breathes in the cottony, blossomy scent of her mother's shirt collar. "Text us when you reach the town." Her mother says *text us* because that's what people do nowadays, but what she really means is *call us*. Call us when you get there. Call us when you wake up. Call us every day. Call us twice a day.

Her dad says nothing, only hugs her for a long moment, then nods once in that way that he does, that squinty, *go-get-'em* half smile on his face. When Ebby looks back from the snaking security line, she sees her parents watching her. Two people so beautiful to look at, they couldn't hide if they tried. Even in one of the busiest buildings in the country, her parents still draw looks. Her dad in his slim-hipped chinos. Her mother, mahogany face glowing above her sky-blue shirt. But Ebby can see right through their casual elegance. Her mother and father are clinging to each other like two people trying to keep their footing on a bobbing life raft.

Ebby calls her mother while walking down the gangway to the airplane.

"You miss me yet?" she says, and she and her mom laugh into their phones. She will call again once she has landed, she promises. And again when she reaches the cottage, yes. The sense of guilt that Ebby feels as she boards the aircraft and shoves her wheelie bag into the overhead compartment has dampened the back of her shirt with perspiration, but the feeling begins to give way as soon as she taps Airplane Mode on her smartphone.

At the first whiff of jet fuel seeping into the cabin, at the upward thrust of the plane, at the ping of the seatbelt sign as it blinks off,

Ebby experiences a new sensation, like a cloak falling away from her shoulders and leaving behind a cool, silken *something* that can best be described as relief. Her plan to run away from home may not be a terribly original idea, but it feels like the smartest thing Ebby has done all year.

# Guesthouse

AFTER ONLY THREE WEEKS IN FRANCE, EBBY HAS LET DOWN HER guard. As she leans over a flower bed outside the entrance to the riverside cottage, she has no premonition, no suspicion, no hunch. She has no idea, when she hears the car door slam, then another, then the sound of luggage being hoisted out of the trunk and wheeled across the gravel, that her life is about to be turned on its head.

Again.

Because the sound of that car is precisely what Ebby has been waiting for. The visitors have arrived at two o'clock on the dot, as promised. The guesthouse out back is ready for them. Ebby smiles to herself as she hears the distant crunch of stone mixing in with the call of the cicadas and the close-by hum of bees in the lavender. It is a blessing, this easy sense of anticipation, this absence of worry. This is why Ebby has come this far, to a village of seven hundred people, a day's worth of travel across the Atlantic. It has been the perfect place to take a breather from the crushing weight of being home.

She owes all this to her friend Hannah, her colleague from London, the owner of the house. Hannah has asked Ebby to welcome these tourists while she takes care of business back in London. When she returns, she and Ebby will take a trip together. But for now, being here is all Ebby needs.

No one Ebby knows has ever heard of this village. And who would, unless they happened to know someone who grew sunflowers or produced Cognac in central France?

"Where, exactly?" said Ashleigh when Ebby told her she was going to stay at Hannah's place. Ashleigh, unlike Ebby, had struck out from home early on, moving all the way out to California for college, studying in Paris on a Fulbright scholarship, and taking postgraduate courses in economics and management in Shanghai. While the village wasn't well known among Americans, this area had managed to draw the attention of foreigners like Hannah, who first gave Ebby a tour of the house during one of their video calls.

Ten percent of the people around here, Hannah told her, were retirees from Britain or other expats, most of whom could fly over in an hour or two. They had set themselves up in old stone houses and refabbed barns, with Wi-Fi service and vegetable gardens and indoor-outdoor cats. Two of them had convinced Hannah to come visit. They were moving north into Brittany and wanted to sell. The summers down here were getting too hot for them. But Hannah had been hungering for warmth.

On the day that Hannah first drove into the village, she stepped out of her car, took one look at the old yellow cottage and little guesthouse, both surrounded by lavender and rosemary, and fell in love. She smiled at the three sunflowers growing in the side yard, their faces turned upward as if watching her, wiped the sweat from her hairline, and said, "How much?"

Ebby and Hannah had collaborated for two years on the same project, emailing and teleconferencing across the Atlantic, before meeting in person. And, yes, Hannah really has become a friend. A luxury. Ebby has never had more than a couple of true friends, having been trailed during her school years by the history of what had happened to her as a child. She's met people who are nice enough for a chat over drinks, but she's never been able to shake the feeling of being observed by others as she was in those first years after Baz's death.

Sometimes, Ebby catches people staring at her. At other times, she thinks it's just her being self-conscious. Either way, Ebby still needs to shield herself from people, to resist the idea that what happened to her brother might be tangled up in the way that others see her. She used to think Henry saw something else in her, someone other than that little girl. But now Henry's gone.

Ashleigh was one of the few who didn't seem to walk on eggshells around her. The first time Ebby saw her after Baz died, Ashleigh didn't hug Ebby, didn't say anything, just walked up to her and plopped down in a deck chair next to Ebby, then leaned to the side until her head was resting on Ebby's shoulder. Ashleigh had practically grown up around Baz. She'd spent part of every summer of her childhood with him and Ebby. And she would come to see the impact of Baz's death on her own family.

Ashleigh's grandparents, the Pittses, had been so shaken by the shooting that, like the Freemans, they felt compelled to move away from the neighborhood where it had occurred. They soon left the town where they had raised Ashleigh's mother, selling the home where they had wanted to spend their retirement.

Ashleigh was the only one who didn't freak out when she was with Ebby in that first year after Baz's death and Ebby was photographed by people on the street without her permission. Maybe it was because Ashleigh's parents were actors. She was used to being around people who got a lot of attention. She, too, had been subjected, at times, to the curiosity of people who did not know her.

Now that Ebby is grown up, people seem more interested in her looks than in her actual life. One magazine writer observed recently that the frightened girl that Ebby had been at ten had grown up to be an "elegant and reserved young woman." And a newspaper article on a scholarship awards event sponsored by her grandparents' foundation mentioned Ebby's "effortless beauty." What makes people think anything about her is effortless?

Surely, there must be people like her everywhere. People who get up in the morning, wipe their children's noses, walk down the street, show up at work, or go to school while calling on every ounce of careful grooming and good manners to make it look like it's no trouble at all. Surely, she is not the only person holding in a world of hurt that pushes against their skin like water against the walls of a dam.

People tended to believe that if you could go through a tragedy like the one that had struck Ebby as a child and not end up being crushed by it, then you could deal with anything else. Even Ebby had come to believe this. She had gotten through those uncomfortable years of being eyed silently by some of the kids who knew about her brother. There'd been eyes on the street where her family had moved after the shooting. Eyes in the hallway at her new school. Eyes at the club for

African American mothers and children over in New Haven. Thank goodness she'd found university and the working world to be easier. The passage of time did help.

When Ebby fell in love with Henry, she felt she'd finally turned a corner in her life. She and Henry were making plans for the future. To say *I will* to a marriage, or to anything that important, when there were no guarantees, was an act of faith, and given what she had been through, having faith felt like a triumph. But after the wedding was canceled, Ebby was back to dodging the periodic look of panic in her parents' eyes.

Her mom and dad were worried about her, all over again, and they didn't even know the half of what she was going through. After Henry left her, there were days when Ebby was tempted to say, *Mom, there's something I need to tell you.* Ebby wanted to be able to confide in her mother, but she didn't want to burden her any further. So Ebby did what she'd always done. She kept the worst part to herself.

The offer to stay at Hannah's cottage couldn't have come at a better time. Hannah had already been bugging Ebby to get away from home, to come meet her in France. Ebby had been tempted but was too proud to put her tail between her legs and run off. She had allowed herself one week alone in Maine, to recoup. Martha's Vineyard had been out of the question. Too many familiar faces up in Oak Bluffs, even if the summer season had come to a close. Too many people who knew her family, who remembered what had happened.

Then Ebby went back to her condo and forced herself to carry on with her work. Effortless beauty and all that. But she felt herself sliding backward, avoiding people, waking up in the middle of the night again. It was as if the old jar, hitting the ground as it had all those years ago, had been like a bomb going off in the middle of her life, and she was still trying to outrun the shock waves from the blast.

Desperation pushed Ebby to make changes. After a few months, she gave up her office at the research journal. She focused on generating the kind of flexibility that home-based editing and ghostwriting would allow. She cut her hair and changed the color for the second time in five months. Anything, she thought, to make her feel that things could be different.

Once Ebby had admitted to herself that none of this would be enough to pull her out of the slide that her mood had taken, she got on the phone and had a long talk with Hannah. She knew, from the start of their conversation, what Hannah was going to say: *Why don't you come to France?* And this time, Ebby was ready to hear it.

This time, Ebby was going to say yes.

Once she and Hannah were done talking, Ebby went online and booked her flights, then took a good look at her schedule of deadlines. She wanted to spend her free time playing tourist and practicing her French language skills, but she didn't intend to give up her job.

"The timing could be good," Ashleigh said when Ebby told her what she was thinking. "Working online from abroad is a thing, now," Ashleigh added. "You could blog about it."

"I don't want to blog," said Ebby.

"You could do just a little bit," said Ashleigh. "Just enough to stay on people's professional radars. To let them know you're not trying to, like, drop out of life."

"But I *am* trying to drop out of life," Ebby said. "Well, not really. I just want to work in peace. Take a break from having to keep up appearances. I definitely do not want to share my expat experience with *the world*."

She was surprised at what Ashleigh said next. She'd thought that Ashleigh would understand her need to keep to herself.

"You can't keep hiding out because bad things happened to you," Ashleigh said. "Okay, so you and Henry had a shitty breakup. And you witnessed Baz's death. That's terrible. No one else can know what that must feel like. But you have to find a way to live with all that without constantly thinking of yourself as a victim and using that as an excuse to cut yourself off."

Ebby felt her mouth fall open.

"What are you going to do about the rest of your life?" Ashleigh said.

Ebby pulled the phone away from her ear and frowned at it. Ashleigh continued to talk, but Ebby was no longer listening. How could her oldest friend not see what Ebby was trying to do? Ebby needed to feel invisible, precisely because she didn't want to be reminded of her past by other people. And she needed Ashleigh to be the kind of friend she used to be, that girl who knew how to be there for Ebby without saying a word. Ebby hasn't really talked to Ashleigh since.

Doing all right over there? Ashleigh texted the other day.

Doing great, Ebby wrote back. She didn't ask how Ashleigh was doing. Didn't say, *Let's do a video call*. She tried to focus only on the summer and fall ahead of her.

Hannah has an extra room and an upstairs terrace large enough for eating, and Ebby has nearly three months to figure out what to do next. Three months to stay without a visa, three months to work remotely, three months to visit the bigger cities and chat with people who know nothing about Ebby, her brother, or her failed love life. All Ebby has to do is look after the place and let vacation renters into the guesthouse.

And now, her first guests are arriving. Ebby washes her hands at the garden faucet and walks around the side of the house, careful not to brush up against the bees in the lavender. Careful not to slip on the muddy grass at the edge of the river. Careful not to kick the stones at the corner of the house where last week a viper reared its slender head in annoyance. *Be careful, Ebby, be careful,* her mother would say. *Be careful,* her mother was always saying. What would her mother say now, if she knew what Ebby was about to encounter?

# Skidding

---

EBBY ROUNDS THE CORNER OF THE COTTAGE AND SEES A RANGE
Rover. A woman, looking to be in her twenties but maybe younger than
Ebby, is standing at the far edge of the parking area, a gleaming sheath of
hair already tilting this way and that for a selfie. Pale-gold hair extensions.
Behind her, the slate turrets of the château at the edge of town stand out
like pointed hats, black against the July sun. A man walks over to take
the woman's suitcase and the sight of him gives Ebby a start. He looks so
much like Henry from that side. Her Henry. Hers at one time, anyway.

Ebby registers the flutter in her chest, the tight feeling around her
mouth, as the man turns and looks her way. By the time Ebby's brain
has absorbed the truth of it, that this stranger who reminds her of the
man she nearly married is, indeed, the man who abandoned her last
year on their wedding day, it is too late. Too late to run back around
the side of the cottage and pretend that she isn't there. Too late to bore
a hole straight into the earth beneath her and disappear.

Ebby steps backward, one rubber boot skidding in the mud. Henry
has nearly reached her. He is gripping the handles of two suitcases,
trailed by the selfie woman, and squinting into the sun. He still is unaware that Ebby, her eyes shadowed by the brim of a straw hat, her hair
now dyed the color of ripe cherries, her mahogany arms covered by a
long-sleeved gardening smock, is Ebby, his ex. Henry always was near-
sighted without his glasses and too vain to wear them unless he was
sitting behind the wheel of a car. And even then, sometimes.

As Ebby loses her balance and tumbles into the river, it occurs to her
that she has made enormous progress. There she was, thinking that this
encounter was the worst thing that could possibly happen to her, when
the very worst, in fact, had already come to pass.

# Henry

———

A PART OF HENRY KNOWS IMMEDIATELY. EVEN BEFORE HE DRAWS close enough to the riverbank to see Ebby properly. There is something about the way she inhabits the space around her that makes the hair on his forearms rise.

*This is not happening,* Henry thinks.

Ebby, of all people.

Here, of all places.

*Well, dammit,* he thinks as Ebby cries, "Oh!" and falls into the water.

# Lucky

———

Baz WAS LAUGHING SO HARD, HE TOPPLED ONTO THE GRASS AND lay there on his back. Ebby threw herself on the ground to imitate her big brother. Dried leaves tickled Ebby's back through her shirt. The sun bore down on her, turning her scalp damp, her skin salty. Kitchen sounds drifted over the yard from her grandmother's house toward the small orchard where she and Baz lay. She could smell the season's peaches ripening in the tree above her. They would end up in a nice big pie before long.

She and Baz were the luckiest kids in the world.

"I heard you two making a ruckus out there," Grandma Bliss said when they went back inside. She was chopping up parsley, her pink-painted nails and diamond ring bright against her long brown fingers. She insisted on making lunch herself whenever they visited, though she left the making of dinner and all the grocery shopping to the cook. Grandma Bliss lowered her chin, now, and looked at Baz and Ebby over the glossy, dark frames of her eyeglasses with an expression that said, *You didn't go out front, did you?*

Their mother's parents lived in a historic house with a wraparound porch that tourists slowed down to gaze at, mostly during the autumn leaf-peeping season, but also in the summertime. Ebby and Baz were never allowed to play in the front yard, on account of the tourists.

"No horsing around out there," Grandma would say. "Let's keep the yard looking tidy."

But they could play in the back, which had all that space, and those fruit trees, and the tiny pond where bullfrogs would make their funny *jugarum* noises. Unless, of course, their grandmother was getting ready to host one of her sorority events, in which case the entire place would be off-limits. Grandma would have the driver pick them all up and take them out for a few hours while the gardeners got to work pruning and raking.

Grandma Bliss liked to remind them that hers was the oldest black sorority in existence, formed at a time when African American university students had to establish their own Panhellenic associations in order to be accepted into one. Ebby understood that the sorors met mostly to discuss community service, a vague label she took to mean helping other people, in the way that their own kids' social club focused on volunteer projects. She just wasn't sure why this required having a pin-neat garden when the women generally met inside and lolled around on sofas in the air-conditioned living room, picking at finger foods.

Earlier, Ebby and Baz had heard the sound of a loudspeaker approaching and had run over to the side of the house to peek. A silver van slowed to a crawl as it passed the broad driveway in front of their grandparents' home, and Ebby and Baz craned their necks over a hydrangea bush to hear the tour guide's voice. The guide was talking about their mother's family. How their grandma's grandmother had been one of the first African American female physicians in the state of Massachusetts. And how the doctor's father had owned so much land that he'd sold some of it to the growing city of Springfield.

"The husband of the current owner," the voice on the loudspeaker said, "is a prominent attorney, but before that, he was one of the famed Tuskegee Airmen." The guide went on to explain that Grandpa Bliss had been part of the elite corps of African American pilots who served in the U.S. Armed Forces during World War II.

"The Tuskegee Airmen flew more than twice as many combat missions, on average, than white pilots," said the tour guide, "and still, they were made to use separate officers' clubs from their white colleagues. When some of them protested, they were arrested. Witnessing these events influenced Lemuel Bliss's professional direction. Bliss later studied law and went on to spend much of his distinguished career teaching, upholding, and working to refine laws related to civil rights."

Ebby followed Baz back to the rear of the house. Baz was nodding as he walked. Ebby knew Baz thought it was kinda cool that Bliss House was a tourist attraction. But not Ebby. When other kids at school asked Ebby about her family, she didn't like it at all. Even at age nine, Ebby felt that people were being nosy, not really interested in her as a kid. Mostly they seemed interested in her father's side of their family, in how the Freemans came to have the kind of money that had allowed her parents to move them into their part of town.

At least, up here in Massachusetts, her family was part of local history. Her parents had always told her and Baz that they needed to watch their mouths and mind their manners, because being the grandchildren of the Freemans or the Blisses meant something in Massachusetts. That it wasn't about their wealth so much as their heritage, education, and social refinement. The Freemans had been in the area long before it had been called Refuge County. They, too, had produced a series of African American pioneers, including their own early contributions to the ranks of local women in medicine.

Their grandfather on the Freeman side had led the campaign to change the county's name, to reflect the role it had played in sheltering people who had escaped enslavement with the help of free blacks, whites, and Native Americans. No matter that the Freemans' historically African American community had never been exclusively so, or that its black population had, in reality, thinned out to just a few families on opposite ends of the county. No matter that everyone else had long since moved east toward Boston or south to other American cities and suburbs.

Their family homes were still there, and the Freemans, in particular, were proud that they still lived in a house that used to stand all alone on a dirt road. The main house was now triple its original size and surrounded by other elegant homes, and their property had been profiled in style and culture magazines. Often enough that Ebby's granny no longer bothered to frame the articles.

"Appearances do matter," Granny Freeman once told Ebby. "I'm not saying that you have to be as fussy about things as your Grandma Bliss." She laughed then because Ebby had opened her mouth wide in a breathy *ohhh* of surprise. "But your mom's mother and I both agree on this point. Because for so long, we colored folks have been made to live with the message that our looks, our lifestyles, and our histories aren't up to snuff. Well, we want to make sure people know that we are proud of our lives."

But in Connecticut, where Ebby and Baz were growing up, her family had no real past to speak of. Even at her age, she could see that the one thing that made them stand out was simply being a well-to-do black family living near the surf club. There were plenty of other students from wealthy families in her class, but Ebby was the only one who was African American.

Sometimes, when Ebby was in the supermarket or at the post office near home, trailing behind her mother, she would see a question flit like a shadow across a person's face as her mom walked by. The question boiled down to something like *What are you doing here?* She could read the question as plainly as if someone had spoken the words out loud. A couple of the kids at school had, in fact, said those actual words to Ebby, and they had made her feel a kind of panic. Ebby was there because she had always been there, living with her big brother, and her mom and dad, in a dove-gray house with a view of the Sound.

Where else in the world was she supposed to be?

# Tumbling

_____

## 2019

Ebby, still sitting in the river, can see from the look on Henry's face that he's finally recognized her. Henry stops and stares, mouth open, then reaches down to help her out of the water. The clasp of his hand is disconcertingly familiar. She feels a ridge of skin on the inside of his thumb, still calloused from carrying his camera everywhere. She used to feel that ridge when he touched her chin or ran his hand along the inside of her leg. She used to dab a bit of lotion into her palm and rub it into that ridge.

Ebby pushes her other hand into the silt of the riverbank in an effort to raise her body fully out of the water. The smell of the mud on her clothes as she staggers makes Ebby think of the musk of clay behind Granny Freeman's house. Her dad's mom would like the soil around here. Good dirt, she would say. There is a town, not far away, that is famous for its clay. Ebby has been planning to visit, maybe buy a souvenir for her grandmother. Granny says clay runs in their family's blood, but Ebby's father sees it differently.

Ebby's dad likes to say it's the sea that courses through his veins, that he inherited a yen for the water from the sailors in his family. His father was descended from men who had worked in shipping and whaling until they'd found more gainful, and less dangerous, ways to thrive. This is why he was meant to live within walking distance of the shore, he says. Because of them.

But Granny and Gramps Freeman, like her mother's parents, have always lived inland, where the nearest body of water is a shallow brook. Where the snow drifts against the banks of trees behind their house

just so. Where they mutter about deer and turkeys raiding their vegetable garden but are slow to chase them away. They hesitate, instead, at
the kitchen window to watch.

"Go on, now," Granny will eventually say to whichever creature
she spots munching on her plants. She'll rap on the windowpane to get
its attention. "You've had enough."

Granny Freeman has a soft, steady way of talking. The thought of
her grandmother's voice, now, helps Ebby to calm her heart, which has
been thumping so hard she wonders if Henry has heard it.

When they were alone, Henry used to rest his head on Ebby's chest,
right over her heart.

Henry used to say, *I'm listening.*

Ebby used to believe that. She used to think that Henry had understood something about her. She used to think her presence in his life
was necessary. Surely, this man who is standing in front of her now is
not the same person. She thinks of Gramps Freeman, who used to
warn her and her brother that most people don't recognize another
person's true value. But Gramps never warned them about this part.
Gramps didn't warn Ebby that she herself might not realize it when
that lack of recognition was happening to her.

"Ebony Freeman," Henry says, in that drawn-out way that Ebby
used to love. "What the heck are you doing here?" Ebby is relieved to
note that she now despises the sound of her name on Henry's tongue.
Though his presence still makes her face burn hot.

# Clay

_____

**1803**

KANDIA DIPPED HER HANDS IN A GOURD FULL OF WATER AND closed them around a mound of clay. She squeezed and pulled, wet her hands in the bowl again, and began to roll the first coil. Later, she would try to recall the quiet of this moment. Her hands, cool in the clay. How it felt to be sitting on the ground in the shade of a karité tree, her mother and sisters working nearby, all of them unaware of what was to come.

Like the other women of her caste, Kandia was born to pull shapes from the soil. Only the pottery women were permitted to climb into the sacred pits and dig out the earth they required, though their men often waited nearby to carry the heavier loads. The women would filter the clay, mold it, and bake it into containers for food and water, or medicines and rituals. People from other villages needed their services, but they were wary of the power that issued from the potters' hands. Raw clay was a living thing that could be reshaped and reborn, until the potters committed it to the fire.

The pottery women were destined to live apart from the others. In Kandia's village, they married only blacksmiths, men who, like the women, could create things from the elements. It was said the pottery women drew their talents from the spirit world. Kandia herself believed this, until the day the people hunters came to her village and treated her like an ordinary woman.

The people hunters seized Kandia and cut down her husband as he fought to defend his family. As they dragged her away from her husband's lifeless body, Kandia could hear the distant cries of her mother and sisters, but when she turned to see where they were being taken, she felt the point of a spear between her shoulders. Kandia would have preferred death to separation from her family, but she knew she had to survive. She was carrying her husband's child.

With a great weight in her heart, Kandia recalled her husband's stories. There were men, he'd warned her, who captured and herded people up and down the coast. But Kandia, like her sisters, had never believed the hunters would come this far inland. She had not believed that anyone would dare to turn her people into prey.

Kandia felt the clay on her hands and clothing drying into a powdery film. The kidnappers were marching her toward the setting sun. Toward the coast. If Kandia truly had possessed the powers of a sorcerer, as often was said of the potters, she could have wielded her magic. She would have made a fortress of clay rise out of the earth to shield her family. She would have kept the people she cared for from venturing beyond its walls. She would have held herself back from the sea.

Instead, at the dawn of the next moon, she found herself shivering inside the rank cavern of a foreigner's ship, a monstrous vessel with wings of cloth, rocking and groaning as it crossed the water. She kept her arms resting over her belly, trying to warm the baby growing within. This was all she had left of her family, now. All she had left of herself.

# If Only

―――――

**2019**

IF ONLY THE WATER WERE DEEP ENOUGH.

Ebby imagines herself diving back into the river and swimming away. Instead, she is forced to stand here, on the riverbank, as Henry Pepper sweeps an arm toward the main house. Henry Pepper, with his long, thick forearms and walnut-colored hair. Henry Pepper, with those gray eyes. Henry Pepper, with his duplicitous ways. He smiles, now, as if they are just old friends, running into each other after a long while.

"So, this is your place?" Henry says. Ebby is slow to respond. She can't get over the fact that this is the man who abandoned her. A man who is about to check in to the guesthouse that Ebby is managing, and with another woman, no less. Ebby steals a glance at the blond woman, who has caught up with them at the riverbank and has her hand on Henry's arm. Ebby runs through a quick list of fitting comments in her head, every one of them a cussword.

"No, this is a friend's vacation house," Ebby says. She resists the urge to say, *You remember my friend Hannah, don't you? The one who flew all the way from England for our wedding?* But no, Ebby will not mention that day. She will not debase herself in front of this other woman. Instead, she says, "My friend asked me to let you in. But I didn't know it was you. I was expecting a . . . Cha. . . ." Ebby shoves a hand into the pocket of her gardening smock. She has the name saved in her phone.

"Chastity Williams?" says the other woman.

"Yes," Ebby says, frowning.

"That's me. Chastity Avery Williams."

"Uh, yes," Henry says, turning to look at his companion. "Ebby, this is Avery. Avery, this is . . ."

"Ebony Freeman, right?" says Avery.

*Oh, merde,* thinks Ebby. She recognizes the tone in Avery's voice. She's heard that tone for much of her life.

Here, in middle-of-nowhere France, is yet another person who has formed an image of Ebby before they've even met her. Someone who knows who Ebony Freeman is, what happened to Ebby as a child, and what Henry Pepper did to her last year.

Ebby wonders how Henry explained away that little episode to this new woman. Or, could it be that this woman is the reason why Henry disappeared that day? Ebby could never be with a man who had done something like that. She grabs a quick up-and-down glance at Henry. She tries to forget their history together and think of him as someone else might see him.

*Well, yuh.*

With Henry's looks, his job, and a family like his, he was bound to creep back onto someone's list of most eligible bachelors. Ebby takes a good look, now, at Avery. She notes the set of Avery's shoulders, the neat arch of each honey-colored eyebrow as she tilts her head to the side to look up at Henry. Avery looks so settled in herself. As if she knows she belongs wherever she goes and can have whatever she wants. Just like Henry. Of course. Someone like Henry would have been on the wish list of someone like Avery from the get-go.

"So, what are you doing all the way over here?" Henry says.

"Same thing you're doing here, I suppose," Ebby says. "Taking a break from Connecticut." Some break, she thinks. How in the world did Henry end up in this town? She and Henry had talked about taking a trip to Paris, maybe even Nice, but not this part of France. But Henry didn't make the reservations, did he? It would have been Avery. And how did she know about this place?

"I'd never even heard of this town," says Henry, as if hearing Ebby's thoughts. "But then Avery found out about it from somewhere."

Wait, was this Ebby's doing? When Hannah came over for the wedding, Ebby encouraged her to leave promotional cards about her vacation rental wherever she went. Hannah left cards in cafés, antique shops, and bookstores. *Of course,* Ebby thinks. Of course.

"So, you're here," Henry says. "You and, uh . . . ?" He looks around as if expecting someone else to appear. Ebby looks at him steadily but keeps her lips pressed firmly together. Henry's clearly fishing. Why would he even bother? Is he feeling guilty? Would he be relieved to think that Ebby has found another relationship already? Well, Ebby has no intention of going down that road with the man who ghosted her on her wedding day. Ebby blinks slowly and ignores the question. She points toward the rear of the building.

"Here, follow me," Ebby says. She leads Henry and Avery around the back of the building to the guest cottage, where she has left a set of keys inserted in the front door lock. Ebby takes the keys and holds them up, focusing on Avery and trying not to look at Henry.

"So this key is for the front door," Ebby says. "The other one is for the back." She hands the keys to Avery and walks ahead of her into the cottage, trying not to smile at Avery's exclamations.

"Look at this place," Avery says. "Hard to believe this was once a barn. Look at these appointments, Henry. The track lighting. The sky-lights. Large windows. With screens! We'll be able to enjoy the smell of lavender and rosemary but keep the bees and mosquitoes out. And look at those luscious floor rugs. That glorious ray of sunshine crossing the patio."

*This Avery woman is good,* Ebby thinks as she points out the coffee maker and shows her where the extra linens are kept. Avery is acting as though she hasn't just met the woman her ex was supposed to marry. As if their aborted engagement hadn't been all over the local news last fall. And she talks like a real estate agent. *Could* she be a real estate agent?

Out of the corner of her eye, Ebby can see that Henry is nodding at Avery. Why is Henry nodding? Ebby was hoping he would come up with a quick excuse to reject the cottage. Clear out of here right away. Move on to some other town. But this is Hannah's house and Ebby is supposed to help Hannah's guests feel comfortable. She wishes Hannah were here with her right now. Maybe Hannah would tell her this is just a bad dream, this isn't really happening.

*This isn't really happening, is it?*

"You can leave the keys in the mailbox," Ebby says, "if I'm not around when you leave." She takes care to stride slowly toward the front door, keeping her neck and back looking relaxed but confident. *Appearances matter,* she hears Granny saying. She does a half-turn, now, and throws them the obligatory parting line: "If you need anything in the meantime, just let me know. My mobile number is on that piece of paper over there."

She points at a cheat sheet stuck to the refrigerator. She is hoping they'll get the hint. *Don't knock on my door. Don't call. Text me instead. Even better, do your own thing and leave me out of it.* There is one moment, just a moment, when Ebby dares to look directly at Henry again. She sees him standing there before her with that other woman at his side and hears the roar of memories and resentment rushing into her head. Suddenly, she feels rooted to the spot. Literally unable to move or breathe. Until she hears the distant trill of a phone in the main cottage. The sound of it grabs her by the collar and pulls her out of the flood of panic.

"That must be the house phone," Ebby says. She knows who it is, too. There is only one person who ever calls the house. An elderly man who rings her every couple of days with the same damn question. Ebby really doesn't want to speak to him right now, but she is immensely grateful for the interruption.

"The house phone?" Avery says. "Someone actually uses their land-line? How quaint."

Henry chuckles. Henry always was easy to amuse, generous with his laughter, Ebby thinks. Ebby used to love that in him. But now Henry is being generous with another woman. He has chuckled at Avery's thoroughly predictable quip.

*Really, Henry? Really?*

The phone keeps ringing, but Ebby needs to stop for a moment and steady herself. She closes one hand over the back of a chair. She imagines pulling it from under the kitchen table and smashing it against Henry's chest. She wouldn't mind seeing Henry suffer a bit. She wouldn't mind seeing a few splinters of wood sullying the blue cotton of Henry's oxford shirt. Maybe a spot of blood, seeping out of a scratch in his skin and into the weave of the fabric. Well, that's an improvement. Ebby used to think she might run him down with her car if she happened to see him out walking somewhere.

"I'd better get that," Ebby says, tipping her head in the direction of the main house and the sound of the phone. Without looking at Avery, she can sense the other woman's shoulders relaxing. Ebby turns again and walks out, slowly, trying not to show how eager she is to leave. By the time Ebby gets back to the main house, the ringing has stopped.

As she closes the kitchen door behind her, Ebby feels her entire body trembling from the unexpected encounter with Henry. Or is it because she's still soaked from the river? She steps out of her rubber boots, takes off the straw hat, pulls off her drenched gardening smock, and walks over to the hallway mirror. Her cherry-colored curls looked better this morning. Sideswept and springy. Confident. Now they are flattened in the middle where the hat has been sitting, calling to mind the image of a clown, the red tufts of hair sticking straight out over each ear, flanking a downturned mouth.

Ebby changes into dry jeans and is blotting her wet hair with a towel when the house phone rings again. This time, she ignores it until it stops. It won't be the last time he calls, she's sure of it. The caller is always looking for some guy named Robert. She has no idea who this *Row-BEHR* person might be. Hannah has never mentioned him. If the man keeps calling, she'll try to find out more, but not today. She is not in the mood.

Ebby plops down at the kitchen table to sip at a cup of tea, trying to get back to that peaceful feeling she had before Henry showed up in the village. She hears a door slam. She moves over to the window and watches as Henry and Avery walk along the river, toward the foot-bridge that crosses into the park. They are ambling across the bridge, now, Avery's arm hooked in Henry's. *How dare they amble!* Ebby gives a short laugh at her own thinking. But trying to make fun of this ludicrous situation doesn't take away the sting.

# Avery

———

LIKE MOST PEOPLE SHE KNOWS, AVERY WENT INTO A PROFES-sion deemed suitable by her family. And like many young corporate lawyers, Avery has other interests. She's done some reading in psychology, for one. And today, she's thinking about the implications of Ebony Freeman's cherry-colored hair. Not dark cherry. Bright, sugary-drink cherry. Not what you would expect of someone like Ebony. Daughter of an elite African American family with a foundation that bears their name. Raised in exclusive New England neighborhoods. Like Avery, Ebony must know there are conventions to be observed, especially when it comes to your looks.

Avery recently read an article called "Survivors of Infamous Crimes: Where Are They Now?" Who comes up with these ideas anyway? There were three side-by-side photos of Ebony. The infamous, award-winning one from the day her brother was killed. Another from Ebony's engagement party as she stepped out of a Benz wearing a sheath dress, her hair smooth and dark. Then a more recent picture of Ebony at a fundraiser, still a stunner in muted, tailored clothing, only this time with cobalt-colored hair tips.

Avery has read about intentional changes in body appearance following multiple stress events. She has noted that not everyone relies on long-term approaches like cosmetic surgery, tattoos, or radical figure transformation through exercise. Avery is intrigued by the idea that some people constantly change their wardrobes or hair in an effort to process their emotions, and she suspects that Ebony may be one of them.

It's been easy enough to draw this conclusion. Avery admits it, she's nosed around the Internet looking at photos of Ebony. When she started dating Henry, she wanted to learn more about the woman who had held his attention for so long. Henry, the handsome and promising son of a powerful banker father and philanthropist mother, had already left a trail of photos on the Internet and in local society columns when he took up with Ebony Freeman.

Together, Henry and Ebony were photogenic, affluent, and unusual enough as a couple to invite attention. He was white, and she was black. He was an outgoing charmer, she was the cool, mysterious type. His life had always gone well, and her life had been marked by her brother's violent death. After the blowup on their wedding day, Ebony went quickly from her sleek, dark-haired looks to the blue-tipped bob. Then she took on a hybrid look of black roots with an emerald-colored Afro puff at the back of her head. And now this. Her natural curls, loosened and lit up, in this *cherry shock* version.

From the start of her relationship with Henry, Avery knew that if she wanted to stay with him, she would have to wrest them free of reminders of her boyfriend's past with Ebony Freeman. Which is why she'd finally muted her digital feed of *all things Ebony* and suggested that she and Henry take a vacation far away. She thought she'd found the perfect getaway when, while paying for a café crème at her favorite bakery back home, Avery saw a small flyer with photos of this guest cottage in France and a view of fields carpeted with sunflowers. Only, this cottage has brought her face-to-face with Ebony Freeman herself.

Avery was more than a little irritated when Henry once admitted to her that he had been so taken with Ebony at their first meeting that he had failed to make the connection immediately between the intriguing black woman and the ill-fated family from the Windward Road shooting. Avery didn't show her annoyance, of course, but she kept thinking about what Henry had said. What Avery didn't understand was, once Henry realized who Ebony was, why in the world did he insist on getting involved?

Ever since Avery's high school days with Henry's younger cousin, she'd had a crush on Henry. She'd moved away and had her share of romantic distractions over the years, but she'd never really stopped liking Henry in that way. More recently, when she realized they were back in the same town, she began to see him as a genuine possibility.

Avery had not expected the *Ebony situation* to last, and she had positioned herself to provide an uplifting and forward-looking alternative once Henry had put himself back in circulation. She did not consider Henry's relationship with her to be a rebound, since he was the one who had dumped Ebony. There was, in fact, nothing for him to bound back from. Or so she'd thought until today. Seeing Henry and Ebony together, even for a few minutes, makes Avery wonder if she had it all wrong.

Every young person needs to be allowed to make at least one colossal mistake in their life. Thinking that he could marry Ebony must have been the biggie for Henry. If Ebony was genuinely surprised that Henry had backed out of the marriage, then she must have been the only one. No matter how influential or admired Ebony's family may have been, they were still black, and Henry's mother was still the kind of mother for whom the Freemans would never have been good enough.

Looking at Ebony today, soaking wet from her fall into the river, droplets of water glinting like fake diamonds on her red pouf of hair, Avery couldn't help but feel a little sorry for her. But Avery hasn't merged onto the partner track at her law firm so quickly by letting sentimentality soften her focus. No, Ebony must not be underestimated.

Avery is busy strategizing. She is wondering how quickly she can move their two-week-long holiday booking—in other words, Henry—to another town.

# Henry

_____

UNTIL TWENTY MINUTES AGO, HENRY HAD BEEN LOOKING FOR-
ward to this part of the trip. Leaving Paris and Versailles behind. Dial-
ing things down for a while. Getting out his camera and wandering
along the river. Having sex in the middle of the day. But then Ebby
turned up. Or, rather, he and Avery showed up and found Ebby here.

Avery understood, instantly, who Ebby was. When Henry realized
this, he turned to look at her. Avery's mouth was tight around the corners, and her eyebrows were raised, but she was being her usual gra-
cious self. She was good at that sort of thing, being diplomatic in her
fury.

The worst part of that incredibly awkward moment was realizing
that, even though he had backed out of his engagement to Ebby last
year, on their wedding day, no less, with no explanation, none of the
qualities that had drawn him to Ebby in the first place had gone away.
Ebby appeared to be the same woman he'd wanted to marry from that
very first night, only with really bright clothing and hair.

What _was_ that color in her hair, anyway?

Bonfire curls aside, Ebby still looked like the woman who, nearly
three years earlier, had responded to his attempt to introduce himself
at a private mixer by saying, "Henry? What kind of name is that?"

It was something that others of Henry's generation might have
thought, but only a person saddled with a name like Ebony Freeman
would have the audacity to ask. Though at the time Henry still didn't
know her name.

"It's a rather common name, actually," Henry said, grinning. "Not
unheard-of in these parts."

"I know," Ebby said, laughing. "What I mean is, who names their

child Henry anymore? That's the kind of name I would expect someone's grandfather to have. Or, maybe, a pirate from the olden days."

Henry laughed. "And you are . . . ?"

"Ebby."

"Ebby?" Henry said. "Well, that's a thoroughly contemporary-
sounding name. Or is that, maybe, a nickname?"

He still didn't know that Ebby stood for Ebony. Still didn't know
that for much of Ebby's life, people had been taking note of her name,
speculating about her, commenting on her most personal struggles. All
he could think of was how drawn he was to the presence of this woman,
this Ebby, reaching for her drink with one long, russet-colored arm.

In that moment, Henry was picking up on much of what continued
to draw people to Ebby's story. Beyond her unfortunate past was her
appearance. She was attractive in a memorable way, which was to say
Henry couldn't stop looking at her.

"I asked you first," Ebby said. "Aren't you a little young to be a
Henry?" she asked.

"Henry was my grandfather's name."

"So your grandfather *was* a pirate?"

Henry laughed. "Well, some people might say so, but no, not really."

It was not uncommon for a man from a family like his to be named
after his influential grandfather. Families of every generation, in every
culture, had honored their ancestors or others of importance in this
way, but it's true Henry had been born at a time when his parents might
have opted for a different sound, or when his formal name could have
been replaced with a more stylish nickname. Something to suit the
trends of the decade. Something more advantageous to chatting up a
stunner like Ebby at a terrace bar overlooking the Sound.

There was a burst of laughter. Henry glanced in the direction of the
noise. A mirthful clutch of people across the room. The place had filled
up noticeably. Everyone here was a professional high achiever of some
sort, or the financially secure offspring of one. They all dressed the
same. Held their drinks up to their mouths in the same way. But not
Ebby. Sure, she dressed in the same kind of clothes but she wore them
differently. Henry admits it. He had approached Ebby because she'd
stood out in the crowd. Who wouldn't have? Just look at her.

It wasn't only her beauty, though, that held his attention. It was that way she had of looking past everyone, as though she had something more interesting on her mind, as though she had no real need for this room full of twentysomethings who were all trying very hard to leave their mark on this flirty, increasingly tipsy gathering. The woman she'd arrived with was already off and mingling, fully keyed into the buzz of energy. Henry still did not know that, while many people liked to watch Ebby and talk about her, and some would aim for a hookup, very few people actually wanted to spend any time with her. Someone might say, *Let's go to that happy hour,* or some other group event, then wander off. Rarely would they want to do lunch, or go walking, or see a play with Ebby alone. And it had become a vicious circle. If Ebby looked comfortable sitting there on her own, it was because she had grown accustomed to it.

But therein lay part of Ebby's charm, the trait that soon pulled Henry fully into her world and led him to say *marry me* two years later. If you could, indeed, catch Ebby's eye, strike up a conversation, and show genuine interest in her, if you could be one of those one-in-a-thousand who could look past the hometown tragedy that had burned itself into her family's identity, or past that reserved exterior, then Ebby would turn her full attention to you. She would be considerate. Ask you questions. Listen to your answers. She would smile. And when she did, it would be like finding the sunny spot in a garden and leaning back in a lawn chair to soak up the light.

"So," Ebby was saying, now, "you're telling me that being called Henry is, like, *name bling*?"

"I suppose you could look at it that way. Name bling." Henry felt himself grinning.

"I get that," she said. "We have one name that keeps getting repeated in our family, too."

"What's that?"

"Edward."

"That's not so bad."

"No, not really. And my dad, for example, calls himself Ed."

"So we've established that Henry, used full strength, is an awful name."

"Not awful. Did I say awful?"

"You implied awful," Henry said, but he was smiling.

"So what do you do when you're not fending off attacks on your name?" Ebby asked.

"Banking."

"Banking? You look familiar. Who are your people?" Ebby asked.

"Pepper."

"Pepper! Not *those* Peppers?"

"No, not really," he lied. "We're a bit poorer."

"But not so poor?"

Henry laughed. "No, *not*."

Ebby smiled broadly, now, and Henry felt, what was the word? Happy? Yes, that was it. He rested one elbow on the counter of the bar and leaned in toward Ebby. He noted something both woody and floral, barely there, in the air around her.

"And you?" he asked.

"Freeman," she said.

"Freeman?" Henry closed his eyes and tipped his face toward the ceiling. "Freeman, Freeman, Freeman. There are some Freemans up in . . ." He stopped. "They're, um . . ." He straightened up. Started to speak again but, unsure of what to say, paused, lips slightly parted. He felt beads of moisture gathering along his hairline. Shit, it was all coming back to him, now. A black family. A terrible tragedy.

"That's right," said Ebby, nodding very slowly. Reading his thoughts. "We are the only Freemans in these parts. And, yes, we are *those* Freemans." Her voice was cooler now, not unlike that bit of chilled air that slips out of a freezer just as the door is shut.

*Oh, great, Henry,* he thought. *Well done.*

"Is there anything else you'd like to know?" Ebby said. "Or have you read all the news reports?"

"Whoa," Henry said, touching Ebby's arm. "Hold on a minute there. I didn't realize. I really wasn't thinking. I was only making conversation. Can we make conversation? Can we just talk? Would that be all right?"

Man, there was that smile again. Look at that. It didn't matter who Ebby was, or what had happened to her family. She was standing right in front of Henry, and he was going to do whatever it took to keep her there. So he tried again.

"There are some seats out there on the lawn. Would you like to join me?"

She nodded, and all felt right with Henry's world.

Henry should have guessed right away that a young woman who had been through what Ebony Freeman had experienced might be prone to sudden displays of defensiveness, as she'd shown that first night. He should have imagined that she might struggle to be around people at times, though she would conceal it well, poised as she was.

Later, when Henry was already too smitten to walk away, he would google Ebby and her family. He would read about the Freemans' long history in Massachusetts and substantial real estate holdings and net worth. At the time of their son's death, the mother was a whip-smart corporate attorney, and the father was a brilliant engineer and inventor who'd sold a couple of patents to the right companies at just the right time.

That the Freemans were African American was something that seemed to be mentioned in every news report, every article, and every social media post that Henry read about their personal tragedy. Nothing like the shooting had ever happened in their neighborhood before, each report would quote people as saying. It felt as though the writers were implying that the Freemans' blackness had something to do with the violence that had been visited upon them, despite the fact that they lived in a wealthy enclave already brimming with temptation for anyone willing to hedge their bets against private security patrols.

But as Henry sat there, facing Ebby for the first time, he was not thinking about the Freemans. He was thinking only of the woman lowering herself into a lawn chair next to him, and of the feeling that a door was swinging open in his life. He wasn't thinking that someone like Ebby might still suffer from trauma, years after a violent event. Might jump at sudden sounds or wake up in the middle of the night, her camisole soaked with perspiration. Might turn down dinners with his friends, more often than he liked, to avoid what Ebby called the *viral curiosity* that followed her around.

He couldn't imagine then that as he approached their wedding day, he would wonder if life with Ebby would always be as thorny as it had become, and that he would be afraid to be honest with her about the doubts he'd been harboring.

Avery's soft chatter pulls him back to the here and now. Avery, walking arm in arm with Henry along the river, tells Henry that they can still change their plans, find a new booking, continue their vacation elsewhere. Henry nods, makes an effort to keep listening. Avery is such an easy person to be around. There's a lot to be said for that. But seeing Ebby has changed everything.

# A Woman Scorned

———

EBBY FORCES HERSELF TO TURN AWAY FROM THE KITCHEN window, to avoid looking at Henry and Avery. They are on the far side of the river, now, moving along the dirt path that passes the campers. The thought of them together leaves a sour taste under Ebby's tongue. She fights the urge to spit in the sink.

The worst part of Ebby's relationship with Henry wasn't the fact that Henry had decided not to marry her. Okay, that was the worst. The second worst was that he had thought to marry her in the first place. In insisting on linking his life to hers, Henry had pulled Ebby back into the spotlight. As it turned out, Henry wasn't as poor a Pepper as he'd suggested on the night that he and Ebby had met. His father's appearance, though brief, on the Forbes 400 list of the country's richest people, coupled with Henry's prior relationship with a retail heiress turned online fitness influencer, had set off a buzz of chatter around Henry that eventually grew to include Ebby.

After living for years in the shadow of her brother's death, Ebby found herself, once again, a character in someone else's story. Henry Pepper, the rising young star of an old banking family, had "taken himself off the market for the child survivor of a fatal home invasion robbery," reported one social media page, which also described Ebby as an "African American stunner." Then Henry left her standing there on her own, on their wedding day. With one shitty move, Henry Pepper had shown the world that Ebony Freeman, try as she might, could not escape the mantle of misfortune that had settled over her.

And Henry had confirmed her parents' fears that they weren't doing enough to protect her. Her mother's persistent plea comes back to her now: *Be careful, Ebby. Be careful.* Ebby walks over to the shoe rack near the front door and starts to slip into a dry pair of pull-on shoes. She wants Henry gone. He should leave today and take that woman with him. Ebby picks up a promotional postcard with a list of *gîtes* and other accommodations in the area. She wants to run outside, hurry over the bridge, and call to Henry. She wants to hand him the list, but then she wills herself to stop.

What's past is past. But the pain feels very present.

Henry left Connecticut in the middle of the night, just hours before Ebby should have been walking down the stone path in her family's garden to marry him. Several days later, an email arrived from Henry. He wrote, I'm sorry, Ebby, I really am. But only that. Then he texted Ebby on her smartphone and asked to see her.

Give me a chance to explain, Henry wrote. Please.

What could Henry possibly say to justify what he had done? Ebby pressed Delete and turned back to what she was doing. By then, Ebby was three hundred miles north in Maine, wearing a baseball cap and large sunglasses, hoping no one would notice her as she stood in a beauty supply store. She knew her mother had sorority friends up that way. They would take note of her thinner shoulders, her puffy middle. She didn't want to look as wholly abandoned as she felt.

Ebby tried to focus on the task at hand. She read through the labels on hair color products, checking for potentially harmful chemicals. She had decided to dye the tips of her hair cobalt blue. Just the thought of the color comforted her. It wouldn't solve her problems, but she would go back to Connecticut looking like a new woman.

As she considered her hair-care options, Ebby could feel someone's eyes on her. She turned to see a trio of women standing in the same aisle. All three of them were holding packages in their hands but looking at Ebby. As soon as she saw them, they looked away. Were they just checking her out, as women did with one another in beauty shops? Or did they recognize her from one of the unfortunate post-wedding-day reports that Ebby herself had seen pop up on her regional news feeds?

——

**SURVIVOR OF VIOLENT HOME INVASION ROBBERY
JILTED BY BANKER FIANCÉ.**

**DREAMY SON OF OLD CT FAMILY A NO-SHOW
ON HIS WEDDING DAY.**

## MORE BAD LUCK FOR AFRICAN AMERICAN SURVIVOR
## OF INFAMOUS HOME ROBBERY.

——

She'd had to turn off her phone to avoid seeing more push notifications mentioning the wedding fiasco. But she was still thinking about the teasers she'd seen. Ebby noticed that no one had thought to describe her, as they did Henry, as coming from an old New England family. Henry's family went back a ways, for sure, but so did Ebby's. Ebby's people on her mother's side had been in Massachusetts since the 1600s. Some had been enslaved. Others had been born free or freed later. Most had purchased land.

Ebby's ancestors had been farmers, craftsmen, teachers, doctors, lawyers, politicians, and investors. Some of the men from her father's side had sailed into and out of New Bedford and Boston on square-riggers and whalers in the 1800s. What could be more *old New England* than that? But the Freemans were black. People saw their skin, not their history.

This thinking only added to Ebby's sense of betrayal. The day Ebby colored her hair ends in blue dye was the day Hannah first urged her to consider a hiatus in France. But it would take her another seven months and two more hair-color changes to act on that idea. When Ebby finally landed in Paris with cherry red curls, Hannah was waiting with a hug and a car.

"In the end, Henry did you a favor, Ebby," Hannah said once they were settled in the car and driving southwest. She glanced at Ebby over her eyeglasses, then looked back at the road ahead.

"A favor?" Ebby said. "Leaving me standing there like an idiot? Leaving me to cancel the wedding on my own? Leaving me exposed to all that media coverage?"

"It was a cowardly thing to do, I know," Hannah said. "But yes. You would have married him, otherwise. And then what?"

It hurt to hear Hannah say it. Even though she knew Hannah had a point, it hurt all the same. She had *wanted* to marry Henry. She couldn't pretend she hadn't, even though he'd let her down big-time. There was no way to get around this awful feeling of having made a bad choice.

Having ended up with nothing for it. But before she could dwell on it, Hannah switched to speaking in French.

"You need to jump into the language right away," Hannah said. "You'll need to fend for yourself while I'm gone."

Chatting in French during the four-hour drive, Ebby found that her language skills weren't as rusty as she'd feared. And everything she saw around her boosted her mood. The stone houses. The vineyards and sunflowers. Even the road signs were charming. Hannah turned the car, now, into a driveway leading to her small compound. Ebby saw a wooden sign at the front of the property, shaped like an arrow. It had one word on it: HIDEAWAY. *Yes,* Ebby thought. Yes. This was going to be *her* hideaway.

Ebby enjoyed twenty-one days of peace before Henry Pepper showed up. Twenty-one days of lavender humming with bees. The soft voice of the river. The comical ducklings on its surface, trying to follow their mother while bobbing sideways over the counterflow of the water. Those long, flat back roads where Ebby liked to ride Hannah's bike. Farms lined with wildflowers and yellowing, summer-baked grass. And the feeling that she could be someone else yet, somehow, still herself.

This was Ebby's new routine: Early morning coffee and gardening. A walk along the river. Breakfast at the village café. Working at the laptop in her favorite room, the one with the large stone fireplace. Listening to the voices of children reaching her from the camper vans on the far side of the river. Taking a break to visit the street market or drive over to another town. Back at the screen in the late afternoon.

Every day, she repeated the mantra her mother's mother had taught her and Baz when they were little. *Hold the moment,* Grandma Bliss always said. Before Ebby had ever heard the term *mindfulness,* Grandma Bliss had a grasp on the concept. Be aware of a beautiful moment as it is happening. Take note of your life as you are living it. Grandma Bliss's advice had been working for her lately, until this afternoon, when Henry and his Instagram envoy showed up and ruined everything.

# Hold the Moment

———

Their grandmother's kitchen was filled with the aroma of something crusty and saucy.

"I made pot pie," Grandma Bliss said.

"Yum!" Ebby said.

Their mom's mother had always liked delicate-looking foods. Puffy and melty-topped dishes that might fall apart as soon as you put a fork to them but still tasted pretty good.

Grandma claimed to have been an attorney once, but as long as Ebby could remember, she had been working on artsy things out of a home studio. The room was filled with swatches of fabric, little rectangles with different paint colors, and before-and-after photos of hotels, hospitals, and houses that were even bigger than hers.

"You two having a good time?" Grandma asked.

"Uh-huh," Baz and Ebby said in unison.

"Uh-huh?" Grandma said. "*Uh-huh?*" Grandma put a hand to one ear and squeezed one eye shut as if she hadn't heard them properly. Baz and Ebby lowered their heads.

"Yes, Grandma," they said.

"Now, that's more like it," Grandma said. "You know I don't tolerate any *uh-huh* kind of speech in this house. How many times do I have to remind you two that you are not donkeys?"

Baz shrugged. Ebby did the same.

"Your grandfather and I," Grandma Bliss said, "and your dad's parents, too, worked very hard to make sure your mother and father had excellent educations. And your parents are doing the same for you.

Not every child has this privilege, even though they should. So don't you ever take your language for granted, children. Claim your language. Love your language. Use it well."

"Love your language," Ebby and Baz said in unison with their grandmother, because they had heard some version of this lecture before.

But at age fourteen, Baz was already questioning the idea of language and what was proper.

"But isn't *uh-huh* part of our language, too?" Baz asked their mother that night. "Can't we love expressions like *uh-huh*?"

"Yes, that is part of our language, too, Baz," she said, nodding. "And unlike your grandmother, I do believe there are times when it's fine to use colloquial expressions. It depends on the context. It's just that, at your age, you need to be sure to master the standard language first. Expand your vocabulary. Embrace the variety of words available to you. Make sure you can command the language in such a way that no one can ever doubt your ability to do so."

Their mom tapped Baz under the chin with a finger. "Don't look down, Basil," she said. "Listen to me. Always look up. You're becoming a young man, now. A young, African American man. People are always going to look for excuses to question your capacity to do things. Fair or not. And then they will use that as a reason to take away the rest, all of those expressions, colloquial or cultural, that make language more interesting."

"Yes, Mom."

"Good. So none of those donkey sounds for now. At least, not when you're talking to your grandma, or she'll send you over to the neighbor's barn to live with the other animals, and she'll put me out there with you, too."

Their mother was grinning. Baz scrunched his shoulders and started into an exaggerated, hee-haw kind of laugh. She mock-slapped him on the arm.

"And please, do not tell my mother that I said saying *uh-huh* is all right. Just be sure to answer her properly. Remember . . . speak better . . ."

Baz joined in now. ". . . walk straighter, be smarter, be kinder."

Ebby, listening from the doorway, mouthed the words with him. Another family mantra. But that was only the first of several times that Baz would ask their parents about language and dialects and what was worthy of consideration. That summer, Ebby saw her brother reading a book. The title was long but Ebby could make out the words *linguistic diversity*.

"What's that?" Ebby asked her brother.

"Library book," Baz said. He looked up from the pages. "See, we have different kinds of English, and this here talks about that. People don't use only one kind of English. Not only the kind that's in the dictionary. We need to embrace all kinds of language."

"Then why do we have the dictionary?" Ebby asked.

"We still have to study the standard, like Mom says. Learn vocabulary and grammar. So we can study for exams and get jobs and talk to people from all backgrounds. The standard is like an intersection in the road, you know, where we all meet. But we're all coming from different directions." Baz lowered his voice now, as if sharing a secret. "Did you know there are entire peoples whose cultures have been supressed because other people keep them from using their language?"

"Uh-huh," Ebby said. But actually, she didn't know. She wasn't sure how such a thing might be done. Did they tape up people's mouths? On top of which, she thought *embrace* meant to hug someone. Could a person hug a language?

"What did you say? *Uh-huh?*" Baz said. He heaved his shoulders up and down and pawed the floor with his feet. "Hee-haw," Baz said, and he and Ebby both laughed, her laughter a high giggle, his voice already on a downward slide toward adulthood.

"And anyhow," Baz said. "Have you ever heard a donkey go *hee-haw*? Donkeys do not go *hee-haw,* but that's what they write in the books. Don't believe everything they put in print."

Ebby frowned. "But you believe what's in *that* book."

Baz frowned back and pointed at her. "I am thinking about the book. I don't have to *believe* everything I read in a book, just think about it." Ebby nodded, though she felt unsure of what this meant. She leaned toward her brother and put her arms around his waist. He pulled her head against his chest and gave her the knuckle.

"Owww!" she said.

"Ha ha," he said. "You walked right into that one. Come on," he said, and Ebby, as she had since she had learned to walk, followed her brother. They went down the hallway, through the kitchen, and into the backyard.

"Can we play hide-and-seek?" Ebby asked.

"Hide-and-seek, again?" Her brother rolled his eyes. "Aren't you getting too old for this?"

But Ebby was grinning. She already knew he'd give in and play. Later that day, Ebby opened up one of her school notebooks and scribbled something in the back. Grandma Bliss always told her and Baz to write down one thing from each day of their visit that they wanted to remember.

"Hold the moment," Grandma would tell them. "Write it down, just a word or two, on any kind of paper you find." On that particular day, Ebby wrote two words in her notebook in uppercase letters: BEST BROTHER. But mostly, she and Baz would write things like SWIMMING IN THE POND or ICE-CREAM SODA or RED SQUIRREL on a piece of scrap paper and attach it to their grandmother's fridge with a magnet. Grandma had a junk drawer in the kitchen filled with pieces of discarded paper that were printed on one side but blank on the other. One day, in the years when there were so few wild turkeys around that no one saw them in their gardens much, Ebby wrote MAMA TURKEY WITH CHICKS!

"Not all the moments will be good ones," Grandma said. "That is part of life. But it's nice if you can hold on to something you have appreciated."

And then just like that, Baz, her brother and number-one friend, was gone. After he was killed, Ebby went to visit her mom's parents and saw the way her cousins and other relatives would follow her with their eyes while pretending not to. She could tell everyone was thinking about Baz but didn't want to mention him when she was around. Ebby had been the only other person in the house when those robbers shot her brother, and this fact lay like a gulf between her and the rest of her family. But not with Grandma Bliss.

Grandma would say things like "I made that cobbler that you and

Baz always loved" or "Are you chilly, baby? Why don't you go get your brother's old sweatshirt from the back room." She must have known that something in the feel of the cotton sweatshirt would comfort Ebby. Remind her of how Baz used to pull her close and bore his knuckles into her head. Of how he could get on her nerves in that way that she missed.

When it was time to go and her parents were loading up the car with overnight bags and leftovers, Ebby pulled open Grandma Bliss's junk drawer, looking for scrap paper. She didn't have to jiggle the drawer to get it open. It was nothing like the ones in her other grandmother's kitchen. Granny and Gramps Freeman were proud of the fact that much of their home's interior dated back to the nineteenth century. But Grandma Bliss had made a point of installing modern drawers that were whisper-quiet and smooth.

Despite the age of the Blisses' house, this kitchen had nothing old in it, and the broad granite countertops were completely free of clutter. The only things sitting on the counters were a food processor and a coffee maker. The only sign of jumble in the kitchen was the fridge, whose exposed right side was dotted with candid photos and a couple of hold-the-moments from the last time Ebby and Baz had been there together. Baz had written GRANDPA'S GOGGLES on a piece of paper because the night before, they'd been looking at Grandpa's old photographs from his time as a military pilot.

There was Grandpa Bliss in a group of trainees outfitted in coveralls and headgear with goggles. There was Grandpa in the cockpit of a P-51 Mustang. There was Grandpa in his dress uniform. And there he was, 153 combat missions and three decades later, giving a talk to high school students in Springfield. The Tuskegee Airmen had not been the first black men to pilot planes in the United States, Grandpa explained. And still, they'd had to prove themselves worthy to join the World War II effort.

It had been fun looking at her grandfather's photos that day, but the moment that Ebby chose to hold closest to her heart was another. One filled with the smell of sunshine on freshly turned earth. She and Baz had gone to a nursery with Grandpa and helped him to choose a tiny maple tree, which they planted in the backyard. Before leaving the house, Ebby took a blue marker and the scrap of paper she'd found in the kitchen drawer and wrote BABY MAPLE, and stuck it on the fridge.

Within a year both Baz and Grandpa Bliss would be gone. Ebby overheard one of her older cousins saying Grandpa had died of a broken heart after what had happened to Baz. But her grandmother said it had been Grandpa's time to pass on, and no wishing otherwise was going to change that. Over the years, the little maple tree grew to be much taller than Ebby, and every autumn, its leaves still turned bright orange. Then the leaves would fall away, and the tree would seal off its branches to protect itself from the onslaught of winter.

# Kandia

———

**1803**

ANOTHER WOMAN WAS SPEAKING TO KANDIA IN A TONGUE
that she did not recognize. Still, Kandia understood. Fear was a language common to all people, and nothing was more fearsome than
being stolen from yourself. They were squeezed into the hold of the
ship with many others, after having been locked up, for days, in that
cold stone house at the edge of the sea. Kandia had hoped to see her
mother and sisters among the people who were shoved into the room,
but she never did.

She closed her eyes, now, and held on to memories of home, murmuring what she could recall to her unborn child. The energy of the
raw clay under her fingers. The tickle of warm dust on her feet. The
voice of her child's father, Mansa. She would give her child his name if
they survived this voyage. *Mansa,* she said, speaking to the center of
her body as her baby stretched and turned inside her. *Mansa.*

Later, the man who purchased Kandia would insist on calling her
newborn child Moses. This was not so important, thought Kandia.
The sound was close enough. And she would know her son by any
name. She could smell the clay and iron in his skin. She and her child
had been stolen from the place she called home, the people she called
family, but on the morning that her son was born she decided that no,
she would not allow them to be stolen from themselves.

# Lookie-Loo

———

**2019**

Avery reaches into her bag for the ipad, then pauses.
She really needs to stop doing this at bedtime. She has read the blogs.
She knows the risks. Blue light and electromagnetic radiation. The
ways they can mess with a person's eyes, and sleep cycle, and cardiac
rhythm. Avery makes a concerted effort to avoid using smartphones
and other electronics once she has climbed into bed for the night, and
she leaves them a few feet away, not right next to her on the nightstand. But this has been, objectively speaking, a very shitty day, and
Avery needs this. She pushes her hand back into her purse and pulls out
the tablet.

Avery presses the button at the top of the iPad until the screen lights
up. She has earned this. She has been diplomatic and patient. Avery is
nothing if not the picture of diplomacy. How many other women
would have handled this situation as well as she has? After encounter-
ing Ebony Freeman unexpectedly at the start of what should have been
a romantic village getaway for Avery and Henry (not Avery and Henry
and Henry's ex), Avery had understood that she needed to take Henry
for a walk as soon as possible. So she took him away from the cottage.
And Ebony.

All day, she kept the tone of her voice light and even. She accentu-
ated the positive, treating their unexpected encounter with Ebony,
though unfortunate, as only a temporary setback and not what it was
starting to feel like to Avery: the crumbling of the dream vacation that
she had spent so much time planning.

"Well, that was embarrassing," Henry said with a low bark of laughter as they walked through the village. Avery didn't want to talk about it right then, but the fact that Henry had finally said something about what had just happened was a good sign. It was better than doing what he'd done initially, simply pulling luggage into the cottage with that synthetic smile on his face, washing his hands noisily in the bathroom basin, and taking out his camera to fiddle with the lenses as if nothing had happened. Avery dreaded the idea that Henry was having thoughts he might have to keep to himself.

Avery's next step is to book another place to stay by tomorrow afternoon. She looks over at Henry, his face partially hidden by the plump pillow, his breathing growing heavier and slower. It's midnight already. She and Henry spent an hour of what should have been lovemaking time swiping away at the tablet, looking for accommodations within a two-hour drive.

More precisely, Avery was the one who spent an hour curled up on the sofa in her frastaglio-trimmed La Perla nightdress and robe, peering at the screen and reading descriptions to Henry, while Henry said *sure, sure* to whatever she read out loud. She had waited for him to come over to the sofa, take the tablet out of her hands, and pull her into bed. But he hadn't. Then he dozed off. After making her way over to the bed on her own, Avery couldn't sleep. Which is why she is back to looking at the tablet. Only she's no longer looking at vacation rentals.

Avery is doing what Avery does when she is stressed and too distracted to read a book or article. She is looking at properties for sale. But she isn't planning to buy anything. She's being a lookie-loo. There's no other way to put it. Back in Connecticut, Avery likes to take note of the addresses with signs out front that advertise weekend open houses and stop by on her way back from putting in extra hours at the office. And whenever she travels, she goes online to search the real estate listings.

Avery attaches the portable keyboard to the iPad, now, and perches it on her book on French châteaux. She types in the search term *annonces immobilières*. Where should she look tonight? So many choices. She moves the cursor and feels her heart rate step up as photos, prices, and property descriptions fill the screen. Versailles. Nineteenth-century mansion. Twelve rooms. 400 square meters.

The home has custard-colored walls with white moldings. *And look at those floors!* There are wooden floors in the hallways and the bedrooms that look like originals and give off that warm feeling that comes with polished oak. Then there is sleek, gray stone flooring extending from the kitchen into the dining area. En suite bathrooms. Study. Cellar. Garage. Avery releases her breath slowly as a sense of satisfaction flows over her. She switches her search parameters, now, to the south. She is looking at a two-bedroom apartment in Nice. Art Deco building. Open-plan kitchen. Plenty of natural light. Harbor view.

Avery could argue that scanning the real estate ads is a great way to get a sense of economic and social trends in a city or region, or that it's an interesting way to get a sneak preview of an area she'd like to visit. But the truth is, Avery simply loves reading the housing classifieds. It doesn't matter whether it's a historic villa in Aquitaine in need of a major overhaul, a sleek, ready-to-move-in apartment in Bordeaux with minimalist furnishings, a comfortable-looking rural bungalow in Brittany with a garden and swimming pool, or one of those ridiculously tiny apartments in the *centre ville* of Paris that are barely big enough for a sleep and a pee. This is Avery's favorite way to daydream.

In every case, Avery can imagine walking into a space with an architect and drawing up a refurbishment plan, or walking over to the window to take in the view, or flipping a wall switch to fill a darkened room with an ivory glow. She sees herself taking off her heels and leaving them near the door, shuffling over to the largest, softest piece of furniture in the house, and letting her body fall back into a place where she can feel comfortable and safe and happily foreign. A place where she is so unknown to those around her that no one has any expectations of her. Where no one would think that she is being any *more* or *less* herself when she is simply being Avery.

Sometimes, Avery imagines she is holding an infant in her arms or pulling herself off a couch to chase after a toddler. Listening to psychology podcasts or books on her AirPods as she navigates the house. Taking calls from legal clients in the afternoon. Billing for way fewer hours than she does right now. But always, she is in someone else's home, someone else's living room, on a sofa that she has seen in the housing classifieds or an issue of *Architectural Digest*. In a place that is somewhere else. Anywhere else.

She clicks, now, on the image of an old farmhouse with stone walls. Great potential, reads the ad. In need of a little TLC. Avery feels like the ad could be talking about her. There are other people like her. She has seen more reports, lately, about people who recognize that being productive doesn't have to mean going flat out, two hundred percent. But the people who are beginning to embrace this approach to work tend to be older. They have fully developed careers and home lives. Avery is still on the uphill climb toward both.

Avery looks over at Henry, sputtering slightly in his sleep. Henry, who can sleep so soundly next to her even when the woman he ghosted, less than a year ago, is just next door. She feels a tinge of irritation. What is that like, she wonders, to go through life being Henry?

# Falling

———

EBBY HEARS HER BROTHER CRYING OUT.

In her dream, she sees Baz lunging for the jar as it falls in slow motion, turning over and over as it nears the ground. She sees the barrel of a pistol, raised. Hears a bullet flying through the air. A kind of drone that slides upward into a whistle. And now Baz is the one who is falling, falling, falling.

And because this is a dream, Ebby is still upstairs, even though she can see what is happening one floor below. She tries to stretch time. Tries to pull at it and mold it like a clump of wet clay. A clock ticks loudly in her head as she turns toward the top of the stairs, willing her feet to move more quickly than the rest of the world. Willing time to take a step back.

Calling her brother's name, her voice unfurling from her mouth as his body lands on the floor.

She is nearly at the door to the study when she is pulled awake by her own shout. She lies there, thinking of Baz, of how for the first time he has appeared in a dream about that afternoon. But why, after all these years? She tries to figure out what has changed. Bit by bit, her eyes adjust to the dark and the scent of her pillow. Damp cotton and lavender. Now Ebby remembers where she is. In France, thousands of miles from home. Trying to forget the good things gone bad. Only, her past is catching up with her. Even Henry. Ebby hasn't moved her life forward at all, has she? No, she's taken a step back.

———

NEXT DOOR, HENRY IS awake. He is certain he's heard a sound coming from the main cottage. A voice, maybe. He glances at the open window. Checks the time on his cellphone. Avery is sleeping next to him, breathing in that feathery way of hers. He thinks of Ebby, of the nightmares that used to wake him up and leave her trembling. Of the weeping fit Ebby had that one time, when he lost his grip on a serving dish and it broke apart on the tile floor.

Henry remembers the curve of Ebby's shoulders that evening as she knelt on the kitchen floor among the blue and white pieces of ceramic and wailed like a child. Eventually, Henry reached the point where he could never be certain that Ebby, who, for long stretches at a time, would seem so contained, might not overreact to something mundane.

During lunch with his parents at the club one day, Ebby jumped up from the table when the wind slammed a door shut. Henry saw how his mother, always cool to Ebby, narrowed her eyes. Even then, Henry was aware of how his mother's reaction, her overall immunity to Ebby's appeal, bothered him more than he liked to admit. And how he wasn't irritated with his mother but, rather, with Ebby.

Toward the end of their engagement, Henry wondered if marrying Ebby would mean having to walk on eggshells all the time. What if they had kids? They'd already stopped using protection during sex. What if she freaked out while holding an infant? Or zoned out during a mixer with some of his colleagues? Henry had been willing to deal with people giving him side glances for having an African American fiancée and, ultimately, a black wife. But dodging the lingering fallout from her trauma was another story. And what if his mom never did warm up to Ebby? What would it mean to live without his mother's full buy-in?

How much of yourself do you have to renounce in order to have the life you think you want?

———

AVERY PRETENDS TO BE asleep. Henry has woken up suddenly and now he is lying there next to her. Avery, in her silky nightgown, with her silky skin and silky hair. If she may say so herself, Avery is silky perfection tonight, with notes of fig and sandalwood spritzed at the nape of her neck. But Henry does not touch her. They lie there, side by side, in the stony silence of this damned French village, just yards away from the woman Henry nearly married, and he does not even turn toward Avery. It would take that little to reassure her. Instead, he remains on his back, still as a rock, and Avery feels the space between them like a weight on her chest.

# Ed

ED FREEMAN CAN TELL SOMETHING IS WRONG SOON AFTER HIS wife answers the phone. Soh is looking at him and frowning.

"Wait, baby, wait," Soh says into the phone, touching a finger to her lips, her signal to Ed to not press his daughter for details. "Your father's here, too, Ebby. Can we do a video call?" Then Soh's face warms up as Ebby appears on the screen from France. In thirty-five years of marriage, Ed has come to know every one of his wife's expressions, and this fact has not always been a welcome thing. But that look, right there, that's his favorite. The way his wife, Isabella "Soh" Freeman, is gazing at their child.

Ebby, who looks just like Ed. Except for that tomato-colored hair. It's her latest look. *Jeez,* he thinks.

"What time is it there?" Ed says.

"It's two in the morning," Ebby says, "but I was still up, reading, so I thought this would be a good time to try you." Ed can see part of the bed and night table from where Ebby is sitting. A buttercup-yellow wall. A quilt and pillows in varying shades of blue, tossed to one side. The massive wooden beam that crosses the room behind her. Ebby is chattering, now, a high tone in her voice. No wonder his wife was frowning before. Their daughter isn't the type to yap on that way, though she does have her lively moments.

"Oh, yes, the weather's really nice," Ebby is saying now. "A little warm, but fine in the shade. And the smell of lavender is everywhere. People keep saying they're worried about the bees dying off, because of the environment, but you wouldn't know it. You can hear them humming all day in the garden."

*Slow down,* Ed thinks. Ebby's speaking so fast.

"I wish you could be here to see it all," she says.

Ed chuckles. But he knows that Ebby doesn't really want him and Soh with her right now. Not after picking up and heading off to France for this . . . what? What should he call it? Hiatus?

The first night after their daughter left for France, Ed and Soh held each other in bed, neither saying a word. They had said it all before, over the years. They had shed tears at their son's graveside and in the therapist's office. His wife had cried the entire first night in their new house, the one they'd purchased even before their previous home had closed escrow.

"I didn't think anyone would want our home, after what happened," Soh had sobbed.

"But did you really think we could have gone back there, babe?" Ed asked. "Did you?" He knew the answer, of course. They had moved into a hotel the night of Baz's death. Gone up to stay with family in Massachusetts after the funeral. Moved into a rental fifteen miles down the coast from their home. A quiet lot on the point where two rivers flowed together and down toward the beach. A place where there was no room for television trucks to park without trespassing on private property or sliding into the water.

And then they had settled on buying the house where they live now, with a different but equally beautiful view of the Sound, a new school for Ebby, and a public library with a resident cat. Ed and Soh have lived here almost twice as many years as in the previous place. Ed loves being just a few steps from a tiny cove. But that other house had been the home of their youthful dreams. The place where they had planned on raising a family. The place where they had lost their son. For that very reason, it remained sacred ground, even if they could no longer set foot on that lot.

After moving house, Ed and Soh managed to raise their remaining child in safety and relative comfort. They couldn't do much to keep her from being exposed to perennial media attention. And they couldn't undo the trauma of her brother's death for her, only hope that therapy would help, along with the distractions of her daily routine. But they taught their daughter to keep going, no matter what.

Ed's parents said the stay in France would be good for Ebby, but his wife couldn't stand the thought.

"If she needed to get away, why didn't she just go back to Maine, or up to Martha's Vineyard?" Soh said when she finally did give voice to her feelings. They have had this conversation several times since, and each time Soh names a new alternative. Why not the Florida Keys? The Arizona desert? Any place on this side of the Atlantic. If she wanted to practice her French, couldn't she have driven up to Montreal?

Ed found himself nodding in agreement. He missed his daughter. He had never gone more than a couple of weeks without seeing her. But he didn't want to keep her in a cage. He wanted Ebby to live a full life. And she was on her way. She had excelled in school. She did useful work that she seemed to like.

There were people who wrote books whose work needed support from a person like Ebby. She had a way with words, and had studied literature and history. Her clients didn't write anything as technical as Ed might, but they did produce material that required fact-checking and the reordering of paragraphs, pages, and even entire chapters. These were people who would say they needed a copy editor to put the final touches on a book when, in reality, they needed someone to help rewrite much of their work. Part editor, part ghostwriter, part researcher. That's what Ebby was.

Ed knew Soh hoped Ebby would go back to school and study law. Or pick up another degree that felt more *concrete,* as Soh put it. But the beauty of Ebby's work was that, like Ed's, it was meant to feel invisible, though it did not lack substance. Ebby did not have Ed's engineering degrees, but her work, like Ed's, still involved a buoying-up of structures and systems that, if successful, went largely unnoticed. Like so much of the valuable work done in the world.

Ebby often smiled when she talked about the reports or books she was working on, and this brought even Soh some satisfaction. Soh didn't want to keep their girl in a cage, either, though often it felt that way. The two of them just wanted to be sure that their daughter would always, always, *always* be safe, and they wanted to keep an eye on her. Not that proximity would be a guarantee of anything. They hadn't been able to keep their son safe in his own home.

In his bleaker moments, Ed must remind himself that what happened to Baz is not the norm, not even in this country, where a young black man is especially vulnerable to unwarranted violence. Children do grow up. Teenagers do survive war, and abuse, and all sorts of misfortune. Too many don't, but millions and millions do just fine. Lately, Ed has needed to repeat this affirmation every day.

So much of life must go forward on faith.

He's missed something on the call. Ebby and Soh are laughing, now. Just the sound of his daughter being mirthful after all that she has been through feels like a small miracle. It never fails to amaze Ed how his heart can soar, even as he still feels the hole that's been blown right through the middle of it by the loss of his son.

The first time he heard Ebby laugh a good, strong laugh again after . . . *Baz,* she was coming up the driveway and around the side of the house with Ashleigh, the Pittses' granddaughter. The two of them had snow up to the tops of their boots and damp spots on the knees of their dungarees. A nor'easter had moved in, causing traffic delays and accidents, and Ashleigh had stayed overnight. That familiar noise, of two children laughing together, made Ed smile as he watched them through a window. They were kicking the steps outside the mudroom, now, to knock the snow off their boots. Just the *uff-uff* sound of their shoes gave him the courage to plod through the molasses of his grief.

But tonight, in Ebby's laughter, Ed hears a kind of frenzy. He thinks of how a smartphone sitting on a desk can vibrate with an unanswered call. How the trembling of the phone against the hard surface can send it inching toward the edge until it falls off. Something about Ebby feels like that buzzing phone.

*Yuh,* Ed thinks, *there's something going on with Ebby.* Something she's not telling them. But who is he to question her? Ed has something he's never told his daughter or wife. He wants to, but he doesn't know how to begin.

# Broken

I*F ONLY THE JAR HADN'T BEEN BROKEN.*

This thought creeps up on Ed in the half-light of the morning following the call from Ebby. It comes to him just as he is doing his usual sunrise walk down the slope from his house and breathing in the smell of the cove. The pungent odor of damp rocks and mollusks and cracked shells. It feels like a betrayal of his son that Ed should think of the jar at all. It goes without saying that more than anything, Ed wishes his son hadn't been killed on that day.

It's just that Baz, in his final minutes of life, saw the jar lying broken on the ground, and Baz had loved that jar. He'd believed in it. For the children, Old Mo had been like an ancient relative, an ancestor from long ago who was still around to share his lessons. Ed and Soh had used the jar to reassure their children that good could come of bad, that comfort could follow strife, that looking at their past could help to guide their future.

Baz had been at that age, that delicate period between boyhood and black manhood, when he had been frustrated by some of what he'd seen going on in his country. Just a month before he died, there had been yet another unjustified killing of an unarmed black man by a police officer, and Baz had lashed out.

"Things aren't ever going to change, are they, Dad?"

"Things are always changing, son," Ed said. "It's true, some of the worst things keep repeating themselves, but things do change. And as citizens, we can do our part to keep things moving in the right direction." Ed saw the skepticism on his son's face, and it saddened him to see it so soon, that emotional armor that Baz would have to carry into his adult years.

"Look at Old Mo," Ed said. "Simply by being made, being carried, being kept by our family, that jar helped to change people's lives." Ed felt his shoulders relax when he saw Baz nodding slowly in response.

Like his father, Ed had shared stories with the children about the jar, but in his own versions, Old Mo was more of a character. Ed had added a good dose of invention to the bits of historical and anecdotal information that his family had passed down to him about the jar's earliest days.

*Tell us about Old Mo and the creek,* his kids would say. *Tell us about Old Mo and the ship!*

The jar stories had inspired Baz, ever the joker, to sketch cartoon scenes for little Ebby and tack them onto the bulletin board in his sister's room. There had been one of Old Mo on stick-figure legs with chunky sneakers up in the air, tumbling down the hill toward the creek. Or Old Mo the fugitive, dressed in a movie-star disguise with a baseball hat, a wig, and oversize designer sunglasses. Or Ed's favorite, the one of Old Mo leaning over his round stoneware belly and whispering in the ear of a woman in a fringed, one-shouldered dress. The woman was a reference to one of Ed's ancestors, who had found shelter in a Wampanoag community on the Massachusetts coast.

The thought of the jar's story, and his family's attachment to it, is all knotted up in the grief that Ed is forced to live with. His little girl, traumatized on the day her brother died, kept repeating the last thing her brother had told her.

*They broke Old Mo, they broke Old Mo.*

If only Baz hadn't seen the jar break. If only Ebby hadn't seen her brother die. If only Ed had been home, *goddamn it,* instead of his kids.

But his son is gone, and Ed needs to believe that their story, as a family, isn't over yet. If Baz is the great loss of Ed's life, then Ebby is his great unfinished work. His hope for the future. During that first year of counseling, the therapist used to remind Ed and Soh that other children had witnessed the violent loss of a family member yet grown up to have healthy, productive lives. Ebby could find her way, too, the doc said.

But back then, all Ed wanted the therapist to do was erase what had happened to their family. Undo the whole damned thing. Ed wanted to see the jar back on the table in his study and his son back on his feet. Ed wanted a guarantee that, he knew, could not be provided. Which is why he stopped going to the therapist years ago.

His wife still goes to therapy. Maybe it's time for Ed to go back. He suspects the doc would understand why he's been obsessed with the jar of late. Ed had been doing all right, really, he had, until he saw his daughter having such a rough time after her wedding fell apart. Maybe Ed could tell the therapist about the jar. Tell her what he's afraid to say to his wife.

But first, Ed would tell the therapist how both of his kids used to splay themselves over the small sofa in his study, jostling each other for space, to listen to Ed's jar stories. Old Mo had always been part of Ed's relationship with his children and his wife. And the children's favorite story was the one where Old Mo had helped their parents to fall in love.

# Old Mo

———

**2000**

THE LAST TIME ED TOLD HIS CHILDREN THE STORY OF HOW Old Mo helped him win their mother's heart, the jar was dressed up in Baz's baseball cap and a silly paper mustache that the kids had taped on its front.

"I knew your mom was special," Ed said, glancing over at Soh. "But she wouldn't pay me any mind." It was a story the kids had heard umpteen times, but they never seemed to grow tired of it.

"It's not that I didn't pay you any mind, Ed," Soh said, giving him the side-eye. "I noticed you. I just didn't think you were *all that*." She wobbled her head and wagged a finger at him and made the kids laugh.

Ed and Soh had grown up in the same county and done community service with the same club, but they'd attended different schools. It wasn't until their families ended up in vacation homes next to each other on Martha's Vineyard that Ed and Soh, halfway through high school and fully in the throes of adolescence, began to spend any real time around each other.

The next year, they were back in the same summerhouses, and this time, there was a kiss. They had climbed up into a red oak and were sitting side by side in the crook of the tree, where they could flirt without being spied on from afar.

"I saw an article about trees," Soh said as she drummed her heels against the trunk of the oak. "It said climbing trees isn't just good for building strong bodies, it's good for building confidence and perseverance, and problem-solving."

"Who knew," Ed said, "an old oak could do all that?" Then he leaned over and kissed Soh.

And Soh kissed him back.

But Ed and Soh were on their way to separate universities and to the kinds of experiences that led teenagers to lose track of each other. There were new places, and friendships, and attractions. Until Soh came home from law school one Memorial Day weekend and went with her parents to a barbecue at the Freeman home.

"Haven't seen you in years!" Soh said when she saw Ed.

Ed looked at Soh. He knew that it had been exactly five years and nine months. Their parents had seen one another, but Ed and Soh had always been up to something else, somewhere else. He didn't want that to happen again.

"Have you met the oldest member of our family?" Ed asked Soh, tipping his head toward the doors off the patio and trying not to slide his eyes down over her backside. Trying not to breathe in the faint whiff of vanilla in her scent. Trying not to reach out and touch her face. He led Soh into the family library, a room that looked a lot like a storage space going through some kind of filing crisis. The shelves running from the oak floors all the way up to the ceiling cornices were fully stacked with books, along with almost every other available space.

Every time the Freemans looked at the mess, they told themselves they were a bookish kind of family and nodded proudly to one another. There were books on the desk, books on the chairs, books piled horizontally inside an old pine sideboard whose doors had been left open. There were art books on one half of a sofa and other volumes laid out on the rug under the coffee table. There was even a paperback perched on a half-full glass of water. But on the coffee table itself, there was only one thing. A twenty-gallon clay jar sat at the center of the tabletop like a small monarch on a throne. The gleam in Soh's eye told Ed that she had some idea of what she was looking at.

"Is that from the 1800s?" Soh asked.

"Yes, it is," Ed answered.

"Georgia? South Carolina?"

Ed raised his eyebrows. It wasn't something he'd ever learned about in school. But Soh had studied history before law school, just as her mother had, and she was a Bliss. She would know something about stoneware produced by enslaved potters in the South. She might have heard of at least one or two of them who had inscribed pieces during a time when they were prohibited by law from learning to read and write.

Ed nodded, pointing to initials inscribed under the lip of the jar. He explained that a potter named Moses had been working in bondage for a certain Martin Oldham at the time. The inscription *MO* was considered a label representing the owner of the enterprise. But the Freemans believed Moses had been making a veiled reference to himself.

When, nearly two centuries later, Soh saw the antique jar in Ed's home, stoneware by enslaved turners had already caught the eyes of historians. Some vessels were distinguished not only by initials but also by designs of rice and other plants that had been painted onto the clay before firing. The MO pieces, dipped in the characteristic alkaline glaze of the region, had also gained attention among a handful of African American families, though few people living up north had ever seen one outside of a photograph.

A couple of these objects had made it all the way across the Atlantic to Liverpool. Still others were believed to have been offloaded at Boston and kept in private homes in Massachusetts. The Freemans' jar was one of those. But more likely than not, if anyone still had a MO sitting around their house or barn, they hadn't given much thought to who had signed the piece. Especially if they were a white family, which was probable.

"How did this jar end up here?" asked Soh.

"Sailed up on a square-rigger from South Carolina," said Ed. "With one of my ancestors."

The Freemans' jar had a small trail of leaves painted over the glaze that actually climbed out of the mouth of the jar and descended from its lip. It curved under the maker's initials and the inscription of the year, 1847, ending at the widest part of the container. But Ed knew that the best part was the thing you couldn't see right off, the secret inscription on the bottom of the piece. Relatively few people had ever seen it because it was never shown to anyone outside the family.

As she stood in the library of Ed's family home on that summer day

in 1983, Soh pulled air into her mouth, slowly, like an *oh,* only in re-
verse. She walked over to the jar and reached out her hand.

"May I?"

"Go ahead," Ed said, placing a hand on the jar and nodding. Soh
glanced at Ed like a child, as if suddenly shy in the presence of a new
toy. She placed her hand on the fattest part of the curve. Ed watched as
she ran her fingers back and forth over the dark glaze, as if reading a
line of braille, then up toward the initials engraved under the lip. Her
lips moved silently as she read the date next to the initials.

"Hello, Old Mo," she whispered.

After that, Ed, too, started calling the jar Old Mo.

"Imagine someone with a name like your mother's," Ed told his
children, "finding Old Mo in a private home in New England!" Because their mother's nickname, Soh, had a story all its own.

Isabella "Soh" Bliss was conceived while her mother, Gwendolyn,
was studying history down in New York. This was before she decided
to go to law school. As an African American scholar who also happened to be female, she was going against everything society was telling her she was supposed to be doing. The same was true of her
marriage to Lemuel Bliss, a widowed lawyer fifteen years her senior.

Eight months later, in February 1960, four black college students sat
down at a Woolworth lunch counter in Greensboro, North Carolina,
and refused to leave unless they were served. Word got out, protesters
joined the scene, and police made the first arrests for trespassing. More
than five hundred miles away in New York, Gwendolyn Bliss doubled
over in pain on the lawn of her university, her thin body jolted by the
force of a premature contraction. The pains came and went over the
next several days until, finally, Gwendolyn gave birth to a tiny baby
girl. As more people joined the sit-in, Gwen decided on a name for her
daughter.

"Let's call her Isabella," she told her husband, Lem, back then. "For
Isabella Baumfree." Lem understood his wife's motivation to name
their baby after the nineteenth-century abolitionist and women's rights
activist. Although Baumfree, better known as Sojourner Truth, had
died in 1883, she remained an inspiration to the contemporary civil
rights movement. Maybe even to those students at the lunch counter.

Still, Lem frowned.

"Didn't we already agree to name her after my mother, Elizabeth?" Lem asked.

"We did," said Gwen, "but don't forget, Elizabeth and Isabella are the same name. One English, one Spanish, right?"

Lem nodded and gave a grunt in assent. He had always been a wise person. Never one to waste his words on an argument unless it was one he was sure to win or that at the very least, merited the effort. Contradicting his wife's sense of conviction in this delicate matter did not appear to fall into either category, especially not after all that Gwen's body had just been through. In the years to come, Lem would merely smile as Gwen repeated the story of how they named their first child after both her grandmother and Sojourner Truth. They quickly took to calling their little girl by the nickname Soh, the name their daughter grew to prefer.

Years later, when Soh first said the words *Old Mo,* Ed felt that the stories of their respective families were entering a new phase, one in which they would tread the same path together. Ed was so sure of this, already, that on the day he showed Soh the jar, he reached down and turned the vessel on its side so that she could read the inscription that distinguished this piece from all others.

Soh leaned in to read the five words carved into the bottom panel, and when she looked up at Ed, her eyes were filled with tears.

# Soh

S OH IS CONVINCED THERE IS SOMETHING HER HUSBAND ISN'T telling her.

There have been some rough days, lately, between them, and she isn't sure how to handle this. Soh and Ed used to have a way of communicating. Even after they'd lost Baz, they managed to muddle through together. They had their daughter to thank for much of that. Watching her grow. *Watching her live!* Because of their daughter, Soh and Ed still had love and laughter and pride in their home, even after everything they'd lost. And wasn't that something? In the beginning, Soh used to wish that she had been the one to die, instead of her son. That she had been the one at home. That her children had already left the house. Now, she thinks, what she really wants is simply for her son to be alive.

Why should she have to wish for one thing, to be spared the pain of the other?

After Ebby's wedding, or, rather, the wedding that never was, Soh began to see a kind of backsliding in her husband's attitude. Outwardly, he encouraged Ebby to keep moving forward. Still cracked his jokes. Cussed at the sound of Henry Pepper's name. Still took his morning walks on the beach, then went to work in his study. But it was as if Ebby's disappointment in love had caused him to lose ground. Ed had been robbed of the chance to ferry their daughter through this important rite of passage. A union of love. The beginnings of a new branch of the family.

And now Ebby has taken off for France, and Soh and Ed don't seem to know what to do with themselves.

Soh, typically a clear-eyed calculator in her legal work, has always been the one to worry more at home, while Ed has been more of a *what can we do now?* kind of person. Ed was the one who had booked them into a hotel on the night that Baz died. Later, he had dared to go back into the house alone to pick up a few personal belongings and to take stock of things for the final move, while Soh couldn't bear the thought of walking into the building. Instead, she wrote lists for Ed. What to look for, what to consider. They had handled that awful period differently, yet together, somehow.

But even before Ebby left, Ed had less to say to his wife. He was spending more time down in the basement by himself. Tinkering with Lord knows what. Spending more time walking on the beach. Alone. He even left town a couple of times on his own, saying he had consultations down south.

"Consultations about what?" Soh wanted to know.

"Just business," Ed told her.

And Soh has been wondering about that. Could Ed have found someone else? Is that what this extra *business* is? Another woman who is easier to be around? A relationship without the history that she and Ed will always have, for better or worse? Soh leaves the house more, to give him space. She goes to volunteer meetings, to choir, to the gym. She's almost always kept a legal client or two, and that takes up some of her time. But the more she stays away, the less Ed seems to notice. Hardly asks her where she's been or when she is coming home. Doesn't ask her, anymore, what she is reading. Doesn't ask her, does she want to go to a film or a concert? No, she has no doubt. Whatever it is that Ed isn't telling her, it's something important.

Of course, there's plenty that Soh doesn't tell Ed. This is the only way she knows to be a woman in this world, by leaving much of who she is unsaid. This is why she still sees her therapist. To be able to say certain things. To admit how bitter she feels at what happened to her daughter on her wedding day. Soh had dreamed of a happy ending for her baby. She had wanted her daughter to marry for love, and she'd been open, even, to accepting someone from a different background.

"Is he white?" Soh's mother had asked her when she'd told her that Ebby was getting serious about a certain young man.

"Well, Momma, most folks around there are white."

"My point exactly," her mother said, pointing an elegant, pink-lacquered nail at Soh. "How could he not be? With you raising my granddaughter in that little *gated* community on the beach."

"It is not a gated community, Mom."

"You know what I mean. It might as well be."

"Plus, who are we to talk, Mom?" Soh said, sweeping one arm around her mother's gleaming kitchen. "Look at your house."

"Oh, so now this is *my* house, is it?" her mother said, smiling. "You mean to tell me you didn't grow up in that room up there?" Her mom pointed at the ceiling, in the direction of Soh's childhood bedroom. Soh tried not to smile. She wanted to be irritated with her momma.

"You know what I mean, Momma, you're deflecting the argument," Soh said. "You are criticizing where I live as if you do not live in an eight-bedroom, five-bathroom home that tour guides refer to as a manor."

It was in moments like these that Gwendolyn Bliss showed herself to be the superior debater of the two. Her voice lost that hint of a smile it usually had, dropped an octave, and became so soft it was barely audible. Because it was not the volume of a voice but the sharpness of its logic and its emotional weight that could tie up an argument. She tipped her head slightly, as if to flirt.

"You, Isabella Bliss, know exactly why my great-grandfather added those extra rooms. You know the story of his large extended family, where they came from, and how all those so-called *relatives* were fugitives from an unjust law, hiding in plain sight."

"Yes, Momma," Soh said.

"Furthermore," her mother said, "you know very well, Isabella, that when I say *gated* community, I am not referring to monetary wealth, I am talking about exclusivity of another kind."

"And our being there is helping to change the racial balance," Soh said, cringing at the petulant tone in her own voice.

"Hardly," her mother said. "You're still the only ones on that stretch of shoreline, aren't you?"

Soh felt like a little girl around her mom. Chastised. She knew better than to go any further down that rocky road. Still, it wasn't fair for her mother to bring this up. Again, and again. Yes, Soh was proud to know that her ancestor, back in the 1800s, took runaway slaves into his home and forged papers to camouflage them as siblings and cousins. This did not mean that Soh had to remain tied to that house for the rest of her life.

"I love this old home," Soh said, "and I am proud of our family's history in Refuge County and proud to be married to a Freeman. And, yes, I wish I had more black neighbors. But if my great-great-grandfather worked so hard and risked so much to flout the Fugitive Slave Act back in the day, then am I not living out his legacy by insisting on raising my family wherever I choose?"

"Your father and I choose to live out that legacy by staying put."

"You and who, Momma? It's only our family, anymore. Almost everyone else has gone to Boston, or D.C., or Atlanta, or what have you."

"But they moved to mostly black neighborhoods, baby. Places where you find other black families."

Soh had thought about this often. Stay put or go? She thought about it whenever she sat down to counsel teenagers of color about ways to improve their prospects of getting into competitive law schools. For Soh, the point was not that she had moved to a place where other African Americans did not live, and her daughter had been the only black student in her class. The point was that other black people might not have access to the wealth and social leverage that would allow them to even consider the choices she'd made. And if they did, they still might not be welcome.

Her mother's principles aside, the house was way too big for one person. Soh had tried to convince her mother to downsize, but her momma had refused. Where, her mother always asked, would people sleep when they came to visit and drank a bit too much to make the drive home? Or got snowed in? Where would the grandkids hold their slumber parties? And what about the tourists? People needed to know about the black families of Refuge County. Especially when there were so few of them remaining.

Soh felt her sense of guilt heating up the sides of her face. Her mother, still in that big house alone. At least her cousins lived close by. Ed's people, too. And it was true, there was always someone stopping by, sitting down for a meal, lolling out back on a deck chair with a glass of something perched on the flat wooden arm while the children ran around the yard, burning off the excess energy that came with growing bodies.

Soh's mother, now, softened her posture.

"Do you at least like the young man?" her mother asked.

"Ebby's happy, Momma. My little girl is happy." She felt her eyes growing prickly around the edges. *No tears,* she willed herself. "And *happy* is all I really care about after everything that girl has been through."

"Come here, baby," her mother said.

Soh kept her lips pursed as she approached her mother, but her mom had that light, floral hug that could melt a person's resolve. It was one of her secret weapons. Soh had inherited a different strength from her mother: her determination. She had made the move to the Connecticut coast because it had been her husband's dream but also because she, too, had wanted to live there. She had stayed in the area after what had happened to Baz. So much of Soh's life was beyond her control. Whenever she could, she would keep on doing things the way she wanted.

In time, Soh's mother grew to like Ebby's fiancé well enough. Henry was, after all, the likable type. He was very good-looking, there was no denying that. He did not, thankfully, have one of those flat behinds, but a boxy, sporty back that gave him a look of substance. And Henry was very kind to her mother when she finally came down to meet him the first time. You would have thought he'd been raised in a black family. Helping Momma out of her coat. Pulling out her chair at the dinner table with a slight bow of his head. Fixing a plate for her. Calling her Mrs. Bliss.

Soh noticed that Henry laughed readily, but never too loudly. And he looked at Ebby in a way that made Soh's heart swell with hope. Still, Soh harbored a secret doubt. She worried that Henry might not have the backbone needed to go through life with her daughter. Henry had always been propped up by the social and financial scaffolding of the Pepper family and he had never faced a personal trauma like Ebby's. Soh worried that Henry might be fine only until truly put to the test. And marriage, if nothing else, had a way of putting a person to the test.

Looking back, now, Soh is grateful that Ebby didn't end up staying with a man who, it turned out, did not have the decency to break up with her in person. Thank goodness Soh and Ed didn't become tied to Henry's parents for life. *Can you imagine?* Those Peppers should have tracked down their son after he disappeared and pulled him by the ear to Soh's front door. At the very least, the Peppers should have shown up alone once they realized that he had run off without warning. Instead, it was left to Ed to telephone the Peppers that morning to find out why they were running so late.

There were many families like Henry's. People who had perfected the art of shying away from blame. They did not understand that as a result of Henry's failure to accept his responsibility in this matter, the Freeman family, automatically, would be considered suspect. Because this was the subtext of every question that had been asked in the media since the afternoon that their son was killed, eighteen years earlier: What had the Freeman family done to bring this upon themselves?

*What had they done?* This was the question that hung in the air above every black family that had ever run into misfortune. And not only. It was a subtext understood by so many women, of any color, who had ever been harmed. It was the question that few dared to ask out loud but many had in mind, with regard to families that struggled to pay the bills. It was the question asked by those who wished to avoid acknowledging that responsibility might lie elsewhere.

*What did you do?*

Henry's parents finally showed up one week later, making the expected noises about "deep regret and embarrassment" that their son had left Connecticut but stressing that it would have to be up to "the children" to sort things out between themselves. And Soh did what she needed to do, cloaking her rage in chilly courtesy. Soh pulls a prayer from deep in her gut, now, and sends it upward. She prays that she will never lay eyes on Henry Pepper again. Except, maybe, once. Just long enough to walk up to that boy and slap him in his face. Which, of course, is just a fantasy. Soh would never do such a thing.

Because this is what it means to be Isabella "Sojourner" Bliss Freeman. Daughter of one of New England's oldest and wealthiest African American families. Top honors at both universities. Attorney and mother. Lifelong volunteer. Champion fundraiser. Still the only black woman in her neighborhood, after all these years, with all that this unfortunate statistic has entailed. Alas, Soh needs to be above slapping that superficial fool in his face, because there are people who are just waiting for a sign that a woman like Soh is beneath them. There are people who still believe that her family and her pride are worth less than theirs.

People who believe that her history is not their history, too.

# Kandia

———

**1806**

THE HUMID, SLITHERING ISLAND WHERE KANDIA HAD BEEN trapped for three years was different from the village where she had grown up, but there was something familiar in the smell of its clay. The people hunters had sold Kandia to a family of sugarcane planters who also operated a pottery. They produced mainly ceramic molds used in the processing of sugar. Strangely, the people who were forced to work there were men, not women. It was yet another sign that this place negated all that was natural.

The pottery men sat on stools and used curious tables that spun around and around, upon which they quickly grew mounds of clay into the shapes they chose. When she could risk it, Kandia would stop at the door to the workshop on her way from the water well to the plantation house. She would watch the men for just a few moments, careful to leave before the overseer came along. If he saw her there, he might push her toward her cabin. Force her to lie with him again. She put down the water buckets just long enough to take two deep breaths and fill her chest with the smell of the raw clay.

On occasion, Kandia and the other women were given surplus clay to hand-build bowls and jugs for their own use. As soon as she wet the clay and began to mold it, Kandia felt the pains in her back and shoulders begin to ease, though her heart never stopped aching from the memory of all that she had lost.

One day, as Kandia rolled coils, she glanced over to see Moses, then three years of age, scratching at the dry dirt with a stick. She pinched off a small portion of the clay and fashioned a piece shaped like a goat.

She would fire the goat in the kiln with the bowls she had made and give it to her son to play with. The child was still small enough to be allowed to play. He was still too young to know what lay ahead of him. Too young to know that he could be taken from her in an instant and sold away.

Kandia tried to forget the terror she felt for her son. She squeezed the clay to form tiny horns and ears. She pulled at the clay beneath the goat's chin to mimic a beard and smoothed the rounded sides of its belly. Perhaps it was not too late, she thought as she shaped a leg. Perhaps her child's destiny was still like the wet earth in her hands. A living thing that could be molded and, if needed, reshaped into something altogether different.

# Keeping Time

———

AFTER ENDING THE VIDEO CALL TO HER PARENTS, EBBY DOES something she hasn't done since arriving in France. She pulls her brother's clock radio out of her suitcase, attaches an adapter to the electric cord, and plugs it into a wall socket. She is already up and moving about the kitchen the next day when the alarm goes off.

Ebby has used Baz's alarm clock for nineteen years, often waking up ahead of time to listen for it, as she did for an entire year before he died. Every morning, it was the same music station, same deejay, same fifteen seconds to run down the hallway to her brother's room. Because Ebby was always out of bed before Baz could reach over to turn off the clock himself.

"All right, all right, I'm up. Go on, get dressed," Baz would say, still under the covers and looking nowhere near ready to leave.

When the alarm goes off this time, the radio picks up a French station. Up-tempo, some rap. Two deejays, chattering. Then the news. Politics, sports, the heat wave. But Ebby's mind is already drifting away from the sound and back in time. She hears her brother's voice, now, and allows herself that little bit of Baz in her head, his sleepy grumble, before easing herself out into a world marked by his absence. Ebby knows what Henry would think if he saw the clock there. *Are you still carrying that thing around?*

Once, during an argument about her nightmares, Henry pointed to Baz's clock.

"That," said Henry, "is proof that your therapist hasn't done enough for you. I mean, after all this time? Isn't it a little morbid to be setting an alarm by your brother's schedule?"

"I don't set the alarm. I just don't stop it from going off, that's all."

"Oh, come on, Ebby. Don't get technical on me, now. Admit it."

"Admit what? That I miss my brother and I like hearing his alarm clock go off every morning? That's not morbid, Henry. Morbid is the fact that two complete strangers forced their way into my family's home and shot my fifteen-year-old brother dead. My parents saved so few things from our old house. I'm lucky to have this. So why can't I keep the fucking alarm clock?"

To Henry's credit, he said nothing more. He moved toward Ebby and wrapped his arms around her. Eventually, Ebby would realize that Henry was more likely to back down from a confrontation than not, and that this would cause big trouble between them. But at the time, his willingness to do so was a comfort.

"And anyway," Ebby said into the sleeve of Henry's shirt. "It's not the therapist's job to *do* the healing for a person. Just facilitate it. Each person is different. Each of us has to follow our own path." She declined to tell Henry that her personal path had included stopping therapy altogether. She hadn't been back in months.

Ebby turns off the radio, now, and listens through the window to the morning sounds around her. This is all the therapy she needs. A smattering of birdsong. The distant, gravelly hum of a tractor. Someone's car door, opening and shutting. A feeling of beginnings. This is what pulls Ebby toward the coatrack, where she puts on a gardening smock and hat, pushes her feet into rubber boots, and steps outside to the smell of wet grass and river muck.

She tries to focus on the sound of the trowel as she shoves it into the earth. Metal cutting into dirt. The rasp of sand grains that Hannah has added to the soil. She wills herself not to think about Henry. But, of course, she is thinking about Henry. She hates to admit how seeing Henry with another woman hurts in a way that she didn't think possible after nearly nine months.

Nine months. The time most people take to grow a baby.

Ebby could have had a child with Henry by now. Their baby would have been three months old. She never did tell him she was pregnant. No one knew, except the doctors. She'd kept the signs to herself.

"What?" Henry would say when he found Ebby, more than once, smiling at nothing in particular. She'd just shake her head and draw him close to her. She had decided to surprise Henry after their wedding with news of the pregnancy. She would give herself a bit more time to sit with the idea. Leave Henry with less to think about before the big day.

When Henry abandoned her, Ebby wasn't sure what to do with her secret. During that first week of escape in Maine, she walked and walked alone, lay awake in the middle of the night, thinking. Sat at her laptop, researching her options. Shed tears into her herbal tea. She couldn't decide what to do, and in not doing anything she was, in effect, making a decision.

The next time she saw her mother, she hugged her tight.

"Baby, what's wrong?"

"Nothing, Mommy, nothing. Just this," Ebby said, planting a noisy kiss on her mother's cheek. Her mother dipped her head to the side and laughed, and Ebby wondered, truly for the first time, how her mother had managed to do it, all these years. She and Ebby's dad had gotten up every day and gone on with their responsibilities. Mom had helped Ebby get ready for school in the mornings, made her breakfast, and even chewed her out if she'd left her bed unmade.

Ebby's mom had left her law firm after Baz's death to be home for Ebby but eventually agreed to go back to handling a couple of its clients. It meant that she might work outside the home, but not like before. She had been there, throughout Ebby's high school years, to pick lint from Ebby's sweaters on winter mornings and tell Ebby *be careful* as she ventured out in the snow. She'd been there to hug Ebby every time she brought home top grades. She had continued to say *oh, look!* whenever her dad's face appeared in one of those articles on engineering, or African American innovators, as if they hadn't all grown accustomed to it by then.

Perhaps the most important thing that Ebby had learned from her mom, and her dad, too, was this: People were wired to persevere. People were wired for hope. People might feel hurt, but they still liked to laugh. They might lose someone dear, but they still wanted to love. Ultimately, the idea of becoming a mother pleased Ebby more than it terrified her.

In the weeks that followed, Ebby wore loose summer dresses to accommodate the swelling of her waist. Tried to eat well. Avoided alcohol. Avoided her parents. Then sat in her bathroom, alone, whimpering, when she saw the blood. She called the doctor, not her mother, when the cramps began. Went to the clinic alone. Sat on the sofa alone and rocked back and forth after the miscarriage. Told her mom, *I have the flu, stay away*. Her parents would never know. She refused to bring more sadness into their lives.

Ebby listened as her ob-gyn reminded her of how common it was to lose a pregnancy in the first few months. She would have other opportunities, the doctor said with a soft smile. Ebby realized that everything would be easier without having the baby of a man who had disappeared on her. Still, she wept. In the doctor's office. In her car. In her kitchen.

Tears rolled down her face and dripped into the sink as she washed the dirt off leaves of kale that she would never eat. As she left pots on the stove until her food burned. Early in her pregnancy, Ebby had secretly tracked the days and body changes on her cellphone calendar. She never did stop counting the weeks to when Henry's baby would have been born.

Ebby reaches for her brother's clock radio, now, and watches as the display flips from one minute to the next. She smiles at the thought of Baz's soupy morning voice. Then she watches the display for one more minute. She is no stranger to keeping time by what she has lost.

# Disquiet

———

AVERY HEARS THE QUIVER OF A SCREEN DOOR AS IT SHUTS. She pushes the curtain aside in time to see Ebony leaving the main cottage and striding across the backyard in her rubber boots. Ebony has a regal bearing, despite the clunky shoes and floppy headgear. Her wide-brimmed hat is different from the one she was wearing yesterday when she fell into the river. Avery feels her mouth tighten as she remembers how Henry reached out to pull Ebony from the water. His hand gripping Ebony's. The tension in the air between them, despite Henry's attempt at sounding mildly amused.

Avery knows that tone. That's Henry doing his *everything is fine* tone when everything is *not* fine. Like the short, cheery peck on her forehead he gave her this morning before slipping out the door with his camera. He winked at her, but Avery could see he couldn't wait to leave. What did he expect to take pictures of when there was so little light out? That was Henry, doing his best to avoid a confrontation.

Ebony is wearing gardening gloves with a conspicuously cheerful floral motif and carrying something sharp-looking in one hand. She crouches down and starts to dig in a flower bed. For a moment, Ebony looks like a very tall child intent on making mud pies. Avery surprises herself by smiling at the sight. But as she continues to watch, a different feeling comes over Avery. A kind of disquiet. She watches as Ebony shoves the gardening tool into the earth, over and over again, stabbing at the soil as if trying to tunnel her way out of a locked room.

Earlier, over her morning coffee, Avery read an article about traumatic bereavement. How its symptoms can affect all aspects of the survivor's life. She should stop thinking about Ebony, stop peering at her through the window, but how can she help it? That article could be

Ebony's life story. Ebony shifts her weight until she is kneeling in the dirt, and her shoulders relax into a slump. In that moment, she looks so vulnerable, and that, right there, could be the biggest threat to Avery. Henry must not see Ebony this way.

Avery has already made a hotel booking in another town for to-morrow night. She needs to keep Henry away from this cottage just for one more day. Avery will convince Henry to drive over to one of the other villages for a late breakfast of café crème and fresh bread with a dollop of jam. Then they can visit a vineyard. There's also a château and a flea market on her list of options. Or maybe they could do nothing at all, as long as they do it away from here.

A full day away from this house. A full day away from Ebony Free-man. Then checkout tomorrow, and they will be gone.

# Henry's Secret

———

Henry tries to chase away his agitation with slow, deep breaths. He leans his shoulder against the trunk of an oak and lifts the camera to his face. He's spotted a fox in a clutch of trees along the river. Amber fur, glowing like gold in a slant of sunlight. He manages to click the shutter a few times before the fox dashes away. He closes his eyes, now, and takes in the smell of the tree's bark, a whisper of laundry detergent on his shirt, and the river's particular odor of life mingled with decay. On any other day, all this would be enough to ground Henry, but not today.

Today, he can't stop thinking about Ebby and how he messed things up. How he should have sat down with Ebby and explained himself.

# Bridge

———

Henry's dad had been playing bridge with the same group of guys since before Henry was born. These men had played twice a month through marriages, children, a divorce, at least two stock market crashes, 9/11, one sexual harassment complaint, and several divisive political races. Four men would play while the other two watched. Then they'd switch out a pair of players, and so on. Henry wasn't really into bridge, but he would stop by on occasion to say hello, as he did one week before he was scheduled to marry Ebby.

Henry knew the bridge group's rules for avoiding conflict in their friendship. They were similar to the ones that Henry's mom had insisted on for dinner-table conversation at family gatherings: no politics, no religion, no shoptalk, no sex. Except for the sex talk. There was plenty of that at the game table down in the basement. And there was some shoptalk. Being two lawyers, two investment bankers, one insurance man, and one physician, they never named their clients or colleagues, but they did share stories, from time to time.

On that evening, the men were ribbing Henry about his pending nuptials. One of them made the inevitable comment about how beautiful Ebby was, followed by a crack that felt somewhat inappropriate to Henry about *producing grandkids for old Charles there*.

"Refills, gentlemen?" Henry asked at that point, eager to move beyond target range until he could make a polite exit. He had just pulled opened the fridge door when he overheard the men recalling the long-ago shooting that had compelled the Freemans to sell their former home, pull Ebby out of her old school, and move to a different town.

Even now, the Freemans' misfortune continued to exert an almost mythic magnetism, Henry thought. The little black girl who had survived a suburban tragedy. The gunmen who had never been found. The victim's parents and neighbors who had never, in all these years, given a media interview about the shooting, their extreme reserve only adding to the intrigue around the crime. They were living in times, Henry thought, when it seemed unnatural to hold one's grief so close to one's chest. Only a family lawyer had ever made a public plea for information in what he and the police had described as an apparent robbery attempt gone wrong.

Henry hoped the bridge group would soon move on from the topic as they shifted their focus back to the cards in front of them. Then he heard the exchange that raised his antennae.

"A real shame about that jar," said one of the guys. Henry looked up, a tray of ice in his hands.

"Jar?" said another one of the men. "What jar?"

"An antique. Family heirloom."

Henry held his breath at the sink, listening. Why would any of them know about the jar? Henry himself only knew because Ebby was obsessed with it.

"The jar was broken, you know, during that robbery."

"Really?"

"Yeah. Seriously historic stuff. Slavery days. Signed by the enslaved man who made it."

"Wow."

The jar had mattered to Ebby's family, of course. And sadly, Ebby now associated its destruction with her brother's death. Yet no one but Ebby had ever mentioned it to Henry. And a broken piece of pottery wasn't the kind of thing that was ever going to make the news when a kid had been shot in his own home. The police had never reported it, nor had the family's lawyer, from what Henry had read. So how would a friend of Henry's father's know anything about something that had never been mentioned publicly?

Unless they knew something about the crime that other people didn't.

There had to be an explanation. Henry wanted to ask, but he didn't have the courage. He didn't want to think there might be some kind of connection between his father's friend and the Freeman shooting.

Those men in the game room had known his dad since they were all kids. Still, there were a lot of unanswered questions about what had happened.

The crime remained unsolved. There had never been any arrests. And it went without saying that when someone went to the trouble of breaking into a home of that value, in that kind of neighborhood, in broad daylight, they had to mean business. And there was a good chance that they weren't operating on their own. That it was part of a larger, well-coordinated effort to relieve victims of significant sums of cash, jewelry, or artwork.

Whatever the circumstances, the only question that mattered to Henry now was, why would someone in his father's close circle of friends know enough about the shooting to say anything? Sure, it was ridiculous to worry about it. Why would anyone in that room need to be involved in a crime like that? Only, Henry did worry. And if he didn't ask, if he didn't clear up his questions, then how was he going to face Ebby, day in, day out, without saying something to her?

But telling Ebby was out of the question. Henry knew this. She was Ebby. She would make a scene. Demand answers, immediately. Threaten to tell her parents. And could he blame her? Ebby had watched her brother die. She and her parents had lived all these years without seeing justice done in Baz's killing. Of course she would want to know more.

Not that Henry had to be one hundred percent honest with Ebby. Honesty in a couple was overrated, anyhow. Every couple had secrets between them. Of this, Henry was sure. But some secrets could not be kept without consequences. And this was that kind of secret. Some things, if left unsaid, could erode the fabric of a relationship, like acid.

Even if Ebby were never to know, Henry would know it.

At first, Henry was convinced it was best to keep his doubts from Ebby until he could figure out what to do. Then he felt guilty for not saying anything to her. And finally, he began to resent Ebby. Strange, wasn't it? When faced with one's moral wobbling, a person often looked about to cast blame elsewhere. That same week, at their rehearsal dinner, even as he stayed by Ebby's side—holding her hand, joking with their respective parents—Henry was wondering why life with Ebby had to be so complicated to begin with.

Looking back, now, Henry sees this was the final push that he had needed to acknowledge his growing doubts over the wedding. He had loved the idea of marrying Ebby. But increasingly, he was worried about what living with her would require of him. Yes, he and Ebby had been through some ups and downs in their two years together. Whose relationship hadn't? It's just that Henry had come to feel that, all else being equal, he would always have to deal with that much more, because of Ebby's traumatic past.

Ebby's nightmares, her night sweats, and her skittishness had all subsided in recent months, but for how long? Then there was her insistence on keeping her brother's clock radio with her and letting the alarm go off in the mornings. And now she was planning to carry Baz's photo down the aisle at their wedding. *How sweet,* Henry had told her, but actually, he disliked the idea. Why did her brother's memory always have to be there in the middle of things?

The night before the wedding, Henry finally admitted to himself that he wanted to call off the ceremony. He needed to know for sure that things could be different with Ebby. He needed things to be easier. Less complicated. But it was too late to rethink their plans. His suit for the ceremony was hanging on the outside of the closet door. It was a late-1950s, Cary Grant–ish kind of look, custom-tailored to go with the dress that Ebby had inherited from Granny Freeman. And if Henry hesitated now, he would lose Ebby altogether. And who, except Henry, had been given the gift of Ebby?

Ebby's thighs.

Ebby's morning pouf of hair, unclipped.

Ebby's overstuffed bookshelves.

Ebby's penciled notes, filling the margins of her favorite books.

Ebby's delight in Henry's photographs.

Ebby's modesty about her own writing.

Ebby's heart.

Ebby had opened her heart to Henry. Confided in him. And Henry was the one who'd insisted on getting married. But his view of things had changed. At two in the morning, the day he was due to marry Ebby in her parents' garden, he packed a bag of clothes, grabbed his camera and car keys, put his smartphone on airplane mode, and drove out of Connecticut. He kept telling himself he could turn back, but he didn't. In all these months since then, he has never run into Ebby, though he's tried to contact her, more than once. Now he's come face-to-face with her, so far away from home. Is this some kind of sign?

Henry's dad had raised him to believe that becoming a man meant learning to take things in stride. Finding ways to forge ahead. He's been trying to do that since he ran out on Ebby, but it doesn't change how he handled things. Standing in the woods on this summer morning, listening to the heartbeat of the world, Henry feels all the chatter in his head falling away, leaving him to face an uncomfortable truth. This, too, may be what it means to be a man: being willing to square your shoulders and look someone in the eye, even if it turns out to be the eye of a storm.

# Moses

————

**1847**

THE LIGHT COMING INTO THE POTTER'S SHED WAS JUST RIGHT. Moses leaned over a disk of greenware and picked up a tool. Looking around to be sure no one was watching, he pressed the slender metal point into the clay and began to write. He told himself he could destroy the disk later. Cut it up. Wet it down. Reshape it into something else. But he did not.

Twenty years earlier, he would never have done such a thing.

# Moses

———

Back when Moses was still learning his craft, he rode all the way out to the port city with Master Oldham and Joe the wagon-maker, his back leaning against a load of new pottery as they traveled due southeast. The sight of the sea after so many years put him in mind of his arrival there as a child, in his fourth or fifth year, he would never be certain which. It took him back to the rocking of the ship in the water. To the memory of the vessel's hull, creaking and stinking with brine and life and death.

It wasn't the first time Moses had traveled by ship. As his mother held him close, she reminded him that he had come across the Atlantic from the savanna of her homeland to Barbados while still in her womb. And there they were again, not heading back across the ocean to the land of the Mandé but this time north to America. His *naa* had told him this story before and she recounted it again, trembling from the sickness as she spoke.

"It was cold but I kept you warm, just like this," she said, hugging her belly where the next baby lay inside her. "You were born three moons later, when the sun was bringing the first light to the sky. And since then, you have always loved the early morning." His mother smiled at him then, but it would be the last time. By the time the ship reached land, his mother and the baby-to-be were gone. They had succumbed to the sickness, and Moses was left alone in the world.

The ship's crew had opened the cargo hold to find little Moses whimpering and clinging to his mother's body, one small hand clamped around the tiny goat-shaped figurine that his mother had made for him. A man with hair and skin the color of sand hoisted Moses into his arms and carried him off the ship. He still remembered his first sight of the docks, the clamor of the market, the large stone room where Moses and the other stolen people were sent to wait until they could be sold. And with a great weight in his chest, he recalled how the clay goat was knocked out of his hand on the way to that room. How he wailed when he saw it crushed under a wagon wheel.

The vessel that had brought Moses up from Barbados must have been one of the last ships to dock at the port city before the ban on the trade of slaves between nations went into effect. Moses would have been too young to know this and, as he grew into a man, it would not seem to matter. Over the years, there were all manner of persons bound with ropes or chains, including children, still being driven or walked or shipped up and down the coast and even, on occasion, from across the seas.

Within days, Moses was taken away by two pink-nosed men and put into a wooden cage on the back of an open cart. Many hours later, they reached a cluster of cabins flanked by a dirt road on one side and broad, tall fields of green on the other. Standing in the doorway of one of the cabins was a woman who looked old enough to be the momma of his own mother.

"The boy will stay here," one of the men said to the woman. She nodded once. She was dark brown like Moses's *naa,* not pale like the planter man who used to come by their cabin on the island.

"You've come a long way, child," the woman said in English, with a slow, drawn-out kind of voice, similar to those of the foreigners who had brought Moses from the port. She cupped Moses's chin with one hand.

"Sit down, now. You eat," she said, pushing a plate of cornmeal mush toward him. When Moses started to cry, she said, "Hush, hush," and took him back outside. She set him down next to a large bucket of water, wetting a cloth and wiping his face and neck.

"Tomorrow, I'll show you how to do the garden," she said. "You can make yourself useful around here."

The woman told Moses to call her Auntie. She taught Moses how to care for the plants, how to tell a viper from a common garden serpent, and how to tend the fire for cooking. He helped her to mix up ointments for use when she was birthing other women's babies. Her husband, Uncle, took Moses hunting for wild game and fishing over by the river. He taught Moses how to build a chair, how to make a man from straw to scatter the ravens, and how to read his Scriptures. In addition to the Holy Bible, Uncle had a little blue book with which he taught Moses to sound out letters and write them down.

"This is just between you and me, now," Uncle told Moses. "Master Oldham won't holler about it, but I can't say the same thing about any other member of his family. This could get you and me whipped. It's against the laws of the state. Do you know what I mean by that?"

Moses shook his head no.

"Well, just do as I say. Don't talk about this, just practice."

Over time, Moses learned to read and write and talk like Uncle and Auntie, who were country-born and had always lived in those parts. He followed them into the rice fields, and then to the trading tree, where they swapped squash and cabbage for things that other slaves had brought. He came to feel that he belonged not to Master Oldham but to Auntie and Uncle, much in the way that he had once belonged to his mother. When Auntie caught some kind of fever after a long day in the rice fields and died, Moses wailed like a little boy. Shed a bucket of tears, even though he was already in his tenth year.

Moses was still living with Uncle when a man whose pants were splotched with a whitish kind of dirt arrived in a wagon to fetch him.

"You," said the man, pointing at Moses. "Come."

Moses looked at Uncle, who nodded.

The reddish man was called Prince. He took Moses to a long, broad yard full of dirt mounds and long buildings, the longest of them spewing smoke out of one end. Moses had seen this place before. It was the pottery.

"You do what you're told," said Prince, raising his voice, "only stay away from the fire and the river."

Moses nodded. He looked over yonder, where two men sank huge shovels into a mound of dirt. Others ground and filtered the dirt, pounding and kneading it into huge logs of clay, before dividing those pieces into small loaves and rolling some of them into long strands.

The smell of the clay brought to mind the scent of his mother's hands. Everyone was busy doing something. One man chopped wood while a woman walked back and forth across the yard with two buckets of water. Finally, he came to a shed where a trio of men worked with their heads and backs bent over tables.

Moses walked up to one of the men and watched, transfixed, as the potter dumped a wad of pale gray mud onto the plate before him. He then kicked at a wheel under the table with one leg. As the surface of the table spun, the man put his hands on the mass of clay. Moses watched as the mud kept changing. Until that moment, he'd thought that he understood the nature of dirt. He had worked in the fields, played with dirt clods, and pulled crayfish out of the mud. He understood that food grew out of the dirt, and that critters could live in the earth, and that dried mud could be formed into shapes, but until that day, he'd had no idea that the soil itself was a living thing that could grow so quickly.

His thoughts turned to his mother, then, and a memory came to him. Her fingers, working with a ball of clay, moving quickly until a tiny goat took shape in her hands. She had made a bowl that day, too. But it had been a slower, quieter process. Moses watched, now, as mounds of wet, filtered dirt were turned and pulled and grew into large jugs, jars, and platters. The arms of the turners working at the wheels seemed like extensions of the mud and the tools they were holding. All parts of the same whole. And now Moses felt it. How the sound of the wheel made his heart pound like a drum. How the smell of iron in the dirt filled his chest with both energy and a great sadness.

By the end of that first week, the clay was everywhere. On his hands, in his hair, on his clothes, and even inside his mouth, leaving a fine grit on his teeth. He oiled his hands every night, but still they grew cracked from the work of digging up earth, grinding it, liquefying it, and filtering it. There were weeks where his back would seize up on him like a scorpion fixing to strike.

For years, Moses went every day to the pottery, until he had grown to be a man and was given his own wheel to work at and bedding to sleep on, in a cabin not far from the kiln. He worked there every day, with only half Saturdays and Sundays off. When he could, he would catch a ride on a wagon hauling stoneware and stop off at Uncle's to sit for a while with the old man, or else he walked the entirety of the distance to and fro.

"Better there than in the rice fields," Uncle told him, and Moses grunted in agreement.

Eventually, Moses worked almost exclusively on the larger jugs. It took two men, sometimes, to add the coils of clay for the larger pieces. Once the greenware had dried long enough to become leather-hard, Moses would take a thin wooden tool and write under the lip. On each piece he would put his master's initials, *M* and *O*, and the date. Moses never signed the pieces in front of visitors or potential customers. He'd wait until they had left. Both he and his master would suffer the consequences if Moses was seen writing, even if all he was doing was labeling the vessels.

Sometimes, Moses would drag the triangular tip of his sculpting tool over the curve of the piece with a delicacy and dexterity that allowed him to leave a small design of a rice plant on its surface before glazing it with an alkaline mixture of wood ash, lime, feldspar, and such. It was a while before Master Oldham made note of the decorative marks that Moses left in the pottery.

"That's a fine-looking detail," the master said more than once. Martin Oldham was not shy to praise a person's work, and he did not mind a bit of innovation. He considered himself a God-fearing gentleman. But Master Oldham also was given to looking the other way if one of his kin had a fit of temper and took to beating one of the slaves or broke up a family by selling one of its members. Moses had seen it happen. In this way, Master Oldham was just like other men. Quick to look away when there was something that he did not wish to see.

# Moses and Flora

———

**1837**

IF YOU THOUGHT IT FINE FOR A MAN TO BE COMPELLED TO WORK for another under the threat of beatings or death, and to be forced to follow his decisions on where you laid your head at night or whether you could keep the children that were born to you, then surely you would say that Moses was living fairly well. Master Oldham had never hit Moses or forced him to take a woman for breeding. And when the time came, Moses received permission to marry a wife of his own choosing.

His marriage might not be recognized in the eyes of the government, but everyone knew they were family. He and Flora had jumped over the broomstick held by her younger brother, Willis, and Joe the wagoner, after which Uncle had written their names side by side in the back of his old Bible. It was the same one he'd used to teach Moses to read all those years before. Uncle nodded in satisfaction as he closed the book and slid it into a clay jar under a layer of rice.

The book had to be hidden. It was one thing to read your Scriptures. It was quite another to record major events in the lives of enslaved persons in the back of your Bible. Marriages, births, deaths. Who had been sold, who had run away. Africans who still remembered their original names, the ones they'd used before they'd been made to take those chosen by the slaveholders.

Moses had known Flora for years. Her daughters from her late husband were both grown, now, and were living with their own children on another farm upriver. Willis had been shadowing Moses at the pottery. The young man had potential. He liked to paint designs on the pottery and he was good at it, too. Moses grew quite fond of Willis, but he took to Flora in a more particular way.

Just to hear the sound of Flora's voice was a pleasing thing to Moses. Always had been, even when she had been another man's woman. And then she chose to be with Moses. She let him fix some broken boards in her cabin. Invited him to sit down with her and Willis for a meal. Let him walk alongside her beyond the rice fields on Sundays, taking in the colors of the wildflowers, their yellows and pinks and violets bright against the green. The two of them would walk nice and easy, as if they were free to keep on going, cross the woods, and find a riverman to ferry them away from there.

# Soh

———

1984

SOH AND ED'S WEDDING DAY WAS PERFECT. SUNNY, BUT NOT too hot for a garden ceremony. Lively, but not too crowded. Soh had been adamant about keeping the numbers down. Her mother had been aiming for more guests, but Soh had convinced her to hold a series of celebratory teas instead, with her parents' extended community of friends, colleagues, and sorors.

Her parents could have a drinks reception for all the others, Soh had reasoned. They could invite the governor, the Blisses' local congress-man, and members of the hospital board on which her father was serv-ing. As Soh continued, her mother nodded. *Closed!* Soh thought, grateful that her legal training had improved her capacity to negotiate such delicate territory with her mom.

On the night before the ceremony, Ed's parents hosted a small din-ner for the wedding party. The betrothed, their in-laws-to-be, and the best man and maid of honor. They had all slid into the languorous mood that typically followed dessert when Soh heard a screech of metal coming from the Freemans' library. Looking around, she real-ized that Ed's father had left the room. Ed's mother stood up.

"Now, Soh," Mrs. Freeman said, "under other circumstances we would have brought a wedding gift to your parents' home." Soh knew she had to get into the habit of calling Ed's mother by her first name, but Soh just couldn't shake thinking of his parents as Mr. and Mrs. Freeman.

"But in the interest of practicality and privacy," Ed's mother con-tinued, "we thought it best to do things this way."

On that cue, the metal screeching started up again and Mr. Freeman emerged from the library pushing a green wheelbarrow. Everyone started to laugh and clap. Soh felt tears come to her eyes. Lodged in the wheelbarrow, with an enormous silver ribbon fixed around its neck, was Old Mo.

"This jar, or Old Mo, as you like to call it, has been in our family for six generations," Mr. Freeman said to the room. "For most of that time, the jar has been right here in this house, or elsewhere on this property. It has been here from the year our ancestors moved out this way. It was here as the family's economic circumstances improved and they became part of a network of people offering support to other black families. And it has been here to see our family grow and achieve things our forebears could never have imagined."

Mr. Freeman turned to Soh, now. "It's time this old fella took up residence in a new home," he said. "Soh, Ed's mother and I have seen how much you appreciate the jar, and it would please us immensely if you would accept Old Mo into your new life with our son."

Soh squeezed Ed's hand.

"Did you know?" she whispered.

Ed shook his head no.

"We didn't want this to wait until we had passed on," said Mrs. Freeman, "since we are planning to be around for a good long while yet."

Laughter.

"The wheelbarrow's included in the gift," said Mr. Freeman, grinning. "Harriet and I don't want to have to lend you ours."

More laughter.

Eyes glistening, Soh stood up and rushed over to Mrs. Freeman to hug her. Later, she would wonder: Would the Freemans have let the jar leave their home if they'd known what their son was planning to do?

# The Coast

———

THEY HAD TALKED ABOUT IT FROM THE START, BUT IT WASN'T until six years after they were married that Ed and Soh finally made the move down to the Connecticut coast. Baz, five years old by then, helped his father to wrap an old sleeping bag around the jar before Ed loaded it into the back of his Volvo. Before Ed closed the hatch, little Baz patted the sleeping bag.

"Have a good trip, Old Mo," Baz said, then climbed into his seat for the drive downriver to their new home.

The smell of the salt air flowing through the car windows put Ed at ease immediately. Ed himself had never been more than a recreational boater, having been raised by two lawyers who considered the seashore strictly a place for summer vacations. Still, he had never made a secret of his yearning to live right on the water. To feel the presence of his seagoing ancestors in the wind as he walked along the shore. To grant himself the privilege of simply loving the beach. It was just that no one had ever taken him seriously.

"But why now?" his mother asked when he announced he and Soh were moving. "We thought you were all settled in up here."

"This is something I've always talked about, you know that," Ed replied. "We prefer the coast. It's a longer commute to work from here. And Soh and I need to make this move now, so that we can get Baz started in school in our new town." There was at least one other reason that he hadn't shared with his parents, but either way, the time was right.

Ed was barely thirty but had sold a couple of key patents to the right company, a once-in-a-lifetime stroke of good timing, and Soh was doing well at her corporate law firm. With their combined incomes, family gifts, and certain contacts, they had the resources to manage what no other black couple had done until then. Ed and Soh were moving into one of the more desirable homes in one of the most exclusive coastal neighborhoods in the state.

"Are you sure?" he'd asked Soh the night before the move.

"You're asking me this now? With everything already in boxes?" Soh said.

"Seriously, Soh, you don't mind being away from your parents?"

"We've gone over this already," Soh said. "It's not even an hour and a half, door to door."

They pledged to drive north every weekend to see their parents, but that plan soon took a back seat to socializing with new acquaintances, and tennis matches, and seaside walks, and spillover work. Not to mention the hunger for catnaps that could sweep over the parents of a young child. But the bottom line was this: They were glad they'd moved.

Waking to the smell of the Sound was a luxury to which Ed and Soh quickly became accustomed. Ed had landed them in a neighborhood that was unattainable even to most white families in the state. He hadn't wanted the status, per se, but he did feel he should be able to live near the shore, not too far from the city, in a quiet neighborhood, and in a place with excellent schooling.

The irony was not lost on him. When he and Soh were still kids, they would not have been allowed to swim at the beaches where they now took long strolls with the children or at the club where they had sunset drinks with neighbors. Some townspeople would wonder why anyone had let Ed and Soh put a down payment on a house there in the first place, but not all. Most people congratulated themselves on their openness to this photogenic, smart, and prosperous African American couple. They were proof, weren't they, that anything really was possible in America?

In the 1990s, elegance, good looks, and a promising investment portfolio had a way of opening doors to newcomers. It didn't hurt that Ed's parents were known for the sizable donations made by their family's foundation. And Soh had strong local connections. She'd worked or gone to law school with two of the governors of the town's beach club, who had told everyone within earshot that Soh's family had been landowners in New England since colonial times.

"Your wife is practically New England royalty," a club member once quipped over a drink with Ed. "Even if she does happen to be black." Ed didn't feel it was worth it to formulate a reply to that comment.

Way back when, an enslaved ancestor of Soh's mother's had actually owned forty acres of property while still held in bondage by a white slaveholder. When he was freed, he went on to accumulate more land and considerable wealth. Ed, too, had come from a family of significant means, but they tended to give away much of what they had. It had been his invention, his sale of the patented designs for a construction-related gizmo to a multinational company, that had catapulted them into that category of homeowners who could live comfortably three blocks from the beach.

People liked to argue otherwise, but deep down, they understood that it was a challenge to level the economic playing field between white and black Americans when one group of people had inherited their wealth over generations by using the other group as forced or low-paid labor. So even a family like his would continue to be regarded with doubt.

Most of Ed's neighbors were numbers men, and in their minds, the color of Ed's skin and his financial ease just didn't compute. After all, they didn't live in the Boston area, or down in Rockland County, New York, or in a metropolitan area like Atlanta or Los Angeles, where Ed might have seemed like less of an anomaly. He'd grown used to that kind of perplexity on the job.

"Got in on the minority track, huh?" a colleague at his first company once said to him. "Well, it's our gain," the guy said right after that, with a grin and a light pat on Ed's shoulder. Ed felt his Adam's apple catch in his throat as he swallowed hard. Not long after that, Ed left and formed his own consulting group.

"Bad-mannered people" was what his mother used to say about the verbal slights that Ed called microaggressions. He understood that his mother hadn't liked his decision to move, but knowing that he could raise his family wherever he chose was part of his sustained response to those *bad-mannered people*.

When neighbors did accept the Freemans and would come to visit, they arrived with certain expectations. And Ed suspected that his family's lifestyle did not fit with what they'd imagined. Despite the impressive double-sided fireplace and large, contemporary kitchen, the rest of the house looked like what it was meant to be: a home where young children could grow and play.

There were no white chairs. Theirs was a home where you could put your feet on the sofa. Where old, ready-to-assemble furniture mingled with family antiques and new flooring. A place where a utility jar like Old Mo could feel at home.

"Look at that," more than one neighbor had been known to say on walking into Ed's study, which also doubled as the family library. Ed could tell from the raised eyebrows, from the forced up-tone in their voices, that they were trying to conceal their surprise at the clunky piece of stoneware clearly sitting in a position of honor on an antique worktable.

"I would have expected something different from you," said Tucker, one of their friendlier neighbors, though they wouldn't have classified him as a friend, exactly. "Something more twentieth-century sleek. Or at the very least much older. Pre-Columbian, say."

"I know," said Ed, chuckling.

"Don't get me wrong," Tucker said. "It's a beautiful jug, in its own way. Really. The more you look at it, the more it seems . . ."

"Jar."

"Huh?"

"It's a jar, not a jug. Made to store food. It belonged to my dad, and to his folks before that, and theirs, too. So it's very special to us."

"I can see that," said Tucker.

Several years later, a similar Mo jar sold at auction for nearly six figures. Eventually, engraved works by Dave, another enslaved potter who later went by the name David Drake, would break all previous records. But at the time, it was unheard-of to pay that kind of money for such work.

"Turned out to be a good inheritance, that old vase," Tucker said the next time Ed saw him.

"I guess," said Ed. He didn't bother to say again that Old Mo was a jar. Tucker told him he'd gone online and looked at the potential appeal of alkaline-glazed stoneware from historic Southern potteries. He'd stumbled onto a couple of articles on the history of these sought-after pieces. He'd had no idea that such pottery, innovative in its day and made with some of the best clay in the country, had been produced primarily by enslaved craftsmen. He hadn't realized that so many practical devices and tools had been made with "slave labor," as Tucker put it.

"Who knew?" Tucker said.

*We knew,* thought Ed.

Ed's old college classmate Harris, who'd come up from New Canaan that day, rolled his eyes behind Tucker's back. He'd worked with Tucker in the past, and Tucker had a way of getting on Harris's nerves. Ed smiled and raised his eyebrows, but the truth was, he was glad that Tucker had come to realize the jar's value, though he never would have admitted that he cared what Tucker thought. In any event, the value of the old jar, for Ed and Soh, lay not in its marketability but in how it had ended up being part of their lives.

If a high price tag for Old Mo meant anything to Ed and Soh, it was only a form of affirmation in a society in which cash, so often, carried greater social weight than a person's history. Ed didn't need a New York auction house to tell him the true value of that jar. And anyway, it wasn't as though he and Soh would ever think of selling it. That jar represented all those stories he could tell his children that most people never told about black folks in America.

Ed didn't think Tucker could fully appreciate this kind of thinking. Still, he would be genuinely sorry, years later, when Tucker was one of the many souls declared missing after the 9/11 disaster. Tucker would leave behind a wife. No one should have to face that kind of loss. By then, Ed himself would have come to understand what losing someone suddenly and violently could feel like.

# Part Two

# Ebby

———

Breakfast in the village feels like an act of defiance to Ebby. To sit outside, in public, and breathe in the absence of attention. To feel the sun on her arms before it gets too warm. To note the sound of an old wooden shop door being unlocked. To listen to the world while hiding in plain sight.

Ebby hears footsteps approaching from the street and looks up to see a man, maybe a bit older than she, glance her way as he walks by. A flash of bright eyes under a mop of dark hair. But he is not imposing. Not intrusive. She revels in the idea of it. That a man might look at her, just to look, without seeing Ebony Freeman. It's rare for her. She likes that he looks at her, then looks away. To be admired, just because, but without pressure.

Sitting there, Ebby wonders if this could be part of the answer to her problems. To stay away from home. Maybe not forever, but for more than just a few months. She would be leaving behind much of what has made her feel exposed. But she'd also be distancing herself from everything that has made her feel loved. Is there a place where she can feel less stress without being isolated? She had thought this village could be that place, with Hannah spending part of her time here. Until Henry showed up.

A bee buzzes near Ebby's cheek. She keeps perfectly still. Breathes slowly and quietly. She doesn't want to agitate the bee. She knows that trying to back away could be a mistake. She hears her mom's voice. *Be careful, Ebby. Be careful.* If Ebby simply stays put, if she allows herself to be part of the bee's world, she should be fine.

Hannah would love it if Ebby decided to extend her stay. And Ebby needs to be around more people like Hannah. Distanced as Hannah had been from Ebby's reality back home, and uninterested as she had been in certain magazines, programs, and websites, she hadn't come into their working relationship with a preconceived image of Ebony Freeman. It seemed that Hannah had been interested in Ebby only as a colleague and, later, as a friend. Not as someone marked by a family tragedy.

Then Ebby met Henry and felt, for the first time, that the same thing might be possible in love.

Henry, with that way he had of pulling her under his arm. Henry, with the way he lowered his head to hers. Henry, scuffing his shoes along the sand and complaining every time he trailed grains into the car. As if the man hadn't been raised on the Connecticut coast. As if he didn't drive a Range Rover. What was the point of a car like that, Ebby reasoned, if not for sand and mud?

"Why don't you just take off your shoes, if you don't want sand in the car?" Ebby asked him the last time they took a wintertime drive together down the coast.

"You ask me that every time," Henry said. "The sand is cold, Ebby. It's *winter*. I can't believe you're walking barefoot."

"It's not like walking on pavement. The sand has a different composition."

"You're just pretending the sand isn't cold to prove a point. It's like that nasty seaweed you insist on eating because it's supposed to be healthy."

"I am not the only person who eats dulse. People in Canada eat it. People in Washington eat it."

"It's algae, okay? It's fishy."

"You eat fish, don't you?"

"Fish are fish. Fish are supposed to be fishy. But fishy vegetables? No, thank you."

"You eat sushi, don't you?"

"Sushi is fish."

This part of every argument with Henry always cracked her up. How Henry, with all his intelligence, education, and professional experience, was, ultimately, an innocent. He never noticed how Ebby's voice slowed down as she came in for the kill. Never saw the logic of it circling his head like a lasso, waving through the air, then dropping around his shoulders before being pulled tight.

"Babe, sushi can be wrapped in seaweed." She nudged him with her shoulder as she said, "A fishy vegetable. Hah!"

The thing about Henry was, he was so good-natured, he'd just make a face in a situation like that one, then laugh it off. He would admit defeat. It wasn't easy to get on his nerves. Henry, for Ebby, had represented a world of possibility. The way he simply listened and nodded the first time Ebony talked to him about Baz. The way he made her stomach flip, just by breathing against her face. The way he made Ebby feel embraced. Up to a point. Until she sensed that the emotional injuries with which she still lived were beginning to weigh on him.

"You can't go on this way for the rest of your life," Henry said one morning, after a particularly rough night. "You need to talk to your therapist about this."

"At what point are you supposed to stop reacting to trauma?" Ebby had asked one day, when she was still seeing a therapist. "At what point are you supposed to stop thinking about it?"

"It's normal to think about your brother and his death," said the therapist. "This was a huge thing in your life. Your challenge is not to erase all memory of what happened, but to find a way to live with it." But Ebby, after years of this, was tired. Tired of being the survivor.

The man who was walking across the café patio a minute before has taken a seat at the far edge of the group of tables. He looks at her and nods slightly. She looks down, shyly, but breathes in the pleasure of it. He's a good-looking guy. This feeling, a kind of buzz, is the feeling she's been trying to get back to since her time with Henry. Henry had noticed her, liked her, wanted *her*, Ebby. Not Ebony Freeman.

Until he no longer did.

Every once in a while, some other man has looked at Ebby in the way that this French guy is looking at her now. His expression has grown hopeful. Every once in a while, she has held someone's gaze and smiled slightly, opening the door to something more. Sometimes, she has allowed herself to be touched by someone who seemed to want only that. Even if only for a night. Usually, only for a night.

"Bonjour, Aline," the man says as the waitress approaches him. The sound of his voice makes Ebby tip her head. What is that sound? It's as if the man is humming the waitress's name.

"Bonjour, Robert!" says Aline, who juts her chin out toward the man before stopping at Ebby's table.

*Row-BEHR!* Ebby thinks. Could this be the famous Robert of the phone calls she keeps getting? Just last night, the phone rang again as she was trying to figure out what to do about Henry's surprise appearance.

"Yes?" she had said, a bit too roughly, perhaps. The person on the other end of the line hesitated, then cleared his throat. That was all Ebby needed to hear to know who it was. That was how often he'd called.

"Robert?" the caller asked.

"No, there is no *Row-BEHR* here."

"Robert isn't there?"

"No, Robert is not here, monsieur. What is your name?"

"Gregoire. Where is Robert?"

"I don't know, Monsieur Gregoire."

"When is he coming back?"

"I don't know. He does not live here," Ebby said.

"*Zut,*" the man said. "*Mais . . .*"

Ebby was thinking she should just pull the cable that connected the phone base to the wall. No one else used this number anyway. They would call the smartphone that Hannah had left for her. But the man had a slight crack in his voice that made her think of her gramps. What if this were her own grandfather, several years older and sitting in a room on his own? Ebby felt a smile creep across her face at the thought of Grandpa Freeman. And just like that, she found herself talking to him, in a softer voice this time.

"And this Robert? *C'est ton fils?*"

Robert, apparently, was not Monsieur Gregoire's son but his grandson. Ebby tried to find out more about M. Gregoire, why he was calling this number, and where he was calling from, but he ignored her questions and launched into a long spiel about his day. Ebby put the telephone receiver on the speakerphone setting and laid it on the kitchen table. She let the man yammer on for a minute while she poured hot water from the kettle over fresh mint leaves. She cut a slice of lemon, twisted open a jar of honey, and he was still talking. She wondered, Was someone taking care of M. Gregoire? Was it Robert? And where, indeed, was Robert?

When M. Gregoire suddenly stopped speaking, she put the phone to her ear, but her mystery caller had hung up.

Ebby squints now in the direction of the man at the café, as if she might recognize him as *the* Robert in question. There must be a million men in France with that name. But how many of them live in this village?

"Another coffee?" Aline says in English.

Aline is used to Ebby by now. Clad in her usual white T-shirt and black apron, she stands there, waiting, with an open face. Ebby can tell from Aline's expression that she knows nothing about Ebby's past, only her present. She knows only that the *américaine* usually orders a second cup of *café* with lots of milk. That instead of the brioche that she ordered the first time, Ebby has become hooked on *la tartine,* a chunk of baguette with butter and jam, the one made from strawberries grown on the Île de Ré. That although Ebby has parked the car nearby, having errands to run, she is likely to linger.

This is all Aline knows about Ebby, and Ebby loves that.

"*D'accord,*" Ebby says, "*un autre café.*" And from the soft upturn of Aline's mouth, Ebby senses that her accent still amuses the waitress.

When the bread arrives, still warm in the middle, Ebby breathes in deeply and focuses on the scent of the baguette as it absorbs the butter. The weight of the jam as she spoons it onto the bread. The sound of two people at the other end of the *place* greeting each other with soft laughter before sitting down, falling silent, and knitting their brows over a chessboard. The little ways Ebby has learned to stay in the moment, over the years. To allow herself the joy of being alive, until the edges of her life grow raw again.

*Hold the moment,* she tells herself.

As Ebby takes another sip of her *café,* she looks up and sees Robert looking her way again. She meets the man's gaze and nods a greeting.

He smiles.

She smiles back.

Ebby pulls at a cherry-colored twist of her hair, then lets it spring back into place. *Carpe diem,* Ebby thinks when Robert stands up and walks toward her table.

# Foreigner

————

EBBY THE FOREIGNER DOES THINGS THAT SHE NEVER WOULD have done at home. On the first full day of Henry and Avery's stay in the guesthouse, Ebby goes home with the stranger from the village café and has sex in the midmorning light. Later, she slinks out of his house while he is running the water in the bathroom, suddenly aware of the huge risk that she has taken. Sure, she's been with guys she hardly knew before, but not like this.

Ebby doesn't even know the name of the street she's on. Worse yet, she is making the oldest mistake in the book. Even as she walks quickly away from Robert's house, she is thinking that there was something between them that went beyond the immediate physical attraction she felt. The way they'd talked and laughed before going at it again. How he had caressed her forehead. How it had seemed just right, for a bit, until she'd felt the need to escape. Either way, she will remain grateful to the soft-spoken stranger with that curly mane of hair and the cyclist's legs for making her forget everything for just a couple of hours.

Ebby spots the roof of the village château, its slate-covered turrets leading her back to the town square and the side street where she left the car. Now she knows where she is, but she can't bear the thought of returning to the cottage after running her errands. She might find Henry and Avery there. Instead, she drives to the train station up in the big town and stands with her back to a wall. The train station is vast and loud. It smells of coffee and pastry and fried foods. It is filled with people coming from elsewhere. Filled with people chattering in languages she doesn't understand. She pretends to be a traveler scrolling through her mobile phone, when all she is doing, really, is trying to disappear from herself.

# Rebuilding

---

BACK AT THE COTTAGE, EBBY WATCHES THE AFTERNOON LIGHT deepen to gold and dreads the approach of another night of troubled sleep. She keeps being pulled back to the past, try as she might to cancel it out. She needs to find a better way to live with herself. To rebuild her relationship with her family's history. There is more to her personal story than hurt. She reaches into her tote bag and takes out a pencil and the lined notebook that she uses as a journal. She curls her legs up onto the sofa. She knows what to do. She has always known, hasn't she?

She feels her eyes grow wet as she writes.

> Dad has been asking me, for years, to write down the jar stories. I didn't have the heart to tell him that I just didn't feel like doing it. He used to tell me and Baz that Old Mo was a reminder that life could bring good things, even in the worst of times. The fact that the jar had lasted as long as it had was like a promise for the future. Then my brother died, and it felt like that promise had been turned on its head. But lately, I've been hearing the jar stories in my mind. And thinking. Maybe it's time I stopped trying to close them out.

Ebby stops scribbling. She hears something that pulls her to her feet and draws her toward Hannah's office. This is her favorite room, the one with the fireplace and the kind of view that compels you to stop whatever you're doing and stare out the window for minutes at a time.

*Yo-ho-ho!*

She hears it again. But where? Ah, there it is. An orangey-brown bird with its unmistakable black-and-white-striped wings and tail feathers. It stops, ruffles its black-tipped crown, then pulls it back down against its head and proceeds to stab its long beak into the grass. That goofy, beautiful little creature reminds her of how easy it can be to love life.

She edited something on birds, not too long ago, and there was something about the hoopoe. *Upupa epops*. Found in Africa, Asia, and Europe. The paper told how these birds had been seen farther north than usual. They had overshot their regular migration path and had lingered, confused, perhaps, by the changing climate. This struck her at the time. How a creature could be in the wrong place but feel all right anyway, and so manage to get by for a while. She thinks of herself, here in France. Is she like those birds? Has she been blown off course? Or is this the path she's meant to follow?

Her work as an editor can be torturous, at times. Many capable researchers are wobbly writers. She's offered a couple of workshops to help people strengthen their academic writing skills, and now her clients are asking for more of the same. But Ebby is not a born teacher. What Ebby really wants, what she needs, is to work on other kinds of writing. Not necessarily educational or technical. Something more story based.

Hannah says she knows people with literary projects that would be perfect for Ebby.

"Think about it," Hannah says. But Ebby's already given it some thought. She just hasn't said. She doesn't want to edit someone else's literary work. She wants to write her own. Create her own body of writing. Now she sees the jar stories could be part of that. Strange to think of it, but Henry once said the very same thing.

"It could be good for you," he said. "To go all the way back to what made you love that jar in the first place."

As if summoned by her thoughts, there he is.

Henry.

Knocking on the kitchen door.

Ebby knows that sound. The particular weight of his hand on the wood. His knuckles, squarish and pale. She doesn't need to see him to know who it is. This is the man she nearly married.

# Moses

———

**1843**

MARRIAGE TO FLORA MADE MOSES MORE INCLINED TO LAUGH when they sat down together. Never mind that he was feeling the day's work in his arms and back. Never mind that Flora's legs and hands were scratched and bitten from working in the fields. Never mind that Master Oldham's nephew Jacob was getting more aggressive with the field hands. Moses was in the frame of mind to welcome a bit of mirth, all the same, when Willis showed up one evening to tell him and Flora and Uncle about the flying alligator.

Word of the alligator had come from the port city by way of the black boatmen who moved goods, people, and secret messages along the riverways of the Lowcountry. It seemed the storm on the coast had sent all sorts of debris flying about the streets in a most frightening way. When the squall moved on, it left behind an alligator, standing on a street corner and looking as stunned as the men who happened upon it.

The first people to see the two-foot-long creature swore it had fallen directly out of the sky. And if not from there, then where else? The alligator was a good walk away from the nearest river. Well, it seemed an unlikely tale at best, the kind inspired by too many cups of liquor, and when Willis related these details, Moses, Flora, and Uncle could not help but laugh. And the pleasure of having a reason to laugh brought forth more of the same.

Moses would remember that evening and the levity shared with the people he most cared for. And he would be grateful for the memory of Flora's laughter when trouble came. That very week, a viper reared up at Flora and bit her on the ankle and made it swell in an ugly way. It happened from time to time in the fields, but it was a worrisome thing because these episodes did not always end well.

"Snake didn't mean nothing by it," Flora told Moses. "I was the one who ran into its burrow by mistake." She chuckled, and Moses made an effort to smile, just to please her, but he could see she was in pain. Uncle sent two girls from up the road to gather some plantain weed. They chewed the leaves and spread the poultice on Flora's wound. The elders had done this many times over the years and the girls, too, were learning the old ways. But they would learn, also, the bitterness of attempting a remedy that did not work. Two days later, after her breathing became more labored, Flora was gone.

The snake sickness had taken Moses's wife away and darned near took Moses's mind with it, too. Moses had lived on that property for most of his life. He had seen people come and go. Babies sold away from their mothers. Couples separated. But this was not the kind of *going* he had been expecting to see just then. How could Moses expect to face the day without Flora? He had come to cherish her role in his life in a way he hadn't known possible. After Flora's burial, he sat outside the cabin with Uncle and Willis, night after night, unable to say a word.

The only thing that seemed to ease the feeling that had come over him was sinking his hands into the clay. It was soon after Flora's death that Moses took to experimenting with a technique for putting designs on the bottom panels of the large jars. Moses would shape a separate piece of clay into a thin disk, carve a shape into it, then attach the piece over the bottom of a jar that had already been formed and dried to a leatherlike toughness.

He began with outlines of flowers, then moved on to making a relief of Flora's head. Her small, flat nose. Her two braids wound tight at the top of her neck. Willis, recognizing his sister's profile, leaned in to watch Moses work.

"That's a fine likeness," Willis said. "Don't much see the use of putting it there, though. Don't know that anyone is going to have occasion to look at the bottom of a jar that big," he added.

Moses nodded. What Willis said was true. Who would tip a twenty-gallon storage container so far over that you could actually see the underside? Likely no one, ever. Which gave Moses an idea. On another day, for the first time, Moses incised a piece of clay with a phrase and affixed it to the bottom of a jar. He couldn't let anyone see that he was writing. It was one thing for him to carve the date or initials, despite the laws that barred people like him from writing. That might be risky, but it was another thing, entirely, to form a full sentence. This was to court danger in the most direct way. But as he drew a tool across the surface, Moses felt the ache in his soul dull slightly.

LORD HAVE MERCY, Moses wrote, then mumbled the words to himself.

*Lord have mercy.*

# Confrontation

———

H ENRY IS PEERING IN THROUGH A GLASS PANE IN THE KITCHEN door, his face yellowed by the lamp above. Ebby exhales slowly. She is thinking about Moses and the kind of love that flourishes despite difficult circumstances. And much as she tries to fight it, the questions come to her, the same questions as always. About love. Had Henry ever really loved her? How could he have shown so little regard for her? And would anyone else who claimed to love her ever be worth the risk? She feels her mouth draw into itself and makes a conscious effort to relax her face.

*Be polite,* she thinks. *This is Hannah's house. This is business.* She pulls open the door.

"Hello, Ebby," Henry says. He makes a move as if to walk inside but Ebby remains in place, still holding the doorknob and blocking the entrance with her body.

Ebby raises her eyebrows. She does not say hello.

"Everything all right?" she asks. She turns her head to get a better look outside. She sees that Henry is alone. No Avery in sight.

"Avery is washing her hair," Henry says, "and I imagine that's going to take a while." He chuckles.

Ebby does not smile.

"What can I do for you?" she says.

Henry clears his throat.

"Well, first of all, Avery has found another place for us, closer to Bordeaux, so we'll be checking out tomorrow."

"I see."

"I mean, if that's all right. We can pay whatever penalty you wish."

"That won't be a problem, though we'll still assess the cleaning fee."

"Oh, of course," Henry says.

"Thanks for letting me know," Ebby says. She starts to push the door closed, but Henry puts his hand on it to stop her.

Ebby is filled with dread at the thought of one more second with Henry here.

*Please, please, let him go away.*

"Ebby," he says. "Could we just talk for a minute?"

"Talk about what, Henry?"

"About us."

"What *us*? There is no *us,* Henry." She can't resist saying, "That was your decision, remember?"

"I know, I know," Henry says. "But you never gave me a chance to explain."

"No, Henry, *you* never bothered to give me an explanation before you *ghosted* me on our wedding day. You didn't even have the balls to show up."

"But I called you, Ebby. I texted you. I asked you to give me a chance to talk."

"That was afterward, Henry. *Afterward.* You had your opportunity. And that opportunity expired once you failed to show up at my parents' house, on the designated day. With one hundred guests in the garden. Would you even be here at this door, right now, trying to talk about *us*"—Ebby raises her arms and forms air quotes with her fingers—"if you hadn't ended up running into me here?"

Silence. Henry looks down at his hiking shoes.

"Of course not."

"Ebby . . ."

"Don't *Ebby* me!"

"Please . . ."

"No, no, no. You, please. Just go away. I am closing this door, right now."

Henry doesn't budge.

"If we need to talk about the guest cottage," Ebby says, "I will deal with Avery. She's the one who booked the room, right? Or would you like me to go to her now and ask her what she thinks?"

Henry steps back and puts up his hands, as if under arrest.

"Would you at least think about it?" he says.

"Think about what, Henry? What part of *no* do you not understand?"

The old Henry would have laughed at the cliché. But Henry's mouth is tight, now, and Ebby admits she feels a bit of satisfaction at the sight of it. But she also feels close to tears. She urgently needs Henry to leave. He turns away, now, and Ebby closes and locks the door. *Breathe,* she tells herself. *Breathe.*

And to think she was worried about Henry, on the day that he ghosted her. She remembers there had been news of a murder on the coast, an unknown victim of an undetermined assailant. The kind of seemingly random crime that had a person wondering, *Could that be someone I know?* Could Henry have gone out to clear his head before the wedding ceremony and run into someone who meant trouble? These things could happen. Every moment in life is a confluence of events and you can't see it all coming. You need to try not to, Ebby thinks. See it all. Otherwise, it leaves no room in your head to simply live.

Ebby closes her eyes now and concentrates. She dares to think of her brother. Baz and her at the beach. Sand in their shoes. Salty air. Grit on their skin. Laughter, laughter, laughter. *Hold the moment,* she thinks. She walks across the kitchen and into an adjacent hallway where a full-length mirror is bolted to the wall. She flips a light on, looks at herself, and fingers her cherry-toned hair, her hand trembling.

This color is all wrong. Her hair looks like some kind of sugary drink. Was it this faded when Hannah saw her? Why didn't Hannah tell her she looked like this? Probably because Hannah is a good friend, that's why. But she wasn't doing Ebby any favors. Ebby needs to take control of the situation. There is a new hair-coloring product that she has been thinking of trying. It has a 4.5 customer-satisfaction rating and comes in twenty shades. Maybe she should drive up to the main town in the area. Maybe she can find what she needs from somewhere around there.

Ebby knows that making a transition to a completely different color is best done with the help of a professional, one step at a time. But Ebby doesn't want to have to wait for that. She needs to make a change now. She checks the time on her smartphone. Probably the stores will be closed by the time she gets up to the big town, but she'll try anyway. She grabs the car keys and goes. She sees that Henry's rental car is already gone. Ebby tries not to think about him with Avery, sitting down at a table outside a cute little bistro somewhere. She shoves her foot down hard on the clutch and shifts the car into first gear.

Ebby doesn't think much of it when, on her way out to the big town, she sees a white SUV turning onto a dirt road alongside the far end of a vineyard, toward a line of trees. Sure, it's late already. The time of day when farmers are done with their work. When a car might be driving in the other direction, toward the asphalt, not away from it. It is the kind of detail that will come back to her later, when the police begin to question people in the area about what they might have seen that was out of the ordinary, and exactly when.

For now, Ebby is thinking only that it is time to make a real change in her life. Seeing Henry with Avery drives home the fact that she has come to France for a reason. To do things differently. Henry seemed so comfortable with Avery. When will Ebby get to feel that comfortable with someone again? For a moment, she remembers Robert. How easy it felt to be with him. She shakes her head. *Wake up, Ebby.* Robert was a one-night stand. Or a half-day hookup, to be precise.

Only it feels like it was more than that. She may not know much else about Robert, but at least they'd established that he is indeed the grandson that her mystery caller was looking for. Before they drifted into a brief nap together, she'd summoned the courage to ask Robert about M. Gregoire.

"Gregoire?" said Robert. "Nooo," he said, shaking his head. "My grandfather? Really? *Oh, pépère!*" He rolled onto his side and touched Ebby's face. Gently. A caress. How long had it been since someone had simply caressed Ebby's face? Not since the week she should have been married. Not since Henry.

"Wait," Robert said then. "Let me see your phone."

"Well, he called the house phone," Ebby said, "so you wouldn't see anything here in my cellphone. You'll have to check with your grandpa. But don't be angry with him."

"I am not angry. I'm glad you told me. He must have used his cellphone. Gotten into his contacts list and changed the number somehow. *Tu vois?* Don't worry, I will take care of it."

Robert's voice keeps coming back to Ebby. And the way his face warmed up when he spoke about his grandfather. The thought of him causes a twinge below her navel. She's not going to stop thinking about him, is she? Well, that's good. She needs to believe that she can be that distracted by someone new. That she won't always feel this bad about Henry. And that one day, she might not mind falling for someone again.

Ebby slows the car. Good, the shops are still open. She buys hair color and a pair of styling shears. When she gets back to the house, she takes about three inches off her hair, snipping in arcs from her forehead all the way to the nape of her neck. She turns her head this way and that to check the results. Not bad. In the morning, she will dye down what's left of the red with a neutral dark brown. She will let her natural hair color come back in. Give her head a rest. Get a hairdresser to give her a proper cut. Then, once she has a few inches of new growth, she'll decide what to do next.

Tomorrow, Henry and Avery will be gone. Tomorrow, things will be much better.

# Love, Again

———

**1847**

LIFE COULD BE STRANGE, THAT WAY. HOW A CHANGE COULD come when you didn't expect it.

When Moses worked on the larger pieces, he needed someone nearby to kick the wheel for him as he stood up to work on the clay. Willis often helped, but one day, when Willis was busy painting slip flowers on a jar, Moses called out to one of the two women at the pottery, the yellow woman who was busy carrying two buckets of water across the yard. Betsey was her name. She was a newcomer who, lately, had been working between the pottery and the big house.

Betsey had a way of speeding up and slowing down the pace of her kicking in a way that made things much easier for Moses. She stood close to him, pushing at the base of the wheel when he nodded. She seemed to have understood, right away, something fundamental about Moses and the way he worked. He asked her to come back again. Betsey was a natural. And Betsey was undeniably beautiful. She had a way of lowering her head when she smiled so that, mostly, all Moses could see was a brief flash of light in her eyes.

When a woman like Betsey smiled at a man, he could forget everything else. He could forget the loneliness of losing his wife. He could forget that he was an old man, more than forty years of age. He could forget the backbreaking labor of turning, throwing, and firing the clay, day after day. The heat on their arms as they loaded all those pieces into the blazing kiln. *Feeding the beast,* the men used to say.

Took a man tall as Moses a good fifty paces or so to walk the entire length of that kiln. It could hold some four thousand gallons' worth of greenware from various potteries at a time, all being cooked in the fires of hell. Keeping up the pace required to produce all that pottery could take away from the beauty of the clay. But Moses was an able turner, and every once in a while, he allowed himself to slow down. Take his time making a piece. Return his mind to the feel of it. Savor the power to shape, to create, to undo mistakes.

To start again.

Betsey was much younger than Moses. And yet, he was sure she had taken a liking to him. For the first time in a long while, Moses looked forward to Saturday afternoon. Lately, he had taken to walking with Betsey over to the makeshift market where they and other slaves would gather to barter their surplus produce. On one particularly fine day, Moses cut some ripe squash out of his garden patch and filled a calico sack. Then he snipped a cluster of blackberries for Betsey. He watched a hummingbird hover near the red cedar as he headed for Betsey's cabin.

This time of year, the hummingbirds would be fixing to nest.

But as Moses neared the small, square building, he saw Master Oldham's nephew Jacob opening the door to Betsey's cabin. Moses held back. The sight of Jacob Oldham entering a slave woman's cabin could mean only one thing. In another world, Moses would have said, *What are you doing over there?* But in this world, Moses belonged to Martin Oldham and Jacob was Oldham's nephew. Not his favorite relation, for sure. Jacob Oldham was known to be a particularly coarse person. But he was Oldham's kin and he was white and he was not a man to be crossed.

"Moses," Jacob Oldham said. "What brings you around these parts?"

"Market, sir," Moses said, holding up the sack containing the squash and jutting his chin in the general direction of the market site. But the younger Oldham wasn't even listening. He had already turned his back to Moses. Moses felt his jaw tighten as the other man stepped inside Betsey's cabin and shut the door behind him. Moses felt his face burning as he continued in the direction of the market.

He met Willis along the road.

"Betsey?" Willis asked.

Moses shook his head.

The next day, Betsey was not at Bible study, and Moses knew better than to go looking for her. On Monday, Betsey turned up at the shed with bruises darkening her forearm and her eyes cast to the ground.

"What happened?" Moses asked, reaching for Betsey's wrist. She pulled her hand away. Didn't speak. Just shook her head and looked at the wheel. No need for her to answer, anyhow. Moses could see everything he needed to know. Around here, a person could lay claim to another person, just like that. Betsey stayed very quiet that day. Didn't come back to Moses's wheel the next. Took to crossing the pottery at the far end of the yard, looking straight ahead. That evening, Moses went out of his way to walk by Betsey's cabin, but he didn't knock. He couldn't risk running across Jacob Oldham there again. Turners like Moses had more leeway than most, moving about and such, but he had to be careful.

Moses glanced down at the plants in the vegetable patch outside Betsey's cabin. There were dried leaves that needed clearing away and weeds that were up to shin level. Betsey had not been tending to them the way she normally did. He hadn't noticed before. It was then that the thought came to him and hit him square in the middle of his stomach: *How long has this been going on?*

When a woman like Betsey touched your arm, you could forget that another man owned you. The problem was, you might forget that another man owned the woman, too. Much later, Moses would conclude that he must have gone temporarily mad, to have blocked such a thing from his mind.

# Betsey

THEY HAD CALLED HER *SLAVE* ALL HER LIFE, BUT BETSEY KNEW better. She was a reading woman, even though it was against the law to show it. And there were people who wrote things. She had met up with some of the other laborers in secret to read the papers that were printed and carried inside people's clothing along the waterways, along the wagon roads, across the fields. She knew that other people lived differently, outside this territory. She knew that things were changing. She knew that just because the law gave a man the power to tell you that you were not a person in your own right, it did not make it so.

When the missus on the plantation where Betsey had grown up ordered that Betsey be sold away, she did not know what to expect. Then she ended up at Oldham's brickworks, and it was different from anything she'd encountered while doing housework at the old place. Betsey spent most of her time fetching water and wood, washing down equipment, and shoveling dirt. She was always covered in mud or a powdery dust.

Betsey learned how to wash out the clay and refine it for the turners, watching as the men created objects out of earth. She liked the smell and sight of the clay as it grew into new shapes. She liked the glow of the long fire tunnel. She liked kicking the wheel for Moses the turner when he worked with the larger objects. And, in fact, she liked Moses, the man, himself. Very much.

Surely Moses was almost old enough to be her father, only he didn't seem like a father at all. And he understood that Betsey had an interest in building pots. He showed her respect. Told her about throwing the clay, timing the wheel, mixing the slip. In time, Betsey found that she wanted to walk with Moses to the market. She wished for him to dance with her when the folks gathered on Sunday at Uncle's after dinner. But mostly, she was shy around him, and so was he, around her.

Betsey began to wonder whether Moses was too old to take her for a wife. Would the master let her stay with him? Would he be able to give her children? She had no time to find out. Master Oldham's nephew Jacob began to spend more time at the pottery. Began to get ideas in his head. Began to stop by her cabin. And what could she do? If Betsey did not do as he said, he hit her. One time, when she refused, he did something so unspeakable as to cast her mind down into a deep, dark well where words could not be summoned.

But time passes, and when time passes, a person can start to think that things will change. The heart of a person, even in troubled times, is a hopeful place. One day, the master's nephew came to get her while she was working in the yard. She refused to go, thinking he wouldn't persist with the other workers close by. But she was wrong. He knocked her down, dragged her into a storage shed, and tied her hands and feet. Then he put another rope around her neck to keep her still.

She could make out the forms of the other workers approaching the open door. Beyond them, the towering form of Moses, crossing the yard. Betsey prayed that Moses would not expose them. Would not show his interest in her welfare to be greater than that of the others. To do so would only make things worse for them both.

"You all stay away from there," Betsey heard Jacob Oldham roar as he stalked out of the shed. "Get back to your work." Oldham yanked the door shut.

It occurred to Betsey, then, that she had been restrained, precisely, in the manner of livestock awaiting slaughter. It was this thought, more than any other, that filled her with an oddly quiet understanding of her destiny. If she was to die, she would die as a woman. As a person.

They had called her slave all her life, but Betsey knew better.

# Trouble

_____

**1847**

He supposed the signs of trouble had been there for weeks, but he had preferred not to think about them. Moses was bent over the worktable, now, thinking of what had transpired four days past. It had been a terrible thing, and now his heart felt like it was lying on its side, struck down by a deep sorrow. This was a world where a person could suffer. Even more so when one had experienced love. It had been a long while since Moses had felt this low.

After everything that had happened, the world felt cruelly normal. He awoke that morning to the usual trilling of the rusty-headed sparrows. That love-hungry woodpecker was out there, too. *Pick-pick-pick-pick-pick*. Now he heard something of significant size rustling around in the garden patch. Raccoon, most likely. He'd have to go and run the animal out of there. Take care not to get himself bitten in the process.

His right knee clicked as he straightened his body. Then he felt a twinge in his neck as he bent to pick up his boots. The nature of his work could have that effect. Moses turned the shoes upside down and knocked them together to check for critters, *one-two-three*. In that moment, he could pretend he was in a peaceful place. He could pretend there was nothing to think of but the cricks in his body and the noises of the morning.

Most days, he would find himself back in that same space in his head when he was at the wheel. Moses would center a lump of clay on the stand and start kicking to turn the table. He would lean in and squeeze the clay with both hands as the wheel slowed. Push in from the sides and down from above. Wet his hand and sprinkle some water over the mound. Then *kick-kick-kick* at the wheel. Press down, lift up. Form a cone, then down again.

When the time was right, Moses would push his fingers into the middle of the mound, then pull the sides up and out. As the vessel took shape, he did not think about who he was, or where he was, or how many pieces he and the other turners would be obligated to produce that day. He thought only of the one piece of clay in his hands, and the speed of the wheel, and how his mother used to hold him and murmur to him about the energy that flowed from the raw clay into her hands. How the earth could give back a bit of what a man could take away.

But on this particular day, Moses was thinking about what his life had come to, and as he looked back at all that had happened, his thoughts would leave their imprint in the clay.

# Ebby

———

EBBY SNIFFLES AS SHE WRITES. SHE KNOWS THAT WHAT HAPPENED to Betsey and Moses all those years ago would go on to forge the connection between Moses's life in South Carolina and that of the Freeman family in Massachusetts. Without Moses, there would be no Ebby. She is dabbing at her eyes with the cuff of her chambray shirt when she sees Avery through the window, crossing the yard to the main cottage at a determined-looking pace.

*What is she doing here?*

Ebby thought Avery and Henry had already left. Henry's SUV wasn't in the parking area when Ebby stepped outside early this morning to check on the garden. She'd assumed, with great relief, that they had left before dawn.

*Rap-rap-rap-rap-rap!*

Ebby puts down her coffee mug, mumbling to herself. *Why won't people use the doorbell?* First Henry, now Avery. There must be something about that old wooden door that makes a person want to bang on its surface. To feel the door rattling in its frame.

*Rap-rap-rap!*

"All right, all right," Ebby calls as she opens the door. Avery's pale eyebrows are pulled together in the middle.

"You know, your doorbell doesn't work," Avery says.

"Oh, no?" Ebby steps across the threshold and reaches for the buzzer. Sure enough.

"Have you seen Henry?" Avery asks.

"You mean since yesterday?" Ebby shakes her head.

"He left early this morning and hasn't come back."

"He's not out doing his photography?" Ebby asks.

There is a moment when Avery blinks, and everything seems to move in slow motion. A full moment before she says anything in response. It is a moment in which Ebby realizes that, in mentioning the photography, she has revealed her familiarity with Henry's personal life, and Avery has registered this fact. The ex-fiancée who knows Avery's lover better than she does. It must have taken a lot for Avery to come knocking on Ebby's door. Or maybe, Ebby thinks, it took nothing at all. Maybe Avery's curiosity about Henry's ex drew her over here.

"But it's been hours," Avery says. "It's almost one o'clock. We were supposed to be in Bordeaux for lunch."

"I haven't seen Henry," Ebby says. "Do you need a phone to call him?"

"I have my cellphone. I've already tried. He's not answering."

"Well, I don't know what to tell you. You don't have to worry about checking out until he shows up."

*Wait*, Ebby thinks. *Did Avery just do a little huff? Do women actually do little huffs?* Ebby thought only characters in animated films did that sort of thing. She presses her lips together to keep from smiling. *Inappropriate affect, Ebby.* Then it dawns on Ebby. Avery knows, as does the entire world, that Henry Pepper ghosted Ebony Freeman on their wedding day. Could Henry have skipped out on Avery, too? Is this what Avery might be thinking? But why? Did they have a fight?

"I'm not worried about checkout," Avery says. "I'm worried about Henry. What if something's happened to him?"

Could something have happened to Henry? A vehicle breakdown, maybe? No matter. The idea of Henry in distress does not particularly bother Ebby. Exactly how much *distress* could a person get into around here anyway? She looks up and across the river, sees the willow trees, their swaying tendrils, bright green in the midday sun. Sees a pair of children running around a picnic table while their parents pull open containers of food.

The only problem that Ebby can see with Henry being gone is the fact that Ebby is stuck with Avery until he comes back. She thinks of what to say to reassure Avery. To make her go away until Henry returns. But Avery, now, is asking Ebby for help.

"Could you, maybe, drive me around a bit? Help me to look for Henry?"

Ebby, look for Henry? With his current girlfriend? She might have taken Avery's question as a joke, if it weren't for the red patches appearing, now, on Avery's face.

"I'm sure he'll turn up soon." She stops herself before saying that Henry used to lose track of time when he was out taking photographs.

"But Henry said he'd be back by ten. He made a point of urging me to be ready to go when he got back."

"Are you really worried? Do you want to use the house phone to call the police?"

"Don't you have to wait forty-eight hours or something before the police will help?" Avery asks.

"I don't know. I don't know the rules in France. But it's true, it's only been a few hours, and he is an adult."

"And you can't, just, you know, take me around?" Avery waves an arm vaguely in the direction of the water. "Drive along the river? Check the edge of the woods?"

*This isn't happening,* Ebby thinks. It was bad enough that Henry and Avery showed up here in the first place. And now this?

"Avery," Ebby says, "I imagine you are aware that Henry and I had a relationship in the past, and that it didn't end very well."

Avery lowers her chin but keeps her gaze on Ebby.

"I just think it would be best for me not to get too involved here just because Henry is a couple of hours late in coming back. Now, I wouldn't want him to be in serious difficulty, so if you really feel there might be a problem, again, I'd be happy to help you call the police."

"Well," Avery says, "maybe I'll wait just a little while longer." She walks away and Ebby goes back to her laptop. Henry is bound to show up. She certainly hopes so. Ebby would be willing to bet that she is even more eager than Avery to see Henry right now so those two can be on their way. Another thought comes to her. *What if something serious really has happened to Henry?* But Ebby pushes the idea out of her mind.

# Avery

―――

A VERY READS THE NEWS ON HER SMARTPHONE AND TAKES A deep breath. A local headline catches her eye. A crime scene. And Henry still isn't back. He's been gone for nearly eight hours. She peers out the window at the main house. She needs to talk to Ebony again, and she knows that Ebony is not going to like it.

You wouldn't know it, to look at her, but Avery is not an overly proud person. Not like some other women she knows. Avery has her self-esteem, sure. She recognizes her accomplishments. She likes the way she looks. But Avery is never too proud to ask for what she wants. She wasn't too proud to put herself in Henry's line of sight last winter, after that messy end to his relationship with Ebony Freeman. She wasn't too proud to be seen with him, knowing that Ebony's name would still be on everyone's lips. Knowing that people would think of Avery as the one Henry turned to on the rebound.

Well, Avery is not going to let pride get in her way now, either.

As she steps outside for the second time today, Avery tells herself that too much pride is a waste of valuable time and energy. She is going to walk across that yard now and knock on Ebony's door again, even if it does irk her to have to plead for Ebony's help.

# Time

————

TIME MATTERS, EBBY THINKS AS SHE TYPES. HOURS, MINUTES, seconds, can make a difference.

They found Betsey with the rope taut against her neck, Ebby writes. By the time they untied her, she was gone. Some folks said that Betsey had done this to herself. That she'd decided it was better than the alternative. But Moses, for one, never believed it.

Ebby looks down at her hands, poised over the keyboard. It is useless for her to wonder, now, whether Moses could have done anything to prevent Betsey's death. But Moses must have felt, back then, the same urgency that Ebby has felt, to step back in time and undo what has already happened.

Martin Oldham was furious. He sent his nephew back to his sister-in-law's estate in the next county over. He gave everyone at the pottery a half-day off to mourn Betsey. Still, he hadn't put a stop to his nephew's cruelty before it was too late. Jacob Oldham's disposition had never been a secret. It was likely that no one had ever dared to say no to him, before Betsey. Surely Betsey must have known that *no* was the most dangerous word in the world. Which made Oldham all the more furious.

Ebby hears a sound and looks up. She can see that Avery is on her way back across the yard, and that the rental car still isn't back. She looks at her smartphone. Two more hours have passed. Maybe she should be worried about Henry, but she doesn't want to think about it. She continues to type.

Later, Moses thought of the last time he and Betsey had walked
back from the market together, side by side. Their fingertips
had touched lightly as they parted ways. With no other place
to put his grief, Moses leaned over his worktable at the pottery and prepared a clay disk for the bottom of a new jar. When
it was ready, he carved five words into it. He knew that no one
was likely to see those words for a long time, but he hoped that
one day someone would. Those words were the only part of his
craft that he could truly claim as his own. Because as much as
he felt that he'd inherited his mother's feel for the clay, all those
hours and days he had put in at the wheel, year after year, had
been under the yoke of bondage, on the orders of a man who
claimed to own him. Someone to whom Moses was not permitted to say no.

Avery has reached the kitchen door and is rapping on the wood
again.

"I need your help," Avery says. "Henry still hasn't come back. It's
been eight hours already. Couldn't we just drive around?"

Ebby is determined to stay out of this.

"I really don't have time now," Ebby says. "I'm going to the doctor."

"On a Sunday afternoon?"

"There's someone on call." Which is the truth, even though Ebby
does not, actually, have plans to go to the doctor. She rummages
through her brain files for some ailment to invent, in case Avery asks.

"Listen," Ebby says. "Just let me know if you decide you want to
call the police. At least to see what they suggest."

"But the police? They won't have time. They'll be busy with that
head on the road."

"Right, sure," Ebby says. "Well, if you change your mind, let me
know." She closes the door as she speaks. Ebby walks toward the cor-
ridor, mentally cursing the abundance of windows in the cottage. It
takes a while to get away from Avery's stare. When she's finally out of
view, Ebby remembers something Avery said and turns back. She pulls
open the kitchen door. Avery is still standing there.

"What did you say?" Ebby asks. "What did you say about a head?"

"They found a head on a farm road," Avery says. "Not far from here." She pulls her cellphone out of her shirt pocket. "See?"

Ebby leans in and reads the first paragraph of a news item on Avery's phone, mumbling a rough translation as she goes. "Body of female victim found between highway and woods . . ."

Ebby grimaces at Avery, then steps aside to let her into the room.

"I'm not saying," Avery says, "that anything terrible like that has happened to Henry."

Ebby breathes in and out, suddenly unsure of what to say. Feeling a bit guilty. Because she is thinking of something else. A woman has been found murdered in a field and Henry, who supposedly went out to take photos, has been gone all this time. Ebby has always thought that Henry's disappearance before their wedding was about her and Henry. But what if it really was about something else? What if this is more than a bizarre coincidence? Is she a terrible person, to wonder whether her ex-fiancé could have anything to do with the crime?

It feels ludicrous and, at the same time, perfectly reasonable in a world where someone you once believed in has turned out to be the kind of liar who could promise you a life together one minute and disappear on you the next. After that, what could she *not* believe? Ebby struggles to banish the thought. Maybe it's all an unfortunate coincidence. But then where the hell is Henry?

Instead of speaking, Ebby raises a water bottle in one hand and an empty glass in the other. A silent question. But Avery shakes her head.

"It's just that, it reminds me that things can happen to people," Avery says.

Ebby raises her eyebrows at Avery. She does not need to say a word. She knows, when Avery's skin goes blotchy pink, again, that Avery realizes she's put her foot in her mouth. Satisfied with Avery's apparent embarrassment, Ebby picks up her purse. Pulls out her own smartphone. Swipes and clicks, to undo the block she has put on the local news bulletins. She prefers to shield herself from services that, from time to time, might fill her phone screen with images from her own life. But blocking push notifications means a person can miss updates like the one that has reached Avery.

"All right," Ebby says, "maybe we can take a drive around town, just to see."

"Oh, thank you!" Avery says, as if it had been Ebby's idea. As if Avery hadn't kept nudging her to do this until she agreed.

"Do you know which way he was headed? What was he planning to take photos of?"

"He was in a water phase," Avery says.

"River water or seawater?"

Avery shakes her head slowly. "What about your doctor's appointment?" she asks.

Ebby says *ahmm* as she tries to recall the exact lie she used with Avery a minute earlier.

"It can wait until tomorrow," Ebby says.

# Searching

———

EBBY DRIVES WEST AND SOUTH WHILE AVERY KEEPS WATCH for signs of Henry. They flank the river until Ebby is forced to turn back onto the main road. Up ahead, now, she sees two police cars parked near the vineyard she passed just the night before. She pulls over behind one of the patrol cars and peers down the long dirt road. There are uniformed officers in the distance, a large van, and the glint of yellow crime-scene tape, one end of which appears to be tied to a grapevine.

"The murder," Ebby says.

Avery nods slowly and turns on the radio. Ebby is surprised at how well Avery seems to understand the French. They listen to a recorded interview with a local farmer and Avery repeats what he says in English.

"It was a dog who found the victim," Avery says. "Early this morning."

It was a farmer's sheepdog, to be precise. He was nosing around among the oak and ash trees along the edge of a neighbor's vineyard when he found something at the base of a tree. The dog stepped back and called out with a series of deep-throated barks. The sheepdog knew his territory. The farmer knew his *chien*. This was something out of the ordinary. It was not a cat or pigeon or porcupine or fox. It was the last thing the dog, or the man, had expected to see. Something no one should ever have to see.

"So," Avery says, "it wasn't actually a head on the road, it's that the farmer only saw the back of the woman's head at first, sticking out onto a footpath. The farmer says he's sorry he didn't walk by last night. Who knows if he might have been able to do something for the woman, or if he might have seen something that could help the police figure out who did this."

"I think I saw something yesterday," Ebby says. "A white SUV. It was headed down toward the end of the field, instead of coming out to the road, as you'd expect at that hour. I remember this because I was rushing to get to a store before it closed." She looks at Avery. "But I was distracted. I didn't think anything of it, just that it was a bit late to be heading into the vineyard. Do you think I should say something to the police?"

"I suppose," Avery says. "Did you see who was in it?"

Ebby shakes her head no.

"Who knows if it was anything," Avery says. "There are so many white SUVs around. Even our rental car is a white SUV."

"Right, I hadn't thought of that," Ebby says. "That wasn't you, was it?"

"No, I didn't come this way last night. I don't know if Henry did. Before dinner, he was out driving around a bit. I was drying my hair. He said he wanted to scout locations for photographs."

A cold feeling sweeps over Ebby.

"Henry?" Ebby says. "Henry was out here?"

"I don't know that. I only know he went out in the rental, then came back to get me before dinner."

On the radio, there are several interviews connected to the murder, and Ebby and Avery remain seated in the car, listening. "Apparently, there have been other unsolved murders in the center of the country," Avery says. "But you know, I think people watch too many of those American crime shows. Not every unsolved homicide is connected. And most are committed by people who know their victims." Avery goes quiet, suddenly, and Ebby feels her look at her, then look away.

"Oh, I'm sorry," says Avery. "That was stupid of me. I mean, you know. Your brother."

"Yes," says Ebby. "It's fine, it's fine." And it is, really. Finally, Avery has come right out and said something. Most of her life, people have whispered within earshot about Ebby, speculated publicly about her state of mind, talked about Baz's death, but rarely has anyone done her the courtesy of addressing her directly about her brother. That takes courage. Henry, at least, dared to do it. And, now, Avery.

"I, of all people, understand," Ebby says. "No one likes to think that they might be caught up in random acts of violence. People want to feel there's a reason for everything. They want to believe certain things could never happen to them, just like that. And, mostly, they don't." Strange, Ebby thinks, how freely she is speaking to this Avery person. The woman who is sleeping with the man that Ebby was supposed to marry.

"Only, sometimes they do," says Avery, quietly. "Happen."

"Yuh, sometimes they do."

They don't need to say any more than this to understand each other. To know that they are not speaking only of what happened to Baz. They both grew up in Connecticut, a few towns apart. Ebby knows, without saying, that they are thinking of the same event. Avery would have been, what? Twenty years old back then? Ebby was in her car when she heard the news on the radio. A school shooting. A living nightmare. The kind of thing you kept telling yourself could not possibly happen around there, only it just had.

*All those children!*

On that day, Ebby had slammed on the brakes. Pulled off to the side of the road. Opened her door and taken in large gulps of air. But she stopped short of doing what she felt like doing next. Because a white woman might have gotten away with running down the middle of the street screaming at the top of her lungs—and even that was a stretch—but Ebby, one hand clasped over her mouth as if to hold in the emotion, trying to slow her breathing, knew that a black woman shrieking on this suburban street could make people react like flame touching a stick of dynamite.

Since Baz's death, Ebby had been coached, by her parents and therapists, to find quieter ways to express rage or fright. And Ebby had always found a way. Even if she knew, in her heart, that going hysterical was the most natural reaction to certain situations. How else should a person feel like behaving when someone had just walked into an elementary school and gunned down a bunch of kids and employees? A person should want to jump out of their car and run down the road yelling.

Run away from this world.

The irony is, of the two of them—Avery and Ebby—Ebby feels she is less worried about Henry's situation, even with her intimate knowledge of tragedy. Ebby has lived through a terrible experience that most people, she hopes, will never have to face. But despite the lingering effects on her mental health, and the challenges to her privacy, Ebby's life has been one of relative safety.

Ebby has never been in a vehicle accident, never broken her arm or a tooth, never had her appendix taken out, never even been pickpocketed on a crowded city train. She has never been in a war zone. She is physically healthy and well educated. If you remove the unthinkable from Ebby's life, if you excise just that one day in the year 2000 from the calendar, if you plug up the hole left in her life by her brother's death, you see a fortunate woman, a life of privilege, a life to be grateful for. Until that day, more recently, when Henry stopped answering his cellphone.

Just as he is doing right now.

There it is again. Another stab of doubt. *Where the fuck is he?*

Ebby senses Avery turning in her seat to look directly at Ebby, and Ebby, too, turns to look at Avery. Until now, they have been looking at the dashboard or out the window as they have spoken. But now they sit for a moment, their faces tensed with the same question.

Without another word, they open their doors at the same time and jump out of the vehicle. They walk, in step with each other, down the access road toward the police scene, each thinking the same thing. How Henry's disappearance has coincided with the discovery of a murder victim barely five kilometers from the cottage. How this isn't the first time Henry has gone missing. How even after sex and flowers and romantic vacations, a woman can never be sure what goes on in a man's head. How this understanding can send a person's thinking in disturbing directions. When a man goes AWOL on his wedding day, you could ask yourself what else he might be capable of doing.

It is Avery who says it first. "You don't think Henry . . . ?" she says, tipping her head in the direction of the crime scene.

"What?" Ebby says, narrowing her eyes at her. Avery doesn't finish her sentence, but Ebby sees, now, that Avery, like Ebby, is wondering whether Henry could, in some way, be involved in a murder. She remembers how Henry used to disappear for hours at a time, keeping his cellphone turned off. But then he'd call and show up at Ebby's place with his camera, eager to have her see what he'd photographed.

And people have instincts, don't they? Ebby's instincts tell her that, despite the terrible wrong Henry has done her, her ex-fiancé couldn't possibly be involved in a situation like this one.

Or could he?

Is Ebby, once again, making the mistake of trusting Henry? Didn't her instincts steer her wrong the last time? He ditched her and she didn't see it coming. Is she falling into the old trap of thinking that anything in her life could go normally for very long? Could be. But just as a police officer turns and approaches them, Ebby shakes her head at Avery's question.

"Henry?" Ebby says. "Nah."

Avery shakes her head. "No. No way," she says.

Still, while Avery speaks to the police and explains that they are looking for a missing friend, Ebby pulls her smartphone out of her tote bag and begins to search. She types in Connecticut, 2018. Murders. New England. Body Found. Just in case there's something there. Anything that might suggest Henry was up to no good when he disappeared on her last year.

*No-no-no, this is crazy,* Ebby thinks. This cannot be. She puts her phone away. But the police are already making suppositions of their own. Which is how she and Avery soon end up sitting with a judicial police officer at a portable card table set up beyond earshot of onlookers.

"You are telling me," the investigator says, "that your friend, Monsieur Pepper, has not been seen since before the discovery of the murder victim's body, and you are concerned that he may be involved?"

"No," Avery says, "we are concerned that something may have happened to him while he was out taking photographs."

"But he was in this area. You say he was driving a white sport utility vehicle, and there are reports that such a vehicle was seen on the access road to the vineyard yesterday evening, in the same area where the victim's body was found."

"We don't know, exactly, where he was. But we are *all* in this area. We're staying in the village, at Hannah Frere's house."

"What about the person who killed the woman?" says Ebby. "Could that person go and hurt someone else?"

"We cannot be sure until we find that person and establish their reasons for doing this. And in any event, we are not at liberty to discuss certain details of our investigation at this time," says the officer. "But until we have more information, we have to consider whether the disappearance of your Henry Pepper could be connected."

Later, Ebby will not be sure whether she merely thought, or actually said, *Oh, shit.*

# Ed

Ed silently curses the internet for the speed at which worrisome news can reach a person. Soh is reading about some nasty killing in the French countryside where Ebby is staying.

"It's very close to Ebby," Soh says. And she would know. She's been studying maps of the area. Soh has reconfigured her news feeds to prioritize regional updates from Ebby's location in France. Even before the Connecticut headlines pop up, Soh's smartphone spits out little bits of French news. Politics, energy prices, emergencies. Which town is having open-air markets, or outdoor concerts, or thunderstorms.

"In case we decide to visit," Soh said when she began to study the maps. "There's a lot to know."

It's true, the article Soh read to him last week about fortified wines was interesting. There's one made from Cognac mixed with unfermented grape must. Seems it's been around since the sixteenth century, but Ed has never tasted this Pineau. Not to be confused with wine made with pinot grapes. It was discovered by accident, as is so often true of the good things in life.

"The French police are talking about an unknown assailant," Soh tells him. "Does this mean the person who killed that woman could go after someone else?" Soh's agitation fills their bed with a humid kind of heat. She tries Ebby's phone but cannot reach her.

"You're worrying," Ed says.

"Yes, I'm worrying," says Soh. "And shouldn't I?"

No matter that they have seen a photo of the unfortunate victim in the prime of her life. No matter that the woman looks nothing like Ebby. This is not enough for Soh. When they finally speak to Ebby, she sounds so quiet that, for a moment, Ed thinks Ebby might have known the victim.

"No, I didn't know her. I don't think she lived in this town," Ebby says. "Anyway, the police are investigating." Ebby sighs, then, and in her breath, Ed hears it. The shakiness he sees in his daughter sometimes. The reminder that any act of violence, however unrelated to Ebby, might take her back to what she lived through as a child. And for all their concern for her, he and Soh have to learn to leave her to find her own way through these moments. The therapist warned them, didn't she?

And what about Ed? What would be the best thing for him? Before he can stop himself, Ed is back to thinking *if only*. If only he hadn't brought his family here, none of this would have happened. And afterward? Should he and Soh have left the state altogether? Moved Ebby back to live near their families? Is it too late to do so? Would Ebby move, too, if they were to leave? Or would she prefer to keep her distance? Who would they be without their daughter nearby to remind them that life, in its own way, has been good?

When his head gets this cluttered, there's only one thing he can do. He peers at the first light of morning filtering through the blinds. He gets out of bed, pulls off the threadbare whale-print pajamas that the kids gave him the last Christmas they were all together. The pajamas always make him smile. He looks over at Soh, still sleeping, as he pulls on a pair of jeans and a sweatshirt. Slowly, quietly, he takes her phone from her hand, turns it off, and puts it on the nightstand. Then he goes downstairs, grabs a bucket and stick, and walks out the back door of the house.

Ed follows a path down to the curve of sand that looks out onto the rocky islands in the Sound, the bucket knocking against his leg as he walks. There's a woman, pants cuffs rolled up, already scratching at the sand as the tide goes out, the rising sun turning her entire back golden. Ed doesn't want to leave this place. Who would want to? But he thinks he should seriously consider it.

# Henry

———

HENRY LIES THERE ON THE BANK OF THE RIVER, WATCHING A terrapin float toward the mud and clamber onto the bank. It would have been nice to have a photo of that little guy, just when it was half out of the water. Webbed feet and tiny claws pressing into the wet earth. Instead, Henry is lying here with a pounding headache and a twisted ankle. How long has he been here? He might have torn something. He tries to get up but between the pain in the ankle and the one in his head, he can see that there is no way he's going to get to his car. The SUV is half a mile up the road and he can't find his cellphone.

In short, Henry is surprised.

Henry is not accustomed to being surprised. Henry has always expected things to go his way. Because they usually do. It doesn't hurt that he was born into a certain family, in a certain town, that he attended certain schools and benefited from a starting push into his profession from his father's associates. He can admit this. It's the truth. It's also true that Henry works hard at his job, despite not being wild about it. And he's pretty darned good at it, too. But, again, he is not surprised when things go well for him. Only when they don't.

Henry's photography, for example, has been going well. Though that, too, involves its share of work. There are things to learn. Adjustments to be made. Techniques to try and retry. Photography is art and technology and instinct wrapped up together. And it's part of Henry. Whenever Henry looks at the world through a camera, he feels more like himself. But he also tends to be less sure-footed, physically speaking. Lost in his thoughts. Which is how Henry ended up tripping on a root, falling backward, and hitting his head against the trunk of a tree as he went down.

As Henry's body rolled into the soft mud along the river's edge, his cellphone must have dropped into the water. The water here is shallow and placid. More like a pond than a river. Henry is sure he could have fished his phone out of the water by now if he hadn't banged himself up so badly. If he hadn't left his glasses in the car. Ebby used to bug him about that. He feels so cold. How is that possible? Isn't it in the nineties today? He needs to rest a bit more. Then he'll try again to find the phone before it sinks completely into the silt or drifts away.

This is how Henry comes to be stretched out on his belly that afternoon, shoulders and face on the muddy bank of a river in southwestern France, feeling around with his arms, when two *policiers* walk up to him from behind. The police have been looking for Henry ever since spotting his white SUV in a parking area near the main road.

# Questions

———

Ebby never thought she'd find herself coming to Henry's defense, not after what he did to her. Yet here she is at the *commissariat,* muddling through her explanation in French, with Avery's assistance. The police have sequestered Henry's rental car, his digital camera, and his smartphone, which they found lodged in the riverbed. They have questioned Henry, but he's still in the hospital.

Yes, Henry is just a tourist, she tells the police. Yes, both she and Avery have known Henry for a number of years. They all grew up in the same part of the United States. No, there is nothing in Henry's past to lead them to believe that he might be connected, in any way, to the recent murder in the area. They say nothing about the day that Henry was supposed to have married Ebby, about the last time that Henry disappeared without warning.

"The car wasn't abandoned, *monsieur l'agent,*" Ebby says. "He couldn't get back to it because he hurt himself. Didn't your *policiers* find him on the ground?"

"Henry goes out every morning to take photos, wherever he is," Avery adds, mimicking the clicking of a shutter with one hand.

The police haven't arrested Henry, but they will send someone to question him at the hospital, once the doctors are through testing him. They ask Ebby and Avery more questions about Henry's exact whereabouts yesterday, and also their own, around the time that they believe the woman was murdered. They ask again about the white SUV that Ebby saw near the vineyard.

"I couldn't see who was driving or anything, just the SUV, turning in to that road around six."

"And you did not think that this could be your friend Henry?"

"No, I . . ." Ebby doesn't want to say, in front of Avery, that she had just seen Henry because he had come to the cottage to speak with her and that she'd been too distracted by the encounter to think too much about what she was seeing. She hears herself repeating the point Avery made earlier. "No. There are so many white SUVs."

Ebby isn't sure what their rights are, exactly. She takes comfort in knowing that Avery is an attorney, even if Avery is not a criminal attorney. Even if Avery happens to be several thousand miles, and six time zones, out of her jurisdiction.

Avery as tourist-attorney is fascinating to see. She is different. Polite but not warm. Her back is even straighter than usual and only now does Ebby realize that Avery has pulled her hair into a low, taut bun. When did that happen? And when, exactly, did she and Avery slip into this tentative alliance?

# Answers

———

EVEN IN A TOWN OF THIS SIZE, THERE ARE SURVEILLANCE CAMERAS, and they will help the police to find the answers they need. By the next morning, the murder has been connected to a vehicle found abandoned nearby. A white SUV, but not Henry's SUV. A car connected to someone who knew the victim. There are images of her and the suspect together. There is word of an arrest and a call from the *commissariat* to go pick up Henry's stuff. The rental car will be released the next day.

Ebby is relieved at the speed with which Henry is cleared of suspicion, and at the thought that Avery will soon be back in her own vehicle. As Ebby drives, Avery turns up the volume on the car radio. Pieces of the murder victim's story are emerging, that of a woman on the run from a ruinous relationship. The suspect in custody is a man who had been involved with the victim. A crime of passion, police say. Avery repeats what they say in English, then turns to Ebby.

"Thank goodness," Avery says.

Ebby nods.

"I mean, it's terrible, what happened to that woman. It's sad. It's just that . . ." She hesitates, and Ebby finishes her thought.

"They don't think it's Henry."

"Exactly. I was starting to worry, you know? The way he disappeared, and all of a sudden, there's this murder. Of course, it was ridiculous to even think it."

Ebby chuckles.

"I feel guilty for laughing, but it's even more ridiculous to think that Henry simply tripped and fell on his butt."

Avery gives a short bark of laughter. "*And* dropped his phone in the river. Henry Pepper, can you believe it?"

Ebby glances over at Avery. Her mouth wide open, her teeth whitener-bright. Still, Avery's eyes are moist with emotion. Ebby gets it. Ebby would hate to think that she had been wrong about everything important when it came to Henry. He's still the man she nearly married.

Ebby pulls the car up to the hospital. There's just enough time for Avery to leave Henry's phone with him inside before visiting hours end. It will be another five hours before the evening visits begin. Henry will be fine, they agree. And, no, they decide, it would not be too tacky to go sightseeing while they wait. They're not that far from a château Avery wants to visit.

"Could we?" Avery wants to know. "We were supposed to see it this week, before we changed our plans." What she means is, before they found Ebby at the guesthouse and cut short their two-week reservation.

Ebby glances at Avery. She sees, now, how awful it must have been for Avery to show up at a holiday place, which she herself had booked, only to find that the person managing it was her boyfriend's ex-fiancée. And knowing how badly things had ended between them. How publicly. How recently. She feels a little sorry for Avery, though she feels sorrier for herself. She's stuck taking her ex's current girlfriend on a sightseeing trip. And the worst part is, it feels like it's the right thing to do.

# Mermaids

———

Snake-ladies. Mermaids. Seal-women.

Avery is standing in a small chapel looking at mermaid motifs on the wall. She looks down at her ebook, then up again. She reads about the family that lived in the château where this chapel is located. The mermaid is linked to a legend surrounding the House of Lusignan, from which the family here is descended.

"Melusine was a two-tailed freshwater mermaid," Avery says, "or part sea serpent, depending on what you read. Anyway, according to legend, she married the founder of the House of Lusignan, Raymond, and used her magic to build their castle. She forbade her husband to approach her while she took her weekly bath, during which she would revert to her original form. But after years together and several children, her husband defied her rule. . . ."

"Naturally," she and Ebby say simultaneously.

"So hubby spied on her, and all hell broke loose."

After reading various tellings of this legend in her tourist pamphlet and on the Internet, Avery has downloaded the translation of a fourteenth-century book by Jean d'Arras, who wrote about the family. Avery stands there, swaying from one beige platform sneaker to the other, reading bits of the book aloud to Ebby.

Avery is glad she came here, but she should have been here with Henry. Henry would have been wandering outside with his camera, most likely, but they would have been together all the same. In this way, Avery and Henry are perfectly compatible. They're both curious. They both like to wander, Henry with his camera and Avery with her reading. Though, lately, Henry seems to have lost track of how well they go together.

"Don't you ever put down that phone?" Henry said the other day at lunch. Henry wasn't given to being short with her, though he had, more than once in their four months of dating, rested his hand on her wrist and pushed it down until her phone was out of reading range. Usually, he would follow up with a kiss on her cheek or neck. But this time, there was no kiss. This time, Henry simply turned and walked away.

Avery chalked it up to *The Ebony Effect.*

Avery has read that couples who don't ever disagree can be as problematic as couples who argue a lot. But Henry came to Avery after the mess with Ebony, and the ease of their relationship should have felt like a gift to him. Avery's mission was to be agreeable until Henry grew attached enough to want to take the situation to another level. She was willing to tolerate any differences that might crop up as they got to know each other better. And until they came to France, Avery had thought it was smooth sailing.

Everyone knows Henry left Ebony, not the other way around. And there had been significant issues in their relationship, he told Avery, things that wouldn't come up with someone else.

"You mean related to her brother's death?"

"Let's just say it would have been a lot for anyone to handle," Henry said. "I think Ebby did better than most people would have."

Avery appreciated that Henry didn't totally slam his ex. Didn't offer too many details. This was a good sign for the future. The man had some discretion. But he couldn't mask the sound in his voice when he said the name *Ebby.*

Well, of course. It was normal. They'd been engaged. But then Avery saw the way Henry's whole posture changed, the other day, when they first saw Ebony outside the cottage. Henry may have been the one to leave the relationship, but his body language told Avery that, maybe, he hadn't really wanted to do so. They'd never discussed it in depth. He'd just told Avery that things hadn't worked out and he was sorry he hadn't handled it in a better way. But what if there was more to Henry's regret? Sometimes, you're convinced you're making the right decision, and later, you're sorry you went with it.

After laughing off their surprise encounter with Ebony, Henry said it was *no big deal* to remain in the cottage until the next place could take them.

"We're going to be out all the time anyway," he said. "It's not like she's going to want to see us." Then he laughed again. A hollow, toothpaste-commercial kind of *hah-hah*.

And now he's had this stupid accident with the camera. Well, Avery refuses to have her entire trip to France ruined by this. Even if it does mean being here, in this romantic corner of the world, with Ebony Freeman.

Avery clicks on a couple of additional Internet sites. No matter which version of the legend you read, the mermaid's fate is essentially the same. Raymond the Count spies on his mysterious wife, after which things begin to go wrong. He blames Melusine and she ultimately leaves the kingdom forever. Her story vaguely repeats the fate of her own mother, who had also married a human, only to end up fleeing with her three daughters after her true identity was revealed. *After she was accused of being some kind of monster*, Avery thinks.

Avery looks up at the chapel wall. The composers Dvořák and Mendelssohn, the authors Proust and A. S. Byatt, and various painters all were inspired in their work by the mermaid myth. In each version of that myth, Avery thinks, the woman-creature who does not conform to the other person's view of her ends up having to leave the relationship. Ends up being rejected for not living up to her lover's view of her.

Is this what happened with Ebony and Henry? Was Ebony, with her past, too complicated for Henry? Did Henry, like the count in the legend, continue to love the woman he had driven away? And now that Avery has seen her boyfriend with his ex, felt the change in him, despite his best efforts, does Avery still have the courage to be with Henry? Because Avery deserves to be wanted. Not settled for. Not second-best. Only, she *wants* to be with Henry. Which is one reason why, probably, she shouldn't be here sightseeing with Ebony.

What was she thinking?

# Ebby

―――

STRANGE TO THINK IT, BUT IT'S NOT HALF BAD BEING AROUND Avery. Despite everything. Now that they've been forced together like this. Sure, Ebby would prefer not to be in this situation, but still. Avery is a people pleaser. Positive. Polite. Curious. Ebby recognizes the type. Always *on*. Service-industry smile. You can't really know the half of what she's thinking. But it's *easy* to be around her.

For one, Avery isn't constantly dropping Henry's name into the conversation. She could do so. Avery could stake her claim to Henry with a thousand little jabs. Go out of her way to remind Ebby that Henry's moved on. In four hours, Avery has mentioned Henry only in relation to the fact that they're due back at the hospital.

"I'll drop you off and go do some work, then come back to get you after visiting hours," Ebby tells Avery.

"Oh, that would be great, thank you."

With any luck, Henry will be out of the hospital tomorrow. Maybe he'll rest up for one more night at the cottage, and then Ebby can be rid of them both. In the meantime, she can handle Avery. In another life, she and Avery might have hung out together. Ebby has only two friends, really, who aren't her cousins. There's Hannah and there's Ashleigh. And neither of them lives in Connecticut.

"So you're actually working while you're here?" Avery says.

"Yes, editing for clients and doing some writing of my own."

"What are you writing?" Avery asks. "I mean, if you don't mind me asking."

Ebby pauses. How to explain, without saying too much?

"We used to have a family heirloom, a historic jar, but it broke." Ebby feels a tug of sadness. "Still, we have all these stories about the jar and how it ended up with our family in Massachusetts. So I've been writing them down." Ebby does not say how the jar broke. She wants to avoid mentioning her brother's death.

*This is the story of our family,* Baz once told her. And their mom, who'd overheard him, said, *That's true, Baz, but not only. Because our history is everyone's history. Our history is American history.* Ebby hasn't thought about that conversation in years. Back then, she was too young to truly understand what her mother was saying, but as it comes to her now, she thinks, *Of course.* Just as people were segregated in America, people's stories have been segregated, too. But it's all part of the same story, isn't it?

"The jar was made by an enslaved craftsman down south," she says. "But it was with my family in New England for more than a hundred and fifty years. It was part of our identity."

"Like an old Bible with family dates and notes inside," Avery says.

"Something like that." Ebby nods, keeping her eyes on the road ahead. "Only not as precise. Either way, we know that our family wouldn't exist without that jar."

"So your brother knew these stories, too?" Avery asks.

Ebby is surprised by the directness of Avery's question.

"He was older than you, right?"

"Yes," Ebby says. "Baz was fifteen when he died." She takes a deep breath and releases it quickly. It feels good to say his name out loud. Another surprise. "He was five years older. But anyway, my brother loved my dad's jar stories. That's what we called them, even though they weren't so much about the jar as about people."

Ebby will not talk to Avery about her brother's death, though this may be what Avery is expecting to come next. Still, as she drives toward the hospital where Henry is staying, she decides there's no harm in telling Avery about the jar.

# Port City

———

To understand the value of the jar you need to go way back, to long before it was made. You could start at any number of points, but a good place would be the year 1670. That was when the first group of planters from the English Caribbean colony of Barbados came up the coast to what would later be called South Carolina.

Sailing inland by river, the newcomers brought slaves and arms. They moved west into the backcountry, taking land away from the people who had always lived there. The descendants of the more fortunate settlers went on to produce rice, indigo, cotton, and sugar for export. Some started textile companies, potteries, or other industries. All of them relied on forced labor to grow and maintain their wealth.

This was the world into which a boy named Willis came to be.

Willis was born in 1817 to an enslaved mother who would die by his twelfth birthday and a father who was sold away right after his birth. He had only ever lived with his mother and older sister Flora in a row of wooden houses between the rice fields and the pottery where he worked, closer to the Savannah River than the sea, but his first trip of consequence took him all the way out to the Atlantic coast. Willis had just turned fourteen, and his deep brown face was still smooth and full on the day that he began the journey. But by the time he returned from the port city, he had sprouted the first thin mantle of hair above his mouth and was already forming a vision of his life that diverged from what had been decided for him by others.

At the start of the journey, Willis loaded jugs, jars, bowls, and cups onto a cart and settled in beside Old Joe, the aging wagoner. It was a long, tough ride. At first, Willis cursed his bad luck. Workmen were still preparing the new railroad, and the horseless wagons that traveled along the rails on a belly full of fire would take some time yet to start carrying goods from the backcountry.

The journey by wagon took days of sitting on that hard, wooden seat, breathing in the smells of horse sweat and manure and hay. It took days of having the bones rattled out of him by the ruts in the road. Took nights of dozing in the back of the wagon or on the ground, taking turns to keep watch over their large cargo. Hours of trembling through a fever after he'd got himself stuck by a scorpion. Later, he would recall Old Joe taking liquor from his flask and patting it on his face and chest to bring down his temperature.

As they neared the port city, Willis had grit in his teeth and so much dust on his person, his clothes had grown stiff. They'd hoped to bathe at a watering hole along the way but had run into two bird-watching men with guns. Had thought it best to move on. But now, there was water everywhere, snaking this way and that. Seawater flowing into fresh. They laughed at all the fish popping their heads above the surface.

Willis and Old Joe walked right into the river, clothes and all, then sat in the sun. As the tide flowed upstream from the sea, they caught a catfish and some crabs for a meal. Willis wished then that he could sit there forever. Not go into the city, not go back to the pottery, just be a boy on the riverbank, with a clean face and a stomach full of food, who belonged only to himself.

He slipped a hand into his satchel and pulled out a pencil Moses had given him and started a sketch on a blank piece of paper he had ripped from the back of a ledger at the pottery. One of the birdmen they'd run into had been making designs on a large piece of paper. It had made quite an impression and Willis would think about that man often, over the years. Willis imagined himself, now, as that man. Imagined himself with all that blank paper and the freedom to draw.

Within minutes of his arrival in the city, Willis's previous ideas of the world flew from his head. There were more people than he had ever seen at the pottery and the farms and the railroad worksites put together. White men talking words he had never heard. African and country-born colored folks walking everywhere and working in every shop. They were banging on metal and wood. Sewing cloth. Pulling wagons full of fruit. Hauling, hoisting, and unpacking goods.

The colored men and women wore copper badges on their chests like the one that Joseph had given him to wear for the journey. The badges announced their various occupations. Porter, mechanic, servant, fisher, fruit picker. The badge Willis wore said **TURNER**.

Willis knew how to read the badges because his sister Flora had taught him his letters. So Willis knew what it meant when he entered the port city and saw a man with a badge that read **FREE**. He had seen free rivermen in the backcountry and he had known of at least one free woman. Most had been yellowish in color, except for one, a man as dark as Willis though four times as old. But in the port city, Willis saw young, dark-skinned craftsmen wearing **FREE** badges. Free young men who looked like Willis. He would think of their faces years later, on the day that he first embraced the jar that, eventually, would come to be known as Old Mo.

# Ebby and Avery

———

Two days ago, Ebby would never have imagined sitting down to lunch in a bistro with her ex's girlfriend. But here they are.

"Go on," says Avery. "I want to hear more about Willis."

"Well, as you know," Ebby says, "Willis worked in a pottery in South Carolina. And that's the pottery where the jar I told you about came from."

A waiter walks by with two plates of a gelatinous-looking dish. Ebby feels her mouth go tight.

"Ooh, look at that," Avery says, putting a palm to her chest. "That looks like . . ."

"*Pieds de porc,*" Ebby says. She knows it well. Her friend Hannah loves eating trotters.

"Pigs' feet!" Avery says, her eyes gleaming.

*Gross,* thinks Ebby.

"Oh," says Avery, both hands over her heart, "just look at the way they've done that." She closes her menu and points at the table where the trotters dish has landed. "That's what I'm having. Do you want to share it? It's a huge portion."

Ebby raises her eyebrows. "No, you go ahead. I don't eat pork."

"Is that for religious reasons or something?"

"I just don't eat meat."

"Oh, what do you eat, then?"

"Anything that isn't meat," Ebby says. "Everything else."

"But how do you manage, here? With all the dishes they serve. The duck. The snails."

"I just eat what I want. There's plenty of good stuff. How much food does a person need?"

"Oh, you don't know what you're missing."

"You're right. I don't," Ebby says, making a face. They both chuckle. "And anyway, I hear the snails are better farther in."

"Oh, yes. In Burgundy, right?"

Ebby nods. Avery has done her research. Avery, Ebby has noticed, is always looking up stuff. At first, Ebby thought Avery was only posting selfies on Instagram or what have you. Since then, she's figured out that Avery actually spends much of her time reading pretty long articles. Still, it's too much time online. Ebby watches as Avery reaches for her purse. She's going for that tablet again, Ebby thinks. Then, to her surprise, Avery stops and pulls her hand away, empty.

"Remind me to look that up later," Avery says. "After we eat." Ebby smiles. Avery flutters her fingers and the waiter walks over. Avery asks for the *pieds de porc*. "But, uh, a half portion?" she asks in French, moving her hands to demonstrate.

"And I'll have this chilled soup," Ebby says, pointing to the menu.

Avery makes actual *mmm-mmm* sounds as she eats. Ebby allows herself to take a good long look at Avery, instead of trying to shield her mind against the insistent prettiness of this woman. Avery smiles at her briefly, raising her eyebrows, then looks down at her plate. Avery, sitting there on the chipped wooden chair in this somewhat dingy-looking bistro, her fingers shiny with grease from that revolting dish on a warm day, her white top already smudged with something, looks perfectly at home.

Ebby tells herself not to grimace at Avery's food.

"So," Avery says, wiping at the corners of her mouth with a napkin. "What happened to Willis?"

# Willis

---

1831

WILLIS HAD NEVER SEEN A TALL SHIP BEFORE. NOW HE WAS STAND-ing near the docks in the port city, looking up at three of them. He tilted his head back to peer at the massive spiderweb of rope ladders and lines that stretched into the sky. Long beams loomed over the decks, wrapped in enormous folds of white canvas. Willis felt his heartbeat quicken at the thought of these enormous vessels, sails un-furled, heading out to sea. Old Joe said the port here was in decline. But you wouldn't know it, to see this place.

"When I was a young man," Old Joe said, "you could find many more ships of all sizes docked here. Sloops, schooners, square-riggers. But those modern ships can cross the Atlantic directly from Europe to cities like New York, without depending on the winds to carry them across by the southern route."

Willis and Old Joe had squeezed their wagon through a street packed with cargo waiting to be loaded onto the ships. On land, dock-workers moved back and forth around them, fetching cotton, rice, and other goods. A dozen oak barrels, bound together and suspended from a long rope, moved slowly from the dock to the deck of the closest ship. This was the square-rigger for which the load of pottery from Oldham's was destined.

Seamen on board the ship tugged at lines and climbed up the rig-ging. Willis watched, open-mouthed, as they called out to one another, raising their voices to be heard above the din.

"Willis," Old Joe barked. He jutted his chin toward the wagon bed, still full of jugs and jars. Willis nodded. He was moving too slowly, he knew, his gaze drawn by the frenzy of labor. As he wrapped his arms around a container, Willis felt a sudden drop in the activity around him. There was a hushing of voices as the ship's crew turned their gazes inland. A small group of men was approaching the docks.

Three black sailors were flanked by a white man in a captain's uniform and another who appeared to be a policeman, his eyes shadowed by the brim of his cap. As the men reached the ship, the policeman turned, without a word, and strode away.

"Foreigners," Old Joe said.

Willis cocked his head to the side, a question in his mind.

"Free sailors from abroad," Old Joe said. "The inspector must have kept them in the jail until their ship was ready to leave port. To keep them from fraternizing with those of us from here. That's the rule."

Willis nodded. He had grown up hearing the story of how a free man in the port city had been hanged for plotting a slave insurrection. Many people had been involved in the plan and, now, all free colored seamen who did not hail from thereabouts were taken into custody on arrival at the port. They were released only when their ship was ready to leave, and only if their captain had posted bond. Otherwise, a Cape Verdean or Gambian who'd been a free crew member on a sailing ship could well be sold into slavery.

"The captains don't like it one bit," Old Joe said. "And the United States government has registered its objections." He gave a short laugh, tinged with a bitter note. "I reckon they all have figured out by now that their opinions don't have much influence over the way things are done around here. So some of those ships won't be coming back."

The ship's captain walked up a plank to the deck, followed by the three black seamen. A couple of the white crewmen nodded their heads in greeting at the black jacks. One of the men called to them and pointed and the colored men immediately fell into activity with the others, as if they had never been gone.

"The authorities want to keep the foreigners from wandering around town and spreading ideas of rebellion to slaves." Old Joe said. "As if a slave who sails the seas with the permission of his master doesn't have eyes and ears of his own. He's a man, is he not? He has a tongue to tell stories of what he has seen and heard, does he not? He has a pocket sewn into his jacket. He can carry the printed word from afar, with news of how men and women live elsewhere."

Old Joe shook his head slowly. "They can't tie up the mind with a rope, but they keep trying anyhow. So they lock up the black jacks."

"What about Frenchie?" Willis asked. He jutted his chin toward a sailor they'd met the night before, climbing the shroud of the next ship over. Moving quickly up the network of ropes, Frenchie did not appear to be more than sixty years old, as he'd claimed to be. As Frenchie held on with one hand and shouted to someone below, Willis wondered whether the police would notice him.

"Shush, now," said Old Joe. He looked quickly from side to side, then resumed moving the pottery from the wagon to Willis's arms. And Willis, though barely fourteen years of age, understood that this was a serious matter.

# Frenchie

———

FRENCHIE WAS ONE OF THOSE MEN WHO MIGHT HAVE BEEN LOCKED up by the authorities, only instead of sitting in jail the night before sailing out, he was sharing a meal with Willis and Old Joe in Enid's kitchen. Enid, Old Joe's sister, had been freed following the death of her mistress and now lived at the edge of town, preparing food for those who could pay and, sometimes, for those who could not.

As Frenchie told it, he had avoided being hauled away by the inspector on the arrival of his ship, in part owing to his ambiguous, ruddy complexion and, in part, thanks to clever timing. The inspector was still on deck, checking the papers of three of Frenchie's colored comrades. Frenchie cast his glance forward, then aft, hoisted a small oak barrel onto one shoulder to obscure his face, slipped a coil of rope over the other, and simply walked down a ramp to the dock and into the crowd.

Willis could barely eat his meal for listening to Frenchie's stories of life on board, for better or worse. The rough seas, the wormy bread, the sickness. The dirty, dangerous work. The satisfaction of a well-coordinated crew. Men of different hues and tongues pooling their efforts, despite the conflicts that could brew on board.

"Not much choice in that," said Frenchie. "When there's trouble at sea, there's no place to go. Either you work together, or you perish together." Frenchie spoke of sailors like him who'd pushed away from the docks and never returned to land. He told of free black jacks being kidnapped and enslaved and having to escape. If they were lucky. Sometimes, the white Europeans were kidnapped, too, and made to labor. Willis found that hard to believe, but Frenchie insisted.

"There will always be men willing to steal the freedom of others if they think it will bring them an advantage," Frenchie said.

Willis was fascinated by the idea that a colored man could push away from the docks and leave the port city. That men like Frenchie could cross the oceans to other lands or travel up and down the coast as they did. That even enslaved men could join them as seamen, stewards, or cooks, and spend so many days separated from the people who held them in bondage. If they did not return, they could be hunted and re-captured, or killed. And even if they did return, they might see their wives and children or other kin sold off as retribution. But in the meantime, they were out there, seeing the world, learning things, and carrying the stories of what they'd experienced from one shore to an-other.

Each story that Frenchie told opened Willis's eyes to new possibili-ties. What intrigued Willis the most was the idea of what men like Frenchie could find when they went home. The different cities, the different ways in which men of color might live. The conditions they faced. Sometimes misery, sometimes loneliness. But oftentimes, such men had families waiting for them ashore. Families with land to farm and workshops to operate and children in school. Families that had never been sold out from under them.

Frenchie himself had a wife and children up in a place called Phila-delphia. Being Martinique-born, he had language skills that had helped him to cross the oceans and back, though he generally avoided routes that brought him this far south. Not only had officials in the port city taken to confining free sailors and seamen, they'd also issued a ban on those who originated in the French-speaking West Indies. The slave revolt down in Saint-Domingue, long before Willis's time, still had the local population of slaveholders feeling nervous. Even Willis knew never to call the country by its post-revolution name, Haiti. But the world was full of contradictions, as Frenchie could attest. Frenchie said he'd once worked with white seamen on a ship that was captained by a black man. There had even been a ship with a woman crew member on board, though no one had realized it at first. Excellent mapmaker, she'd proved to be.

"The hardest trip," Frenchie said, "was my very first. We are going back twenty years, now. I was the cook, and the only colored man on board. There were men who tripped me as I walked by. Men who referred to me in most uncharitable terms. Men who hit me for not delivering the food fast enough. I would prepare the food, with my own two hands, for every man on that rigger, but when the time came to sit down to a meal, I was made to eat on my own."

Then the vagaries of nature forced a change in their relations. A terrific storm rose up during that voyage. The ship and crew were in danger, and all hands were needed on deck.

"That was when those other lads saw what I was made of," Frenchie said. "When they needed me to help keep that ship from rolling over and cracking apart." Frenchie unleashed a low, undulating laugh. "After that, I was hired on as a deckhand. And the year after that, the captain took on a few more fellows like me."

No matter his provenance, Frenchie said, the seafaring man often was disrespected by others who did not know his work. He was seen as a man apart from others.

"Men without ties to a family or a town. That's how some people see us," Frenchie said. "There are people who believe all sailor-town districts are places of ill repute. But sailors come in different shapes and sizes and needs, like anyone else. Over the years, I have come to see that we mariners often band together, across languages and cultures and colors, despite our prejudices, not only to stay alive but also to protect ourselves against the disdain of others."

Sometimes, Frenchie said, a determined young slave would escape bondage by stowing away on a ship, and they'd all look the other way. If he survived, they'd absorb him into the crew. Make him work for his keep. Willis leaned forward, listening carefully, as the idea of running away by sea began to steer his imagination in a new direction. But Frenchie, who must have recognized in Willis this hopeful kind of agitation, shook his head. It was almost impossible now, with the inspections, Frenchie said.

"Are you never afraid?" Willis asked Frenchie. "You sail on ships similar to the ones that have kidnapped people from far away." Willis had heard, from the oldest slaves, how men and women, taken forcibly from distant shores, had been bound and stacked like stolen logs.

Frenchie smiled. "How old are you, now?" he asked.

"Fourteen years of age, sir," said Willis.

"Four-teen," Frenchie said and gave a hoot. "What you have seen in your short life is only one small part of the truth. Don't you forget that, young Willis. If you live long enough, you will find that the rest of the truth is out there," he said, pointing in the direction of the bay. Willis turned his head to look toward the coast.

Frenchie lowered his voice and leaned in toward Willis. "Our ancestors have been going to sea for as long as anyone can remember. It is only natural that some of us return to ride the waves. To listen for the voices of those who went before us. We cannot undo the worst days of our past, but we can always look to better days. A man might have fear, young Willis, but he lives all the same."

To Willis, it seemed they were still in the midst of their worst days, even though Africans were no longer being brought across the ocean. Even as he moved about the port city with relative ease, Willis saw a market building where a group of men, women, and children were fixed in place by ropes. They were being auctioned off along with cattle and furnishings.

Willis had seen people brought to the backcountry in wagons, chained together or bound with rope. His heart pounded at the thought that he, too, might be stolen away and sold, despite the fact that he was already in bondage. There were slaveholders worse than the Oldhams, Willis knew. All his life, people had told him so.

The next day, Willis watched as the crew on Frenchie's ship pulled on the clew lines and buntlines from the deck, adjusting the sailcloth. Soon the vessel moved away, buoyed by the incoming tide and towed by longboats. Frenchie and another seaman, still holding fast to the ropes high above the deck, each raised one arm in salute to the people on the docks. Willis waved back and watched as first one, then another sail was raised and the vessel turned fully toward the horizon.

# La Mer

———

**2019**

Okay, Ebby's had enough. She's been practicing a little spiel while waiting for Avery to come out of the hospital. She wants to find a polite way to ditch Avery. Her plan is to make herself one hundred percent unavailable until tomorrow sometime, when the rental car is ready to be picked up from the police. Then Avery can take things from there. If Avery were anyone but Henry's girlfriend, Ebby wouldn't feel odd about spending more time with her. But she does.

"Henry's doing all right," Avery says. "He sends a hello."

*That feels weird,* Ebby thinks. "When is he getting out?" she asks.

"The doctor plans to discharge him by tomorrow afternoon."

"Great," Ebby says. "Um, listen, Avery, while you're waiting for Henry, I'm going to . . ."

But Avery interrupts. "Oh, I really don't want to sit around waiting for him," she says. "I was thinking to head out to *la mer* tomorrow morning."

"The seaside?"

"Maybe it was your story about those sailors, but I'm just feeling a yen for the sea, and I thought you might want to go to the coast with me. The rental car will be back, so I could drive."

The word *coast* is all Ebby needs to hear to forget her plan to call a halt to sightseeing with Avery. Ebby has never lived this far from the shore. Wherever you go, you can find beauty. But living a good two-hour drive from the water feels *off* to her.

Ebby feels the absence of the sea. Much as she likes this village with its lazy, duck-filled river snaking through the middle of it. Much as she loves seeing a million willow leaves rippling in the breeze. Much as she loves that absurd little hoopoe bird that pounces and preens and calls out in the yard.

"All right," Ebby says slowly, "but I'll drive." She wants to be sure she's in control of the situation.

This odd state of affairs.

The next day is hot, sunny, and filled with the smell of sand and salt water. They are only there to walk and take in the views, not lie on the beach like everyone else.

"I missed this smell," Ebby tells Avery. She looks out over the water in the direction of a series of colorful fishing huts perched on stilts.

"Oh, yes, all that dimethyl sulfide," Avery says.

"Mhmm," Ebby says, nodding. She tries not to smile.

"Algae farts, essentially," Avery says, enunciating each syllable.

Ebby can't stop herself, now. She laughs outright, and Avery joins in with a *yap-yap* sound that makes Ebby laugh again. She looks at Avery. At the pale pouf where the extensions lift the hair at the top of her head. At the neat curves of her pale brows. At the shell-colored ovals of acrylic covering Avery's nails. Avery has surprised her, once again. That sound, coming out of her mouth.

Ebby googled Avery last night, she couldn't resist. Apparently, she is one of the tri-state area's young attorneys to watch. Exactly how one assesses the quality of an attorney at such a young age, Ebby isn't sure. The point is, Avery is no lightweight. She suspects Avery is the type to read legal articles while waiting all those hours to have her hair extensions done. She suspects Avery is damn near perfect.

Avery's quirky little laugh is a surprise, but so is the ease with which Ebby finds herself joining in. She feels a current of sadness run through her as she thinks what a relief it must have been for Henry to be with Avery after two years of Ebby. Two years of restless nights. Two years of being gossiped about. Two years of being called and texted repeatedly by Ebby's mother every time they went away on a trip. And suddenly, painfully, Ebby sees, so clearly, the tone of her relationship with Henry. She glances at Avery again. Well, of course.

*Of course.*

But Ebby sees this too: that nothing excuses Henry's behavior. No matter that it might have been difficult for Henry to be with Ebby at times, and that the prospect of being linked to her indefinitely might have come to feel like too much. People fall in love, they dream, then adjustment kicks in. Sometimes disillusionment. Fine. But Henry was a shit about it. That hasn't changed. Nothing excuses the fact that he didn't call her on their wedding day. That he didn't show up and face her like a man.

Ebby grew up with little privacy, but she still craved it. When Henry ghosted her, knowing, full well, that the media would be following their nuptials, it was as if he had stripped off her clothes in public. He hadn't even tried to protect her. She looks over at Avery. Doesn't that set off alarm bells for her? Once again, she wonders what woman would want to be with Henry after knowing what he's done.

And isn't it outrageous for Ebby to feel as she does now, overcome by a tremor in her chest as she thinks of Henry and his pending return from the hospital? Love leaves a memory in the heart, even when your head tells you it shouldn't. Ebby must not be at the house when Henry comes back. She will make a plan for the evening. She will grab a book, she will take a sweater, she will drive in the opposite direction from the hospital. By the time Ebby returns, Henry and Avery will have settled into the guesthouse for the night.

"Do you think you love the sea so much," Avery is saying now, "because it's part of your heritage?"

"My dad thinks so," says Ebby. "He thinks we're tied to the water because we had mariners in our family."

"No, I mean, you know, the whole African water-spirit thing."

"*African water-spirit thing?*" Ebby says, frowning at Avery. She sees where this is going. People see her skin color and decide that her heritage is more *foreign* in nature than theirs. No matter that Ebby's family have been in New England for four hundred years. Probably longer than Avery's. No matter that their ancestors were all foreigners, at some point, if they weren't from one of the indigenous peoples. Which, come to think of it, part of the Freeman family was.

"I mean the idea," Avery says, "of water being a link to the spirit world."

"Could be," says Ebby. "But in my case, I think it's mostly the fact that I grew up on the Sound." Ebby stops and turns to Avery. "How about you? Do you love the sea?" She tries not to sound sarcastic.

Avery nods.

"Is there, like, a water-spirit thing going on in *your* heritage?" Ebby raises her hands to form air quotes as she says this. Can Avery hear the irritation in her voice? Probably, because Ebby sees those pink splotches appearing on Avery's face. Didn't Avery stop to think that Ebby might feel uncomfortable with that kind of question?

"Actually, yes," Avery says. "My mother's side is German. Going way back. She says the sea is in our blood. She used to tell me these stories about shape-shifting sea deities. But I have my own view."

"Which is . . . ?" Ebby says.

"That it goes beyond culture," Avery says. "That it's in our nature as humans. Our world is more sea than land. We came from the sea, we eat from the sea, we travel across the seas. We seek out the salt water to soothe our bodies and our worries. The sea is part of us. Whether we live at the shore or not. I believe this is what that Willis guy must have felt when he reached the port city for the first time. The moment he saw the bay and breathed in the coastal air, he may have recognized a part of himself that had been missing."

Ebby nods.

"My father would agree, for sure. But I think the initial attraction was a more practical one. Even for a boy whose ancestors would have been dragged across the ocean to the Americas, against their will, the sea raised the possibility of a different life for Willis."

Ebby knows this, for a fact, because Willis himself told this to his grandchildren. And one of Willis's grandsons was Ebby's great-grandfather.

# Words

———

1847

WORDS HAD A KIND OF POWER. ANYONE WHO HAD READ THE Scriptures knew this. Anyone who had ever been freed from bondage by a bill of sale or a final will and testament knew this. Teaching an enslaved person to read and write was against the law in this territory. Enslaved persons caught studying could be lashed, and a plantation owner known to teach them to read or write could be fined or jailed. But like many of his brethren, Moses had learned his letters anyway. Martin Oldham believed that a certain familiarity with the Scriptures was fundamental and had chosen to look the other way when he came to know that Uncle was teaching the young ones to read.

Martin Oldham also was a practical man, and ultimately, he saw fit to make use of Moses's reading and writing skills. Moses had begun by writing initials, dates, and sizes on pieces of pottery. Soon, he began to make note of inventories and pricing and deliveries in the pottery's register. The only thing was, everyone knew better than to acknowledge it. Words had the power to feed resistance, and for this, an enslaved person who could read and write words would continue to be feared.

After Betsey's death, Moses decided to carve five words into a piece of greenware that, unbeknownst to him, would go on to change lives. He contemplated the size of the disk and the space that would be required for him to fit all the words onto it. He broke up the phrase into three lines and attached the disk to the bottom of a twenty-gallon storage jar. Then he added the jar to the kiln with the next batch of stoneware.

In the days after Betsey's death, everyone had been feeling particularly low. Distracted. As the jar was fired, glazed, and fired again, the uneven heat caused a slight distortion in the structure that no one, not even Moses, would notice. Everyone who saw the jar would take a second look, though. There was something about that particular piece, not only the leaves added by Willis. They did not realize that it was the slight asymmetry of the jar that had caught their eye. Moses himself felt it to be the most beautiful thing he'd ever made.

While loading the jar onto a wagon bed one day, Willis accidentally knocked the piece off the edge of the platform and had to lunge for it. He had parked the wagon too close to the creek. The earth was damp over there, and the soil being what it was, it didn't hold his shoes. Willis skidded and the jar continued to roll toward the edge of the water. As Willis caught up with the vessel and bent to pick it up, he caught sight of the words incised on the bottom.

Willis had not been there when Moses was inscribing the words on the bottom of the jar. Still, he understood exactly what had inspired the phrase. He read the full inscription three more times, moving his lips silently.

A fortnight later, Willis was gone.

# Badge

———

At one time, the port city sold as many as four thousand badges a year to people who wanted to hire out their enslaved laborers. And, as it had always been the way of the world to counterfeit things of value, there was an underground network of skilled enslaved workers who had learned to copy just about anything, including those badges. It also was the tendency of people to subvert rotten systems by taking advantage of them, and Willis had been giving the matter serious thought for some time. He had already begun making inquiries when he saw the inscription on the bottom of Moses's jar.

As he prepared to take a load of stoneware to the port city, he acquired a badge that read **PORTER**, delivered in clandestine fashion by one of the rivermen down the way. On the outskirts of the city, he removed his regular **TURNER** badge and pulled the leather string holding the new counterfeit over his head. He then drove the wagon all the way into the city and down to the docks. His fake badge would give him an excuse to linger in town, should it be necessary, rather than return immediately to the pottery. But Willis hoped that it would not be necessary to stay.

By that time, the decline of the once-great city was in full swing. The rails from the backcountry stopped far short of the docks, leading to the costly and time-consuming transfer of cotton and other goods to waiting vessels. Increasingly, merchandise was traveling to and from rival ports in the region, or directly to Northern cities like Boston, New York, and Philadelphia.

In less than twenty years, the city would be ravaged by conflict and fires, and, later, a powerful earthquake. But on that particular day, no one at the docks could know this. On that day, the arrival of an enslaved porter with a handsome-looking load of alkaline-glazed jugs and jars was a small sign that commerce was still alive, if not well, in those parts.

Willis, now thirty years of age, had been hiring himself out on small jobs, with his owner's permission, and keeping a small portion of the income he produced. He built and painted signage for buildings and ships and was skilled in the repair of wagon wheels, something he'd learned from Old Joe. He knew of men who had saved enough to buy their own freedom or that of relatives. He also knew of men who had pretended to be free and had been caught without a badge. Everyone knew what could happen to an enslaved man who was picked up by the guardsmen and sent to jail. Everyone knew what would happen to a woman if she was caught without a badge.

Willis had saved nearly enough to buy his freedom. But after what had happened to Betsey, he was scared. He couldn't be sure that, even with sufficient funds, he would be granted his desire. It was time to make a move, no matter what the consequences. After unloading most of the pottery, Willis rode the wagon away from the wharf and to a riverbank outside the city. He watered and fed the horses and tied them up in the shade of a large tree, where they would be seen by one of the rivermen. Before his passing, Old Joe had made Willis promise to take good care of those mares. He patted their necks, then began the walk back to the city, carrying a small sack on his shoulder and a single storage jar in his arms. Moses's special jar.

Willis looked at the ramp leading onto the ship. Could anyone hear his heart, pounding as it did? Just a few more steps, he thought as he mumbled, over and over, the words that were written on the bottom of the jar. He felt his limbs trembling but held his back straight as he walked up the ramp. Willis had layered dried beans over the items inside: a jacket wrapped around pieces of bread, salted meat, and other provisions. Unable to resist, he'd also tucked a few sheets of paper and a pencil against the inside wall of the jar.

He stepped onto the deck and headed straight for the hold where food and other goods for export would be stored for the voyage. When he heard footsteps coming his way, he scurried to the farthest point of the hold, deposited the jar, and crouched behind a row of large barrels.

Willis had reached the point of no return.

# Monster

———

IT WAS THE SHOUTING THAT DREW WILLIS OUT OF HIS HIDING place.

For three nights and four days, Willis had kept himself squeezed into a dark space in the ship's cargo hold, knees folded against his chest behind rows of sealed jugs and barrels, his back leaning against Moses's jar. The containers in the hold were stacked in such a way as to avoid being rolled or spilled whenever the ship rocked. These goods seemed to require no particular attention, but closer to the entrance there were piles of ropes and what looked like bolts of sailcloth, along with other items whose purpose Willis could not determine. It was this collection of items that, on occasion, would draw a seaman into the room.

The first time someone stepped inside to lift a bulky metal object from near the door, Willis's chest felt as though it would collapse from the fear. He closed his eyes, stilled his breathing, and told himself that there was nothing he could do about it now. He had made the decision to run and now he was trapped on a square-rigger headed north. If they found him, so be it. Willis pictured Betsey on the day she'd died. He remembered the loss of his sister Flora, bitten by that snake because she'd been tired to the point of carelessness. He recalled being whipped as a child solely for making designs in the blank pages of a ledger he'd found in the master's office. If it came down to it, he would jump from the deck of the ship rather than return to bondage.

At first, Willis did not touch the food he had hidden in the jar, so roiled was his stomach from the rocking of the ship. When his appetite returned, he would reach his hand down through the top layer of beans and feel around for a strip of dried meat, a pecan, or Old Joe's green glass bottle, which he had filled with river water. Otherwise, he urged himself to sit immobile, even when a rat jumped over his shoes. Even when he felt like retching at the tipping of the ship's floor. Even when he needed to piss.

Willis would hold his water all day and sneak onto the deck to relieve himself in the middle of the night, careful to stay out of sight of the single watchman on duty. The sky out there was like nothing Willis had ever seen. Even in his fright, he would stop to gaze up at the points of light that blazed above and gulp at the air that stirred along the length of the ship.

Willis looked out over the sea, its inky waves visible in the moonlight, and thought of the Scriptures. He imagined the Spirit of God as described in the book of Genesis, hovering over the waters as He brought forth light and land. This must be something like the world that God had generated in those first few days, Willis thought, before He created man to rule over the other creatures of the earth and sea. Before everything went wrong.

Surely this was the world that God had intended, for the place Willis had come from was not.

By now, Willis's escape from the pottery would have been noted and reported. There would be signs posted on trees and outside shops. Logic told him he could not make the whole trip without being found, but he knew that others had done it. Other men had escaped by sea and sent word to the backcountry through coded messages. After those first few days, he had begun to feel that he might have a real chance. That is, until the shouting started.

Willis thought the ship was going down or about to run aground. It was known that a nasty gale up north could wash a dozen ships ashore in a day. He stood up and approached the doorway to the deck.

"Starboard!" a sailor cried.

Willis pulled open the door just enough to peer through at the men who ran past him.

"Whoa!" shouted another man. "What a monster!"

Monster? Willis opened the door just a bit farther, and what he saw pulled him fully out onto the deck. A spray of water shooting straight out of the sea. Mesmerized, he ran toward the bow. He had heard stories of this sort of thing. He had seen an illustration on a map posted on a board at the docks and, still, he could not believe his eyes. He watched as a gray-black creature leaped out of the water and twisted itself in the air, its body the size of a large boat, its hide covered in cuts and crusts.

*A whale!*

The splash that followed doused Willis with salt water. It was a fearsome thing, to be sure, to be so close to that big fish. The other men were still shouting, eager to avoid a collision with the creature. Willis felt the ship heel outward as it turned away from the whale. But this was no monster. Willis had lived among monsters. Willis was running from monsters. No, this was one of God's creatures. Like those stars at night, this was the world that God had intended. This was the world as it was meant to be.

The whale was larger than any animal Willis had ever seen. As it flipped over and back into the depths of the sea, another of its kind came along, breaching the water like the first and seeming to stand up among the waves. Willis ran to the side railing and looked toward the stern, now, tears flowing down his face.

"Oh!" the other men shouted in unison, laughing now and pointing. Willis wiped at his eyes.

Distracted from his bleak circumstances by this spectacle, Willis had not seen two men approaching him.

"Who in blazes are you?" one of them said. Willis looked up to find two Negro seamen facing him, hands on their hips. For one moment, he had forgotten that he was a stowaway.

"Who are you, I say!" He grabbed Willis by the shirt and punched him, threatening him in a foreign-sounding accent. Later, several of the men would question Willis thoroughly and, too frightened to lie, he would tell them the truth.

"Don't send me back," Willis cried. "Please don't send me back. I can work. I can repair wood and metal. I'm good with paint. I can make designs." And then, in his boldest statement yet, he said, "I know my letters." The seafarers looked at one another.

That night, still in the hold, but now furnished with some old rags to rest his head, he pulled a piece of paper out of the jar, laid it on the floor of the ship, and drew a whale. One of the seamen had told him that whales were not like other fish. They laid no eggs. They bore their young directly out of their bodies. Like cattle. Like people.

The same mate had told him about small fish that flew over the surface of the water, south of where Willis had grown up, in the seas beyond Florida. They flew like birds scouting for food, only much faster, as if propelled by a feeling of pure happiness. This new awareness of the immensity and mysteries of the sea and its creatures was daunting and energizing at the same time. It made Willis feel alive.

It made Willis feel free.

Willis felt this way even when the mariners shared stories of great sadness. Of losses and disappointments. To tell your story was to experience a kind of freedom. To be able to share news of your adventures, to name your relations and favorite places, was to be a man.

# Potential

——

At first, the black jacks had threatened to throw Willis overboard. They couldn't afford to get into trouble, they said. But in the end, they put him to work washing down the deck and helping the cook. They pretended to the others that Willis had always been one of theirs. An apprentice, of sorts. He seemed capable enough, and he was strong.

They did this, they said, because they had known others like Willis.

Because they could have been someone like Willis.

Because they knew they still could end up like Willis.

And the others pretended not to have realized the truth.

Soon, Willis showed his potential on deck. He was capable at knotting rope and repairing things. He was learning to work with the sails. The first time they ordered him to climb the ship's shroud, he clambered all the way up, without hesitation. The smell of the salt water, the sound of the canvas billowing in the wind, the sight of the world, seen from up there, convinced him that he had been right to board the ship after all. Climbing back down that first time, however, was a different story. It put the fear of God in him, to see the deck so far below.

Whatever happened next, though, Willis was ready to risk it. He might fall to his death from the rigging. He might drown. But he kept in his mind the thought of the jar and what was written on its bottom panel. Those words had given him courage, even though he knew that a man like him could not reveal or repeat them. Not a colored man who was trying to stay alive. Not for now, anyhow.

In Boston, Willis was given clean clothing and offered paying work on board. In time, he grew to understand the ways of the wind and the currents. Other crew members started calling him by his new name, which they had advised him to choose immediately. In the world of the free, he would need two names. And so Willis from the South Carolina backcountry became Edward Freeman in Massachusetts. Because words had the potential to remake a man.

Still, Edward Freeman would continue to think of himself as Willis, because words also had the power to hold memory. Although the name had been chosen by a slaveholder, it was the only moniker he had ever known, and it held the memory of his sister's voice. It held memories of Moses and Old Joe. It was a reminder that despite all he had run from, Willis had been cared for by others. He could not be sure that, if he survived, he would ever find that again.

# Part Three

# Encounter

———

THE THING ABOUT VILLAGE LIFE.

Sooner or later, you run into everyone a second time. Including the person you picked up at a local café one morning. Usually, those flings don't lead to anything lasting. Except, sometimes, for biological consequences, but Ebby and Robert had used protection that day they were together. Both times. So nothing should come of it, right?

Still, Ebby can't help but smile when she sees Robert, crouched on the shoulder of the road, examining a flat tire on his bicycle. Can't help but feel warm about the face as he loads the *vélo* into the trunk of Ebby's car and settles into the passenger seat beside her. Can't help but laugh out loud as Robert tells her about having to scroll through his grandfather's smartphone on the sly and remove the record of Ebby's number from the list of recent calls. Now, his *grand-père* can't call the holiday cottage by mistake.

But there's more. His grandpa, that very morning, asked him what had happened to *la femme sympa,* that woman who used to answer the phone.

"Oh, poor *grand-père!*" Ebby laughs. "You didn't explain that he mixed up the numbers?"

"He should have been the one to explain it to me! I don't know how he managed to get that number saved under my name. But I'll tell you something else. He insisted that you knew me, that you asked about me, so it could not have been a wrong number. It's your fault, of course, for being so nice to him."

Robert trails his fingers down Ebby's torso, following the thin, dark line that runs from her navel down to the triangle of fuzz below.

"I have one of these, too," Robert says, pointing to his own linea nigra.

"I've noticed," Ebby says. She props herself up on an elbow and smiles at him as she begins to run her own hand down along the line that connects his navel to the part of him that is unfurling now, like a shoot, stretching upward. "I didn't know men could have these."

"I didn't know women who had not had children could get them."

That line on Ebby's belly has been there as long as she can remember. Still, at the mention of the word *children,* she feels a pang of sorrow for the baby that she has lost. For the line that might have grown darker had her pregnancy lasted. She keeps these thoughts to herself, but as if he can sense a longing in her, Robert leans over and kisses her there. Ebby wraps her arms around his head. She wants to cling to him for a bit. But the emotion scares her.

This is not a *thing* between them, she tells herself. But she really likes Robert. And she can't help but say *d'accord* when he invites her to go listen to a jazz band outdoors the next night. It's only music, Ebby thinks. And it's an excuse to stay away from the house, since Henry and Avery have decided to stay an extra night.

"The food truck with the crêpes woman will be in the *place,*" Robert says.

"Mmmm," says Ebby as Robert cups her face in his hands and leans in to kiss her, his lips warm in the cool night air. It's only food, Ebby thinks, and people need to eat. She puts her arms around Robert's neck before kissing him goodbye.

"Okay, jazz and crêpes," she says from her car window as she drives away, grinning.

# Henry

———

WHERE IS SHE?

Henry has been listening for the sound of Ebby's car. She wasn't at the cottage when Avery brought him back from the hospital last night, and she was gone again today. He needs to talk to Ebby before he leaves the village tomorrow. Even after everything that has happened— Henry's fall by the river, the police questioning, the *rapprochement,* as Avery put it, between her and Ebby—it's clear that Ebby is avoiding him. He rubs his bandaged ankle where it hurts. This is Henry's last chance. Avery has gone to wash her hair and pack. Henry picks up his camera and fiddles with it, listening.

Waiting.

True, Ebby has refused to hear him out already, but he needs to try again. Not only for himself, but also for her. She needs to know why he did what he did. He has thought of writing Ebby a letter or leaving her a long voicemail, but he owes it to her to stand and face her this time. Plus, it's a delicate issue. He doesn't want to leave a paper trail or digital record about anything connected to the death of Ebby's brother. What if his father's friend really does know something about the crime, as unlikely as that may seem?

Better to talk to Ebby here, in this hamlet far away from home. If Henry Pepper were to approach Ebony Freeman's apartment back in Connecticut, or meet her in a coffee shop, or even nod at her while passing her in the parking lot of a supermarket, their encounter might end up being fodder for gossip, and he doesn't want any more of that.

When he ran off on their wedding day, he wasn't thinking straight, and he sure as heck wasn't thinking about social media. He knew there was bound to be a local news headline somewhere. But things kind of blew up when he took off. It has always perplexed him how, with all the big-name celebs running around, and with all the scandals popping up, anyone found the time or energy to be that curious about Henry and Ebby.

There she is.

Henry hears Ebby's car pulling onto the gravel outside the cottage and rushes out the front door. He still has a few minutes. Avery's shower is still running in the bathroom.

"Ebby," Henry says as he approaches her. Ebby is shaking her head *no* and waving him off, but he persists. "Could we please just talk for a minute?"

Ebby stops. Henry tips his head in the direction of the main house.

"Can we go inside?" he says. Ebby doesn't say yes, but she doesn't say no, either. When she turns toward the house, Henry follows.

Ebby isn't making this easy for Henry. She stands there, in the kitchen, with her arms crossed. And she won't look at him. This is the worst part, he thinks, that Ebby won't even lift those velvety eyes of hers in his direction.

"I know there is nothing I can do to make it up to you," Henry says. "But I do owe you an apology, and I was hoping you'd let me explain." Ebby flicks her eyes up at him, now. He takes that as a *yes* and lets his story spill out.

The thing about people is, they will surprise you. Ebby doesn't interrupt Henry. She doesn't raise her voice or shed tears, as he expected. She locks her hands together and brings them up to her mouth, looking down toward the floor, as if in silent prayer. Nine months have gone by since they last saw each other. A lot can happen to a person in nine months. When Henry is done talking, Ebby just stands there for a while, nodding slowly, before speaking.

"That is weird," Ebby says slowly.

"Exactly," Henry says. "You told me no one knew the jar was broken."

"Well, my family. Maybe some of our friends. But it wasn't, like, public knowledge. And you believe your father's friend knew something about it?" Ebby asks.

"I don't *want* to believe it, but it made me feel very uncomfortable to hear him mention the jar being broken during the home invasion. I mean, how did he know? I was uncomfortable enough that I didn't have the guts to ask. He's one of my dad's best buddies. I kept thinking there had to be an explanation that wouldn't be so, you know, incriminating."

"Who is this person?"

"I told you, a close friend of my father's, but I'd rather not say his name."

"Well, you should have asked him," Ebby says.

"I know."

"And you should have told me."

"No, I couldn't. You would have gone ballistic. You would have wanted to know right away."

"And could you blame me?"

"No, not at all. But you wouldn't have given me time to find out for myself. And that could have been very awkward for my family, as well as upsetting for yours. So I didn't tell you, and then I just couldn't face you, Ebby."

"You couldn't face me?" Ebby says. "This is why you skipped out on our wedding? Because you felt guilty not telling me?"

"Yes," Henry says. "I mean, no, not only that. It's that, I didn't know, anymore, how to be around you without worrying about how you'd react to things."

Ebby turns one side of her face toward him as if trying to hear something.

"You didn't know how to be around me anymore? Are you saying you wanted to leave me anyway?"

Henry opens his mouth, but nothing comes out. And as his reaction sinks in, Ebby opens her mouth even wider. A silent *ohhh*. Then an endless moment in which Ebby breathes in and out.

"And you couldn't have told me this before the day of our wedding, Henry?"

Henry reaches for Ebby, now, but she steps back and puts her arms up as if to deflect a blow. She shakes her head *no-no-no-no-no* as if responding to an internal voice, until, finally, she lowers her arms and her face grows still as stone. Henry recognizes that look. This is *aloof Ebby, private Ebby, deep-down-hurt Ebby*.

Henry's heart is breaking, not only for her but for himself. Maybe he could have asked Ebby to postpone their wedding plans, instead of running off. Maybe he'd only needed some time to figure things out for himself. Maybe Ebby would have understood if he'd been honest with her.

"Your father's friend," Ebby says slowly, now, and Henry sees that she is sidestepping the issue of their relationship altogether. "I agree there's got to be an explanation. It just doesn't make sense he'd say something like that, openly, if he'd been mixed up in something criminal."

"Exactly. And I don't think he needed the money."

"Maybe not, but you already know what I think."

"That this wasn't necessarily about money."

"Right," Ebby says, and they nod simultaneously.

Early in their relationship, on one of Ebby's more difficult nights, she awoke from a nightmare and confided in Henry. As her tears soaked his T-shirt, she told him about her brother's death and how he had seen the jar fall and break.

"That was the last thing he saw," she sobbed. "Everything that jar represented. Our family's pride. Our history. All the stories that used to entertain us. Gone. That jar had been there before us, and our parents, and their parents, and it was supposed to be there, no matter what."

Henry held Ebby in his arms and listened. This woman, who had brought her own special light into his life, sounded like a broken little girl in that moment.

"That wasn't the last thing your brother saw," Henry said, wiping her wet cheek with his hand. "*You* were the last thing he saw. His little sister. He knew he wasn't alone. Don't you think that counts for something?"

Ebby nodded. Wiped her nose with her forearm.

"But there's more," Ebby said. And still in the voice of that little girl, she made him swear not to tell anyone before she told him the rest.

Not even her parents knew, she said. She told Henry she was sure the robbers had gone to her family home to take the jar. And she told him why she believed this. Henry nodded and listened, and he kept his promise to Ebby. He has never shared the details of that conversation with anyone. But he has failed to keep a different promise to her, his promise of marriage. And look at them now.

# Treasure

____

## 2017

WHAT EBBY TOLD HENRY WAS THIS: EBBY AND BAZ WERE PLAYing hide-and-seek and Ebby was hiding upstairs off the landing when she heard an unfamiliar voice downstairs. She ran to the banister and looked down. She saw two men in work overalls, their faces covered by ski masks. One of them was pointing a gun at her brother and talking in an aggressive way. *Where is it?* the man said to Baz. *Just show us.*

"He said *it*," Ebby told Henry, "not *the jar*. But I knew what he meant. He meant Old Mo." The twenty-gallon piece, she explained, had been kept on a table all by itself in her dad's study. It had a name of its own. Like a person. It was so special, a historian friend of her parents' had come to see it. Ten-year-old Ebby was certain that even in a house like theirs, full of nice things, Old Mo was the only *it* of any real consequence.

But Ebby never told her parents. When the police questioned her, she said she'd run to the banister after hearing the gunshots, then gone downstairs. She was terrified that the men who had entered her family home might find out she'd seen them from above and come back to hurt her and her parents. She had grown up living with a kind of terror that she hadn't been able to express.

As Ebby grew, the fear gave way to rage. In centuries past, people had kidnapped some of Ebby's ancestors and taken control of their bodies and lives. And in the twenty-first century, Ebby's identity continued to be shaped by what had been taken from her family. Her brother. Her first home. Her family's privacy. Their heritage.

But alongside these feelings grew something else, a sense of guilt at not having told everything to her parents and the police. Ebby was certain she would never have been able to identify the people who committed the crime. But what if it could have helped the police? At least they would have known that the people who broke in had been looking for the jar.

When, a year later, Henry heard his father's friend Harris mention the jar during that bridge game, he couldn't help but think about what Ebby had told him. There were people who might covet a historic piece of American stoneware enough to have it stolen. Or to have it taken then returned to the original owner for a fee. And unlike Ebby, he actually knew the name and face of a person who might know something.

Holding art for ransom was a thing. It happened all the time. Robbers stole tens of thousands of pieces of art and artifacts every year, worldwide, and much of the loot could never be sold through legitimate markets. But who would know enough about how special that jar was to think of taking it? His father's friend Harris might be the person to know. Harris was in the insurance industry. Not an agent. More like an executive and majority shareholder. But still. He knew these kinds of things. Only there was no way to raise the question with his father's friend that wouldn't be incredibly awkward, at the very least. It was Harris who had mentioned the jar during that bridge game. *How had he come to know about it?*

If he'd had doubts about anything else, Henry would have gone to Ebby with them. They used to talk about a lot of things. She knew how Henry felt when he put his camera up to his face. Which meant she knew more about him than most. She knew something about how Henry could be when he was at his best. But she also knew how much he hated confrontation. That he had given in to his father's insistence that he go into banking instead of entering a fine arts program. That it had cost him to go up against his mother's reservations about him marrying "outside of the community," as she had put it.

Ebby knew Henry well enough to know that in a pinch, Henry might take what felt like the easier way out. Had she known what was going on, she might have been able to predict what would happen next. On the night before Henry should have married Ebby, he was freed from his dilemma by the following line of logic: The jar was gone anyway, and the robbers had run away empty-handed. Ebby's brother was already dead, and Henry couldn't do a damn thing to bring him back. Ebby was sexy and smart and kindhearted and she would find someone else to love her soon enough. Sooner than he liked to think. Breathing much easier, he slid behind the wheel of his Rover and drove off.

But when Henry saw Ebby by the river that first day at the cottage, tugging her boots out of the mud, he felt a rush of nostalgia for the woman with whom he had fallen in love. Then came the deep embarrassment of recalling his failure to show up on their wedding day. Henry thought he'd already paid the price for backing out of their engagement by giving up all possibility of a future with Ebby. But now, he sees the true cost of what he has done. It isn't the *what* that counts so much as the *how*. The way in which he's handled things.

Henry has taken himself down a notch as a man.

# One More Night

———

IT IS HENRY AND AVERY'S LAST NIGHT IN THE VILLAGE. THEY HAVE packed all but the essentials. Put gas in the car. Lolled on the sofa together, looking at maps on Avery's tablet. But now, Avery has stepped out of the shower to find Henry gone. She wants to be sure that he's feeling all right. The doctor has warned her to keep an eye on him, since he'd hit his head. She sees that Henry has left the front door ajar, but his camera and phone are still sitting on the dining room table. Avery walks outside and heads toward the only light that she can see from the darkened yard. The kitchen in the main house is blazing with light, and Henry and Ebony are clearly visible inside.

Funny, Avery thinks. Just that morning, before going to the beach with Ebby (as Ebony asked her to call her), Avery was reading a new article about relationships. Many rebound relationships had been known to develop into love and long-term commitments, the author wrote. But there was a *but*. For the person on the rebound, lingering, often negative, feelings from the previous love story could stand in the way.

While the partner on the rebound might be seeking only relief and a boost in confidence from the new affair, the other person might be wholly invested in building a long-lasting relationship. Nothing new there, thought Avery. But the article quoted actual figures. A study that reflected a fundamental imbalance. Rebound relationships rarely lasted more than three months. Avery pulled the cap off of her felt-tip pen and wrote an *X* next to that last point in a paper notebook. She nodded to herself. She and Henry had already been together for four months. They were still on vacation together. They'd been making new plans.

But now, approaching the open windows of the main cottage,

Avery sees Henry holding Ebby by the shoulders. Henry has raised his voice. She can hear him saying *never stopped . . .* and she can guess the rest of the sentence. He is shaking his head, now. He panicked, he says. He was a shit. *Yes, Henry,* Avery thinks, stepping closer to the house, *you are a shit. And you, Chastity Avery Williams, have been deluding yourself.* She turns to go back to the guest cottage.

Until Ebby begins to shout.

And because Avery has always been a curious person, always driven by a need to know how people's minds and hearts work, she stops and turns back, stepping closer to the window, just beyond the reach of the light.

———

EBBY REALIZES SHE'S YELLING. She promised herself she wouldn't make a scene, whatever Henry had to say, but she wasn't expecting any of this. At first, she absorbed the full hit of learning what had led him to abandon her on their wedding day. But the more she thought about Henry's omissions, the less she was able to control her reaction.

"You just walked away," Ebby says.

"Let me explain," Henry tells her. Ebby turns her back to him. He puts a hand on her elbow, but she keeps her arms folded tight across her middle. Henry moves to face her and ducks his head to try to look her in the eyes, but she refuses to meet his gaze.

"So you changed your mind about our relationship. A little *late,* I might add. But you still could have demanded answers about the shooting."

Henry is murmuring now. It is a wordless kind of contrition that only a lover should be allowed to use.

"This is how you treat someone you were supposed to marry?" Ebby is fighting the urge to cry.

"I didn't have a choice," Henry says. "I told you, he's my father's childhood friend. I needed to find another way to learn more."

"And when, exactly, did you try to learn more? Was that before or after you left me and my parents standing there, in our garden, like fools?"

Henry is pulling at Ebby's crossed arms, now, but she bats him away.

"No!" Ebby says. She hears how her voice has sunk into her chest, weighted with bitterness. "You did have a choice. You were supposed to choose me, but instead you chose some guy who played poker with your father."

"Bridge," Henry says.

"What?"

"Bridge, not poker."

"Are you kidding me, Henry? Do you think I *care* which game?" Ebby feels a wave of sadness wash over her at the thought that Henry has found yet another way to disappoint her.

————

WHY DID HENRY SAY THAT? Ebby's right. It doesn't matter. Henry looks down, now, feeling the heat in his face rise to his forehead.

"Don't do that," Ebby says. Her voice unnerves him. "Don't look away from me. You're the one who wanted to have this conversation. You chose your family's comfort over my family's desperate need—no, our fundamental *right*—to know. You decided that your people were worth more than my people. And there I was, thinking that I *was* one of your people."

"Just give me a chance to finish, Ebby?"

"Finish what? Making excuses? My brother was murdered. He was just a kid."

Ebby is weeping, now, and Henry wants to hold her, but she keeps pushing at his chest, pounding a fist against his breastbone. She's not really hitting him. It doesn't hurt. But she is breaking him apart.

————

LOOKING THROUGH THE WINDOW, Avery sees that Ebby is crying, and Henry is trying to wrap his arms around her. Ebby keeps pushing him away but Avery sees it all anyway. She sees how well Henry and Ebby must have fit together once, even as they are struggling with each other now. She sees what love must have looked like for Henry and feels the dagger of disappointment sink deep into her chest.

Once again, Avery turns away, and this time, she vows she won't turn back. She has been so engaged in the scene unfolding before her that she does not notice, until she turns, that there is a tall, narrow-looking man with a head of frizzy curls standing next to her. She sees something soft and pastel-colored dangling from one hand. A sweater, maybe.

"Bonsoir," he says.

Avery opens her mouth but finds she cannot speak. She swallows and nods. She has no idea who this stranger is, but she doesn't feel threatened. The man is beautiful, and physical beauty has a way of disarming people. She is merely speechless. She walks toward the guest cottage. When she reaches the front door, she turns back to see the stranger leaving the yard and stepping into the road that leads back to the village's main *place*. Avery hears the faint strains of music coming from that direction. There is a band playing out there tonight. She had thought to convince Henry to go. But now, she goes into the bedroom to finish packing her bags.

# Robert

———

*M*AIS OUI, ROBERT THINKS AS HE TURNS AND WALKS AWAY from the cottage where Ebby is staying. He knew better than to expect anything else. He has been very foolish about Ebby.

This village has too many expats and tourists. People who come for a while, then go. Even the foreigners who own property here tend to call some other place home. The way things work is this: If you find someone who appeals to you, you don't waste any time. You embrace the opportunity. But then what? What if you want to keep seeing someone? What if you don't want them to leave? And how is it possible that he feels this way about Ebby after so little time?

Robert isn't an adolescent. Robert is thirty-two years old. And already a widower. When his wife grew sicker, she made him promise not to close off his heart. But it did not feel as though there could be anyone else for him. Still, after a while, the loneliness came to be too much. It felt good to be around people with open smiles and energy. It felt nice to be held by someone, however fleeting the experience.

Robert has known from the start that Ebby would be here for only three months. But then she talked about, maybe, staying on, and for one entire day, Robert had begun to imagine it. He hadn't told Ebby about his wife, but Ebby had a way of listening closely when he spoke that left him feeling he could do so. He was thinking to suggest a day trip together. Until he walked by Ebby's cottage to pick her up for their evening out and saw her standing in the kitchen with a man. A man who clearly knew her very well. And Robert is surprised by how bad that feels. He hasn't felt this strong a pull toward a woman since his wife.

# Ebby and Henry

———

EBBY HATES TO THINK HOW MUCH SHE LIKED HEARING THOSE words.

*I never stopped loving you.*

Hearing Henry say this, a minute ago, made her feel that, maybe, she hadn't wasted her time with him. Not altogether. But Henry, his face open and questioning now, mustn't know this. No good would come of it. She lets the air out of her chest slowly, feeling it whisper through her nose, incredulous that she needs to spell things out for him. Does Henry really believe that he is less accountable than another person would be in his position? Why is it that some people in this world feel so little responsibility toward others? How is it that the man she loved turned out to be one of those?

"Is there any chance, Ebby?" Henry says.

"Is there any chance?" Ebby says. "You mean any chance to go back to a time when you did not have the decency to come see me—to call me, even—to say that you were leaving me alone, and pregnant, on what was supposed to be our wedding day?" Ebby says. "Now, why would I want to go back to that, Henry?"

Henry looks at her in silence, as if unable to understand her words. As if they are speaking two different languages. Ebby wonders, has she misinterpreted something? Was Henry asking to get back together, or only asking her to forgive him?

"Pregnant?" Henry says finally.

*Oh.* Did Ebby say that? She didn't mean to say that. Ebby has never meant to say it to anyone.

Had Avery still been outside, watching them through the window, instead of packing up her toothbrush and toiletries and shoving the last of her belongings into her luggage, she would have seen Henry take a step toward Ebby. She would have seen him stop, then back up, then drop into a chair. Avery would have seen Ebby walk over to the sofa. She would have seen Ebby talking, tears streaming down her face, legs folded under her, while Henry put his elbows on the kitchen table and buried his face in his hands.

She might have seen everything that happened afterward.

# Despite All

DESPITE ALL, EBBY STILL YEARNS FOR THE HENRY SHE WAS supposed to have married. Ebby understands that this man before her now is not that Henry. This is the Henry she is better off without. The one Hannah says she was fortunate not to have married. Ebby is sure that this Henry is a man she could never again kiss, never again hold. But as she sits on the sofa, watching her tears wet her hands where they rest in her lap, she tells him anyway. She tells Henry about the pregnancy, about the miscarriage, about never having said a word to anyone. She tells him everything, the way she used to.

Henry makes a grunting noise. When Ebby looks up, she sees that Henry is crying. Actually weeping into his hands. Shaking his head back and forth. *Really, Henry?* Tears? And where was he when she needed him? She feels the full force of the grief and humiliation wrapped up in her history with Henry coming back to her. And the anger. This is the emotion that surges through Ebby's limbs, now, pulls her to her feet. Henry, too, stands up and turns toward her. She sees the look on his face but it only makes her angrier. Ebby rushes at Henry, pushing him back.

"You fool," she says.

"I know, I know," Henry says.

"You fucking idiot."

"I know, Ebby, I'm sorry."

Ebby is screaming now. "You ruined us!" She pushes Henry again and he drops to his knees, covering his head as she keeps pushing at him. He wraps his arms around her knees but she kicks him away. "How could you?" She stalks over to the kitchen door and pulls it open. Stands there, chin held high, not looking at Henry. Waiting for him to walk through the door. Henry approaches slowly, but instead of walking out, he puts a hand over hers. Gently. A glimmer of the old Henry. Ebby feels her legs trembling. Henry pushes at Ebby's hand until the door is closed again.

"Don't," she says, walking away. "Don't. Just go." But she says it softly. And when Henry turns her around, she doesn't fight. She knows that this is what she wants. She thinks, for a moment, that she should feel ashamed of giving in to a man who has treated her the way Henry has. But it is only a moment. Henry is kissing Ebby's face, now. His hands are on her shoulders, on her thighs. Ebby doesn't even know how they end up in the bedroom, only that when they lie on the bed, they lie down together.

Ebby sees the Henry she knows in this man's eyes. He is gentle, now, as he tugs at her tank top. Asking with a tip of his head, not insisting. He would stop, now, if she were to tell him to, but she does not want him to stop. She wants to know that she did not imagine *this* Henry. She has missed him. She wants to believe what he's told her, that it was not so easy, after all, for him to walk away from her. He is more urgent, now, and she is there with him. She is still wearing her skirt, pushed all the way up, when she lifts that part of her body to meet his. And he is still wearing his T-shirt. It used to happen this way, sometimes, between them. They used to laugh about that.

This feels like love.

Henry, next to her, in bed.

This feels like belonging.

Henry's scent on her skin.

But love without trust is something less than that.

Henry, like this, is less than what she wants.

Afterward, Ebby lets him kiss her and nuzzle her until she can take it no longer. Until she feels strong enough to push him away. She sits up and shrugs her body back into her top and juts her chin toward his pants, discarded at the edge of the bed.

"Wait? What?" Henry says.

"I think it's time for you to go."

"But I thought . . ." Henry says.

"I know."

"Couldn't we, could we just . . ."

"Just what, Henry? Pretend you fought for our relationship? Pretend you didn't want something easier? That, faced with a choice, you didn't choose me?"

"I wanted you. I never stopped."

"You may have wanted me, but you didn't care enough about me to keep me from going through what I had to go through on my own."

"I've already explained to you, I was trying to protect you."

"You were running from confrontation, Henry. You were more interested in protecting your own interests."

"It's not that simple, and you know it."

"Oh?"

"What was all this about, then?"

"*All this* is about what we used to be, Henry. Not what we are now."

"After everything that has just happened, you can't find a way to forgive me?"

"This is not about forgiveness, Henry. It's about trust. It's about me not being able to forget."

"But, Ebby, I thought you still loved me."

"Everything I've loved about you, Henry, everything I've admired about you, hasn't really changed. But the rest is the rest, and it makes a difference. It makes me really sad to see that you don't get that. You just finished telling me that you had all these doubts about staying with me."

"That was before."

"Before what, Henry? Before you brought Avery to France for a romantic vacation?" She reaches one arm out, pointing in the direction of the guesthouse.

Ebby shakes her head. This time, she is not shouting at Henry. This time, she is not crying. She feels strangely tender toward Henry. She has seen Henry shed tears for the first time since knowing him. She believes he, too, is mourning the baby they never had. She has felt his desire to be with her and his willingness to be vulnerable to her anger. She has heard him, in effect, ask for another chance with her. But this man, who has just made love to her, is still the man who failed her in too big a way for her to get past it.

This time, Ebby feels truly ready to see Henry leave. When he does, she locks the kitchen door, goes back into the bedroom, and changes the sheets.

# Ebby

———

EBBY FEELS LIKE A BIT OF A CRIMINAL, STANDING IN THE HOUSE with the lights out, eavesdropping on Henry and Avery. Not that she intended to do so. The door to the guest cottage is wide open and she can't help but hear them raise their voices. She feels embarrassed, thinking that Avery, too, might have been able to hear Henry and Ebby. Things grow very quiet for a while. Then she hears a stomping of shoes. A wheelie bag on the gravel. Avery, out in the yard, and Henry following her through the door. The Rover, pulling away. It is well past midnight. She looks out the window and sees Avery at the steering wheel, lit up in the glow of the vehicle's interior light, and Henry, standing in the yard, watching.

Henry looks toward the main house and Ebby ducks away from the window. Ebby feels bad for Avery. But Ebby and Henry came before Avery, and Ebby and Henry had unfinished business. Still, Avery has left in the middle of the night. What will she do? Beyond every expectation, Ebby finds herself smiling.

*Of course,* Ebby thinks.

Everything that Ebby has observed about Avery, up to this point, tells her that Avery would not drive off in the middle of the night, just like that, without a plan. Knowing Avery, she will have booked a place to stay already. While Ebby and Henry were arguing, while Ebby and Henry were making love for the last time, Avery will have been swiping at her tablet, booking something, somewhere. Avery might be upset, but she will not be out of control. Avery does not come across as the kind of person who does *out of control*. Avery will be all right.

Henry is still standing at the door of the guesthouse, looking in the direction of the main building. Ebby dreads the thought that he might come back across the yard, but within minutes, he has closed the door and switched off the lights. Ebby puts on her headphones, finds some music, and pulls the bedcovers over her head. Tonight, she does not dream of the jar falling. She does not dream of Henry. She dreams of love stories that stand the test of time.

# Finding Aquinnah

———

Because the love between a daughter of their tribe and an African slave was not a desirable thing, they drove the man off their land. He was no longer a slave, by then. They had bought the African, along with other goods, from his European enslaver, then freed him to work among their people, as was their way.

They believed that the risk of being captured and enslaved again would help to keep the African loyal to their tribe and useful to their territory. He was a skilled worker. He built canoes and all manner of things from wood. And he was a strong young man in a tribe where so many of their own had been killed. Later, they would see that it had been inevitable, the visceral pull between the stolen son of a faraway king and the daughter of their chief.

When, in 1829, the chief's daughter saw her father cast out the man whose child she was already carrying, she chose to follow the thrown-away man north into that fearsome world beyond the community where she had always lived. She knew that she would never return. She understood that she might not survive. But the kindness of strangers would give her hope.

A farmer with skin the color of oak found the young couple hiding in his barn. They were muddied and shivering and clinging to the side of a cow for warmth, looking more like a bundle of cloths than two people.

"What is this?" the farmer called. He watched the gathering of rags pull closer to the beast, as if to hide among its teats.

The farmer was a rarity in those parts, a country-born former slave who had purchased his own freedom, then acquired the land on which he now worked.

"You cannot stay here," he told the couple. But he gave them a cup of broth and bread and sent them on their way with a sack of provisions, a glass bottle filled with cow's milk, and a list of instructions to help them reach safety.

"Don't go that way," he said, pointing to the northwest. "Never go that way. Go toward the coast but stay inland." He handed them a small piece of wood with an *X* burned into it and told them where to stop next. There would be a wagonmaker who could help. There would be another man with a canoe. All they had to do was show the right people that piece of wood. The wrong people would think nothing of it.

The more dangerous things became, the more generous they found people to be. They hadn't realized that there were so many free men and women, including the pale ones, who were inclined to help. The world beyond the confines of the woman's tribe was confusing. But it was a world where she and her man might be able to raise their child.

They did not speak of their past, though anyone could see they'd been running. The daughter of the tribe refused to say the name of her people, but the couple found another tribe up north whose elders understood where she had come from. Some of their ways were similar to hers, though not all. Still, they welcomed the young foreigners into their community, as was their way.

Massachusetts was frigid. The smell of the sea a shock. They found themselves seeking outside work in a raucous place with streets of stone filled with odors of brine, whale oil, and horse manure. But there was work to be found at the docks and in the stables and workshops. The husband made the acquaintance of men who looked like him but who hailed from Cape Verde or Barbados or England, while the wife sewed sacks and other materials, eventually growing skilled in the making of sails.

One day, a large sailing ship approached the shore after more than twenty months away. It was ragged, but laden with oil and wax and baleen from the whales that the crew had slaughtered. One sperm whale, one blue, and two bottlenose. A foul-smelling, but essential, cargo. The seafaring men, their faces creased and caked from exposure to the elements, told stories of the enormous creatures they had fought and conquered. But three of their mates had been lost. The young couple did not want that life for their children.

In time, the wife and husband would purchase a plot of land farther inland, though they would keep their ties to the port. They would teach their children to make sails and pots and tools of use to the men who traveled at sea. They would take their wagon to the coast when necessary. They needed to remain flexible. They had found a place with good dirt, but they could not be sure of holding on to it.

But first, the daughter of the tribe gave birth to a baby girl in the ancestral lands of another people, just as her father and the rest of her family were being forced off their own land. They were made to leave the place where her people had been rooted and cross the great river, along with many others, toward a vast territory where, legend had it, the winds could rise up like monstrous spirits and suck entire wagons into the air. Her mother and one of her sisters would die along the way, but she would never know this.

All over America, the winds of change were rising up like those dust monsters and sweeping through people's lives. But the runaway couple's children would manage to remain where they were born, in a place that, years later, would come to be known as Refuge County. One day, their firstborn daughter, now a young woman, would meet a sailor who was running from his past, much as her parents had escaped theirs. He would stop at the workstation where she sat stitching sailcloth and look at her like a thirsty man drawn to water.

His name was Edward Freeman, he told her. But once they were married and living within the walls of the cabin where she had grown up, he would tell her to call him Willis. And he would call her Aquinnah. It was a favored name with the tribe that had sheltered her parents. Willis liked the sound of her name, but sometimes, he would simply call Aquinnah *wife,* because the idea of having found a woman who had chosen to make a family with him pleased him so.

# Messages

———

WILLIS DIDN'T WANT TO HAVE TO RUN AGAIN.

After landing in Massachusetts, he went to sea three more times, reveling in the cut of the air against his skin and that feeling that looking off the deck of a schooner could leave in his heart, a sense that the world was much larger than the one in which he had been forced to grow up. But the work at sea was dwindling, and it was mostly the whaling that was open to Negro men. Willis needed work, but he knew he wasn't cut out for the hunt. He believed he might perish if he boarded another whaler.

Fortunately, Willis's growing attachment to his wife and the arrival of their first child made it easier for him to stay on land, in the house that Aquinnah's parents had built. Aquinnah stitched clothing instead of sails and helped her parents with their farming. Willis used his skills as a carpenter and worked with a local wheelwright, but soon he started his own enterprise doing fancy painting around town. He put designs on signs and wagons and buildings and such, and it brought him great satisfaction to know that the same compulsion to draw that once led Willis to be whipped as a child now provided a source of income.

It had started quite by accident. Willis had taken to decorating the front entrance to their home, covering the space between one step and the other with flowers, then moving on to the balustrades and porch railing. He painted the flowers he'd seen in the meadows nearby. The pink-petaled mayflower, the bright yellow trout lily, the raucous violet of the hepatica. The house he shared with Aquinnah and her parents was not the type of abode that would normally cause a person to stop and look, but stop they did as Willis continued to paint whatever he could.

"That's a very interesting design you have there on your wagon," Reverend Arundel said one Sunday as members of his congregation stepped out of the church and gathered around. Rather than decorate his cart with flowers, Willis had gone back to his earlier inspiration of seafaring themes. His lowly one-horse cart bore a seascape with a sailing bark on frothy seas. Willis had painted the vessels heading toward the shore, with the city shown in the background. His designs grew in popularity and became quite lucrative.

But Willis was still Willis, even though he went by the name of Edward Freeman in public. The ships that came north from the Carolinas and Washington, D.C., were bringing worrisome stories of a new law aimed at people like him who had escaped slavery. There was muttering all around about people in free states being taken away in greater numbers, and then confirmation of a worsening situation came by way of his stoneware jar.

By then, the jar made by Moses, standing on the floor just inside the Freemans' kitchen, had become known as a safe place to leave notes and other items that would not be seen except by those who knew to go looking. Sometimes, the missives came by way of regular visitors. At other times, a stranger would come to the stoop at their front door and ask for a cup of water. That was the code. Aquinnah would push the jar with her foot and use it to hold open the door. Then she would turn her back while fetching a cup of water or coffee and a bit of bread. Once the visitor was gone, Aquinnah would reach her hand into the jar to see what had been left behind.

The riskiest delivery had been a letter from an enslaved woman in the South to her freed husband, but most missives were disguised as everyday objects. A blue hair bead, a knife, a wooden toy, and the message that brought Willis to tears: a small plate with cobalt glaze on one side, inscribed with a large letter *F* and a tiny flower on its bottom. Willis recognized Moses's hand and understood it to be a greeting from the man who had once been married to his sister Flora. That night, he showed the plate to his wife and talked about Moses and Flora and Old Joe, and even Betsey. He laughed. And then he wept. Moses had found him.

But this meant that someone else with less loving intentions might do the same.

True, there were free men and women, both black and white, who were willing to help, as well as members of the native tribes. But the risk of separation from his family was greater than ever. A visit from Reverend Arundel confirmed this.

"Can I offer you a bit of sweet tea, Reverend?" Willis's wife said when the reverend stopped by one day unannounced, and without his wife.

"A cup of water would do just fine, thank you."

This was the sign. Aquinnah turned her back as she asked after the reverend's wife and children. Once he had finished his water and was gone, Aquinnah reached one arm down into the jar and pulled out a folded piece of paper. It was an announcement, of the kind posted in public places.

CAUTION! COLORED PEOPLE . . . it began.

Aquinnah read on. Police officers and watchmen in Boston had been empowered to take colored people into custody under the Fugitive Slave Act and were acting, in effect, as slave catchers. It could only get worse. Her eyes began to swim with tears. She steeled herself for her husband's departure. The best option was for Willis to leave for the Canadian border without his family. Aquinnah, who looked more like her mother's people than her father's, would stay behind, working and tending to their young son and her parents as though nothing had changed. If anyone came looking for Willis, she would say that he was away for work.

Later that week, they filled a sack with provisions and Willis planned a route. Before daylight the next morning, he pulled open the door of his home and looked out onto the shimmer of dew in the waning moonlight. Caught a whiff of calamint and clay. He turned back to look at his wife and her parents, then looked down at Moses's jar. He did not want to go, not now that he had found himself a family. He did not want to let go of what was in his heart, not again. He dropped his sack to the floor and sat down at the kitchen table.

"No, this is what we'll do," said Willis. They could afford to purchase more acreage, he said. Add a barn and study room among the trees to the west. If it came down to it, he could hide in one of the outbuildings or even run, but not now. Willis would earn his living from there. He could build wagons in addition to painting them. And in the winter he could make sleds. Yes, he told Aquinnah, he would stay, and they would have more children, and raise them together.

# Henry in the Morning

————

H ENRY IN THE MORNING IS AT HIS BEST. HENRY, WATCHING THE light shift. Wandering, looking, waiting. Clicking the shutter, again and again. But this morning, Henry is not on his usual walk. His camera sits unused on the dining table. Henry is sitting at the window of the guest cottage, looking for a sign that Ebby is awake. Maybe the kitchen door will open and Ebby will step outside. But there are no lights on in the house, no sign of activity. Henry has only a few more minutes. The driver will be here, any time now, to take him to the airport.

Of all the things that Henry has wondered about in the past ten months, about how Ebby was doing, about what Ebby was thinking, not one of those even came close to the idea that she might have been pregnant before the wedding. Even though a man had to assume this kind of thing could happen. *Basic biology, Henry.* But truly, it had never occurred to him that Ebby could be pregnant so soon.

Henry had wanted children with Ebby. Really, he had. Though, to be honest, he had wondered if it would be such a good idea for someone with Ebby's background. It was his mother who had raised the question.

"So you're thinking of children?" Henry's mother had said while buttering a scone.

"Well, sure," Henry said, smiling, but looking down. He felt shy talking about these things with his mom. Especially when he knew she wasn't wild about Ebby.

"You know Ebby's background," his mother said, now.

"Yes," he said. "I mean, well, what do you mean?"

"Meaning, women of color are more likely to suffer post-traumatic stress disorder," Henry's mom said.

"I think anyone would suffer PTSD, Mom, if their brother had been shot to death in their home."

"Exactly, but that hasn't happened to anyone else we know. Plus, I've seen studies."

"I think I know what you mean, Mom," said Henry. "Studies about the disproportionate burden of PTSD among women of color? Part of the reason for that is in this country, they don't have the same level of access to the proper care or support they need. There may be some social and economic situations going on. But bear in mind that these don't really apply to someone like Ebby."

"Someone like Ebby?"

"Well, Ebby's family isn't exactly destitute, you know that. The fact is, Ebby has had all the advantages."

"I don't know, it's not always about money," Henry's mom said.

"It's not always about color, either, Mother."

After that conversation, Henry's mother gave him the silent treatment for two weeks. Which was saying a lot, for her only son. For her only child. Henry knew that his mother was more than a little bent out of shape by the fact that Henry was marrying a black woman. He hated to admit it, but this was the simple truth. But his mom's comment had touched a nerve. Privileged or not, black or not, Ebby still exhibited the effects of her childhood trauma. Was this likely to cause problems if she became pregnant?

But all that is past, now, and Henry's last half hour has come and gone. He does a final check of the cottage, finds a lip thingy of Avery's near the foot of the bed, turns it over and over in his hands for a moment, holds it up to his nose, then tosses it in a trash basket. Ebby isn't coming outside, is she? Ebby is doing this on purpose, isn't she? Avoiding him until he leaves. Henry thought that last night, everything that happened, would have taken them forward somehow. After Ebby told him about the miscarriage and he told her about his worries over the jar, it seemed there wasn't anything they couldn't say to each other. There *wasn't* anything they didn't say.

There wasn't anything they didn't do.

But in the end, she asked him to leave anyway. She pushed the door shut behind him, turned the lock, and immediately switched off the light in the kitchen. Refused to reopen the door when he turned back and knocked. Called her name. He could hear her shut the bedroom door. Well, Henry thinks, a clearer message than that he isn't going to get. And it's not right to insist any more than he already has. What's important is that Ebby sees, now, how Henry feels. These things take time. There's still Connecticut. He'll find a way to make it up to her. And he's got a heck of a lot to take care of before he faces Ebby again.

Henry hears car wheels now, rolling over the gravel. It's the airport limo. It's time to leave Ebby behind.

# Ebby in the Morning

----

At dawn, Ebby hears a vehicle approaching and peeks through the blinds on her bedroom window. She sees a car with a driver pull into the parking area. Henry comes out with his luggage, stops, and looks toward the main cottage. Ebby pulls back from the window and hides behind the wall until she hears the car doors slamming. First the trunk, then two more doors. As the limo drives away, Ebby feels a great sense of relief. But also sadness.

Not long after, Ebby steps outside to tend to the flower beds and is shoving a trowel into the dirt when she notices a cardigan draped over a garden chair. She thought she left that cardigan at Robert's. She walks over to the garden chair and sits, holding the cardigan in her lap. Yes, she did leave this sweater at Robert's. She's sure of it. Robert must have been here.

*Oh, no,* she thinks. She was supposed to go out with Robert last night. She thought that Robert hadn't bothered to show up. But he must have come by when she and Henry were arguing. Did Robert see Henry in the house with Ebby? He must have. As had Avery, probably. But how much of what happened between Ebby and Henry did they see?

There is that feeling again. The feeling that Robert elicits in her. It matters to her what he thinks. She wants to see him. But how could she go to him now, after what has just happened between her and Henry? And only one day after she was last with Robert. No, no, no, she needs to be alone. She needs to regain some sense of control over her actions. She's already seen the consequences of letting Henry get close. *Dammit, Ebby.* She shouldn't have opened that kitchen door.

The following day, Ebby tries to keep the tone of her voice even when she talks to her parents. She still hasn't told them about seeing Henry. She is trying to forget what happened between her and Henry. What they said. What they did.

# Carpe Diem

——

AFTER A WEEK, EBBY STILL HASN'T SEEN ROBERT IN THE TOWN square. Or the café. Or the market. As each day goes by, Ebby is increasingly aware that she keeps hoping to catch sight of him. Back at the cottage, she pulls the cardigan off the coat-tree and holds it up to her face, searching for the scent of Robert's hands. Of the mint he grows in his garden. The yearning she feels draws her out to her car.

Ebby feels a bit like a stalker, driving around, looking for his house. She's been there twice and she still doesn't know the name of the street. She zips up to the high point of town to look across at the château, down at the network of streets, then back across the river. Maybe this is a sign that she should forget about Robert. So it didn't go well. How much was it reasonable to expect? Wait, she sees something familiar. Backs up the car. Turns down a side street. She reaches Robert's house just as he is walking out through his front door. He looks her way then turns to lock the door.

"Robert, I'm so sorry," Ebby says as she gets out of the car.

"Sorry about what?" he says, too politely.

"That I couldn't go out with you last week. My ex was here. It's a long story. Anyway, he wanted to talk."

Robert nods. Says nothing.

"I saw the cardigan," Ebby says now. "Thank you."

"So you came here to thank me?"

"And to apologize."

Robert's face is softening now. She recognizes that look. Feels a stirring below her belly button. Oh, she does like this man.

"I'm going to the café for some breakfast," Ebby says. "I thought, maybe, you might feel like joining me."

"I need to make breakfast for my *grand-père,*" Robert says. "The woman who takes care of him has an appointment this morning."

"Oh, okay," Ebby says. She nods and takes a couple of steps backward in the direction of her car.

"Do you want to meet him?" Robert says.

"Huh?"

"*Mon grand-père.* Do you want to go with me to see him?"

Ebby feels her face break into a grin.

If someone were to look through the ground-floor windows of the *manoir* where Robert's grandfather lives, they might see the following: Ebby, trailing *papy* around his living room as he points out framed photos, telling her who's who, while Robert pours coffee and collects milk, butter, and jam from the fridge. And if someone were to look through the living room window at Robert's cottage that evening, they might see small plates and wineglasses sitting on a long, low table. Nothing but olive pits left on the plates. They might see Ebby and Robert sitting close together on the sofa.

"I had no idea you were married," Ebby says. "When your grandpa showed me that photo, I had a moment of panic. I mean, we'd . . . you know. Then I noticed he was talking in the past tense. I'm so sorry."

Robert nods. Pulls Ebby close.

"She looks lovely."

"She was."

"But you didn't say anything."

"We've only seen each other a couple of other times. What should I have said? *Bonjour, my name is Robert and I am a widower?*"

Robert chuckles and Ebby smiles. When a man who has lost his young wife is speaking with a woman who lost her brother as a child, they can be this way with each other. Only, Robert doesn't know about Ebby's past.

"Your wife . . ."

"Mireille," Robert says.

"*Mee-RAY?* Is that right? Yes? Was she from here, too?"

"No, Paris. But she was living in the U.S. when I met her. We both went to university there. Then we came back to France together, to Bordeaux. It was a great city for young people, but not so far from *mes grands-parents*. We visited often. They were always happy to see us."

Robert falls silent. It is a silence that Ebby understands. Certain memories cannot be put into words. Ebby leans her head against Robert's shoulder and they sit that way for a while.

"The doctors say she may have been sick for some time before we realized," Robert says. "She was twenty-eight when she died."

Ebby swallows hard. She knows what she must do. Because she knows what it is like to lose someone. To miss someone. She must ask him more.

"Was Mireille a translator, like you?" Ebby asks. She feels Robert breathe in, his chest rising against her face. He releases one of his arms from around her and reaches down to take her hand, rubbing his fingers over hers.

"No, she worked in software," Robert says. "And Bordeaux was a very good place for that."

"So you liked it there?"

"Oh, yes," Robert says, smiling. "Good energy."

"Would you ever go back?"

"Two years ago, I would have said no, but maybe I would. It's just that, well, things change. Right now, I am here for my grandfather. And my mother will come out in the winter."

They sit again in silence, until Robert pushes her back from his chest and looks at her.

"What about this ex-boyfriend of yours?"

"It's complicated."

"Do you still love him?" Robert says, his voice so low, now, it is almost a whisper.

Ebby sits up and looks at Robert. She wants to say *no*. Instead, she tells him what happened the previous year.

"What a jerk," Robert says.

Then Ebby tells Robert what happened in the year 2000 and how that affected her relationship with Henry, with Connecticut, with everything. She tells him as little as possible but the revelation strikes them both silent. Then Robert pulls Ebby's face to his chest and kisses her hair, then her forehead, then her nose.

"Why are you making excuses for that man?"

"I'm not making excuses, I'm just saying . . ."

"Saying what? He was very unkind to you. I don't like that man."

"Oh, I think you're just jealous," Ebby says, teasing.

"Yes, I am very jealous," Robert says, nuzzling her neck until she laughs.

# Escalators

———

AVERY IS BACK IN PARIS AND RIDING THE ESCALATOR UP FROM the ground level of the Musée d'Orsay. She is typing into her iPad. *Former Beaux-Arts railway station renovated and converted . . .* She looks up at the beams that crisscross the barrel-vaulted interior. She wonders how many old buildings in this city have been reimagined for completely new purposes. It can be more difficult and costly to rework a historic structure than to tear it down completely and start all over. But the results are like nothing else. It is somewhere between the ground floor and the upper level that Avery understands she needs a personal renovation. She needs to reimagine her own life. She is not getting on that plane tomorrow. She is not going back to Connecticut. Not yet.

———

HENRY IS HALFWAY UP the escalator on his way to passport control at JFK when he realizes two things. He's glad to be home, glad for the familiar, and yet not. Nothing is quite the same. By the time he steps off the escalator he already knows what he must do as soon as he gets back to his apartment. There's an artists' residency he's heard of. It's a program where aspiring and practicing artists go to concentrate on their work. Henry has a project in mind for his photography. He thinks he may have a shot at getting in. He could take a leave of absence from his job. He'll find a way. But first, he needs to do something else.

———

EBBY HAS GONE BACK to the coast on her own. She is somewhere between the bathrooms on the upper level and the first step on the

down escalator when she makes a decision. Looking down at the Atlantic Ocean, she watches the waves come and go, and wonders how
long it takes for water here to make it all the way across to North
America. She thinks about waves coming and going and feels her body
being pulled toward the water. And she understands that she needs to
go back to Connecticut. She needs to go see her parents. She needs to
talk to them.

But not yet.

# Hesitation

———

EBBY KEEPS PUTTING OFF LEAVING FRANCE. SHE REALIZES THAT much of her hesitation is linked to Robert. To the way he is with her. To the way he treats his grandpa, even. But it's more than that. She likes waking up in the morning in this cottage by the river. And she'd rather wait for Hannah to come back. She'd hate to miss the trips they'd planned to take together. But if she doesn't leave France now, she will have to call her parents and tell them that Henry was here, before they get wind of it from somewhere else.

Three weeks have gone by, already, since Henry left. Ebby picks up her phone and scrolls through to her mother's number, then remembers that it's still the middle of the night in Connecticut. There is nothing that Ebby can do right now anyway.

So she sits down to write.

# Refuge County

————

WILLIS DIDN'T LIKE THE IDEA AT ALL. HIS SONS WERE HEADING west to the treacherous whaling grounds of the Pacific. And he feared for them. If they went north, their bark could be trapped in the Arctic ice. If they went west into the ocean, they would be perilously far from land. But his boys were men now, and they had made their choice.

Everything was supposed to have been better following the Civil War, but this thing they called *the economy* was toppling over like the mast of a ship fractured by a gale. Later, the experts who spent their time making proclamations on such matters would say the great fire in Boston, preceded by another in Chicago, had contributed to the dramatic situation. And there had been that terrible horse disease. It had hobbled transportation and brought orders for the Freeman wagons to a halt.

There was so much competition for work. Skilled colored craftsmen and workers were facing racial quotas, exclusion from craft unions, and other forms of discrimination. Massachusetts men were competing for work with new black migrants from the South and white newcomers from abroad. Feeling they had no other options, Willis's boys decided to leave for San Francisco.

Willis, too, had done whatever he could to make do in his day. But he had sought every alternative to the whale hunting that he could. One run had been enough for him, and he had managed to stay clear of the whaleboats, that one time, remaining instead on the ship. There had been much work to do on deck. The repairing of harpoons and sails, the dreaded handling of the whale carcasses after a hunt. One sailor had lost his life, another his leg. When he could, Willis drew what he had seen, but he later learned that he could sell his artwork if it showed more of the triumph of the whaler and less of the grit and terror.

He'd heard stories, too, about what could happen to a colored man while traveling across the country. Harassment and violence. It felt as though things were getting worse than before. After the boys left, Willis and his wife fell into a silence that lasted for days. Then, one day, she called to Willis.

"Look," she said.

It had just occurred to Aquinnah to look inside the stoneware jar, which had continued to occupy a space near the kitchen door all these years. She had reached into the jar and pulled out a new piece of paper. Their sons had left them a note, which she showed to Willis now.

"Our Dearest Father and Mother," Willis read. "We pray, keep watch over one another and trust in the guidance of the North Star to bring us home to you before long. Your faithful sons, Edward Moses and Basil." He nodded at Aquinnah. She read it to herself again, moving her lips silently, then folded the note and put it back in the jar, weighing it down with the small piece of wood marked with an *X* that had helped her parents to freedom.

Aquinnah remained crouched by the jar, one hand resting on the trail of leaves painted by her husband all those years ago. Neither of them could have foreseen exactly how the jar would take on new layers of significance in their lives, but Willis had understood from the start that it would be part of their family. And that piece of wood was now part of the jar's story. She and Willis linked arms and stood together at the open door, turning their gaze to the west, as they would every morning and every evening, training their thoughts on their sons.

# Reckoning

—

EBBY DOESN'T KNOW WHAT THIS THING IS BETWEEN ROBERT and her, only that life feels good when she's with him and she wants to keep it that way. But her growing feelings for Robert have been pushing her toward a reckoning. Who is it, exactly, that she wants Robert to care for?

For some time now, Ebby has told herself that therapists can do nothing more for her. But she can't keep leaning on Hannah when things weigh her down. Or waking up in the middle of the night, the bedclothes damp with her perspiration. And she doesn't want this to ruin things with Robert. Ebby is getting tired of being this way. Something has to change.

Ebby opens the Web browser and writes *France* and *expat services* in the search window.

*We are beginning our third year as a happy expat family!* shouts one blog. There are photos of wine and cheese and bicycle trips against flowery, sun-dappled backdrops. There's an article about why people become expats. For work. For love. To study. Another feature profiles someone who came to France to visit their ancestral village and stayed. That sort of thing. Nothing about people like Ebby. No one she's read about admits to wanting to hide out. No one talks about the challenges of finding an English-speaking therapist.

Articles about being an expat always had a cheery, glossy kind of feel to them, even when talking about the downsides of moving far away from home. Being an expat felt like a high-end or privileged thing, even when it wasn't. Being an expat had nothing to do with being a migrant or refugee. Being an expat had nothing to do with the reasons that landed Ebby's ancestors in New England. Being an expat had nothing to do with what Ebby needed in her life.

Or did it?

Ebby types in *France English-speaking psychotherapist* and watches as a number of responses to her search terms pop up on the screen.

Bingo. Simpler than she'd thought.

She picks up the phone and makes an appointment. Now that Ebby has a plan, she feels ready to call her mom. She's ready to tell her parents about Henry.

"Hi, Mom."

"Hello, Ebony. I was just about to call you."

*Uh-oh.* Her mom only calls her Ebony when she's in trouble.

"Oh, yes?" she says slowly.

"Is there something that you forgot to tell us?" her mother says. "Something about Henry Pepper?"

*Oh, shit.*

"Oh, Mom. Oh, no," Ebby says. How did her mother find out? "I'm sorry, Mom. I was going to tell you."

"Well, there's no need to tell us anything now, Ebony, because Henry Pepper was here."

"Henry? Henry went to see you? I didn't know he was going to do that." *Why did he do that?*

"But you *did* know that he was in France, and you didn't tell us."

"Mom, really, I'm sorry."

"We've already established that."

Ebby hates it when her mom uses her attorney voice.

"It's like, I didn't want to believe it. It was so strange. That he was here, at all. And with another woman. Though she was nice enough." Ebby stops for a moment. What a strange thing to say. But it's true. Avery was a nice person. "It just seemed like some kind of a bad dream. I didn't want to talk about it, I just wanted it to be over."

"Well, Henry has told us everything."

"Everything?" Ebby has a moment of panic. Did Henry tell her parents they went to bed together? No, that couldn't be.

"Henry has told us about the jar. About Harris."

"Harris?"

"Your father's old college buddy. The insurance exec. He's also a childhood friend of Henry's father's, and he's the one Henry overheard talking about the jar. He's the reason Henry was so upset."

Her father knows that man?

"If Henry had come to your dad ten months ago," her mother says, "he could have cleared up everything and saved us all a lot of trouble." Ebby's mother proceeds to explain. "I didn't know this, but way back when, your dad asked Harris for his opinion on our home insurance."

"This is very confusing, Mom."

"I know, Ebby. All you need to know is that Harris knew about the jar being broken because your father had told him. But Henry did not know any of this. When Henry finally talked to Harris, he sent Henry over to our place. Well, you can imagine how that conversation went."

"Oh, Mom!"

"Actually, I felt kind of sorry for Henry after that." Ebby's mother laughs and Ebby joins in, but she can't shake the current of nervousness that has been running through her body since her mother first mentioned Henry.

"Seriously, though, what a mess. Are you okay, Mom?" she says. "Do you need me to come home? I was already looking into earlier flights. Is Dad there?"

"That's another thing. Your dad is gone."

"Gone? Where?"

"He said he needed to get away. He needed time to think." Ebby hears her mother's voice crack. "Things have been a little rough between your dad and me, lately."

"Oh, Mommy."

"He's been brooding for a while."

"Dad? Brooding?"

"Yes, your dad broods sometimes. He doesn't let you see it, but he does. He's always blamed himself for your brother's death."

"Dad? But why?"

"He doesn't talk about it much, but soon after Baz was killed, your father said that maybe it was his fault for insisting that we move to Connecticut, all those years ago. That maybe we wouldn't have stood out so much in a different community, with more black folks around.

That maybe no one would have thought to break into the house. Then Henry showed up and it just dredged up all sorts of stuff. Your dad and I had words after Henry left. Then, when I was in the shower the next morning, he just drove off."

"Oh, Mom."

"Well, Granny Freeman called to say he was up there with her and Gramps."

Ebby can't help but smile. She can just imagine Granny giving Dad a piece of her mind and insisting on calling Ebby's mom.

"Okay, Mom, I can come home early," Ebby says, though she's just not sure she's ready for that. She wants to see that therapist she's found, at least a few times. And she'll need to talk to Robert.

"Well, at this point," her mother says, "you might as well take your time getting back. You went all that way for a reason." Ebby is surprised at her mother's reaction. She pumps a fist in the air and mouths the word *Yes!*

# Words

—

WORDS HAVE POWER. SO DOES THE ABSENCE OF WORDS. SOME-
times, when people choose not to speak, their silence can block out the
sun. Take, for instance, Henry Pepper, who has caused more hurt than
he'd intended because he'd thought it would be worse to speak up than
not. Worse to point a questioning finger at someone close to his father
than to get to the bottom of an uncomfortable question.

When Henry returned to Connecticut, he decided to speak with
his father about what had set him off the previous year, on the eve of
his wedding to Ebby. His father found Henry's concerns about what
had happened to the Freemans' jar to be so preposterous that he refused
to talk about them. So Henry, now veering into what felt like reckless-
ness, went directly to the source, his father's friend Harris. But unlike
Henry's dad, Harris wasn't bothered at all.

"Shit, me and my big mouth," Harris said. "I wasn't thinking. I can
see why you would have been concerned, Henry. I knew about the jar
because Ed Freeman told me about it. He needed some advice. We go
way back, you know that."

Henry shook his head and frowned.

"Sure you do. We're old college buddies. Studied math together.
Then we reconnected in Connecticut. Anyway, the whole jar business
really isn't mine to discuss. I shouldn't have made that comment that
afternoon. Does Ed Freeman know you're here?"

"Ebby's father?" Henry said. "I haven't seen him, you know, not
since the whole wedding mess."

"Yup, I figured. I've known you since you were yea high, Henry. I
think it's time you got your butt over there."

"I don't think that's up to me, Harris. I don't think Ed Freeman is going to want to see me."

"This is exactly what I'm talking about, Henry. This isn't about what Ed Freeman wants. This is about what you should be doing. This is about you and how, for whatever reason, you were willing to let go of your fiancée there. You are the one who chose to handle things the way you did. Your dad would be pissed if he heard me saying this, but your parents let you get away with this. You think you can just pull a stunt like that wedding-day thing and still get to stay in your comfort zone?"

Henry looks away.

"Okay, lots of people do, I'll give you that. But come on, Henry. You're better than that."

At this point, Harris, taller and larger than Henry by quite a bit, stood up.

"You should have asked me, right then and there. And even if you didn't, you should have gone and talked to that girl. Told her everything, or anything at all. Whatever. Even if there was other shit going on. Even if you had other reasons for ditching the wedding, you should've talked to her. How did you not see that?"

After speaking with Harris, Henry sat outside in his car, thinking. Then he pulled out of Harris's driveway and drove over to the Freemans' place, where Soh Freeman, looking out a window, saw him pull up to the house. Before Henry could get to the front door, Soh stepped outside. Just as Henry was thinking how relieved he was that he wouldn't have to knock, Soh walked straight over to him and slapped him in the face.

# Henry

———

HENRY DRIVES AWAY FROM THE FREEMANS' HOUSE FEELING BET-
ter, if not about himself then about the fact that he had, finally, gone
to see them. After Soh Freeman slapped his face and said, *How dare you,*
*Henry Pepper,* Ed Freeman came downstairs, the expression on his face
tight. For a moment, Henry thought Ed was going to hit him, too.
Instead, he stood there, looking at Henry in a way that made Henry
wish Ed had hit him after all. Ed and Soh glared at Henry until he realized they were waiting for him to explain himself.

So Henry talked. He told them everything. About what he thought
he'd overheard the week he'd been scheduled to marry Ebby. About
being afraid of Ebby's reaction and potentially defaming a close friend
of his father's. He admitted, even, his doubts about being up to the
challenges of living with someone who still exhibited signs of trauma,
as Ebby had. He could tell from their expressions that they hadn't realized that Ebby still suffered so often from nightmares. How she was
always tired. He saw how Ebby's mother looked when he said that. He
felt awful.

"I want you to know I'm really sorry," Henry said. "I was a shit,
there's no way around it."

To their credit, the Freemans continued to listen. And then it was
Henry's turn to listen to them. To understand that sometimes you can
save yourself a lot of trouble by daring to have a difficult conversation.
How would their lives have been different, Henry wondered, if he'd
only spoken up before? He watched Soh, one of those women who
was so lovely to look at that it was easy to believe that nothing truly
bad could ever happen to her. That straight back.

Henry looked at Ebby's parents, now, and marveled at how they had gone on after what had happened to their son. This was the true miracle of life, he thought. Not so much to be born as to bear up under what came your way. To find a way forward. To embrace what was good.

"So your mom is a top corporate lawyer," Henry had said the first time he'd gone to Ebby's apartment. He was nosing around, peering at photos of her family on the mantelpiece.

"Was," Ebby said. "Mom left her full-time work with the firm to take care of me after my brother was killed. But she still has clients."

"And your dad is a famous engineer."

Ebby nodded, but said, "Not so much famous as, well, valuable. People in his field know him, but if he weren't my father, I certainly wouldn't know anything about his work."

"But he's on the cover of that magazine," Henry said, pointing to a picture frame. "And that one, over there."

"Well, they profile him because his work is important. Or, more precisely, because his work has made him all that money."

"I'll admit I don't quite get what he does."

"Various things, but, mostly, he's known for joints."

"Joints?"

"Yeah. Look, for instance, at our bodies. They're held together by joints, right?" Ebby held out her arms and bent them back and forth at the elbows. "We are able to move, in part, because of joints. So those joints are used, and over time, they may wear out or suffer damage from an accident or illness. Well, my dad does a lot of thinking about how to make joints that function well and stay strong, even when they suffer trauma."

"For example?"

"For example, a bridge. You may think of a bridge as something that helps us to go from one place to another, right? Well, my dad can't look at a bridge without talking about how it's made up of a series of connections. And how those joints reduce trauma by moving back and forth under daily, monthly, and yearly pressure."

"So in a way, your dad specializes in trauma prevention."

"More like resilience under trauma. You can't prevent it, but you can find ways to hold up under the pressure, to continue to function well."

"So your dad's technology is what's famous."

"That, and the fact that he's a successful black engineer and people don't expect that. We are surrounded by black scientists and doctors and lawyers and other highly skilled professionals, but still, people are surprised. They continue to be surprised at African American achievement, even though it's all around us. Even though it's always been there, holding up society at every level."

Henry nodded.

"And then," Ebby continued, "when my brother was killed, you know, everyone started paying attention to my family. So my dad became more famous, only for the wrong reason."

"That's a real shame," Henry said. "I mean, I'm really sorry you lost your brother that way."

Ebby shook her head. "We didn't really lose him," she said.

"Sorry?"

"We didn't lose my brother. They took him from us. They *took* him."

Henry noted the bitter tone in Ebby's voice. He should have thought, then, about what it would mean to be with a woman who had gone through all that. But in that moment, he was only thinking that he needed to be with her, period. Plus, Ebby was right. She was absolutely right. Something had been stolen from the Freemans that they would never be able to get back. The family they should have had. Henry wondered, then, about the mechanics of the heart. The heart was a muscle, right? Did the heart, Henry wondered, have something like joints?

# Unhinged

WELL, THAT BOY DESERVED TO HAVE HIS FACE SLAPPED. AND THE sight of his wife doing the slapping made Ed bark with laughter. At first. Then, as Ed turned away from his bedroom window and started down the stairs, he found himself slipping back toward that dark corner he'd been inhabiting of late. Because the mirthful satisfaction produced by what he'd just seen gave way to the disturbing realization that his wife was not the type to slap someone, not even if that someone was a spoiled brat who had broken their daughter's heart in the most public of ways.

In short, it felt like Ed's wife was becoming unhinged. And that wasn't Soh's style, despite her worrying over Ebby. In the first months after Baz's death, amid the grief that seemed to fill every crevice in their lives, Ed and Soh had managed to move house, go back to work, and put their daughter in a new school. Soh later arranged for a leave of absence, which would later morph into her years as a stay-at-home mom and part-time attorney.

Ed and Soh had been, if nothing else, organized and disciplined in their grief. Determined to do what they could to protect Ebby and each other. To counteract the image that most people now had of their family life. The image that they themselves had, of a life that had been torn apart and appeared to be irreparable. Without discussing it, they'd both decided that if they could undo this impression, then reality might just follow.

They went through the motions, based on memory. And this rote behavior had its value. Sometimes, all a person had was a routine, or a series of rituals, to hold things together. Without structure in their lives, Ed, Soh, and Ebby would have been like crumpled pieces of paper being buffeted about by their emotions. Drifting here and there. Before Baz was killed, the four of them together had formed a unit, each one linked to the others. Without that fourth section, without Baz, they no longer knew the shape of themselves. Their old habits at least provided them with a kind of container until they could figure it out.

Soh was the first to move toward the new form that her life would have to take. She regained the impeccable appearance for which she had been known and made sure their daughter followed suit. She made Ebby study hard and go back to practicing the piano. In her daughter, she honed the unflappable air with which their family would become associated in public. For the most part, it worked. Except late at night, when their daughter's mask slipped away in her sleep and she revealed the full extent of her distress.

Still, Soh persisted. She seemed to have understood, sooner than Ed and Ebby, that their lives would never again be private. Whenever an article or a photograph of their family would pop up online, or appear in a printed newspaper or magazine, Soh would bat her hand in the air as if sweeping away a fly.

"Let's see, is this actionable?" the lawyer in Soh would ask. "Hmmm, hmmm, hmmm, hmmm," she would say as she read. "Nope," she would say most often, because usually such things were not worth going to court for. Whenever she did think it was worth a legal complaint, she wouldn't handle it herself.

"Oh, heather," Soh would say, instead of *oh, hell,* and get on the phone. "Heather, heather, heather." She'd long ago told Ed that one key to her mental health was letting someone else be the attorney on family issues.

In the early years after Baz's death, Ed would feel compelled to rip up offending news pages, stuff them in the trash, and take a walk down to the beach to stomp out his agitation. But over time, he, too, grew to ignore most of what he saw. Took to straightening his back when the paparazzi showed up. At events. At restaurants. At the botanical gardens. Ed was learning from Soh and her cool public demeanor. It was only when it came to any kind of separation from Ebby that Soh became wobbly.

Ebby was twenty-nine now. She'd been living on her own for several years, but, still, Soh could barely tolerate her absence. Where was Ebby going? What was Ebby doing? Should they do this for Ebby? Should they do that for Ebby? *Be careful, Ebby,* Soh was always saying. *Be careful.* And now, with Ebby in France, things with Soh felt like they had gotten out of hand. It wasn't that Ed didn't worry about his daughter. It wasn't that he didn't think, *Be careful, be careful.* It was that he tried not to say everything he was feeling. He didn't think a person could, constantly, voice that level of distress.

What if Ed were to say the half of what he was feeling?

Yes, seeing Soh slap Henry's face had unnerved Ed. But then Soh slipped back into her old groove. She tilted her head toward the side of the house and said to Henry, "Come." Henry followed her and Ed around to the back of the house and they sat down together on the deck. They let Henry fold his tall frame into an Adirondack chair and talk. They had little choice. Wouldn't look good to have a white man standing out in the front yard getting worked up the way he was doing now. There were some loud words. And Henry actually had tears in his eyes at one point. It couldn't undo what he had done to their daughter. But it was better to know the boy felt bad about it.

Somehow, it had escaped Henry's notice that Ed and Harris knew each other as well as they did. Around these parts, everyone's dad had been at school with someone else's father, so he might not have remembered, or even known. But not even Soh knew that Ed felt comfortable enough with Harris to have talked with him about the jar and the day on which Baz had been shot. They'd never really talked about that with anyone, except their own parents.

Ed felt better after the conversation with Henry, and Henry himself left the house looking relieved. Soh, on the other hand, did not look happy at all. After Henry left, she was very quiet. Ed knew they would have words, eventually. Ed had talked with Harris about the day of the shooting but he hadn't told Soh. Ed, who lately had refused to talk to a therapist or even his own wife much. But for the moment, Soh was focusing her energy in another direction. When she finally spoke, she said, "We need to go to France."

*Shit,* Ed thought. "No-no-no-no-no," he said.

"But you heard what Henry said. Ebby is still suffering from nightmares."

Ed was still shaking his head.

"She's been keeping this from us," Soh said. "She's been having a tougher time than we thought but she didn't feel she could talk to us."

"I know, but maybe she simply didn't want to talk to us, baby."

"You mean the way you haven't wanted to talk to me? So you talk to Harris instead?"

"I already explained to you. I was talking to Harris about our home insurance. It was right after Baz had been killed and it just came out, you know? We were talking about Baz and I told him about the jar being broken. Harris is my buddy. I'm allowed, aren't I?"

Ed looked down to avoid the expression he knew he'd see on his wife's face. He fought to keep his voice even, now, as he looked up again.

"Listen, Soh," he said. "About Ebby. She wanted to go away, don't you see? Maybe what she needs is the chance to figure things out for herself."

"What do you know about what people need?" Soh said. It was the way she said it that struck Ed silent.

The tone in his wife's voice.

After so many years.

A bitterness.

In that moment, Ed understood that Soh might blame him for the death of their son. Ed was the one who first spotted the FOR SALE sign on the house where, ten years later, Baz would be killed. It was the thought that Soh, the love of his life, might have these feelings that she had never voiced that led Ed to pack his overnight bag and put it back in the hallway closet while his wife was down in the kitchen. It was this thought that led him to drive away the next morning while Soh was still in the shower.

# Promises

E BBY HOLDS ROBERT TIGHT AND SPEAKS INTO HIS SHOULDER.

She explains.

How you can want to be with someone but feel you're not ready.

That you can still be tied to a previous someone, though you no longer want to be.

That recovery takes time.

That Ebby has something she needs to do first.

That, yes, she would consider coming back to France.

Back to him.

But no promises, please?

She needs to not make any promises.

She needs to not hear any promises.

She doesn't like people who make promises, then break them.

# Reentry

———

Ebby sits for a while in the car with Hannah.

"I'm really sorry we had to cancel our trip."

"That's all right," Hannah says. "And anyway, you're coming back, aren't you?"

Ebby shrugs, but smiles.

"Good. You owe me. But I know I'm not the one you're coming back for."

They laugh. Standing at the back of the car, they unload Ebby's luggage. Ebby hugs Hannah for a long time. Holding one of Hannah's hands, Ebby promises to text her as soon as she lands.

"Just keep my mother at bay until I text you, okay?"

"Don't worry, I can handle her."

Ebby laughs. "That's what you think."

But two months away have made a difference. After two months, even with the Henry mess, Ebby has found that her mother doesn't bother as much with the texting. After two months, Ebby is able to get away with fudging the truth. And after two months, Ebby can allow herself to take a few days for herself, even knowing that both her parents are distressed. The challenges they are facing right now aren't new. The challenges they are facing go back nearly two decades. And they're not likely to be gone soon.

Hi Mom, I'm all booked for next week, Ebby texts now. But I won't be on the phone much this week, she writes. Coastal trip. Bad signal, she adds. Hannah's at the cottage, if you need anything.

Two months away can make it easier to lie.

Ebby boards a flight to JFK in New York. She's already booked a hotel near the airport. Tomorrow, she will rent a car and drive all the way up to the Pittses' holiday home in Rhode Island. Ashleigh has given her the code to get in. It felt a bit awkward to call Ashleigh, but once she did, it was as if they'd never had a rough conversation. Sometimes, people let you down, but they're still your people.

In a boutique at the airport hotel, Ebby buys a hat with a wide brim. She hopes to be incognito. She needs to sleep near the water. She needs to get out and walk on the sand. She needs to breathe in the odor of life and decay. But she wants to do all this alone.

Ebby needs a soft reentry.

# Hide-and-Seek

―――――

Ebby WATCHES A COUPLE WALKING ALONG THE BEACH. JEANS cuffs rolled up. Zigzagging, laughing, holding hands. Young women who might be adolescents still. Nuzzling like puppies. One of them has dyed her hair a cerulean blue. That's a tough color to pull off on dark hair like her own, Ebby thinks. Maybe impossible? Still, Ebby makes a mental note. Cerulean. Like a rich daytime sky. Free of mist. Free of pollution. Full of possibility.

Ebby thinks of the Swiss chemist who developed the color from cobalt stannate. Playing with chemicals to re-create a natural atmospheric phenomenon. The irony of it. She chuckles to herself, but soon, she turns pensive. Ebby is thinking about how to talk to her parents. About her doubts, her fear, her guilt. About the fact that she has never told them everything about the day Baz was killed. How she'd been terrified to say how much she'd witnessed.

At the start of their game of hide-and-seek, Ebby had taken off her sandals and scurried along the floor, her bare feet clammy against the cool wood. Baz was still downstairs, but she knew that at any moment, he would stomp upstairs and start calling for her, checking closets, peeking under her parents' bed, because that year Ebby was still small enough to squeeze under there. But Ebby, though only ten, was old enough to figure out that she needed to do something different, something unexpected, to elude her brother's search for as long as possible.

Her father had been fond of saying that their entire family had been built on people who had done the surprising thing. People who had been underestimated. Well, Ebby was a Freeman, wasn't she? She was the daughter of a Bliss, too. Ebby had just reached the farthest point on

the upper floor, her parents' bedroom suite, when she decided to double back and go in the opposite direction.

Ebby went back toward the staircase to find a place just beyond that
to hide. Baz would underestimate her. Baz would walk right past her
hiding place and never think to look for her so soon. She smiled to
herself with satisfaction as she pulled open the upstairs broom closet.

Ebby didn't hear the front door of the house open. When you lived
in a house like theirs, it was entirely possible for people to enter and
exit the house without being heard from upstairs. It was possible for
people to be in the kitchen cooking or making noise with silverware
and plates at the dining table and not be heard from above. But there
was a funny point on the ground floor, in the hallway, near the entrance to the study, where the sound traveled up in just such a way that
you could hear every word. *Acoustics,* her dad had explained.

Acoustics.

This was the part that Ebby had been too afraid to tell the police or
her parents. That she'd heard a man talking in the hallway. He'd
sounded surprised. He'd said a bad word. Her mother would have said
*young man!* in a threatening tone if she'd ever heard Baz say such a thing.
Then Ebby heard a short, soft sound from Baz, not really a word. She
crept out of the closet and leaned over the banister to look down. She
had been thinking to run downstairs, but what she saw and heard made
her freeze.

"Where is it?" a man with a ski mask was saying. Ebby saw a gun,
and the gun was pointed at her brother's face as he walked backward
into the study with two men following him. *They were being robbed!*
Ebby knew what she should do, she should call Emergency, the way
her parents had taught her. She only had to run for the phone in her
parents' room. She was barefoot. They wouldn't hear her. She only had
to run. But Ebby was so scared she couldn't move. Not even Henry
knew this part. No one knew that on that day, the day her brother was
shot, Ebby froze instead of calling the police.

Then she heard the jar fall.

# Home

———

Ed is still trim enough to sit on the swing where he and his sister, Kandy, used to play. It dangles from an oak tree that has been in his family for as long as anyone can remember. He listens to the creak of the swing. Remembers his own kids playing here. He loves this yard. Loves his hometown. He drove here seeking relief from the doubts that have been tearing him apart. He was certain he would tell his parents he was ready to move back to Refuge County. But by the time he pulled into the driveway, he realized it still wasn't what he wanted.

Ed believes there is something at the core of each person that works like a compass. It should tell them who they are and where they belong. But compasses can malfunction, and lately, Ed has been feeling as though the directional needle in his head has gone awry. Of one thing he is sure: More than anything, Ed's home is with Soh. Only he's messed things up with his wife. He came to his parents' house without telling her first. Kept his phone turned off all the way up here.

Ed could have changed his mind while he was still on the Post Road. He could have told Soh he'd gone to the grocery store earlier than planned. They were supposed to be having friends over that evening. He even went so far as to stop and pick up a half dozen oranges, two bottles of wine, and a sack of barbecue briquettes.

After putting the groceries in the trunk, he sat in his car, engine idling where the parking lot met the street, thinking. But instead of turning left to head back home, Ed turned right and just kept on going. The next thing he knew, he was two towns over and heading up Route 9 along the Connecticut River. Later, he would see all the unanswered calls from Soh and think of Henry. Had it been this easy for Henry to drive away on the day he was supposed to marry Ebby? When, finally, Ed tried to call Soh that night, she wouldn't answer. She'd already talked to his mother.

And his mother has been giving him the side-eye ever since.

"These things happen," Ed's father said. "You stay as long as you need to work things out."

His mother said nothing. Her mouth looked tight.

His kids used to have fun playing in this garden. Both his folks and Soh's parents had yards far bigger than their own. But Ed was always certain nothing made Baz and Ebby happier than when he took them down to the water back in Connecticut. There was a gamy smell that used to come up from the beach as the tide went out. It was the smell of marine life exposed, and when the children were small, they would hover near the door like hungry young birds stretching their beaks out of a nest.

*All right,* Ed would say, *let's go clamming.*

*Yaaay!* the kids would cry, and skip down the garage steps to grab a bucket and a short rake or stick. The older the children got, though, the rarer those moments were. Moments when there was no tennis, no piano practice, no kiddie groups, no fundraisers, no working late. Nothing pressing enough to keep them from walking down the road and striding across the sand as the tide reached its low point.

Ed nods to himself as he thinks of his great-grandfather. He and his brother were seafarers in their youth, just like their father before him. But the truth is, by the time Ed was born, none of his ancestors had worked on board a ship for nearly a century, and places like Martha's Vineyard, Nantucket, and New Bedford were no longer dependent on whaling. For Ed's parents, being at the seashore was a purely recreational pursuit. But for Ed, it became essential.

Every summer, his parents would take the whole family over the water to Oak Bluffs, on Martha's Vineyard, which was especially popular with middle-class and well-off black families. There was a particular stretch of coastline that welcomed them at a time when black folks were discouraged from congregating at most beaches in New England. And Ed could not remember a time when his summers weren't marked by a longing to live on the coast permanently.

When Ed and Soh finally started looking at real estate in Connecticut, they found the search to be simple enough, as most homes were not being shown to African Americans, not even in 1989. Still, there were a few nice possibilities. Later, Soh would tell people she knew which house she wanted the moment Ed pulled the car to the curb. Ed thought that sort of thing happened only in the movies, but no. Soh gazed up at the five-bedroom, split-level home with gray siding and white shutters, and as they breathed in the scent of fallen pine needles mixing with the salt air, she nodded.

"Why there?" Ed's cousins would ask periodically. Like Ed's mother, they never did approve of his move to the overwhelmingly white coastal enclave, though he noticed his cousins weren't above driving down for a barbecue on a holiday weekend. Which was a good thing. Ed didn't want to lose touch with his family. His roots. He just wanted to live in that house near the beach.

His sister, who still lived in the same county as his folks, never said anything. Kandy would just show up once in a while and hook her arm in his while they walked along the sand. And for this rare quality of hers, this ability to refrain from adding her voice to the perennial debate, he cherished her all the more. She was the quiet one in the family, which likely meant she was the wisest one.

His mother had been more specific than his cousins in expressing her misgivings, even years after he and Soh had moved.

"I am not trying to live like a white man, Momma," Ed told his mother one day, during one of their more frustrating discussions. "I am living the life that I would like to live. As a black man. Which I have the right to live, by the way."

"No one is saying you don't have the right to make that choice," his mother said.

"Well, good, because I *choose* to be in that particular house, not too far from the trains, where I can walk down to the shore and sit on the rocks and put my feet in the water. This is fundamental for me. Is that too much to ask? Isn't this what you and Dad have always wanted for us? The freedom to live where we wish, and to make a living as we choose, no matter how people think African Americans should be living?"

"Now, Ed, you know your dad and I have wanted many things for you and your sister, and we have been blessed because you have had access to it all. But the thing we want most for you is your safety. If you move down there . . ."

"*Down there,* Momma? Less than two hours away?"

But you could not tell a mother who had raised black children in the sixties and seventies, not even in their prosperous, quiet corner of New England, that her children would always be safe. You could not grow up to be a black man, no matter how successful, without knowing, in some quadrant of your brain, that you were more vulnerable to potential harm than other men. You had to watch your back. You had to teach your son to watch his back.

Ed had seen this firsthand, even in his own county. This was the other reason he'd left when he had. The thing he would never tell his parents.

# The Road Home

———

## 1988

Ed was going seventy-five miles an hour and there was little to see but the headlights of his own car on the macadam. He eased off the gas pedal as he dropped down toward the Refuge County line and cracked open the window. He wanted to smell the night, the way it settled in at that hour. The air was cool, there was no traffic to speak of, and for just a few minutes, he felt as though the world was his alone. Until he saw the headlights of another car behind him grow very close, and very quickly.

The other car, a station wagon, switched to the fast lane and pulled parallel to his. The passenger rolled down his window and extended his right arm as far as it could go. A young man with blondish hair, holding something like a business card. Ed squinted and even smiled briefly as he tried to read it. *Crazy kid,* he thought. On the card, written in dark ink, were three large letters. Actually, now that they were coming into focus, Ed could see that they were the same letter, written three times. Ed didn't think that anyone really used those letters anymore in those parts, except in news reports or books about hate groups of the past. But there they were.

Ed was no longer smiling. He lifted his foot off the pedal, slowing his car significantly as the other vehicle sped up and flew into the darkness. The white men in the station wagon were barely adults, more like teenagers. Like the college sophomore, an engineering student, who'd been interning with Ed for two months. But that young man on the passenger side of the other car, holding the business card out for Ed to see, had made Ed's blood run cold.

Ed checked his rearview mirror. Thank goodness, Soh hadn't seen anything. She was still sleeping, her head leaning against the car window while her hand rested on the seat holding their three-year-old son. Ed wanted to chase the other car and yell at the men. *It's 1988, for Chrissake!* he wanted to shout. "And this is my road," he whispered to himself. "This is my home."

# Together

―――

1877

Iт тооk four years for willis's sons to return home from their whaling work off the Pacific coast. When they did, the older one, Edward Moses, brought a wife with him. The other son, Basil, never married, though he became a favorite of his brother's children. He was always surrounded by the kids and their friends. Uncle B, as they called him, was generous with his time, engaging in such essential tasks as building and fixing tree houses, playing his violin, and telling stories that made the children squeal with laughter. Every family needed someone like Uncle B.

Willis's boys preferred not to speak of their time at sea, the whaling having been such a drawn-out and bloody affair. Still, there was one occasion, when the three generations of Freemans were gathered for a meal, that Uncle B described the first time he'd ever seen a whale. The beast had risen straight out of the water and flipped itself back down into the depths, he told them. It had frightened and thrilled him to see the size of that thing.

"That whale," Uncle B said, "was the most magnificent creature in the world. It was larger than the longboats that chased it." At this description, the children said, "Ohhh!" in unison. Uncle B's eyes took on a gleam as he continued, waving his arms dramatically.

"The creature had a waterfall coming out of the top of its head!"

"Ahhh!" the kids yelled.

"Well, that whale," Uncle B said, picking up his spoon, "was living proof of the greatness of God, I tell you." Uncle B took in a mouthful of soup. "It was not an easy task, ours, to have to hunt those creatures.

It was a nasty job, to have to process them later for their oil." He made cutting gestures and grimaced, and the children made the same face back at him. "But we needed the work, and it was a privilege to ride the seas. To see the Lord's wonders. That whale was only one of them."

Grandpa Willis listened to his son, nodding, a big grin on his face. What a fortunate man he had turned out to be, he thought. To be here, alive still, and free. To witness this gathering in his kitchen. To hear his own youthful impressions echoed by one of his sons. There had been bleak days without his boys, though the occasional letter had arrived from San Francisco. But here they were, now, all together. And they were doing well.

Willis's family was growing. He had enough land to feed them all. His wagon wheels and sleigh runners and decorative painting were back in demand. There was less need for sailmaking, though Aquinnah still had plenty to do. But all the talk about being at sea made Willis think of his very first days in Massachusetts. He looked over at Moses's stoneware jar, which was sitting by the kitchen door, as it had for years. On that evening, he decided that if he was still around when his grandchildren established households of their own, he would pass the jar down to a new generation.

It would be nearly twenty more years before the stoneware jar changed hands. Willis's youngest grandson had just married a minister's daughter from Springfield, and Willis decided they should move the jar into their home.

"No sense waiting until I'm gone," Willis said. "It won't be going far anyhow."

In five decades, the jar had rarely been used for its intended purpose, namely food storage, but Old Willis and Aquinnah directed their children to stock the jar symbolically with food to provide for the young couple as they began their union. Amid much noise and laughter, they loaded the ceramic container with a series of smaller glass jars that had been filled with fruits, dried beans, and pickled meats and sealed shut with glass lids and metal clamps.

The jar was then hoisted into a wheelbarrow and pushed from the kitchen of the house where Willis and Aquinnah had raised their boys to a much larger home down the road, but on the same property. Once the original store of canned foods had been removed from the jar, it became an occasional receptacle for whatever suited the family. The post, newspapers, parasols, jackets, and, at one point, a hunting rifle.

The jar would remain in the big house through childbirths, wars, the Spanish flu, stock market crashes, and house renovations, until 1984, when Edward Freeman III moved into the first home he would share with Soh. By then, the Freemans had become a family prosperous beyond the wildest hopes of Willis and Aquinnah. Still, they understood that the old jar was the most valuable thing they had, apart from their freedom.

Ed, like his father, left the jar mostly empty, with the exception of one item, which had always remained in the bottom of the vessel, no matter what else was placed in there. Every once in a while, someone in the family would reach their hand all the way down to the bottom of the jar and twirl their fingers around until they found the old piece of wood with the X burned onto its surface. Invariably, they would pull it out to look at it, smile, then let it fall back in. That piece of wood was still helping the Freemans to find their way through the world, along with the hidden message carved into the bottom of the jar.

# MD

## 1910

"SEE HERE, GRANDPA?"

Eliza leaned over her grandfather's chair and placed a piece of paper in his hands. He could barely see the writing on it, but he liked the feel of that paper. The weight of it. Eliza held his left hand and moved his fingers over the words.

"These here letters, *M* and *D,* stand for *Medical Doctor.*"

"And that's what you have become."

"That's right, Grandpa."

"And that's why you have been in Pennsylvania all this time."

"Yes, sir."

"Have you come back home to stay now, Eliza?"

"Yes, Grandpa, I have come back home to stay. I will see my patients right here, in our old schoolhouse. And I will stop by to say hello to you every day on my way over there. Will that suit you all right, Grandpa Willis?"

"Yes, dear, that will suit me just fine."

# Ed

———

A PRAYING MANTIS LANDS ON ED'S HAND. HE UTTERS A SHORT laugh. He grew up with these things all over his backyard but he still can't get over how funny they look. Those bulby eyes. Those legs. He read somewhere that people believe a mantis landing on your hand meant you were going to meet someone important. Ed doesn't see the logic in that. But he does wonder about the timing when, just as the mantis jumps down to disappear in the grass, he hears a car door slam.

A part of him is hoping his wife has come to order him home after his three weeks of hiding out at his folks' place, but that wouldn't be Soh's style, would it? No, Soh will continue to give him the silent treatment until he figures out how to make amends. He was so sure he needed to get away, to be anywhere else. But once the initial comfort of being back with his parents had soothed him, all he wanted was to go back to Soh. Now he hears the yip of female voices in the front of the house. Footsteps coming this way. His sister, perhaps? Ed pushes himself out of the Adirondack chair and starts walking toward the house.

It would have surprised him to see Soh here, but it's an even greater shock when he sees that it's Ebby. The old Ebby. His daughter's bright-red cloud of hair is gone, replaced by short, dark curls. Soon, he will learn that Ebby has been back in the U.S. for more than a week, mostly on her own, and that his father has just picked her up at a train station.

"Hey, Dad," Ebby says, opening her arms for a hug.

# Burdens

——

E D AND EBBY ARE SITTING SIDE BY SIDE IN THE DIRT, NOW, UNDER the old oak, while his mother clears glasses from the back porch, pretending she's not watching them.

"I should have moved us back here, after Baz died," Ed says.

Ebby sits up straight, looks him in the eye.

"But why?" Ebby says. "I mean, I love this place and all, but no."

"But our roots were here."

"Our roots are still here," Ebby says, putting her head on her father's shoulder. Few things please Ed more. She used to do that all the time when she was a little girl.

"You had to grow up all alone. At least you would have had your cousins, here."

Ebby says nothing, merely nods her head.

"I wish we could bring your brother back, but we can't."

"I know, Dad." He hears her voice break.

"It's been hard for you."

"For all of us. I feel like my mistake was trying so hard to forget what happened, you know? When my engagement to Henry fell apart, it put too much of a spotlight on me. It just brought back too many memories of what it was like after Baz died. That's why I took off for France. I kinda wanted to forget who I was. I wanted to live like someone else. But I didn't want to forget about Baz. Just everything that happened to us right at the end."

Ed nods.

"I think I caused you a lot of worry," Ebby says. "Because I never liked to talk about that day."

Ed holds his breath. This may be the first time, in all these years, that his daughter is choosing to talk about the impact of her brother's death without being prodded by Ed and Soh, or by a therapist.

"You know how the media always talked about us being the only African American family in our *exclusive coastal enclave* and that sort of thing? Well, as I got older, it really bugged me. As if they were trying to say that what happened to us wouldn't have happened to a white family."

"Right."

"Even though we know it does."

"I felt that way, too. Your mom and I both did."

"It's just that," Ebby says, "Dad . . ."

Ed's shoulder feels wet. His daughter is crying.

"Baby girl," he says, touching her chin.

"No, no, I'm okay. I just need you to listen."

Ed sits back. Ebby lifts the hem of her shirt to pat her face dry.

"In a way, it's true, Daddy. That it happened to us because we're black."

Ed tips his head to one side. Ebby hasn't called him *Daddy* in that little-girl voice in years.

"Because of the jar, Daddy," Ebby continues. "Those robbers? They were looking for Old Mo."

"We don't know that," Ed says. "We may never know. Though I have wondered about it."

"But *I know*, Dad, for sure. I heard them."

"Heard them? Who?"

"The men. The robbers."

"But you were upstairs."

"I was, but I heard voices, and looked over the banister, and saw them from up there."

"Wait, you actually *saw* them?" Ed says. He stands up. "But we asked you. The police asked you. You saw them and you didn't tell us?"

"I couldn't really see them. They had their faces covered. Two men with ski masks."

"Could you tell if they were white?"

"I think they were white. Just from what I could see around the eyes, you know? Light-skinned, for sure."

"Would you recognize them if you saw them?" Ed asks.

Ebby shakes her head.

"I've asked myself that a million times, but I'm pretty sure I wouldn't know them if they walked into this yard right now. And that was part of what scared me. Who were they? What if they knew I'd been up there? That I could hear them?" Ebby is on her feet now, pacing.

"I kept thinking, what if they were to come back? What if they tried to hurt you and Mom? Or me? I'm sorry, Dad, but I was petrified. I saw how they treated Baz. They pushed him into the study and then I couldn't see any more, but soon after that, I heard the shots."

Ed realizes he's been holding air in his lungs for too long. He exhales heavily, now. Finally, he has confirmation of what he has long suspected. Even his friend Harris suggested it. Whoever came into their house all those years ago came looking for the jar. And now he knows that his daughter witnessed more on that day than she'd ever admitted.

"I didn't want to tell you and Mom," Ebby says. "But all these years, I kept thinking that they wouldn't have come to our house if it hadn't been for Old Mo."

Ed hugs his daughter. Ebby may not think she knew enough to make a difference, but even the confirmation that the robbers had been looking for Old Mo might have helped police in their investigation, early on. He's not sure it would make much of a difference now. So many years have passed. But Ed won't say that. His daughter looks miserable enough.

"You would have been too young, at the time, to know any of this, but the jar had become very valuable, all of a sudden. It had always been historic. But most people had no idea how special it was. Then someone sold a similar jar for a lot of money, and the experts started doing interviews in the news about pottery produced by enslaved craftsmen, and people we knew started making comments about Old Mo's value."

"Word must have gotten around."

"Yes, word must have gotten around."

"And whoever came for that jar killed Baz," Ebby says quietly.

"And none of this would have happened, we wouldn't have been at home, if I hadn't insisted on playing hide-and-seek one more time. Baz kept telling me we had to go, but I convinced him to stay. We were still there because I begged him to play one more game. Baz is dead because of that, too, Daddy. Baz is dead because of me."

"Oh, no, baby, no," Ed says. "What happened to our family happened because someone came looking for something that didn't belong to them. They came into our house uninvited, they brought a weapon into our home, and they were willing to shoot a defenseless child. That is why this happened to your brother. The rest is all variables. You do know this, don't you? You know that this is about the people who did this, and not about what you did or didn't do?"

As Ed hears himself say it, he finally, finally, finally believes it. The same thinking applies to him. You can't separate out one event from another, one choice from another. His son wasn't killed because Ed chose to live on the coast or because his daughter wanted to play one more game. His son was killed because other people made the decision to interfere with their lives. His family had a historic jar, but it might have been something else, or someone else, on that day.

"But, Daddy, there's something else I never told you."

And then Ed's twenty-nine-year-old daughter cups her hands over his ear and whispers into it like she's ten years old again. When she is done telling him, Ed pulls back and looks at her.

"Nooo," Ed says. "You can't tell yourself that. It could have happened to anyone, and you were only ten years old. People freeze all the time when they're scared."

"But you and Mom taught us . . ."

"Sure, we taught you to call 911, but things were happening so fast. You're not a machine. And no one could have gotten there in time to stop what was happening, don't you see?" Ed hugs his daughter. "You called them afterward, Ebby. You tried to get help. But the doctors told us your brother wouldn't have survived anyway. I'm so sorry you had to live through that, baby girl, but probably it was over the moment they shot him." Ed hears his voice break. "The damage to his body was too great."

"But he talked to me, Daddy. He was still alive."

"I know, baby, I know." Ed's heart is breaking. To think of all that his daughter has carried with her all these years.

"And they broke Old Mo."

Ed nods, now, at a loss for words. His daughter's doubts have been mirroring his all this time, and he didn't realize it.

"They took everything from us."

"They didn't take everything, Ebby." Ed puts his arms around his daughter again. "They didn't take you." He glances up at the kitchen window and sees his mother, watching them from inside. And now Ed knows what he needs to do. It is time to tell his family the truth about the jar. But first, he needs to patch things up with his wife.

# Book Game

———

E BBY WALKS INTO HER GRANDPARENTS' LIBRARY. THIS IS THE ROOM
where Old Mo used to be kept when her dad was a kid. The room is
still filled with books as it was when she was a child, only now most of
the volumes are filed away on one of the floor-to-ceiling shelves.
They're no longer piled on the furniture and floors as they were when
she and Baz used to play there. Travel books and maps used to block
the path of the rolling ladder that her grandfather had installed to reach
the highest shelves, but it hasn't been that way for years.

Ebby sinks into one of the two sofas and leans her head back to gaze
at the room. She can smell the wood oil used to clean the furniture and
that particular odor a vacuum cleaner can leave when it has sucked at
the fibers of a rug. The amber-toned shelves are beautiful. The spines
of all those books, inviting. Still, she liked it better before her grandparents had it tidied up.

There was a game she and Baz used to play at Granny and Gramps's.
The book game. It was the same game her father and Aunt Kandy used
to play when they were growing up here. A large mason jar was filled
with strips of paper holding clues. The players would form teams of
two and take turns pulling clues out of the jar and reading them out
loud.

One teammate would read a clue referring to a book and the other
would scurry around the room looking for the title in question. But if
someone knew for a fact that the book was not in the room and instead, say, upstairs on someone's bedside table, they were supposed to
speak up right away. It would be the sportsmanlike thing to do.

During the hunt, teammates weren't allowed to talk to each other
about which book it might be, or point to it if they happened to know

where it was. There'd be a lot of raised eyebrows and meaningful stares and throat clearing. And, sometimes, a bit of bickering afterward. The first team to have more than two books would win. They would play this game a couple of times a year, mostly on cold winter nights or rainy summer days. Then Ebby and Baz would go back home, knowing that their grandparents would throw out some of the old clues and write up some new ones for the next time.

After Baz, there was no *next time*. It's not that her grandparents didn't make holiday meals, or take her and her cousins to the ballet to see Alvin Ailey or to a concert at Christmastime. It's not that the kids didn't play, or that the adults didn't gossip and laugh together. It's just that they never again played that game. No wedging of one's body between piles of books on the sofa. No sitting cross-legged on the rugs. No jumping up to scan the titles all around them.

All the years that she and Baz had been going there, that room must have looked to other people like nobody had ever bothered to tidy up. But you only had to look at the rest of her grandparents' home to know that it wasn't a lack of care. And if you knew her grandmother's profession, you would know it was intentional. Granny Freeman had been one of the first African American librarians in New England. She certainly didn't reach that position leaving books all over the place.

No, these books had been left to inhabit the library like people. They had been left lying where they were to be picked up during the game, to be flipped through on quiet afternoons. To be sat among, the way you sat with relatives and friends. To be conversed with.

Her grandmother walks into the room now.

"We still have some of the clues, you know," Granny says. "Did I ever tell you that?"

"Really? No, I didn't know."

"Open that drawer over there."

There are cassette drawers running along the lowest level of the bookcases. Ebby pulls one open to find a sea of small strips of paper.

"Oh!" She looks at her grandmother, who nods.

Ebby crouches down and picks through the pieces of paper until she finds what she is looking for, even though she didn't realize what she wanted until now. She finds a couple of strips with her brother's handwriting on them. THE GIVING TREE, reads one. The other reads NARRATIVE OF THE LIFE OF FREDERICK DOUGLASS, AN AMERICAN SLAVE.

"Go on, take them," her grandmother says. Ebby stands up and hugs her granny for a long time.

# Neighbors

————

E D AND EBBY ARE WAVING AT ED'S PARENTS AS THEY WALK toward his car.

"Should we stop by Mr. and Mrs. P's on the way down?" Ebby says.

They're already due to drive up to see Bob and Adelaide Pitts in a few weeks' time. Bob Pitts has a big birthday coming up. Eighty-five. His wife, Adelaide, is planning a surprise party. But Ed misses the Pittses. When they still lived on adjoining properties, Bob would walk with Ed down to the beach, sometimes, the kids running out ahead of them.

Now that the Pittses live up here, they often stop by when they're headed back from Massachusetts. Ebby always goes first to Adelaide. She lowers her head into the crook of Adelaide's neck and gives her a long hug and says, *Mrs. P.*

Ed thinks back, now, to the day of the shooting. Bob had called him to hurry home. He told him that it was serious, that Baz had been hurt. Ed and Soh couldn't get up their own driveway, it being blocked by two police cars. He recalls how he and Soh jumped out of their car and ran across their front yard as Ebby walked toward them, clinging to Adelaide, unseeing. She pulled away only when her mother dropped to her knees in front of her, arms out.

When Ed and Soh first moved in across the backyard from Bob and Adelaide, the Pittses came over right away to introduce themselves.

"And who is this young man?" Bob asked.

"I'm Baz," Ed's son said, looking down at his feet.

"It's short for Basil," Soh said.

"Well, that's a fine name," said Bob. "Not like my name." He frowned.

Baz looked up, curious.

"You can call me Mr. P," Bob said. "Because my name is the pits!" Baz grinned and Ed breathed in a lungful of relief.

"Like olive pits," Bob said, and Baz giggled and squirmed.

"Like peach pits!" Baz shouted.

"Shhh," Soh said. "Keep your voice down."

"Like tar pits!" Bob said, his voice a low growl.

"Like an orchestra pit!"

"Oh, that's a good one, isn't it?" Bob said, nodding at Ed and Soh. "How old are you?"

Baz held up five fingers.

"Five? You're only five and you already know what an orchestra pit is?"

"We took him to a musical."

"And a ballet, remember, Mom?"

"He saw the orchestra down in their space."

"He's already playing the recorder."

"Wow," said Bob. "Do you like that? Playing an instrument?"

Baz nodded. "Mhmmm."

When Ebby was a toddler, the Pittses started bringing their grand-baby over to play. And that's how Ebby and Ashleigh got started. In the early days, the two couples would push the girls' strollers all the way down to the surf club together, then onto the sand. Ed quickly grew to love that neighborhood. Though he had to work to keep his cool when his young family drew stares in the town center. Or when a new member at the beach club, who did not recognize him from the article in *Forbes* magazine, or from the dais at a benefit dinner, mistook him for a waiter. Or when people at parties were clearly trying to get to the bottom of how he could afford to live where he did and he had to trot out his elevator speech about his inventions.

Living next to Mr. and Mrs. P had made things easier. Had helped to make their beautiful house on Windward feel like their forever home.

Back then, Ed could never have imagined that one day he'd wake up in the morning feeling like he was falling into a deep well.

Falling, falling, falling, into a pit.

*Like a bottomless pit, Mr. P.*

Ashleigh is supposed to be at the birthday party. The last time they saw the Pittses' granddaughter was when she came in from the West Coast for Ebby's wedding.

Ebby's *non-wedding*.

After Henry failed to show up for the ceremony, Ashleigh and a couple of Ebby's cousins stayed with Ebby all that afternoon and evening, then drifted back to their own lives, though Ed gathered that Ashleigh still talked to Ebby regularly from California. Ed isn't sure exactly what Ashleigh's job in entertainment entails, only that she's not an actor like her parents. She's into something more focused on people management.

When Ed and Soh sold that first house in Connecticut and moved farther, to where they live now, they found themselves in a town where several of the other children were growing up in the public eye because they had been born to parents who worked in fields like entertainment or high-profile finance. One girl's mother has since evolved into a social media beauty influencer, now that such roles exist. But no one else had been thrust into the media spotlight at only ten years of age for the same reason as their daughter.

"Are there at least some black folks in your new neighborhood?" was all his mother wanted to know when Ed told his parents where he and Soh were purchasing their next home. "Is there even one black person living there?"

"Well, there will be at least three of them, now," his father had said with a chuckle.

Ed shakes his head, now, at the memory. His mother is never going to like him living where he does. But he still likes it. Before climbing into the driver's seat, he turns to Ebby.

"Sure, why don't you give Mrs. P a call and see if we can stop by?" Then he gets out of the car again and calls to his daughter. "I'll telephone your mom. See if she wants to drive up to meet us." His daughter walks over and kisses him on the cheek. Ed waves her away with a laugh. But the pressure on his chest feels lighter.

# Mrs. P

———

THIS BEAUTIFUL GIRL.

Ebby hugs Mrs. P the way she always does. Her face in the curve of Mrs. P's neck, as if she were still a little girl and not a woman a head taller than Mrs. P. Same height as her granddaughter Ashleigh. Same age. She's glad that Ebby still keeps in touch with Ashleigh. When Ebby hugs her like this, she thinks of her granddaughter, too. Mrs. P looks over at Ed. She can tell from the look in his eyes that they've been thinking too much about the past.

Mrs. P knows all about that. Thinking about the past. Wanting to undo what they can't.

When your neighbors gave you the keys to their back door, this was not what any of you had in mind. You didn't know that being a good neighbor, being a friend, would lead to what it did that day in 2000. What you had in mind was letting the kids inside if they'd locked themselves out. Or checking on the house as a favor while the Freemans were away. You did not imagine seeing a van speeding away from their home. You could not, in a million years, imagine what would come after.

You hadn't seen the van in the driveway beforehand. From your garden, you could see only the Freemans' backyard and part of the street that led away from the house. You remember noting the ripening corn and squash in their vegetable patch, and a late-summer brood of wild turkeys hobbling after their mother as she picked at crab apples.

You'd been gathering seeds with your husband and taking note of the number of turkey poults for the government's wildlife survey. Wild turkey populations had been way down in the 1970s. Non-existent, really. But they'd been improving ever since. And just as you were thinking, *Now there's a hen with six poults,* the entire lot of birds jumped and scattered, *chirp-chirp-chirp-chirp-chirp.* That was the first sign that something was wrong.

When you hurried next door and found the front door open, you ran straight into the cool, cedar-scented hallway that led toward the stairway. You knew this house almost as well as you knew your own home. The sun-filled living room was to the left, and farther down, the tiled kitchen and a guest bathroom. But you stopped, now, at the study, to the right. This was the long, book-lined room where Ed Freeman worked. This was where you found the children.

Little Ebby was kneeling on the floor and pushing, pushing, pushing at Baz's blood-soaked arm, as if to rouse him from a deep slumber. A cordless telephone receiver lay on the ground, and you could hear a voice squawking from it. You picked it up. On the other end was an emergency dispatcher.

"Yes," you said. "My name is Adelaide Pitts. I'm a neighbor." You felt your chest constricting. "A friend of the family."

Only later, as you put your arm around Ebby and followed the police officers out of the room, did you notice the broken pottery on the floor. It was that olive-colored, open-mouthed thing that the Freemans loved so much. A real piece of Americana. In all these years, in its journey from south to north, in its sojourn in this room within frequent reach of young children, the jar had never been damaged, but there it was now, its belly split open on the floor.

By the time your neighbors gave you the keys to their back door, you were already a grandmother. You had given birth to your first child the week Martin Luther King, Jr., was killed, which also happened to be the year the U.S. registered its highest death toll ever in the Vietnam War. You'd had your second child the year Nixon resigned, having suffered a miscarriage once before that. And your granddaughter was born the year the Hubble Space Telescope was launched, the World Wide Web was formally proposed, and a paleontologist found the fossilized skeleton of a *Tyrannosaurus rex,* which later bore the scientist's first name, Sue.

By the time you first hung the Freemans' house keys on the hook near your kitchen door, you thought you'd seen it all. The Freemans were the first black family that had ever lived in your section of town. They turned out to be a lovely pair. And you couldn't help but grow attached to their children. Their second-born had been the cutest baby. Sure, you thought you'd seen it all, but you hadn't. What happened to the Freemans changed everything. After that day, you and your husband sold the old house and moved away.

# Ebby

E BBY HEARS HER MOTHER'S CAR. SHE RECOGNIZES THE DISTINC-
tive hum of the hybrid auto as it slows to a stop at Mr. and Mrs. P's
house. Ebby and her dad head out the front door with Mr. and Mrs. P
following close behind. Her mother is approaching with a basket full
of blackberries. With a cool air, she turns her cheek for Ed to kiss it,
but does not linger. Then there are exclamations and hugs. Mrs. P and
her mom reach for each other the way a person might reach for a life-
saver in a stormy sea. They are each other's proof of survival.

Ebby, suddenly, feels very tired. Her mind takes her back, to where
it always goes. To the study of her first home. Mrs. P is there, checking
Baz's pulse and breath. Then she is speaking into the phone with the
911 woman. She puts the receiver back on the floor, pulls off the cotton
jacket she is wearing, balls it up, and pushes it against the wound high
on Baz's chest.

"Ebby," she says, "can you hold this in place? Yes? Keep it there,
even when I move around."

Mrs. P pinches Baz's nostrils shut, puffs two breaths into his mouth
then shifts her hands to his rib cage, near his stomach. She puts one
hand over the other, links her fingers together, and starts to push at his
chest. Then another two breaths. Then back. She mumbles to herself
as she presses down. *One one thousand. Two one thousand. Three one thousand.* Mrs. P keeps doing this, over and over again, until the paramedics
arrive.

But Mrs. P knows already, doesn't she? Just as Ebby knows. Baz has
already left them. Later, her mom will say that Baz has gone to heaven.
And Ebby will wonder, if God was the one who made heaven, then
why couldn't he just send Baz back to them?

Ebby blinks, and she is back in the present, sitting in the Pittses' living room. The smells of coffee and pie drift in from the kitchen. She watches as her father reaches for her mother's hand. Her mother lets him take it but doesn't look his way. Her mom is still pissed. But Ebby feels herself exhale. There is something about looking at those two together, even with the tension between them, that makes her feel grounded.

*Will it ever be that way for me?* Ebby wonders. Will she ever be so far into a relationship, one that works, that it will be able to bear up under the pressures that life can bring? Later, when she is alone with both of her parents, she will tell them how sometimes she feels guilty for wanting to be happy, even though Baz is gone.

But she does.

Want to be happy.

She does.

After Ebby and her parents say goodbye to their old neighbors, she says, "Dad, do you want to ride back in Mom's car? I could drive yours." Her father's face brightens at the suggestion, but her mother cuts in.

"That's all right," her mom says. "I'm all right on my own. You two go ahead."

*Oh, dear,* Ebby thinks. *Oh, dear.*

# Part Four

# Avery

———

Is this what it means to be a woman? To be nearly thirty years old and still afraid to say what you want in life? Or, at the very least, what you don't want? Sometimes, Avery thinks, one of the hardest things in life is, simply, to sit with yourself and allow yourself to *be*. Listen to your instincts. Admit that you don't always know how to move forward. Or, rather, that you think you know how to move forward but are afraid to take that first step.

Avery is not the scaredy-cat type. It's not like she has to make life-or-death decisions in order to get by. Hers is not that kind of life. So she wasn't afraid to negotiate her salary and conditions at the law firm. She wasn't afraid to suggest the firm hold two staff meetings a week during the lunch hour to avoid consuming billable client hours in the morning. She wasn't afraid to say to the partners that it would be more cost-effective to offer the staff a catered meal on those occasions. To build morale.

Ultimately, Avery had gained respect by daring to point out that the partners were wrong in assuming that their administrative staff, working as they did for some of the top lawyers in the country, would be satisfied merely with the prestige of it. The attorneys expected good incomes and benefits for their own efforts. Why shouldn't their staff have a nice meal on the company? More vacation days to compensate for the lunchtime work. More money, period. Thoughtful compensation would yield greater productivity, she argued.

So Avery has not been shy about speaking up. And when it came to it, she wasn't afraid to cut her losses with Henry and drive away in their rental car alone.

What does make Avery nervous is the thought of admitting what she wants now. She has been changing her mind about a number of things. She thought she wanted Henry. Thought she wanted a child with someone like him. Thought she wanted to make partner at the law firm above all else. But now, after thinking she was done with school for a good while, she knows she wants to go back to university.

Avery can see herself picking up another degree. Switching careers and going back to her original professional interest. Avery did a major in psychology before going to law school. Studies show that older university students tend to be focused and successful because they know what they're trying to achieve. But the fact remains that Avery is afraid to no longer be the person people expect her to be.

Avery suspects she would sound like a green Miss America hopeful if she were to tell her parents that she is insatiably curious about people, about what makes them function. About what helps them to heal. She is afraid to say that she believes she has a calling and that this calling is not what consumes most of her working hours now. She wants to be brave enough to say to her parents, *I could help people. I could still make you proud of me.*

She finds herself wishing she could talk to someone like Ebby about this. Someone who must be accustomed to not quite fitting other people's notions of who she is. She wonders, should she go back to calling her Ebony? Does she still get to think of her as Ebby if they're no longer talking? Not that there was an official rift of any sort with Ebby. Avery simply drove away the last night she saw Ebby without saying goodbye. In fact, she has nothing against Ebby, per se. It's just that Avery doesn't know what she would say to someone whose very existence has dashed her hopes, however misguided, of a meaningful relationship with Henry.

Avery is sorry, in a way, that things ended as they did between them. She and Ebby might have been friends, under other circumstances. But she can't see how a real friendship would have been possible had Avery continued to see Henry. And now that she is *not* with him, a friendship feels just as unlikely. Avery cannot shake the image of

Henry, that final night at the cottage, hands on Ebby's shoulders, try-ing to get her to look at him.

The way he bowed his head toward hers. The way she, so clearly, struggled to resist looking up.

Those two have a kind of history that Avery never did have with Henry. Avery sees, now, that no matter how messily things ended be-tween those two, it had begun with love. Henry had loved Ebby. And, it seems, Henry now regrets having left Ebby. Probably, it is beyond the scope of Henry's imagination to consider that Ebby is not likely to take him back. But it is clear to Avery. Because the problem between Henry and Ebby wasn't about affection or attraction. It was about the kind of man that Henry had been with Ebby. It was about Henry let-ting go of Ebby when he should have done whatever it took to hold on to her.

Sometimes, when a person comes around, it's simply too late.

Avery remembers hearing a door slam that last night at the cottage before Henry trudged into the guesthouse. She figured whatever he and Ebby had talked about hadn't ended well. On the other hand, Avery has been questioning her own judgment in getting involved with Henry. For Avery, finding a way to get close to Henry had been a bit like her quest to go to Yale Law School and get on the partner track at a corporate firm in Connecticut by age thirty. She had decided that Henry was her goal and that she was going to make it work with him.

Avery had told herself that Henry would be different with her. That he would be more considerate. And, in a way, he was. That last night in the guest cottage, after Avery had finished yelling at him, Henry pulled Avery by the hand and sat her down next to him on the sofa. He stroked her arm and apologized for any embarrassment or dis-appointment he had caused her. He explained that he had tried to em-bark on a relationship too soon after Ebby. And then he said the thing that, looking back, now, Avery can see was an act of generosity on Henry's part.

"Avery, I'm sorry. I didn't want to give up the chance to be with you." On that note, Avery stood up, grabbed the keys to the rental SUV from the kitchen table, slung her handbag across her torso, put her tote bag on her shoulder, hooked the straps of her beauty case over the handle of her wheeled suitcase, and, above that, the elastic bands of her travel pillow. She would have preferred to hear that it never would have been a go with her. That she hadn't been his type to begin with.

"No, Avery," called Henry. "Please, don't do this. Maybe I just need some time." Henry followed her around the room, his voice getting louder. "Can't we talk about this?"

Avery felt a half smile cross her face. A kind of tenderness warmed her chest. But no. Avery was not an overly proud person. Still, she had more pride than that. With a shake of her head, she pulled open the front door and walked away. Henry called her name as he followed her out the door but then stopped in the middle of the yard. As Avery loaded the trunk of the SUV, she congratulated herself on the efficiency of the baggage and travel accessories that she had put together for the trip. She got behind the wheel without looking back.

But having enough self-esteem to walk away from Henry doesn't mean Avery doesn't have her issues. Avery still needs to be cared for. To be admired. To be supported. She knows she's been lucky. At home, Avery has always been cared for, admired, and supported. And she doesn't like imagining a world in which she might have to do without those things.

You don't spend all that time, plus your parents' money, going to Ivy League institutions and finishing two degrees only to say, *Sorry, I changed my mind,* and expect your parents to say, *Okay, fine.* Especially not when they'd gone to the very same schools themselves. Avery was a legacy student, and in her parents' minds, this comes with a sort of reputational responsibility to the previous generation. In Avery's case, the previous two generations.

Avery doesn't need her parents' support, at this age, to embark on a new course of study. She is not short on cash. What she does want, though, is her mom and dad's approval. Because this is part of who Avery is. This is why Avery, waiting for a train to Versailles, is still unsure of how to tell her folks that she has rented a two-room attic apartment in a suburb of Paris. She wants to tell them about the wooden floors and all that light. She wants to tell them not to worry. She wants to hear them say, *Are you sure that's what you want?* And she wants to be on a video call, so they can see her smile when she says yes.

She has told her boss. This morning, she wrote an email to tell him she's taking a leave of absence from the law firm. Potential career killer, she knows. But she needs to figure things out. When she gets back to the apartment, she clicks on the links she's been saving in a Word document. Links to graduate programs in psychology. Links to information on the GRE testing required of applicants. She stretches her legs out on the velvet chaise longue and props her laptop on her thighs. The chair is cobalt blue with gray piping. The flooring is a gray herringbone oak. The doors to the terrace are filled with handblown glass panes. This room energizes her.

Before wading into the GRE instructions, Avery clicks on a news site and checks the headlines. Maybe she should have gone to a real estate site instead, because all she can see are people in trouble. She reads about student protests and a boycott. Xenophobic attacks. A double bombing. The hottest September on record. The French say their honey production is down because of the impact of global warming on bees. The scientists say the planet is in trouble, just look at the bees.

Avery stands up, walks over to the window, and looks outside. She watches as bees float above a bank of lavender. In this little corner of this garden, there appears to be some hope for the bees. Avery goes back to her laptop and sits down. Now, where was she?

# Soh

E BBY IS SLEEPING IN HER OLD ROOM FOR THE NIGHT AND HER presence fills the house. It makes Soh think of the before times, in their former house, when both their children slumbered down the hallway from her and Ed. Even back then, Soh and Ed would have their disagreements, but it was easier for them to find their way back to each other. This time, Ebby's confession about the day Baz died, and Ed's own talk about his feelings, have helped to soften everything around the edges. But Soh and Ed still have a lot to work out.

Ed turns to Soh, now, but she's really not in the mood to talk. She's had enough revelations for the day. She pulls the duvet up toward her chin, but Ed ignores the hint.

"You know," he says. "Harris said something that I've been thinking about."

Soh tips her head, listening despite herself.

"Do you remember our neighbor Tucker?"

"Tucker? The one who died on 9/11?"

"Right. Remember he brought a few buddies and their wives over to our place for that benefit event, the one for the science education fund? Well, they ended up doing right by us. Made some very respectable contributions. I was surprised because I thought he was the kind of man who was all talk. But there was more to the guy."

"Mhmm."

"Harris never could stand Tucker. Thought he was too self-satisfied." Ed shakes his head. "Anyway, back then, Harris said word had gotten around that Tucker had a private gallery somewhere in his home, filled with art and artifacts, that no one ever got to see."

"How did anyone know, if they didn't get to see it?"

"Well, you know how these things go. Someone must have seen it, or Tucker maybe said something. Back then, we both laughed at the idea of Tucker as the clandestine art coveter. But it makes me wonder. Was he the kind of person who might have wanted the jar enough to commission a robbery?"

"Are you saying Tucker could have been involved?" Soh says. "But Tucker is dead."

"Yeah, poor bastard. But remember, he died a full year after the shooting. He was still around when it happened. And he'd even said something to me, before that, about the jar and its value. He'd been reading up on it."

Soh sighs. "Still. That's difficult to believe."

"Not any more than what happened to our family."

Listening to Ed, Soh thinks back to that time when Tucker's widow sold their Connecticut house and moved out west. Sixteen, maybe seventeen years, now. Said she was going to set up a new real estate practice out there. They never did hear from her again, but then, they hadn't really been friends in that way.

"The point is," Ed says to Soh, "Harris says he's been thinking about that, too. Poor guy, he really feels bad about the whole mess with Henry. He keeps calling."

Soh snorts. "I think Henry brought that whole mess upon himself."

Ed chuckles.

"It's not funny."

"No, it's not funny."

They're both laughing, now. Even in the worst of times, she and Ed have always seemed to find their way back to humor. The thought lightens her mood.

"But Harris also told me something else after Henry showed up."

Soh raises her eyebrows at the softening of her husband's voice.

"His exact words were, 'Stop with the guilt trip already. You're gonna give yourself a friggin' heart attack.'"

"Guilt trip?"

"I'm sorry, Soh."

"What for?"

Ed takes a deep breath. "I did something I never told you about."

Soh feels her mouth grow tight.

"After Baz died, I collected an insurance payout on the jar. I couldn't tell you. I thought you might have said any money coming from that day wouldn't be right. But I thought at the time that our family could use the money to do good. Maybe something to honor Baz. Then the years went by, and still, you didn't know."

"But Harris knew."

Ed nods.

He turns to Soh, now, and touches her face, but she pulls away.

"What?" Ed says.

"So that's it?" Soh says. "That's why you've been acting strange all these months? Not talking to me about things? Taking off on trips without warning? All this, over an insurance payout?" Soh is irritated, though she doesn't feel the same deep resentment that has threatened to derail their relationship of late. Probably, Ed was right not to tell her until now. She would have reacted exactly as he's said. At least, he doesn't seem to be having an affair. Or is he? She can see from Ed's face that he's holding something back.

"What else aren't you telling me?" Soh is surprised at how quiet her voice sounds.

"It's not only about the money," Ed says.

"What do you mean?" Soh braces herself for a shock. Ed, instead, looks relieved. He sits up straight and jumps out of bed.

"Put on your robe," he says. "I want to show you something. Something I've been wanting to talk to you and Ebby about."

"At this hour?"

"Yes, it's important. Look." He reaches into the back of one of his dresser drawers and pulls out a hard case for eyeglasses. When he opens the case, Soh is certain she's imagining things. Inside is a small, rough-hewn piece of wood, half the length of Ed's hand, with a black *X* burned into it.

"That's not . . . ?" Soh says.

Ed nods.

It is the piece of wood they used to keep inside Old Mo. The one marked with an *X* that had been used as a secret signal by Ed's ancestors, Aquinnah's parents, as they fled toward Massachusetts. All this time, Soh thought it was gone, along with the jar. Along with her son. She pulls it out of Ed's hand.

"You had it all this time and you didn't tell me?" She feels the recent resentment toward Ed coming back, remembering her husband's silences. His distance. She looks down at the piece of wood. Its chipped edges. The sight of it should break her heart, but instead, Soh feels something unexpected, a kind of lightening of a weight in her chest. She closes her hands around it then opens her palms again to look. *It's still there!*

"Why didn't you tell me?" she says.

"Would you have wanted to know?"

Soh looks around at the room where she and Ed have slept since their son's death. No, she thinks. She would not have wanted to know. She would not have wanted to see anything from the room where her son was killed.

Ed puts a finger up to his lips.

"Come," he whispers, and takes her hand. They walk down the hallway until they reach the room where Ebby is sleeping. Soh pauses outside the door. She can hear her daughter breathing. Short puffs that sound almost like snores. Soh smiles as she thinks of her daughter dreaming quietly. Often, her daughter has dreamed noisily, engaging in warfare with her thoughts.

Soh must fight the urge, now, to open the door, walk over to the bed, and lie down beside Ebby. Or, at least, to gaze at her daughter, just as she used to watch both her children while they slept. Her husband is tugging at the sleeve of her robe now. He is no longer distant. He is eager to talk.

# Breaking and Entering

———

## 2000

THEY WERE SHAKEN UP BIG-TIME.

How did it come to this? They had always been careful planners. They had worn gloves and masks and shoe coverings for the burglary. They had returned their rental van as if nothing had happened, after removing the magnetic sign and fake license plates. Plus, they knew they were dealing with a town that had very few surveillance cameras anywhere, private or public. All they had to do was drive out of the state in their Benz and change the plates on that car, too, just to be safe. It should have been a piece of cake. A simple case of breaking and entering—no harm done, folks. But the getaway was the only thing that had gone according to plan.

Within minutes, they had slid from burglary to home invasion to murder.

Murder. Assault. Robbery. The town had registered zero crimes in all these categories for several years running. That's what they said on the news that night. Burglaries and other kinds of theft were many times below the national average. Theirs was supposed to have been a middle-of-the-afternoon job in a sleepy neighborhood. They were equipped with a diagram of the house and a summary of family schedules. They had spent several afternoons observing the residence on Windward and would be in and out before anyone knew it.

The only people coming and going at that hour were folks who made a living making things clean and functional for families like the people who lived on Windward. Two men in a white service van would fit right in. They only had to drive up, step out of the vehicle in fake uniforms, and knock on the front door, keeping their heads down to hide their faces from anyone who might see them and blocking the view of the door while they fiddled with the lock.

One always had to assume that there might be a surveillance camera somewhere inside, even if they couldn't see one. Even if there'd been no information to that effect. They would pull on their masks as soon as the door was open. They would pretend that they were being greeted by the cleaning lady, who they knew did not work that day. They would walk into the house in an unhurried manner and close the door behind them. They'd have to take a quick look around, because their client hadn't provided a photograph. Apparently, there weren't any in circulation, but the guy who'd hired them said he had seen it with his own eyes.

Everything went as planned until they entered the front hallway and found the fifteen-year-old son of the property owners in the house. It was hard to say who was more surprised, them or the boy. The men knew that no one was ever home at that hour, that the family's two children had their various extracurricular activities, depending on the day. What in the world was this boy doing at home?

The whole thing was an accident. But who would believe that, or care, when they had entered the home with guns? Who would care, when a fifteen-year-old kid was dead? No matter that he was a black kid. He was still a rich kid, living in a beach-club community. They had noticed the flooring on entering the house. What a color. They had been aiming to have something of that sort in their own home, someday. But their motivation for accepting one more job had not been to spend their money on décor. Their client had real money and they were looking to be set for life.

The guy who'd hired them was smart. He knew to look for people without a record. People with decent day jobs. Not someone desperate for quick cash. They'd already made a good amount with the most re-cent robbery. An art-for-ransom scheme. They were all going to wrap it up after this job. While no one would ever suspect the two of them, the alpha dog, the guy who'd hired them, had been too close to the insurance industry, and he'd done this several times. One more job and his colleagues might figure it out. So this would be it. They'd make it work for all of them, then scatter. It should have been easy enough. The alpha dog wanted the piece for himself. He would pay them outright, and that would be that.

They'd thought to arm themselves only because, nowadays, that's what you did. In case someone walked in on you or some neighborhood security patrol passed by earlier than usual and pulled into the driveway behind their van. They'd had to park in the driveway because that's what a service company would have done. Made it easy to walk up to the front door. Would make it easier to walk out with their item in a thirty-five-gallon trash bag.

"Don't get nervous, now," they told the kid. "We just want the antique vase. Where is it? Just tell us where it is." They had studied the diagram but they were too flustered to remember. Left, or right? But the boy wouldn't answer, even when they pointed a gun at his chest. Still, if you watch a person closely enough, you can tell what they're thinking. They saw his eyes shift to the right. They saw a room full of books.

The study.

Once they entered the room, they saw the piece right away. Just think, all that fuss over a big old brown jar. They had taken ancient Chinese, Greek, and Roman stuff in their other jobs. Much older. And a heck of a lot prettier. Hard to believe someone else had sold a similar piece for six figures, which is what the man who'd commissioned them said. But it was historic. A part of American history that not that many people knew. That's why their client wanted it.

One of them reached for the jar while the other shook out the folded trash bag. Then the boy did something unthinkable. He reached for the jar and tried to stop them. That sullen-looking boy, almost as tall as they were but a kid, nonetheless, had suddenly sprung to life. He lunged at them like a viper. Shouted at them. *No!* Scared one of them into firing their weapon. The fool kid. What was he thinking, doing a thing like that?

Everything happened so fast. You would think you'd remember every millisecond of what happened on a day like that, but you don't. It could have been that jolt of back pain. It could have been the pills you were taking for the injury. Or it may have been the surprise of it all, the discrepancy between what you'd forced your way into the house to do that day and what you'd actually encountered. Any one of these things could have muddled your brain. Left you with only a few details to remember. The sound of a gun going off, and a teenager falling backward.

Stupid kid.

Stupid, stupid, stupid.

Point-blank.

Fuckin' hell.

Well, of course they ran. And forget the old vase, it had fallen over and broken apart. Needless to say, they never heard from their client again. That had been the agreement, should something go wrong, should something end up in the news. Their careers in commissioned art theft had come to a full stop, just like that. Thank goodness, they still had their day jobs and all of their take from the most recent robbery. They still had the home they'd shared for five years. And they still had each other. They would bide their time, act normal, then move to another state someday.

Strange how things had turned out since then. Their client, who had orchestrated all those art thefts, would be gone a year later. He was up in his office in the Twin Towers when those airplanes hit. They read his name in the papers later. He had never been linked to any of the crimes he'd commissioned.

Even though they hadn't earned a dime on that job, they had turned out to be the lucky ones in that whole mess. There'd actually been another kid in the house, but she'd been upstairs and apparently didn't know anything until afterward. So there'd been no real witnesses. No investigation that had come even remotely close to them. Yeah, they'd been lucky, all right. Or maybe not. That kid was fifteen years old when he died. And they were going to have to live with that knowledge for the rest of their lives.

# Places People Go

———

Because this was the way of the world.

There were places.
Where a man with money could hide his resources
    from public scrutiny.
There were places.
Where a man could go to hide himself.
There were ways.
That a man could disappear.
Be feared lost forever amid a disastrous event.
Be searched for, but never found.
Find himself walking away from a coffee shop,
    stunned, but safe.
Then running in the other direction.
There were times.
When a widow might leave her old life behind.
To distance herself from a tragedy that had left her alone.
To retire to a quiet offshore estate.
Far from the unrelenting gaze of the media.
Take her jewelry with her.
Take her late husband's art collection.
Take a lover who resembled her husband.
Though he was different.
Tucker's hair had been the color of a darkened room.
Black with hints of gray.

Her lover's hair was blond.

Bleached bright as the midday sun.

Glinting above his middle-aged forehead like the promise
   of a second chance.

There were places.

Where, throughout the ages, people have been able to go.

To live without accountability.

# The Jar, Again

———

E D LOOKS AT SOH AND SHE NODS.

"Ebby," Soh says, "your father has something he'd like to show you."

Ebby tips her head to the side and looks at them with a frown. They've just finished the crêpes that Ebby has made them for brunch. Smoked cheese and chives for the filling. Very French. It's good to have Ebby back again, though barely a month has passed and she's already talking about going back to France for a while. Hannah will be there, too, Ebby says, so not to worry. But Ed hopes that after he shows her what's in the trunk downstairs, she will change her mind.

Soh links her arm in Ebby's, now, and leads her across the kitchen toward the basement entrance. Ed pulls the door open and walks down the flight of stairs ahead of them. He removes an old stereo and a lamp from the top of the chest. Soh takes a rag from the laundry area and wipes the dust from the top and sides of the lid while Ed pulls a key out of his pocket. He can tell, from the narrowing of Ebby's eyes, that she might have figured out what's inside, only her hunch must seem, to her, to go against all logic.

Nineteen years ago. After Baz was killed in that other house, Ed went back there alone. The crime-scene tape had been removed, but the professional cleaners had not yet shown up. On entering, Ed walked straight into the study and dropped to his knees at the sight of his son's blood staining the carpet. He stayed there, rocking back and forth, struggling to breathe, until the tears came. As he wept, he saw that the police had left the broken jar lying on the ground, along with a couple of books that had been knocked off a side table. He picked up a piece of pottery that had split off the base of the jar, then, without stopping to think it out, he gathered all the smaller pieces and put them into an old tote bag.

Ed then fetched a plastic trash bag from the kitchen and put the base of the jar in there. He laid both bags in a large cardboard box that had been set aside to be recycled. He taped up the box and marked it STUDY and FRAGILE and took it to the trunk of his SUV. The box would become part of their house move and Soh would never know the difference. The only thing that wasn't sealed in the box was the small piece of wood marked with an X, which Ed had found some distance away, under a chair. From Aquinnah's side of the family. On impulse, Ed had slipped it into his jacket pocket.

Ed lifts the lid of the trunk, now, to show his daughter a mound covered with a flannel cloth. He hears Ebby gasp as he pulls the cloth back to reveal Old Mo, damaged, but repaired. Ebby puts her hand up to her mouth, now, and Ed tells her what he told Soh the other night.

"I'm sorry I didn't tell you, all these years," Ed says. "I couldn't bear to let go of it, but I couldn't bring myself to tell your mother or you that I had saved it. It was too much of a reminder of your brother's death. I didn't think any of us could stand to look at it again. Your mom had refused to go back to the old house, so I simply told her that the jar had been discarded with everything else."

Ebby puts her hand on the jar. She looks so sad, his little girl.

"After your broken engagement," Ed continues, "I thought of how you'd spent so many years with such sadness, and I kept wondering, would it have been easier on you, to see that we still had the jar? Or was that twisted reasoning on my part?"

"To know that they hadn't taken everything from us?" Ebby said softly. "Even though Baz *had been* everything?"

Ed turns in surprise to look at his daughter. She is nodding. She gets it. Just as Soh understood when he showed her the jar.

"You were right," Soh had told him last night. "I would have told you to get that thing out of my sight. But things are different, now. I think we need everything that helps us to remember who we are, even without Baz. Because we're still struggling with that."

When, nineteen years earlier, Ed opened the cardboard box and laid the pieces of Old Mo in this trunk, he didn't think he'd ever put the jar back together. But last year, feeling helpless to ease his daughter's misery after her failed engagement, he was desperate to do something with his own distress. He began to research South Carolina stoneware, looking for the right person to repair the jar. He enlisted the help of a historian friend, who in turn called Ed when he thought he'd found someone. When Ed arranged for the repair, it felt like he was finally getting some use out of that insurance money. Only, once Old Mo was back in one piece, Ed didn't know what to do about it. Until now.

Over dinner last night, Ebby had surprised him and Soh by saying she'd finally written down some of the jar stories.

"I can read you some tomorrow, if you'd like," she said. Ed hugged her, and took it as further confirmation that it was time to tell his family about Old Mo. But he knew that, first, he had to show it to Soh alone.

"All those times you were down here in the basement," Soh said last night as they crouched, side by side, in front of Old Mo. "You were looking at this?"

"Mostly no. I was on my laptop, doing research. Making calls. Trying to get help."

"And those trips down south?"

"I went to see an expert potter," Ed said. "I took the jar."

Now, together with Soh and Ebby, he calls his parents and tells them about Old Mo. Hears his mother exclaim through the phone. He tells them about the stories Ebby has been compiling and a proposal he has in mind. Ed, Soh, and Ebby have written up a list of possibilities. They have calls and appointments to make. Professionals to consult. But if his dad and mom are in agreement, he says, they can take the next steps. Their family has the connections to make it happen.

His father is silent. Ed wants to be sure he's convinced him.

"Dad, you taught us that our family's connection to the jar was special. And I believe that. I respect that. But maybe Willis was wrong about something. Maybe Old Mo was never meant to be ours alone.

Maybe the Freemans were only meant to be caretakers of its story until it could be shared with others."

Ed hears his father clear his throat.

"What do you think, Dad? Now that the jar is whole again, don't you think it's time we let it go?"

# Home, Again

———

E D'S PARENTS AREN'T WILD ABOUT SEEING HENRY PEPPER ON their property, though they are mollified somewhat by the sight of the jar, which is back in their home for the first time in thirty-five years. When Ed first removed Old Mo from the wrapping, his mom and dad said, "*Ohhh!*" then fell silent, running their hands along the seams where the jar had been repaired. Ed knew they were thinking of Baz. They all were thinking of Baz. But they were grateful, too, for this one thing that had been reclaimed from what they had lost.

After that, his folks began to move about the house with half smiles on their faces, though Ed has seen his mother throw cutting glances in Henry's direction. The last time Ed's folks saw Henry, he was getting ready to marry Ebby. Days before he disappeared from her life. Ed doesn't like having Henry here, either, but this is what Ebby wants. Ebby says she and Henry have had a long talk about things. Henry himself told Ed he feels like a shit for what he did to Ebby and wants to help the Freemans with their project.

Ebby says Henry has the skills they need at this point, and she knows she can trust him to keep quiet about their family's plans for the jar until they're ready to make the announcement. Henry is good at not saying anything, she says. And, no, the irony of that isn't lost on her.

"See?" Ebby says, pointing at Henry. Henry has his camera anchored to a tripod and is asking Ed's father to shift the position of the old jar. Its surface seems to glow, now, except where delicate shadows of oak leaves quiver against the stoneware. "Henry has this way of capturing light," Ebby says.

Ed nods and tries to smile, but he feels his brows pull together as

Ebby walks up to Henry. She looks so pleased with him. Not a good thing, Ed thinks, though he notices that Ebby never touches Henry, never quite looks him in the eye. Not like last year. Not like before. It's as if there is some kind of shield separating their former lives from their current ones. Yet there they are now, standing side by side, facing the jar, their heads tipped in the same direction. This breakup is too damned civil for Ed's taste.

Ed's back feels damp under his sweater. The seasons are not what they used to be. His cousin's son, the one in climate research, says the temperatures in New England are rising faster than the global rate. Before long, he says, the timing of rainfall and cooler temperatures might not be right for the autumn colors this area's trees are famous for. Not that you need a mathematical model to figure that out. Anyone over forty can see it. Hotter summers. More chaotic storms. More bugs. At least the hummingbirds are coming north earlier. Still, some things about autumn in this backyard haven't changed. The feel of dried leaves underfoot. The fat glow of squash reaching its prime. The scent of the season's first logs chopped and stacked.

Massachusetts in autumn will always feel like home, even if Ed still doesn't want to come back to stay. The feeling of home isn't tied to one place only.

Ed watches as Henry moves around Gramps Freeman, now, clicking the shutter. By lunchtime, everyone here will have had their turn before the lens. Ed isn't accustomed to seeing a man of Henry's generation with an actual Leica, with the bulk of it in his hands, as opposed to a smartphone. Ebby is the one who is using a cellphone camera. She shadows Henry, taking photos of him as he aims the camera. Ebby moves behind Henry, in step with him, bending her own legs as he crouches down.

"Excellent," Henry says. The shutter sounds repeatedly, though faintly. Ed finds the mechanical sound soothing as he imagines the blades inside the device clapping open to take in the light, then slipping back into their original position. He likes the tangibility of it. But Henry says it's a digital camera. The shutter sound can be turned off. Though Henry, too, likes to hear it. Ed watches Henry, trying not to look too impressed, and hoping to God that boy does not convince his daughter to get back together with him. Soh follows Ed's gaze, and as if she can read his mind, she leans in and whispers.

"She met someone, you know," Soh says.

"Oh, yes?"

"Someone in France."

Ed rolls his eyes. In *France*? A lot of good that's going to do Ebby here.

"Lord help us," Ed whispers. Soh gives him a friendly slap on his arm. It feels good, the return of a certain jocular ease between the two of them.

"Shhh," Soh says, taking his hand and turning to walk farther into the garden. "As for him," she says, jutting her chin toward Henry. "With any luck, he'll do some growing up. Find his stride."

"I really don't care," Ed says. "As long as his stride doesn't take him back into our daughter's arms." When Soh laughs, Ed kisses her. He thinks back to late summer, when Soh surprised him by slapping Henry. Until then, he would have been willing to bet the cost of his Rover against seeing that happen. This much Ed will say about Henry: That boy did muster enough nerve to drive all the way up to the Freeman place and look Ed's mother in the eye. That took guts. Or stupidity. He's not sure which.

They are all sitting on the screened-in porch, now, sipping on drinks and riffling through the contents of his mother's ubiquitous canisters of salted mixed nuts. Ed's dad is talking about Willis, the first Edward Freeman. How he had a way with sketching and painting.

"He told my grandfather," Gramps Freeman says, "that when he was still a boy, he met a man on the road back from Charleston who inspired him to draw more things from nature. He swore it was the same fellow who did that famous bird book."

"Who?" says Henry. "You don't mean Audubon?"

"That's the one. Well, he didn't know the name of the man at the time, but that's who he later claimed it was, and it's been documented that Audubon was working on illustrations in the area at that time."

"Seems a little far-fetched to me," Ed's mother says, "but this is the story that's been handed down through the years."

Ed's father nods and stands up. "As you know, Willis used to deco-rate pottery. He put that trail of leaves on Old Mo, and once he got settled in Massachusetts, he painted animals and flowers on wagons and buildings and furniture. But he also drew things he'd seen at sea." He leaves the room and comes back with the large, flat wooden box that Ed knows well. It holds some of the drawings his ancestor Willis left with his grandchildren, including Ed's grandfather.

Opening the box releases the scent of years gone by. Years when his grandfather's grandmother, Aquinnah, a farmer and sailmaker, met Edward "Willis" Freeman at a workstation near the docks. The Free-mans have all heard the stories of how one day, after returning from another sea voyage, Willis rode a wagon inland to see Aquinnah's par-ents, removed his hat, offered them a sketch of a seascape, and bowed his head before them. A plea for their daughter's hand. When Willis first saw Aquinnah, he had little more in his possession than the jar, a few sketches, and a new name.

Gramps Freeman removes the sketches carefully and lays them side by side on a coffee table. They all lean forward to peer at the pencil draw-ing on the first sheet of yellowed rag paper in front of them. It shows a square-rigger, sails raised, pitched at an angle in stormy seas. The next image is a detail of a ship's rigging, sails neatly folded against the cross-trees. Its intricate system of ropes, cables, and chains rendered in such de-tail. The sight of those sketches sets up a thrumming under Ed's rib cage.

There are people, nowadays, who still take voyages on tall sailing ships to learn their workings. When the kids were little, Ed used to say that one day he would take them on just such a trip, and Baz and Ebby would raise their arms in the air and yell, *Yaaay!*

"When you two are bigger," Soh would say. She didn't want them taking risks. Then Baz died, and Ed's view of the world shifted so radically that he no longer recognized himself. One day he looked at his image in the mirror, at his neatly trimmed, graying temples, at his long, manicured fingers, at the powdery-blue collar of his oxford shirt, at the muted, mustardy tone of his cable sweater, and saw right past it all. He saw through his skin, through the jumble of sinews and arter-ies and bones beneath, to the only thing he knew to be true. To the wounded heart at his center.

"Why don't you go?" Soh had said to him more recently, after Ebby left for France. "You've always wanted to do that ship thing." Ed knew Soh wasn't interested. Wouldn't even humor him by saying she would consider going. Still, she kept telling him to sign up. He just didn't see the point anymore. He had meant to do that with the kids. Now, looking at these old sketches, Ed is thinking about it again. He swears he can smell the sea from here, though he knows it's more than seventy miles away. Maybe he'll go after all. Or maybe it'll be enough for him to simply drive back down to their petroleum-blue clapboard house on the Sound and walk down to the beach. Who is he kidding anyway? He never was a sailor, he just loves being by the water.

"Wow, look at that," says Henry, his voice cutting through Ed's thoughts. Ed's father has placed a sketch of a whale, blurred in some spots, on the table in front of them. The bulk of the whale's body towers over the surface of the water at an almost ninety-degree angle, waves frothing around it.

"Wait, should we be taking photographs of these, too?" Henry asks. "And what about the tintype?" he says, waving a hand toward the living room, where a nineteenth-century painted tintype of Willis, Aquinnah, and their grown sons hangs from one of the walls.

Henry's enthusiasm seems genuine. Which makes his presence here all the more irritating.

# Lens

———

Henry hooks up his camera to his laptop and scrolls through some of the images for Ebby and her family.

"Mmmm," says Granny Freeman. Ebby recognizes that particular *mmmm* sound and waits. Sure enough, her grandmother asks her, now, to help her in the kitchen. Granny opens the oven door and Ebby, mitts on both hands, reaches in to pull out the roast that the housekeeper has cooked for them. Together, they transfer it to the oval, ivory-colored serving plate that has been in Granny's kitchen for as long as Ebby can remember. The smell of the roast mixes with the aroma of a pound cake that has been cooling on the counter.

"The photographs," Granny says. "They're not bad." She sticks a fork in the side of the roast, nudging it this way and that. "I'm not saying they're not nice. I'm just wondering why there isn't a black photographer here instead, taking those photos? Or at least someone from around here? Someone who didn't, say, abandon you on your wedding day?"

"Henry left me, in part, because he couldn't handle all of who I was, Granny. And he already knows how I feel about the way he left me. But also, there are reasons why I wanted to marry him in the first place. Qualities that can be helpful to us right now. For one, Henry was the only man I'd ever really confided in. Henry knew how much the jar meant to Baz and me. He encouraged me to write the jar stories."

Her grandmother's mouth looks tight. Ebby swallows hard and continues.

"Henry tried to be there for me, Granny. He was there for me for a long time."

"Two years is not a long time, baby. Sixty years is a long time. Two years is a cop-out."

"All right. Yes, Henry let me down, big-time. But I really do believe that a person should be able to say, *Okay, I can't handle this. This is something I'm not up for.*"

"Well, sure, honey. I agree. But it would be advisable to take such action well before the day of one's nuptials, and have the courtesy to advise the bride in the process."

Ebby bursts out laughing. Her grandmother frowns.

"I'm glad you find that funny."

"No, it's not, it's just . . . well, it is. It's that you sounded one hundred percent the professor when you said that."

"Well, I'm retired now," Granny says, her voice softening. "And I only taught library sciences in the beginning. So this is just your grandmother speaking. It was unforgivable, what he did, and I'm just concerned that you may be forgetting that."

"I haven't forgotten, Granny. But you've seen it for yourself. Henry has a good eye. He owes me a favor, big-time, and he's someone I can trust to be discreet until we're ready to say more."

What Ebby doesn't say is, if she doesn't allow Henry to help her with this, he may never let her be. Henry thinks he wants Ebby back, but what Henry really wants is to be able to forgive himself. But her grandmother has figured this out.

"Life is too short, Ebby," Granny Freeman says. "You don't owe that boy anything. You owe yourself a person who can be with you through thick and thin."

"This is not only personal, Granny. It's strategic thinking. Look at Henry's family. They have people on the boards of institutions that might support our idea for an educational project if they see how enthusiastic Henry is."

Her grandmother grows very still. It is that certain type of stillness that Ebby has learned to read as *don't rile me, now.*

"Do you not suppose," she says, with a hint of a chill in her voice that Ebby has never heard, "that our family is sufficiently equipped to find the right institutions and sponsors to support this project? We have owned land in Refuge County since the 1600s. Our family has doctors, lawyers, and judges. Engineers, professors, military officers. A city mayor and a state senator. And, more importantly, various people with excellent research and secretarial skills. All of whom have telephones. I believe we have what it takes to round up the support our foundation needs."

Ebby lowers her head. Feels her face grow hot.

"We need those photos, Granny."

"I have talked to another photographer," Granny says, "who is available to come by after lunch."

"Wait, what?"

"Your grandfather and I have already discussed this. If you still want to use some of the Pepper boy's photographs after you have seen the others, I'm not going to be the one to rule that out. Maybe you could get your ex-fiancé to take photographs of the other person photographing the jar. An African American who is looking at their history and identity through the lens of the jar's story. Now, there's something Henry Pepper could do for us."

It's pointless to argue. Ebby looks up at the clock on the kitchen wall. Good, they still have several hours of sunlight.

"We want people of all backgrounds to appreciate the history behind the jar," Granny says, "but we must not lose sight of the fact that the jar is ours, and its story must be shared with others by our family, first, and by people from our community, not the other way around."

And with a wave of her two-pronged serving fork, Granny Freeman ends the conversation.

# Calendar Reminder

———

E BBY'S PHONE IS BUZZING. AN EVENT NOTIFICATION. SHE SWIPES to stop the vibration, then taps on the calendar icon. As if she needs the reminder.

> EVENT: BAZ'S BIRTHDAY.
> REPEAT: YEARLY.
> DURATION: FOREVER.

Her eyes tingle but she doesn't cry. She sits there for a minute, bolted in place by the weight of what she is feeling. Then she stands up.

Today will be different.

When Ebby and Baz failed to leave the house on schedule that afternoon twenty years ago, their bicycles waiting for them beside the gardening shed, they could not have known. As Ebby begged her brother to play one last game of hide-and-seek, she could not have known. When Baz said, *Just one more time, but then we're going,* he could not have known. The therapist and her parents have told her this a million times. They could not have known that two strangers with firearms were on their way to the Freeman home. A hundred different things could have happened in those few minutes after Ebby ran upstairs and none of it would have been Ebby's fault.

No, it's not Ebby's fault her brother died. Of course she knows this. But it's true he'd likely still be alive today if they hadn't played that last game, if they'd only walked out the back door of the house just fifteen minutes before. She still wishes she hadn't been frozen with fear at the top of the stairs, even though surely no emergency call could have stopped her brother from being shot. There was too little time.

And yet.

To keep these thoughts from consuming her takes a daily effort. Ebby sees, now, that she must follow the example of Moses, the man who carved those words on the bottom of the jar in a time of great pain. Moses channeled his grief and anger into words of perseverance when he must have felt like giving up. For generations, her family has drawn strength and reassurance from that one simple line. And now, they are ready to share it.

Today will be different.

Perhaps the only way to cope with loss, or guilt, is to name it and defy its potential to destroy you. Not run from it, as Ebby has tried to do. Her brother's death is as much a part of who she is as her brother's life, as are the things she prefers to remember about him. His alarm clock. His photos. Old Mo. The fun they used to have playing a few rounds of hide-and-seek.

Maybe all you can do is give yourself permission to embrace the rest of your life. To play, to love, to risk. To take the beauty that someone brought into your life and share it.

# Soh

———

TODAY IS BAZ'S BIRTHDAY. TWENTY YEARS SINCE HIS DEATH. IN other years, Soh would have avoided the television news, kept the radio turned off in her car, blocked the news pop-ups on her smartphone, and, back when her parents still had newspapers delivered to their door, thrown the day's edition directly into the recycling bin without reading it. Just in case. She would have gone to visit Baz's grave, then stayed indoors for the rest of the day. She would have avoided answering phone calls from anyone but family and the Pittses. Always, the Pittses.

Adelaide Pitts had been the first one to reach Ebby after Baz was shot and she had understood that Soh needed to hear everything about what Adelaide and Bob had seen at the house that day. Quietly, but without holding anything back.

Adelaide also got something that many people didn't: that Soh needed to be able to talk about Baz's life, not just his death. How Baz had run into the Pittses' house the week before to tell them about joining the debate team at his high school. How every week he seemed different, rapidly moving toward manhood. How Baz had doted on his little sister. Always giving in to her almost constant schemes to play. That this was the way that Soh would live from then on. Between tears and laughter. Between loss and love.

This is why Soh has never gone back to the group meeting for grieving families, despite her therapist's recommendations. That first time, everyone was encouraged to talk about how they had lost their children. That was natural. That was helpful. To be in a room of other people who would not flinch at the tears. At the anger. But as time went on, as new people with fresh wounds joined the group, Soh wanted to talk more and more about how her son had lived.

Soh also wanted to ask that most terrible of questions, which not everyone was ready for. Not why did this happen to her son, but how could she be sure that nothing bad would ever happen to her daughter. The one who had been left behind to face public curiosity. The one who had to cross the street to go to school, who had to use the school bathrooms where meningitis might be lurking. The one who would soon be drawing the attention of boys and men twice her age. The one who would be learning how to drive.

Soh's daughter was the only reason she was still alive. Soh had never stopped loving her husband. Not even when he had closed in on himself. But Ed was not the reason why Soh had kept herself from driving her car into a tree all those years ago. She had aimed right for the bank of trees one night, so desperate was she to simply turn down the volume of the rage in her head. But she'd had Ebby to think of. Her second-born. Her baby. And Soh had willed herself to be there for her daughter. It was the only thing that she felt she could offer Ebby. Her presence. Her determination to keep her daughter alive.

But things are different now. And today will be different.

# Ed

*First of all, I would like to thank the director, the museum council, curators, staff, and volunteers for their belief in this project. My family and I look forward to the day when we will be able to gather here again for the opening of the new gallery. For now, I would like to share a few personal thoughts with you about the planned inaugural exhibit and the genesis of this idea. Please bear with me, as some of what I have to say will not be easy.*

*Thirty-five years ago today, our son, Edward Basil Freeman, was born. We called him Baz for short. Fifteen years later, armed persons who have never been identified broke into our home. They shot Baz and left him to die in front of my ten-year-old daughter, Ebony. On that terrible day, something else happened that held significance for my family. Somehow, a treasured heirloom was broken. It was a nineteenth-century stoneware jar, crafted by an enslaved potter, and it had been in my family for six generations.*

*The jar came to Massachusetts from South Carolina with a man who had escaped slavery by stowing away on a sailing ship. That man was my great-great-grandfather, Edward "Willis" Freeman. For years, his story, and the story of the potter who built the jar, was a source of education, cultural pride, and even amusement for my children.*

*We don't know everything about the jar, but my family has handed various stories down from one generation to the next, and these conversations have helped to keep the history of the jar alive, along with a few letters and other items that have survived over the years. My ancestor was close to Moses, the enslaved potter who built the jar and who had*

been married to Willis's sister. Willis himself played a role in decorating
the jar, having been, from an early age, an able artist. If you look at the
photograph projected onto the screen here, you can see the raised trail of
leaves on the side of the jar. That is Willis's handiwork.

But there's more. When you see the exhibit, you will understand
why Willis held on to that jar even after escaping to freedom, and why
he insisted his family protect it always. There is an inscription on the
bottom of the jar, which Moses must have written into the clay before the
final firing of the piece. I will come back to this thought in a minute.

As I mentioned, the jar was damaged on the day of the crime. For
years, my daughter and wife believed the jar had been thrown out, but I
had saved the broken pieces and locked them away in a trunk. I could not
bring myself to let go of the jar, but at the same time, the grief of losing
my son kept me from saying anything to my family or doing anything
about it for years. How could I think of the jar when I had lost my son?
At the same time, how could I give up on the jar after everything it had
meant to Baz and the rest of our family?

Then I thought about the risks that my ancestor Willis had taken to
seek freedom, about the hardship he and his family experienced even
when they were free, and about the good fortune and generosity of others,
black, white, and native, who helped my relatives along the challenging
path from adversity to prosperity. I consulted with experts about how the
jar could be repaired and provided with a new home and went as far as
South Carolina in search of help. Still, I said nothing to my family until
I was sure we could do something.

Thanks to the funds provided by an insurance policy and our sponsors, we are now in the position to prepare a dedicated space for an educational exhibit centered around the jar.

As mentioned by the director, the jar is of historic interest for a number of reasons: The fact that it was made by an enslaved potter. The
type of clay and glaze used, which are specific to the fine tradition of
stoneware production developed in South Carolina. The markings and
decoration on the jar. The fact that this piece has been here, in New England, since the mid-1800s. But for my family, it is the inscription that
gives this piece its greatest value.

The words written on the bottom of the jar helped to give Willis the *courage to escape bondage, but it is a phrase that most people have never seen. For a long time, an African American in possession of a jar with those few words written on it might have ended up being punished or killed for having written them, or simply for being able to read them.*

*Even today, those words have a kind of power that, until now, we have been reluctant to share beyond the Freeman family. But in his short life, my son gained so much from those words and from learning about the jar. And we, as a family, have come to realize that it is time to share this legacy. For better or worse.*

*We have always loved this jar because it reminds us of what our family has achieved since it was made, and it tells us something encouraging about the human spirit, in general, no matter what your origins. But make no mistake about it: The jar, like so many other works of craftsmanship from those times, was created through forced labor.*

*We are told that Moses loved to work with clay, as did his mother, who had been a potter in a village somewhere in West Africa before she was kidnapped and enslaved. But Moses, despite his work as a highly skilled turner, lived with the daily risk of harm or alienation from those he cared for. He must have woken up every day knowing that he or the people he loved could have been sold away or killed. We may think of love as something that cannot be quantified or held in one's hands, and yet we know that through that system, love could be stolen from people, for a fee. And so, too, their future.*

*For years, my ancestors either toiled under bondage or struggled to survive as free people who did not have the advantages of inherited resources, government compensation, significant schooling, or protection from violence and discrimination. During the same period, many former slaveholding families were able to enjoy access to these benefits. We Freemans have done all right for ourselves, and we are grateful for that. But so many others have not. And it's no secret that we continue to see the repercussions of those times today.*

*I'm looking over at my mother, now, because I know what she's thinking. She's thinking I'm getting too preachy. Sure, go ahead and laugh, but look at her. She's nodding. All right, Momma. Well, once you are able to see the jar for yourselves, you will be able to reflect on some of what I've said.*

Sadly, none of this can ever make up for the loss of my son. We cannot undo what happened to him or what our daughter, Ebby, had to go
through. But I think that Baz would have been proud to see us here
today, knowing that soon, we will have a way to share the jar with all
of you.

The story of the jar is not only the story of the Freeman family, or of
African Americans. These stories are part of the complex fabric of this
country. History, too often, has been told from only certain perspectives.
This is not good enough. History is a collective phenomenon. It can only
be told through a chorus of voices. And that chorus must make room for
new voices over time. When the exhibit is ready, there will be a way for
each visitor to add their own touch to the story that will be told. Every
person who comes to see the jar will alter its history.

All right, I'm going to stop here. I won't tell you any more. Let the
rest be a surprise.

# Henry

———

HENRY GETS A KICK OUT OF SEEING HIS PHOTOGRAPHS IN THE paper. He loves the contrast between his images and the ones taken by Carrie, the art school graduate that Ebby's grandmother lined up. To the left is Henry's portrait of Old Mo sitting on a tree stump like a little patriarch, surrounded by three generations of the Freeman family. To the right is Carrie's brilliant version of the same group as they break out of formation, going every which way, except for Ebby. The sight of Ebby standing there, looking at the jar, head tipped slightly as if she's listening to it, makes Henry's stomach pull into itself.

At the end of the article on the planned exhibit is a photo Henry took of the jar by itself under the oak tree, its leaves lit up by the afternoon sun and casting their undulate shadows against the jar's surface. The tree, like the jar, is older than anyone alive. The tree, like the jar, has touched the lives of many people, including Henry. After everything that's happened, it's strange to think that Henry's strongest feeling toward Old Mo, right now, is pride. He takes greater satisfaction in having worked on this project than when he received his MBA.

After the photos were taken and chosen, Ebby made it clear she didn't really want to deal with Henry when they weren't working on the project. She didn't think it was a good idea. But at least they've managed to do this together. Ebby came to Henry for support because she knew this was something she could trust him to do, and Henry felt he owed Ebby a huge favor after the way he let her down. Instead, it feels like Ebby is the one who has done Henry the favor. Look at his portfolio. It's finally showing some promise. And Henry feels a little less like a shit than he did before.

Henry turns the page and is struck by another news item in the arts section. A big auction house listed a salt-glazed stoneware jug from down south that turned out to have been stolen years ago, along with other antiques, from a home in Maryland. The widow of a broker and former insurance man had tried to sell the items through a representative. It's not clear whether she realized the pieces had been stolen, as she'd taken them from her late husband's collection. Her husband had been one of the victims of the Twin Towers collapse in New York. His was one of the many bodies that had never been found.

Henry's mind begins to make a series of connections, now. The article is talking about another stoneware piece from the same geographic region and time period as Old Mo. The guy who died was a Connecticut broker who lived in the same town as the Freemans. Is it possible the auction-house jar was stolen by the same people who invaded the Freeman home twenty years ago?

Henry's immediate impulse is to call Ebby, but to say what, exactly? No, he'll have to wait. He can't bring this up, after all the years the Freemans have had to live with unanswered questions about their son's death. He doesn't want to make the same mistake he did last time but he needs to know more before he says something. There are other people Henry can go to first. The police, for one, or an art-recovery organization. Or maybe Henry just needs to bide his time for a minute. This auction-house case is already being investigated. One thing may very well lead to another. Or maybe not.

Henry picks up the phone and calls his father's friend Harris.

# Ebby

---

IN ALL THESE YEARS, EBONY FREEMAN HAS NEVER HELD A SOCIAL media account. No Facebook, no Twitter, no Instagram, no TikTok. You name it, she's never even considered it. And why, ever? Why would Ebby, after the impact that photographs have had on her life, even think of drawing more attention to herself than necessary?

She can think of only one reason to do it now. The museum that acquired Old Mo for its collection is reopening its doors to the public for the second time since the start of the pandemic. They can't be sure how many weeks or months they'll have, this time around. But the new gallery is ready and the jar is about to go public.

Ebby rubs a dab of oil between her palms and smooths it against her hairline. She likes the dark-brown, close-cut hair with emerald tips. She is satisfied with her decision to go back to green. The word *green* is related to the Old English word *growan*. To grow. Ebby puts on a bit of lip gloss now. *Good.* She walks over to a houseplant near the window, catches the sun on her face, and holds her smartphone high. When she is done, she opens her first social media account ever.

Ebby's first post includes a series of snapshots from the preparation of the exhibit. The removal of the jar from a crate. The cleaning and mounting of the piece. The museum's catalog photo of Old Mo. She types in a list of hashtags like #oldmo #thejar #jarstories #family-stories #blackhistory #americanhistory #craftsmanship #enslaved #identity #legacy, and adds a link in her bio to a page on the museum's website. Her caption reads: This stoneware jar is 174 years old. It is part

of my family's history. And it is part of the story of the United States. This is
why we want to share it with you.

She hears Robert beeping the car horn. Time to leave. Sometimes,
it's still hard to believe that he is here with her in Connecticut. He has
moved into her condo with a very large suitcase and both his laptops.
He knows he might not be able to travel back to France when he wants,
or even across the U.S. to his mother's place. He's learned this from
Ebby's own experience in France during the first virus-related *confine-
ment national*. But Robert, like Ebby, is lucky. He still has his work.
Translations are home office–friendly.

After visiting France that second time and being stuck there with
Robert during the first lockdown, Ebby grew comfortable again with
the idea of a longer-term relationship. She didn't hesitate when Robert
suggested coming to the U.S. last fall. It has been good, between them,
despite the urgency of the pandemic. But Robert is on Ebby's turf,
now. Will he continue to like who Ebby is when she's here in Connecticut?

It just might work. Or it might fall apart. But Robert has his own
interests. His own work to do. His mother here in the States. Dear old
*grand-père* was from his father's side. Robert misses his grandpa. Ebby
does, too. How grateful they were for the uneventfulness of his death
in a year like this one. A drifting-away one night, in his sleep. As it
should be.

Robert says he will want to go back to France at some point, but
with his grandpa gone, he's in no hurry. And he doesn't want to let go
of Ebby. Strange, how easily they can talk about these things with each
other. They have gone into this phase of their relationship with their
eyes wide open. Even if they cannot see a foot ahead of themselves.

# Emergency

——

MORE THAN ONE MILLION PEOPLE HAVE WATCHED ED FREEMAN'S news conference from last year on the Internet. About fifty of them are lined up, now, on a walkway outside the museum, wearing face masks and waiting to be let in, two at a time, to see the exhibit on its first day. One of them is a sixty-year-old woman, a longtime emergency dispatch operator and instructor. She squints in the morning light, thinking she's been spending way too much time inside. She closes her eyes, now, and tilts her face toward the sun. Feels its strength, despite the chilly air.

One of the dispatcher's roles is to make sure whoever calls in an emergency stays on the line, if possible, until help arrives. She is good at her job. But sometimes the caller drops the phone or cuts the line. She thinks back to the year 2000. October, it was. When the ten-year-old child called, upset but lucid. She gave her name and explained that her brother had been shot by two men who had come into their home. He was now bleeding on the floor of their father's study. She gave her brother's name and age. You could always tell when a child's parents had drilled them on how to call emergency services for help.

"Ebony, are you injured?" the dispatcher asked.

"No, I was upstairs."

"Did you get a good look at the men who shot your brother?" the dispatcher asked.

The girl hesitated. "No," she said quietly.

The dispatcher recognized that kind of *no*. It was the kind of *no* that you say when you're afraid to tell what you've seen. Part of the dispatcher's job is to glean pertinent information. But the dispatcher, too, must tread carefully. Must keep the caller on the line.

"Ebony, I'd like you to answer me, now, with just a *yes* or *no*, all right? Is there someone else in the house with you? Besides your brother, I mean?"

"No, I don't think so."

"Do you know for sure that those were two men who shot your brother? Did you see them?"

A small intake of breath. Then silence.

*She saw them, didn't she? And she's terrified.*

The emergency dispatch operator was forty years old at the time. A seasoned professional. She had heard some dramatic situations over the phone in her career. But this one would stick with her. This one would haunt her. She remembers how the girl, Ebony, began to call her brother's name quietly, then grew more agitated. Then she heard the phone receiver collide with a hard surface. The floor. Ebony had dropped the phone.

"Ebony? Ebony?" The dispatcher couldn't get the child to answer, but she could still hear her.

That's when that poor little girl began to shriek. *Baz! Baz!* she kept shouting. Then the words left her altogether, and her voice mushroomed into a kind of keening that hit the dispatcher square in the chest, funneled down through her veins and into her feet. The dispatcher pulled off her eyeglasses and wiped the sweat off the bridge of her nose.

In this world, there were too many things that a child should never have to witness.

She heard a woman's voice, now, and muffled sobs, as if someone had embraced the girl.

"Hello? Hello?" the woman said. She identified herself as a neighbor and friend of the family. The dispatcher was back in contact, but she was shaken. One of her responsibilities was to be ready to take the next call with a calm and communicative disposition, no matter what had gone before. She was proud of the dedication she brought to the job. But after what she'd heard that day, the dispatcher had to ask to be excused for twenty minutes from her duties. This, too, was professionalism. To understand when you needed to step away.

At the end of her shift, the dispatcher skipped going to the supermarket and drove, instead, straight to her own daughter's high school. She was early. She sat in the car for an hour. She sat there until her daughter had finished band practice and came walking out of the main entrance with two other girls. She watched the fifteen-year-olds walk down the steps of the high school, toothy and leggy and beautiful. She took in a deep breath, filled with relief and love.

The Freeman family are standing off to the side now, greeting the first visitors from a distance, as the dispatcher enters the exhibit hall. She sees an elderly white woman and a white man in a wheelchair with them. She recognizes the woman from the old news photos. The next-door neighbor.

None of the photos the dispatcher has seen have prepared her for how lovely the Freeman girl is. She would be, what? Thirty, thirty-one? Young, but mature. Composed and smiling. Ebony Freeman turns toward her now and nods at the emergency dispatch operator, unaware, of course, of who she is. Their eyes meet and the light in Ebony Freeman's eyes is a gift. It eases some of what remains with a person who must listen, every day, to other people in distress, knowing that she cannot undo what has been done to them.

# Baz

———

## 2000

"Ebby, you're really bugging the heather out of me," Baz said. That was what their mother always said. The *heather,* not the *hell.* You didn't get to say *hell* in their household.

"Oh, come on, Baz, just one last time?"

Baz put his hands over his eyes. "All right, just this one—last—time," he said.

"Edward Basil Freeman," Ebby said, crossing her arms over her stomach, "stop peeking through your fingers, I see you." Baz made a face and put his hands back over his eyes and turned away, counting as Ebby skidded over the polished maple floors and ran out of the living room and down the hallway. This being a wood-frame house of a certain age, you could hear and feel folks as they moved about. Ebby was barefoot, but Baz could tell that she had run upstairs and was headed toward their parents' bedroom, which was right above the spot in the living room where Baz stood, counting down to the chase.

Baz grinned. As he stepped into the hallway that separated the living room from the study, he could hear his sister coming back now, maybe looking for a hiding place closer to the stairs. But he would pretend that he didn't know. He would make a fuss of looking for her, calling out and stomping back and forth, though not for long. They really needed to go. They were running late for Ebby's piano lesson, and it was Baz's job to get her there.

Baz had just put his foot on the lowest step when he thought he heard someone at the front door. The door sprang open and a shaft of sunlight flooded the hallway floor. Baz was still smiling as he turned toward the door, thinking, *Huh, who's that?* And he would keep smiling, even as he watched two men walking toward him, pulling something over their faces.

*Masks? Are they wearing ski masks?*

You see, it could take a moment for the brain to catch up, to make sense of something that made no sense at all. Baz was getting ready to climb the stairs. That was what made sense at the moment. Because he was playing hide-and-seek with Ebby. Because nothing made her happier. And there wasn't much that made Baz happier than his little sister.

She was such a goofball, that kid.

# Old Mo, Again

———

THE FIRST MEMBERS OF THE PUBLIC TO SEE OLD MO IN THE MUSEUM are surprised by how close they can get. The much-heralded jar is positioned in the middle of a large room, with no apparent protection. It is not enclosed in a display case, nor is it cordoned off by a rope or an electronic alarm system. Instead, Old Mo is merely anchored to a broad base and tipped to one side on metal supports. Visitors can step up and peer through a magnifying glass to see the inscription on the jar's bottom panel.

A sign next to Old Mo invites visitors to touch the jar, to run their fingers along the painted trail of leaves, to feel the ridges in the alkaline glaze that has dried in long, thin lines. There is a camera mounted on a tripod nearby, wired to a large green button on the floor, and everyone smiles when they see this part. Visitors can step on the button to take selfies with Old Mo for inclusion in a digital display. Everything else, contributed mostly by Gramps Freeman, is enclosed in a glass case or framed: two letters from Willis and Aquinnah's sons, a letter from Moses to Willis, and various household objects from the nineteenth century.

In a case all on its own is the small piece of wood with the black *X* burned into it that Aquinnah's parents used as a silent plea for help two centuries earlier. On the wall next to it is a panel based on text written by Ebby, in which she tells the story of their desperate journey to Massachusetts.

Some of Willis's sketches have been framed and displayed on each of the walls, alongside photographs from different generations of the Freeman family. The last photo in the exhibit shows the jar in September 2000, dressed up in a baseball cap and paper mustache, flanked by

Baz, Ebby, and their parents. They are all laughing. If a visitor looks closely, they will see a small gap on one side of Ebby's smile, where she has just lost her last baby tooth.

Ebby and her parents stand to the side, greeting people as they come in. In the line that runs down to the street and then curves around the corner of the museum, Ebby sees a familiar figure. Blond hair pulled tight in a ponytail, rising in a slight pouf on top. Gucci sunglasses above her surgical face mask. Pivoting now, with her smartphone held high, to show the line of visitors from behind, all standing at the required distance from one another.

"Avery," Ebby says when Avery finally steps inside and pulls off her sunglasses.

"Ebby," Avery says. They nod at each other and Avery continues past her into the exhibit hall. Ebby lowers her face and smiles to herself.

# A Sailor's Story

———

AMONG WILLIS'S SKETCHES IS A PORTRAIT OF AN OLD SAILOR whom he met during his first voyage on a ship, after his attempt to stow away had been discovered. His grandchildren told their own children that Afam had managed to purchase his freedom from enslavement but had been known to weep at the thought of all that he had lost. A speaker near the sketch emits the sound of Ebby's voice as she reads from a story based on the anecdotes handed down by each generation of the Freemans.

For most of his life, Ebby explains, Afam had been referred to by another name, the name the *oyibo* had given him. He remembers being a boy and watching his father and older brothers digging a boat out of the trunk of a sacred silk-cotton tree. The vessel they produced was as wide as their house. They would push off in their long wooden boat, staying away for many days. Going as far south as the coast of Angola, though Angola, his mother told him, was very far away, and teeming with people hunters.

Afam knew he was destined to join his father and brothers someday. He had the sea in his blood. But during one of his father's long trips, everything changed. The boy was on his way to market with baskets made by his mother when he heard a commotion up ahead. Moving in closer to see what was happening, he saw people being cut and hit and grabbed. He ran back home to look for his mother. He found her outside their hut, bleeding and trying to pull away from a man with a cutlass. She shouted to him. *Run!* But someone threw a cloth over his head and picked him up. He never saw his mother or father or brothers again.

It was not safe for Afam to go back to his homeland. There were too many perils along the way. He might be sequestered and enslaved again. Still, he could not forget. At night, he dreamed of the people who lived on the far side of the Atlantic, who still traveled up and down the coast as free men. In his slumber, he watched as they rowed their cotton-tree vessels from one port to another, fishing and trading and gliding among the spirits of their ancestors. They were not bound by ropes or chains. They were not stacked, one upon the other, like pieces of wood. They were living as men were meant to live.

After being called by another name for years, Afam reclaimed his original appellation. The ship's manifest listed him as Afam Efuna, a broken-up version of the name he had been given at birth. Each time someone had called him Paul over the years, he had repeated his original name in his head, and every night he had whispered it to himself and promised his ancestors that, one day, he would insist people call him Afam again. And he would live out the full meaning of his Igbo name.

Afamefuna. *My name will not be lost.*

# Soh

———

Before leaving the new edward basil freeman gallery, soh takes one last look at the jar. It is surrounded by admirers. When Soh first saw Old Mo sitting on the large, squat pedestal in the museum, she stepped up to it and ran her hand along one of the seams where the jar had been repaired. She drew close to the vessel with her nose and breathed in. Soh loved thinking that in the beginning, when it was just a mound of clay, Old Mo could have been anything at all, until that critical moment when it was placed in the kiln and heated to more than two thousand degrees Fahrenheit.

In the beginning, Old Mo had been full of possibility, just like a person. Even in its final form, the jar has continued to transform people's lives, just as they, in turn, are leaving their mark on the life story of Old Mo. Soh loves that jar more than ever. She loves to think that something that has been broken can be pieced back together.

"So long, Old Mo," Soh whispers as she walks away. She stops outside the entrance to the hall, where her son's name is fixed to the wall in raised bronze lettering. She reaches up to run her fingers across the BASIL, then steps back. She stands there, breathing in and out, for how long, she doesn't know. There are no words for this moment.

There are no words to capture the meaning of a person's life.

# Legacy

———

THE OLD MO EXHIBIT IS A HIT. THE SIGN NEXT TO THE JAR REMINDS visitors that while they are invited to touch its surface, the piece is damaged, so they are kindly requested to refrain from hugging or leaning on it. But after reading the informational panel about Old Mo's history, and after seeing the inscription on the bottom of the vessel, many people simply cannot resist.

By the end of the first several months, when the museum is forced to shut its doors for the third time due to the pandemic, Mo's Selfie Bank is filled with rotating digital images of people with their arms wrapped around Old Mo. There are children, retirees, and people of various colors in all manner of headdress.

Someone has their face pressed against the side of Old Mo. Someone else is kissing the jar. In one image, someone has positioned framed photographs of their ancestors around Old Mo on the stand built to support the jar. That one makes Ebby laugh out loud. In another photo, three students, one of them in tears, hold up a large piece of paper with five words written out in large black letters. Ebby catches her breath. She recognizes the phrase. They are the words from the bottom of the jar.

They are the words that Moses wrote after Betsey lost her life. They are the words that Willis saw before he decided to make a run for freedom. They are the words that Ebby's dad showed to her mom on the day that he led her into his family's library. The students have written the words exactly as they appear on the jar:

THE MIND

CANNOT

BE CHAINED

Ebby nods as she reads the words again. *At least, this,* she thinks. *At least, this.*

# Epilogue

———

## Moses

**1867**

The war had ended and messages were getting through. Willis sent word to Moses, urging him to move to Massachusetts. There were potters up that way, too, Willis wrote. Their clay might not be as fine as that of the South Carolina backcountry, but it was of good quality, he assured him. Still, Moses could not see himself moving to that distant territory at his age, when he had spent most of his life out this way.

After being freed from bondage, Moses had walked southwest from the Oldhams' and found paid employment as a turner for a competing pottery, one of the few nearby that wasn't owned by the same family. The stoneware producers had done better than most during the fighting. Even the army had needed jugs and plates and such, and pottery was still in demand. Then, the following year, the son of a former associate of Martin Oldham's rode over in a wagon and approached Moses with a business proposal.

Together, the two men opened a pottery and brickmaking enterprise in the next county over and soon had a sizable clientele among both white and colored folks. They had good dirt, out that way. Moses had decided to take Willis's surname after emancipation, so the new pottery was called Lewis and Freeman. One white owner, one colored owner. Unheard-of in these parts, only five years ago. But now, there was a colored man on the local county commission and freedmen settling over on the border with Georgia in a town that used to be a major slave-trading post. Moses wrote all this down in a letter to Willis and imagined Willis laughing in satisfaction as he read.

By the time he turned seventy, Moses Freeman was no longer producing large pieces. Instead, he spent much of his time keeping the ledgers and training younger turners while his partner focused on the bricks and other production. At home, he had Abigail, a companion of nearly the same age whom he'd met at the market. He was grateful for the new affection and purpose that he had found so late in life, but he worried that the situation had grown more dangerous for men like him, rather than less so.

There were stories going around about the terrible things that could happen to colored folks around there. Violent things. Attacks on freedmen who had been able to prosper or hold political office. Attacks on colored people to keep them from voting in elections. Still, there were many people who hadn't fled north, or down to places like Bermuda. For better or worse, Moses felt he was part of a community. And that community was changing.

At Abigail's urging, Moses took on two local girls as apprentices. It caused a bit of a ruckus among the men, but he shushed them. Wasn't going to have any of that here, he said. He liked working with the girls. They had a way of watching and learning things that you didn't even have to explain. They made him think of poor Betsey. How keen she had been to acquire turning skills of her own. How she seemed to understand that clay was a living thing. How back then everybody was sure that Betsey could not have taken her own life, as that no-good Jacob Oldham had claimed. But Moses wasn't so sure anymore. He only knew that, in any event, Betsey had gotten herself killed through a final act of resistance.

Moses and one of the apprentices watched the other girl, now, as she centered a wad of clay on the table.

"Good," Moses said. "Go on."

She pulled the clay upward, then pushed the thumb of her right hand into the mass and added her forefinger.

"Keep it watered," Moses said. The girl wet her hand in a bowl of water and moved it back to the clay.

"Yeees."

Moses smiled. This girl was barely fifteen. He thought of where she and the others might be in a few years, if they could learn the craft well and keep themselves safe. The latter, in particular, would be a challenge. But there was reason to hope. Over in Charleston, there was a colored barber who was stirring things up. He was fixing to get himself into Congress. And he wasn't the only one.

Moses looked at the face of the girl at the potter's wheel. How her eyes focused on the spinning table. How she nodded to herself as she pushed the clay to take on new shapes. He thought of his mother, all those years ago, living as a free woman in a village of potters, on the far side of the ocean. Moses should have been born over there. Should have become a blacksmith, like his father. Should have known his father, to begin with. But there was no turning back now. All he could do was keep moving forward and help the younger folks to gain back some of what had been taken away from him, his mother, and others like them.

Moses watched as the wheel sped up, then slowed, and a small jar took shape on the table.

*Just look at that! The girl is able.*

Yes, Moses thought, these were precarious times, but he was keeping his eyes on the future. And these young people would be part of it.

*At least, this,* he thought. *At least, this.*

# Author's Note

———

THE IDEA FOR THIS NOVEL BEGAN WITH A THOUGHT, AND THAT thought took the form of a character. Ebony "Ebby" Freeman sprang from my imagination and landed on the page as I wondered about the ways in which a personal tragedy could shape a person's identity—especially when their trauma had been played out in the public eye. In my first profession as a journalist, I had often encountered people as they experienced some of the worst moments in their lives. Writing about Ebby was one way to explore the human capacity to thrive and love despite unspeakable hurt.

I knew, early in the writing process, that Ebby's emotional journey following a major romantic disappointment would be affected by other influences on her identity, including a treasured heirloom and her family's long history as African Americans in New England. To build her backstory, I researched historical details from nineteenth-century Massachusetts and South Carolina between site visits, museum exhibits, and university and library reading lists, and spent much of that time learning about two areas of labor that regularly relied on both enslaved and free black people but were rarely, if ever, seen in fiction: the mass production of pottery in the American South and the crewing of ships sailing to and from American ports.

I would like to share with you, here, a few of the titles that crossed my desk during my research. They include *Black Jacks: African American Seamen in the Age of Sail* by W. Jeffrey Bolster, *Carolina Clay: The Life and Legend of the Slave Potter Dave* by Leonard Todd, *Great and Noble Jar: Traditional Stoneware of South Carolina* by Cinda K. Baldwin, and *Black Lives, Native Lands, White Worlds: A History of Slavery in New England* by Jared Ross Hardesty.

As I developed the history of the fictional Freeman family, another nonfiction book that I'd read out of general interest bolstered some of my thinking about the impact of inherited stories and objects on identity. *All That She Carried: The Journey of Ashley's Sack, a Black Family Keepsake* by Tiya Miles revolves around a simple cotton sack given by an enslaved woman to her daughter before they were forcibly separated and the impact of that object on subsequent generations.

In reading Miles's book, I was reminded of the importance of a longtime family possession in one of my favorite fictional works, *The Piano Lesson* by August Wilson. This play, which I first saw performed on stage more than twenty-five years before writing this novel, had me thinking about how personal experiences, family lore, and American history can come together to form or shift a person's ideas of themselves and the world around them and, ultimately, affect their destiny.

Many thanks to those educational and cultural institutions that provided online and in-person resources. They include, but are not limited to, the New York Public Library's Schomburg Center for Research in Black Culture, the S.C. Sea Grant Consortium in South Carolina, the Museum of Fine Arts in Boston, the Library of Congress, and the David Ruggles Center for History and Education in Florence, Massachusetts (a facility on the U.S. National Park Service Underground Railroad Network to Freedom).

In the novel, the name of the fictional birthplace of most members of the Freeman family, Refuge County, was inspired by real-life stories of assistance provided by multicolored mid-nineteenth-century abolitionist groups in Boston and smaller communities in Massachusetts like Florence, today identified as a village in Northampton.

In the mid-1800s, David Ruggles ran the nation's first African American bookstore and journal in Florence and is said to have assisted more than six hundred fugitives on the Underground Railroad. The formerly enslaved abolitionist and women's rights activist Sojourner Truth lived nearby for years, and prominent black and white abolitionists like Frederick Douglass and William Lloyd Garrison were known to visit.

While writing the story of Moses, I visited an exhibit of nineteenth-century stoneware that originated at the Metropolitan Museum of Art in New York and traveled to other cities. The show, *Hear Me Now: The Black Potters of Old Edgefield, South Carolina,* included key pieces by the real-life potter Dave (called David Drake following the end of his enslavement). Much like Moses, the character from the novel, Dave inscribed stoneware pieces with phrases despite the laws designed to keep enslaved persons from reading and writing. Pottery from Edgefield and surrounding areas in South Carolina and Georgia was known for its quality, due in part to the prized attributes of that region's soil and the availability of skilled, though forced, labor.

While Moses and the other main characters in *Good Dirt* are fictional, as are several locations in the narrative, the research was eye-opening. Overall, the experience of writing this novel has helped to expand my general awareness of the American story. One example is the fascinating book *Root of Bitterness: Documents of the Social History of American Women,* a scholarly compilation of letters, inventories, and other writings edited by Nancy F. Cott, Jeanne Boydston, Ann Braude, Lori D. Ginzberg, and Molly Ladd-Taylor. The book was filled with details from the daily lives of women, black and white, who lived between the seventeenth and late nineteenth centuries.

As one character says in the novel, history can be told only through a chorus of voices. Fictional storytelling can be part of that chorus. It is my hope that the details shared in this note will serve as a starting point for readers who wish to explore evolving accounts of the past by doing further reading.

# Acknowledgments

———

THE OPPORTUNITY TO PUBLISH MY SECOND NOVEL HAS BEEN A gift. I am grateful, as always, to my agent, Madeleine Milburn, and to her incredible team, for believing in my ideas and providing support in so many ways. Thank you, also, to my editors and publishers and their amazing colleagues. They include Hilary Rubin Teeman of Ballantine Books and Jessica Leeke, formerly of Penguin Michael Joseph, who embraced this story early on and saw it through various revisions, along with Lily Cooper and Clio Cornish, also of Michael Joseph.

Many thanks to Kara Welsh, president of Ballantine Books; Kim Hovey, senior VP and deputy publisher; and Jennifer Hershey, senior VP and publisher, for offering a home to this novel.

I can only begin to thank the talented people in production, design, copyediting, marketing, and publicity who work tirelessly to take an author's story, transform it into a book, and find ways to share it with readers everywhere. Many thanks to Andy Lefkowitz, Pamela Alders, Katie Zilberman, Hasan Altaf, Elena Giavaldi, Kathleen Quinlan, Emily Isayeff, and Hope Hatchcock. Caroline Weishuhn, thank you for being there through much of the process.

In the U.K., a heartfelt thanks to Gaby Young, Ella Watkins, and Madeleine Woodfield for the support that you have offered throughout.

I won't mention everyone here, but you know who you are. Your expertise, insights, and generosity are part of my life as an author and this book would not be possible without you. Finally, many thanks to those family, friends, readers, and fellow writers who supported me through the work on this book and the publication of my previous novel. By *friends,* I mean to include all those booksellers, librarians, book bloggers, and bookclub organizers who bring writers and readers together every day and help to build community through the sharing of stories.

## ABOUT THE AUTHOR

CHARMAINE WILKERSON is the *New York Times* bestselling author of *Black Cake*. She is an American writer who has lived in Jamaica and Italy. A graduate of Barnard College and Stanford University, she is a former journalist whose award-winning short fiction has appeared in various magazines and anthologies.

ABOUT THE TYPE

This book was set in Bembo, a typeface based
on an old-style Roman face that was used for
Cardinal Pietro Bembo's tract De Aetna in
1495. Bembo was cut by Francesco Griffo
(1450–1518) in the early sixteenth century for
Italian Renaissance printer and publisher
Aldus Manutius (1449–1515). The Lanston
Monotype Company of Philadelphia brought
the well-proportioned letterforms of Bembo
to the United States in the 1930s.